PRAISE FOR DONNA GRANT'S BEST-SELLING ROMANCE NOVELS

"Grant's ability to quickly convey complicated backstory makes this jam-packed love story accessible even to new or periodic readers." - *Publisher's Weekly*

"Donna Grant has given the paranormal genre a burst of fresh air..." – *San Francisco Book Review*

"The premise is dramatic and heartbreaking; the characters are colorful and engaging; the romance is spirited and seductive." – *The Reading Cafe*

"The central romance, fueled by a hostage drama, plays out in glorious detail against a backdrop of multiple ongoing issues in the "Dark Kings" books. This seemingly penultimate installment creates a nice segue to a climactic end." – *Library Journal*

"...intense romance amid the growing war between the Dragons and the Dark Fae is scorching hot." – *Booklist*

DON'T MISS THESE OTHER NOVELS
BY NYT & USA TODAY BESTSELLING AUTHOR DONNA GRANT

CONTEMPORARY PARANORMAL

DRAGON KINGS® SERIES

Dragon Revealed ~ Dragon Mine ~ Dragon Unbound

Dragon Eternal ~ Dragon Lover ~ Dragon Arisen

REAPER SERIES

Dark Alpha's Claim ~ Dark Alpha's Embrace

Dark Alpha's Demand ~ Dark Alpha's Lover

Dark Alpha's Night ~ Dark Alpha's Hunger

Dark Alpha's Awakening ~ Dark Alpha's Redemption

Dark Alpha's Temptation ~ Dark Alpha's Caress

Dark Alpha's Obsession ~ Dark Alpha's Need

Dark Alpha's Silent Night ~ Dark Alpha's Passion

Dark Alpha's Command ~ Dark Alpha's Fury

SKYE DRUIDS SERIES

Iron Ember ~ Shoulder the Skye ~ Heart of Glass

DARK KINGS SERIES

Dark Heat ~ Darkest Flame ~ Fire Rising ~ Burning Desire

Hot Blooded ~ Night's Blaze ~ Soul Scorched ~ Dragon King

Passion Ignites ~ Smoldering Hunger ~ Smoke and Fire

Dragon Fever ~ Firestorm ~ Blaze ~ Dragon Burn

Constantine: A History, Parts 1-3 ~ Heat ~ Torched

Dragon Night ~ Dragonfire ~ Dragon Claimed

Ignite ~ Fever ~ Dragon Lost ~ Flame ~ Inferno

A Dragon's Tale (Whisky and Wishes: *A Holiday Novella*,

Heart of Gold: *A Valentine's Novella*, & Of Fire and Flame)

My Fiery Valentine ~ The Dragon King Coloring Book

Dragon King Special Edition Character Coloring Book: Rhi

DARK WARRIORS SERIES

Midnight's Master ~ Midnight's Lover

Midnight's Seduction ~ Midnight's Warrior

Midnight's Kiss ~ Midnight's Captive

Midnight's Temptation ~ Midnight's Promise

Midnight's Surrender ~ A Warrior for Christmas

CHIASSON SERIES

Wild Fever ~ Wild Dream ~ Wild Need

Wild Flame ~ Wild Rapture

LARUE SERIES

Moon Kissed ~ Moon Thrall ~ Moon Struck ~ Moon Bound

WICKED TREASURES

Seized by Passion ~ Enticed by Ecstasy ~ Captured by Desire

Books 1-3: Wicked Treasures Box Set

HISTORICAL PARANORMAL

THE KINDRED SERIES

Everkin ~ Eversong ~ Everwylde ~ Everbound

Evernight ~ Everspell

KINDRED: THE FATED SERIES

Rage ~ Ruin ~ Reign

DARK SWORD SERIES

Dangerous Highlander ~ Forbidden Highlander

Wicked Highlander ~ Untamed Highlander

Shadow Highlander ~ Darkest Highlander

ROGUES OF SCOTLAND SERIES

The Craving ~ The Hunger ~ The Tempted ~ The Seduced

Books 1-4: Rogues of Scotland Box Set

THE SHIELDS SERIES

A Dark Guardian ~ A Kind of Magic ~ A Dark Seduction

A Forbidden Temptation ~ A Warrior's Heart

Mystic Trinity (a series connecting novel)

DRUIDS GLEN SERIES

Highland Mist ~ Highland Nights ~ Highland Dawn

Highland Fires ~ Highland Magic

Mystic Trinity (a series connecting novel)

THE SHIELDS SERIES

A Dark Guardian ~ A Kind of Magic ~ A Dark Seduction

A Forbidden Temptation ~ A Warrior's Heart

Mystic Trinity (a series connecting novel)

DRUIDS GLEN SERIES

Highland Mist ~ Highland Nights ~ Highland Dawn

Highland Fires ~ Highland Magic

Mystic Trinity (a series connecting novel)

SISTERS OF MAGIC TRILOGY

Shadow Magic ~ Echoes of Magic ~ Dangerous Magic

Books 1-3: Sisters of Magic Box Set

THE ROYAL CHRONICLES NOVELLA SERIES

Prince of Desire ~ Prince of Seduction

Prince of Love ~ Prince of Passion

Books 1-4: The Royal Chronicles Box Set

Mystic Trinity (a series connecting novel)

DARK BEGINNINGS: A FIRST IN SERIES BOXSET

Chiasson Series, Book 1: Wild Fever

LaRue Series, Book 1: Moon Kissed

The Royal Chronicles Series, Book 1: Prince of Desire

MILITARY ROMANCE / ROMANTIC SUSPENSE

SONS OF TEXAS SERIES

The Hero ~ The Protector ~ The Legend

The Defender ~ The Guardian

COWBOY / CONTEMPORARY

HEART OF TEXAS SERIES

The Christmas Cowboy Hero ~ Cowboy, Cross My Heart

My Favorite Cowboy ~ A Cowboy Like You

Looking for a Cowboy ~ A Cowboy Kind of Love

<u>STAND ALONE BOOKS</u>

That Cowboy of Mine

Home for a Cowboy Christmas

Mutual Desire

Forever Mine

Savage Moon

**Check out Donna Grant's Online Store at
www.DonnaGrant.com/shop
for autographed books, character
themed goodies, and more!**

READING ORDER
THE CHIASSON AND LARUE SERIES STORIES ARE INTERTWINED.

A generations old family of hunters fight the many evils that abound in the bayous of southwest Louisiana and New Orleans.

Chiasson & LaRue intertwined series reading order:

Wild Fever, Chiasson Series

Wild Dream, Chiasson Series

Wild Need, Chiasson Series

Moon Kissed, LaRue Series

Moon Thrall, LaRue Series

Wild Flame, Chiasson Series

Moon Struck, LaRue Series

Wild Rapture, Chiasson Series

Moon Bound, LaRue Series

PRONUNCIATIONS

Arcineaux (are-cen-o)

Chiasson (ch-ay-son)

Davena (dav-E-na)

Delia (d-ee-l-ee-uh)

Delphine (d-eh-l-FEEN)

Dumas (dOO-mah-s)

Lafayette (lah-fai-EHt)

LaRue (l-er-OO)

GLOSSARY

Andouille (ahn-doo-ee) & **Boudin** (boo-dan)

Two types of Cajun sausage. Andouille is made with pork while boudin with pork and rice.

Bayou (by-you)

A sluggish stream bigger than a creek and smaller than a river

Beignet (bin-yay)

A fritter or doughnut without a hole, sprinkled with powdered sugar

Cajun ('ka-jun)

A person of French-Canadian descent born or living along southern Louisiana.

Etoufee (ay-two-fay)

Tangy tomato-based sauce dish usually made with crawfish or shrimp and rice

Gumbo (gum-bo)

Thick, savory soup with chicken, seafood, sausage, or wild game

Hoodoo (hu-du)

Also known as "conjure" or witchcraft. Thought of as "folk magic" and "superstition". Some say it is the main force against the use of Voodoo.

Jambalaya (jom-bah-LIE-yah)

Highly seasoned mixture of sausage, chicken, or seafood and vegetables, simmered with rice until liquid is absorbed

Maman (muh-mahn)

Term used for grandmother

Parish

A Louisiana state district; equivalent to the word county

Sha (a as in cat)

Term of affection meaning darling, dear, or sweetheart.

Voodoo (vu-du) – New Orleans

Spiritual folkways originating in the Caribbean. New Orleans Voodoo is separate from other forms (Haitian Vodou and southern Hoodoo). New Orleans Voodoo puts emphasis on Voodoo Queens and Voodoo dolls.

Zydeco (zy-dey-coh)

Accordion-based music originating in Louisiana combined with guitar and violin while combing traditional French melodies with Caribbean and blues influences

CHIASSON SERIES

BOOKS 1-5

DONNA GRANT

WWW.DONNAGRANT.COM

A CHIASSON NOVEL
WILD
FEVER
DONNA GRANT
NEW YORK TIMES BESTSELLING AUTHOR

CHAPTER
ONE

Southwest Louisiana

June

VINCENT CHIASSON CLOSED his eyes and remained hunched down at the end of the dock. The air was heavy, the heat oppressive even at midnight.

He heard the telltale splash as a gator on the other side of the bayou entered the water. Off to his right was a hiss from a water moccasin, and all around him the sounds of the bayou filled the night.

But none of that was what he searched for. It was the creatures of the night, the beings people only thought lived in imaginations and movies that he hunted.

It was what the Chiasson's had done throughout the

centuries. It began in France, continued in Nova Scotia, and followed them all the way to Louisiana.

A scream split the air. Vincent's eyes snapped open as he jerked his head to the left. He stood and rushed back down the pier until he reached solid ground. He knew the land as well as he knew himself.

He knew every stump, every curve in the swamp. Vincent ran as fast as the wind to find the woman before the creature could attack again.

Another scream rent the air, this one full of fear...and death.

Vincent pumped his legs faster. He jumped over a log and slid to a stop next to the water's edge. Every instinct told him he had to hurry to the woman, but stealth was all that would get him close to the creature.

With his breathing ragged, Vincent silently stepped into the bayou. The water reached to his knees, but didn't so much as ripple as he entered it.

Off to his right, a gator eyed him. Vincent moved farther to the left, hoping to come around and behind the creature he hunted.

"Please!" a woman yelled. "Someone help!"

Vincent ground his teeth together and reached down to the outside of his right thigh where his machete was attached. He pulled out the blade and kept his gaze ahead. His three brothers would be closing in on the beast as well. It would end this night.

The woman and the creature were about fifty feet from him on a small outcropping. The full moon shed enough light that Vincent could make out the woman trying her best to climb to her feet. Her hands clawed at the earth, and she kept looking behind her.

Vincent was determined to kill the being that night. He crept to the left were a grove of cypress trees nestled. As soon as he climbed out of the bayou, Vincent was ready to kill.

He slunk closer, keeping his legs bent and his body in the shadows. When he was just twenty feet away he saw the creature. It was hulking with dark fur and unimaginable claws, and yet he couldn't get a look at its face.

It loomed over the woman, and Vincent knew it was now or never. He burst out of the trees, his machete raised as the woman's scream echoed through the bayou.

Vincent skidded to a halt when he came to the woman. The creature was gone, and blood coated everything. He knelt next to her and winced.

"Molly Guidry," Lincoln's voice said from behind him. "That makes three in a week."

Vincent stood and faced his brother. "I don't need a recount, Linc. I know exactly how many have been killed."

"Son of a bitch," Beau mumbled as he came out of the bayou.

Lincoln ran a hand down his face. "I thought we had it for sure this time."

"So did I." Vincent had set everything up perfectly. They should have had the creature.

Beau looked around. "Where's Christian?"

All three began to search for their brother. It was a whistle that had them looking to their right.

"There," Lincoln said.

While his two brothers went to Christian, Vincent remained with Molly. He had known her since the day she was born. Their parents had been close, and consequently they were often together. At one time Molly had been infatuated with Christian.

Vincent looked over at Christian. Did he know it was Molly? Damn, but this mess was getting out of control. All three victims they knew.

That wasn't too rare in the small Cajun town, but it didn't make things easier. Just like contacting Molly's parents and telling them what happened was going to be one of the hardest things he had ever done.

Lincoln walked back over and squatted beside him. "I told Christian it was Molly. Did you know they went out last week?"

"No." Vincent didn't like the unease that rippled through him. Was it coincidence that Molly had been killed? "I thought she had given up on Christian."

"We all did." Lincoln blew out a breath. "He's not taking this well."

Vincent stood and shook his head at the gruesome sight of Molly. "What did Christian find?"

"Claw marks."

"We're hunting a creature we haven't even identified. We're completely fucked."

Lincoln slapped him on the back. "We've always figured it out in the past. We will this time as well."

"I have my doubts. We were in perfect placement to find this bastard. How the hell did it get away without us seeing or hearing it?"

Vincent didn't wait for his brother to respond, because there was nothing to say. He bent and gently lifted Molly in his arms.

"Want me to go with you?" Lincoln asked.

Vincent shook his head. "You three see what else you can find. I'll meet you at the house."

"Mom and Pop always knew what to say to the families. You've got their gift as well."

He sincerely doubted it. Most in the parish knew what the Chiassons did, but that didn't always mean they were welcomed into houses. Chiassons were respected, but feared. It made for a lonely life.

It was a long walk through the bayou to the Guidry's. He heard crying before he even saw the house. When he moved out of the tree line and the edge of the light caught his shape, a man stepped forward.

Hank Guidry, Molly's father. Vincent drew in a deep

breath and continued until he reached Hank. On the porch the crying grew louder, wracked with pain.

"I knew something was wrong when she didn't come home from locking up the store," Hank said as he stared at his daughter. "She's never late."

Vincent looked at the ground. How he hated this part of the family business. No matter how many times he did it, it never got easier.

"Did you kill it?" Hank asked.

It was the viciousness in his voice that drew Vincent's gaze. The need for revenge, the yearning to hurt something as he had been hurt shone in Hank's eyes as clearly as the moon in the sky.

"We almost had it." Vincent knew it wouldn't be enough. It never was, and it was what made them hated throughout the parish.

"Almost!" Celine screamed from the screened porch. "You almost had it? Isn't that your job, Vincent Chiasson? Don't you hunt these evil things? How could you have let it get my baby? My only child?"

Each word was like a knife to his gut. Vincent moved past Hank and made his way to the porch. He shouldered open the screen door, walked past Celine, and then into the house.

Vincent carefully set Molly on the couch and turned to leave, only to have Hank block his way.

"This was never supposed to happen to my baby girl," Hank said as tears coursed down his face. He pulled off his glasses and shook his head. "I'll help in any way that I can to kill this creature you hunt, Vincent. I helped your father on occasion. I'll do the same for you."

Vincent rested his hand on Hank's shoulder. "Be here for your wife. Bury your daughter. If God's willing, we'll have killed this thing by then. If not...I'll give you a shout."

He walked to the doorway and paused. When he looked back, Hank and Celine had their arms around each other as they mourned their daughter.

By the time Vincent returned home, he was in a foul mood. He let the screen door slam behind him. Next to the door were three sets of boots, one for each of his brothers. The only thing missing was the smaller pink pair.

That was his doing though. To give Riley a chance at a normal life that didn't include hunting in the bayous in the middle of the night, Vincent had sent her off to college in Texas.

That had been three years ago. It felt more like three lifetimes, but it had been for the best.

Vincent began to remove his muddy boots when the door opened and Beau walked out on the back porch. He handed Vincent a bottle of beer and took one of the rocking chairs.

There were no words as they both took a long drink of their beers. Vincent sprawled out on the swing with one leg hanging down.

"Tough one. You should've let one of us go with you," Beau said.

"Did y'all find anything else?"

"Not a goddamn thing. I tell you, Vin, this thing knows us. It knows what we're looking for."

Vincent squeezed the bridge of his nose with his thumb and forefinger. "Let's hope to hell you're wrong."

"We've not even figured out what it is."

He wasn't saying anything Vincent didn't already know. "We need a new plan of attack. If we can find where this thing is hiding out, we can kill it before it hurts anyone else."

The door to the house was thrown open and Christian walked out, followed by Lincoln. They each took a chair, though Christian chose the one farthest from all of them.

Vincent didn't know how close his brother had been to Molly. It was rare that a Chiasson dated anyone from the parish because of the family name. It was even rarer when a Chiasson found a woman he wanted to ask out. But as their father had often said, they had to keep the line going so more creatures could be killed.

"Riley called," Christian said to break the silence.

Lincoln let out a string of curses while Beau just shook his head as he peeled off the label to his beer.

Vincent looked at Christian to find his brother's gaze on him. "What did she say?" Vincent finally asked.

"She was checking in."

"You didn't tell her about what was going on, did you?" Beau asked.

Christian gave him a droll look. "Do you think I'm that

thick? I was in agreement about sending her off. Of course I didn't tell her anything."

Vincent scrubbed a hand down his face. He was the eldest of them, the one who was supposed to keep everyone in line and focused. It had seemed like an easy job when he was younger.

And when their parents had still been alive.

"What's the plan?" Lincoln asked.

Vincent drained the rest of his beer and looked at the amber colored bottle. "We go back out at first light. We split up and search every inch of the bayou. That thing is somewhere out there. I won't rest until it's dead."

For the next hour, the four discussed which sections of the bayou they would take, as well as individuals they knew they could get to help.

Lincoln was the first to call it a night, and Beau soon followed. Vincent rose from the swing and stood at the edge of the porch, staring through the screen to the bayou beyond.

"I didn't know you had found someone, Christian. I'm sorry it ended the way it did."

Wood creaked as Christian rose from the chair and came to stand beside him. "I liked Molly. I'd probably have asked her out again, but I wasn't in love with her."

"It doesn't make it hurt any less. You knew her."

"Do you ever wish we had been born to a normal family? The kind that goes to the movies, bails kids out of jail for buying beer underage, and staying out past curfew on Friday nights?"

Vincent rested his forearm against a wood beam and chuckled. "For most of my life. It's not easy being a Chiasson."

"Dad was married and had you and Lincoln by the time he was your age. How long until you marry, Vin? Do you think you ever will? Hell, will any of us?"

Vincent wished he had answers for him, but he didn't. "Let's focus on one thing at a time. We need to find this creature and see what it is so we can kill it. There is also Molly's funeral we'll need to attend, and then Deb's on Sunday after church for lunch."

"That's a lot to do in three days," Christian said with a hint of a smile. He raised his beer bottle to Vincent before he lifted it to his lips. "Do you really think we can catch this creature?"

"Yes."

"Always so sure of things. That must make sleeping easier for you. Me, I'm not so certain. This...thing...is quick. It attacks differently every time, and we've barely gotten a look at it."

Vincent ran his thumb around the mouth of his empty beer. "Everything can be killed. Remember that, little brother."

CHAPTER

TWO

OLIVIA BREAUX ADJUSTED her hands on the steering wheel as she took the exit off I-10 toward Crowley. The closer she got to the small town she had left behind the night of her high school graduation, the more she felt as if someone were sitting on her chest.

She drove through Crowley, taking in the sights, and was amazed to find that very little had changed. To her, Crowley had been the "big town". She hadn't understood just how small Crowley was until she saw Dallas for the first time.

Olivia had sworn then and there not to ever go back, and yet, nine years later where was she? Going home.

With Crowley behind her, the buildings gave way to pasture and rice fields. Life seemed to slow to a crawl in the bayou, matching the movement of the water.

She noticed several new homes built on what had once

been farmland. Fewer of the fields had rice growing, but other than that, it all seemed the same.

As she drove, she found her thoughts returning to the life she had once led. It seemed an eon ago, and yet she could remember Vincent Chiasson with a clarity that was startling.

She had always been infatuated with him, even going so far as to do almost anything to get his attention—to no avail. Vincent, like his three other brothers, kept themselves apart from others.

The only one of the Chiasson's that didn't was Riley. The youngest of the five, she was wild and beautiful. And completely protected by her four older siblings.

She smiled as she recalled a party her senior year where someone had brought Riley. The best part of that night had been when Vincent had shown up to take Riley home.

He had looked like an avenging warrior with his bright blue Chiasson eyes glaring at anyone even close to Riley. What Olivia would have done to have him protecting her.

She wondered what he was doing. She knew he and his brothers would never leave the area, but after all this time she was sure he was married with children. And yet, she held out hope to get a glimpse of him, to look from afar as she always had.

Olivia frowned when she saw traffic stopped ahead. With only one main road to and from Crowley, what little traffic there was could get backed up quickly.

She stopped the car and put it in park before she rolled

down her window and leaned her head out. There was a group of people standing together and looking farther up the road.

Olivia recognized two of the women, which stopped her from getting out and seeing what was going on. She rolled her window back up not to waste the air conditioning and inwardly groaned at her cowardice.

She was going to have to face everyone eventually. It wasn't as if she could live there and not come in contact with others, especially those she went to school with.

With a puff of her cheeks, she blew out a breath and lowered her visor to look at herself in the small mirror. She ran her hand through her board straight black hair and grimaced.

Olivia pulled her sunglasses down her nose so she could see her black eyes as she asked herself, "What do I tell them? Do I just say that I wanted to come back?"

She snorted. "Yeah. That won't work. The truth? Nah. I'd rather not. I'll have to come up with something."

A shriek flew from her lips when someone knocked on her window. She fumbled as she raised the visor and tried to find the button to lower her window.

"Hey," Sean Hebert said as he leaned down. He pushed back the Stetson on his head full of blond hair as the sun glinted off the sheriff's badge on his chest. "Just wanted to let you know things will be moving along soon."

"Thanks." Olivia tried to raise her window in the hopes that she could get away without him realizing who she was.

Unfortunately, he put his hand on the window and pulled down his sunglasses. "You look familiar." He studied her a moment with his dark eyes and then suddenly smiled. "I'll be damned. Olivia Breaux has come back to Lyons Point."

"Hi, Sean. What's in the road?" she asked, hoping he would forget any questions he might have. Sean had always been good looking, the guy every girl wanted to date in school—her included, for awhile.

"Gator," he responded with a wide smile. "You know how they like to cross this area to the other canal. So, what's brought you back home? We figured never to see you again. Are you married?"

Olivia found one question she could answer. "Nope. Not married."

"Want to go out while you're in town?"

She pushed her sunglasses back up and forced a smile. "I need to see to a few things."

"Of course, of course," he hurried to say. "I know where to find you."

"Alrighty then." She rolled up her window when she saw the tail of the gator disappear over the other side of the road. The cars began to fire up and drive away.

Olivia, however, couldn't move her car since Sean was

still leaning against it. He kept smiling as he straightened and patted her car.

She drove away hoping every encounter would go as smoothly, if not as strangely, but she knew there were old friends who hadn't forgiven her for leaving. Friends who would love to rub it in her face if they knew why she had returned.

Her heart was still hammering by the time she turned onto a dirt road. It was just as bumpy as she remembered, which, oddly, brought a smile to her face.

Cows and horses grazed peacefully in the pasture on her left while on her right a new house was being built. How she missed the rice fields. Strange, since she had thought she hated them.

She had to slow the car to a crawl as some parts had slag while others had so many holes she had nowhere to drive. It was thirty minutes later when she spotted the mailbox with the immaculate flowerbed around it.

"I'm home," she murmured.

Olivia turned in the drive and found herself grinning wildly when she saw the old wooden house on stilts, just as it had been nine years earlier.

She parked her car behind her grandmother's old Chevy truck and turned off the ignition as she sat there looking around. She could almost pretend it was the day after graduation and the last years hadn't happened.

Sitting in a parked car without AC in the Louisiana sun

was a great way to get heat stroke. Olivia opened the car door and stood.

The first thing that hit her was the humidity. The second was the smell of the bayou and her grandmother's cooking. There was nothing that could match it.

"It's about time you arrived. Now get on up here," her grandmother said with a wave of her wooden spoon from the steps of the porch.

Olivia let out a laugh. She might have spoken to her grandmother every week, but she hadn't seen her in years. Her silver hair was pulled back in a loose bun, and she wore her favorite apron, which had roses embroidered on the edges.

She didn't hesitate another second in grabbing her purse and one of her bags before she was running up the steps. Olivia paused long enough to look over the bayou and the cypress trees.

With a shake of her head to dispel memories, she turned and opened the door to the screened porch. She didn't dwell, because there would be enough time for that later.

Olivia hurried into the house. As soon as she entered, all her cares dropped away just as they used to. She shut the door and dropped her bag and purse seconds before she was enveloped in a hug.

"It's so good to have you home, sha," her grandmother whispered brokenly.

Olivia felt tears threaten her own eyes as she returned the embrace. "It's good to be home."

She hadn't realized just how much she had needed her grandmother until that moment. It wasn't just her words, but the woman herself. Her house had become Olivia's home after her parent's death when she was seventeen. As horrific as that was, it was as if nothing dared to come near her as long as she was in that house.

Everything changed the day she left Louisiana.

"Now, none of that," her grandmother said, and stepped back to look at her. "You need some rest and food. You're too skinny, sha."

"Only you would say that, Maman."

Her grandmother looked at her with the same black eyes as her own before she turned to the stove and began to stir something in the pot. "Then it's a good thing you've come home."

"Yum. I smell gumbo."

"Sha, as if I'd let you come home and not greet you with proper food."

Olivia opened the fridge and pulled out a Coke. She sipped the beverage as her gaze caught the loaves of fresh bread her grandmother baked every day.

"Anything interesting happen on your drive in?"

"Why didn't you tell me Sean Hebert was a sheriff's deputy?"

Her grandmother's sly smile said it all. "So, you ran into Sean. He always asks about you when he comes out here."

"He comes out here?" Olivia asked in shock.

Her grandmother tasted the gumbo and put another pinch of pepper in. "He checks in on me from time to time. He's not the only one who asks about you. Now, what had you running into him?"

"Gator in the road."

"Ah," she said with a nod of her silver head. "That does tend to stop traffic."

Olivia took another drink as she debated on whether to tell her grandmother the rest. "Maman, he asked me out."

"Good, good," she said with her back to Olivia.

She pulled out a chair at the table and sat. She knew better than to get in the middle of her grandmother and cooking. "Is that all you have to say?"

"You could do worse. Sean has made a name for himself in the parish. He's respected, and he'll be sheriff one day."

Olivia just couldn't see herself as the wife to a cop in any form. "I think it might be too soon."

Her grandmother placed the wooden spoon down too gently. When she turned, Olivia saw that determined glint in her dark eyes, the one that said she was about to get an earful.

"I hate what happened to you, my girl, but I'd be lying if I said I wasn't happy you're home. That man you had in Dallas is no man. If he was, he would have admitted his guilt instead of letting you take the blame and getting fired for his actions."

Olivia knew she was right, but it was still hard to accept. Calvin had been all she wanted. He was successful, gorgeous, and well-off. He'd treated her as if she were a princess.

Right up until funds went missing from their work and he placed the blame on her. It didn't matter how much she professed her innocence, Holbert and Dobbs Incorporated believed him—a man who had been with the company for ten years—over her.

To make matters worse, that's when she learned he was married. With three kids.

It was as if the kicks wouldn't stop coming. The final jolt had been when she ran out of money and she had to choose between paying for her car or her apartment.

Olivia had no alternative but to pack up her belongings and return to the only place she could to lick her wounds and try to piece together her life.

"It wasn't his mistake, Maman," Olivia said. "I think he targeted me because I worked in accounting. He stole those funds and put the blame on me. Everything he did was done through my computer, at my desk, with my access code. Who else could the company blame?"

Her grandmother rubbed her hand up and down Olivia's arm. "Are they still going to press charges?"

"Oh yeah. That's a given. I may go to jail, Maman."

"Not going to happen, sha. Now get some bowls. The rice is done and so is the gumbo."

Olivia let her grandmother take over with talk of her flower garden, town gossip, and unimportant things that kept her listening as she ate.

It wasn't until they were sitting on the porch drinking wine with the crickets singing and the smell of gardenias that Olivia realized her grandmother had gone out of her way not to mention a single person Olivia knew in Lyons Point.

"You don't have to protect me, Maman."

Her grandmother snorted, not even pretending not to know what she was referring to. "Of course I do, my girl. It's what I've done since the moment you came into the world."

"I hired an attorney," Olivia said. She didn't want to bring it up again, but she wanted her grandmother to know that she was going to fight. "I told her everything. I gave her texts, emails, and even phone messages."

"Is she capable?"

"I wouldn't have hired her if she wasn't. She has roots in Louisiana as well. Her father's family is from near Lafayette."

That made her grandmother smile. "Do you think she can get the charges dropped?"

"If you met her, you'd understand why I chose her. She's like a pit bull in the lawyer world."

Her grandmother threw back her head and laughed.

"We'll have to invite her down. I'd like to meet her. What's her name?"

"Ava Ledet."

Her grandmother nodded and sipped her wine. "I want Calvin's balls in a bag."

That caused Olivia to spit out her wine she started laughing so hard. Leave it to her maman to say something like that. "I think Ava will get them for you."

They sat on the porch for another twenty minutes in silence until her grandmother rose and kissed her on the cheek before she went off to bed.

Olivia couldn't go yet. It had been too draining of a day to try and turn everything off and find sleep. She pulled her legs up against her in the chair and thought back to nights in high school when she and her friends would sit on her porch late into the night.

Not once had someone gone into the kitchen and not found a plethora of food to choose from. Her grandmother loved to have a house full of people to feed. Olivia hadn't comprehended until then how lonely her grandmother must have been, to go from a houseful to no one in a day.

Olivia hadn't been thinking about her grandmother the night she left. She had been thinking of herself. Just as she hadn't been thinking about her job when she was busy kissing Calvin or running his errands while he went in and stole from the company.

She was paying for her sins now, and rightly so. After all

her grandmother had done in taking her in and raising her, Olivia hadn't done well by her.

That was going to change. Olivia might have wanted out of the small town, but she had a chance to start again. She wasn't going to thumb her nose up at it now.

She stood and walked to the door of the porch. The screen kept the mosquitoes out so that they could enjoy the night, but Olivia wanted a closer look at the water.

The moonlight had always been so pretty on the water. Not even that could compare to the way the beams shown through the moss hanging from the cypress trees.

Olivia walked through the door and down the steps to the dock. It was narrow and long with several boards having been replaced recently. She walked to the end and looked down at the still water.

The bayous scared some people, but she had grown up with it. There were terrors out there like gators and cottonmouths, but there was beauty as well.

Olivia didn't know how long she stood there before she realized the crickets had ceased. Suddenly the hair on the back of her neck lifted and she knew she was being watched. It was predatory, threatening.

And it scared the hell out of her.

She backed up a step as her gaze skimmed the area looking for what it could be. There were plenty of shadows for it to hide in, which didn't make her feel any better.

The low rumble of a growl made her heart hammer

against her ribs. That wasn't any animal she knew. Olivia spun around and ran up the dock. She tripped on the steps, slamming her shin against a board as she reached for the handle to the door. Even then she didn't stop until she was inside the house with the door locked.

She backed away from the door, waiting for something to bust through. Seconds turned to minutes, but nothing happened. She checked the locks on the doors but left the lights on as she walked to her room in a vain effort to find sleep.

VINCENT WAS CLOSING in on the creature when he caught sight of Olivia Breaux. He was so shocked to see her standing at the edge of the water with her long hair loose and her long legs bared by her shorts. He was struck senseless by her beauty, struck dumb at having her so close again.

She had always had that effect on him. It was just one reason he had kept his distance from her. It hadn't helped that he wanted nothing more than to kiss her.

Vincent forced his gaze away, but the creature was gone before he realized it. He let out a silent curse as he once more looked at Olivia.

He was afraid the beast had found its next target.

CHAPTER

THREE

IT WAS the smell of bread baking that woke Olivia. She rolled onto her back and yawned as she stretched her arms over her head. It had taken her hours to fall asleep after that eerie feeling the night before.

She wanted to laugh it off, to toss it aside as her imagination, but she couldn't. The fear had gripped her tightly and hadn't loosened its hold until the wee hours of the morning.

Olivia blew out a breath and looked to the window where the golden rays of the morning sun filtered through the blinds. The soft whirl of her ceiling fan mixed with the sounds from the kitchen and her grandmother's humming took her back to her childhood in an instant.

If only she could go back and relive the night she had left. How different her life would be if she had stayed. Hindsight, however, was 20/20, and there was no use thinking of the could've-beens or should've-beens.

Olivia threw off the covers and rose to pad into the bathroom. She walked out fifteen minutes later, showered, dressed, and ready to face the day. Whatever it might bring.

"Oh, good. You're up," her grandmother said as she flashed a smile before she turned to the stove and the eggs she was scrambling. "Bacon is on the table."

Olivia grabbed a piece and took a bite. She reached for the bread knife and began to slice a cooling loaf. "What's the plan for today?"

"I need to head to Grace's. I've baked her some bread, and I'll be taking some gumbo over to her as well."

Grace had been her grandmother's best friend since they were young girls. Ever since Grace fell and broke her hip three years earlier, her grandmother had been bringing food and doing some cleaning.

"There're some items I need from town. Want to pick them up for me?" her grandmother asked.

Olivia stilled. She knew exactly what her grandmother was doing—forcing her to face the world and the small town she wanted to hide from.

She set down the knife and turned. "Maman, I—"

"You're a Breaux," she interrupted and dumped the eggs into a bowl that she set on the table. She placed her hands on the back of the chair and regarded Olivia. "We're fighters, Olivia, even when we don't think we can."

Those words stayed with Olivia long after breakfast was over and her grandmother had departed for her visit with Grace. Olivia left the list of groceries on the table, trying her best to ignore it as she cleaned the kitchen.

She finished drying the last of the dishes and put them away only to turn and see that damn list. Olivia smoothed the dishtowel on the edge of the sink.

With a frustrated growl, she grabbed the list and her purse before she headed to her car. The entire drive to the small grocer, Olivia kept praying that she could get in and out without anyone recognizing her. It had been almost a decade since she had left. Surely she had changed enough people wouldn't know her.

To prove just how awful her luck was, Olivia had no sooner walked into the store than she literally ran into Sean. "I'm so sorry," she hurried to say.

"I'm not." His smile was too bright, alerting her that their bumping into each other hadn't been an accident. "How does it feel to be back home?"

Olivia licked her lips and slid past him to grab a basket and looped it over her arm. "It's been good."

"I'm glad you're settling in nicely."

She pursed her lips trying to think of a way to get him to leave. When nothing came to mind, she walked to the produce section and stood looking at the bell peppers.

"I could throw a party and invite everyone over."

Olivia began to feel sick. No doubt Sean had been telling

everyone—and he knew everyone—that she was back. So much for her hiding out and taking baby steps back into the world she had left behind.

"Sean, I think someone just hit your car," came a deep voice from behind Olivia.

She remained staring at the bell peppers. It had been the worst idea to stop here. She should have gone into Crowley. At least there she had a chance to get in and out without being recognized.

"He's gone. You can let go of the pepper now."

Olivia looked down at her hand to find she had picked up one of the bell peppers and squeezed it so hard her fingers had punctured the skin. Dear God, what was wrong with her?

"Thank you," she said. She turned around and looked into bright blue eyes. There was only one family she knew to have eyes that distinct color—the Chiassons.

Excitement coursed through her as she thought it was Vincent. Even though the man had the same dark hair and the same Chiasson good looks, he wasn't Vincent.

Her disappointment was palpable.

He smiled softly as his gaze held hers. "Olivia, right? I'm Beau Chiasson."

"Beau, yes," she replied with a nod.

He glanced behind him and shifted his basket from one hand to the other. "Sean will be occupied long enough for you to get in and out. Good to see you, Olivia."

She watched him walk away before she pulled out her list and hurried through the store grabbing the items her grandmother needed.

~

It was Beau's whistling that alerted Vincent that he was up to something. After another unsuccessful night, he was in a foul mood. It didn't help those three deaths weighed so heavily upon him.

Vincent poured a cup of coffee and lifted the steaming liquid to his lips. He had barely taken his first sip when he saw Beau glance at him out of the corner of his eye.

Beau deftly cut the onions, bell peppers, and ham into pieces for the omelets. "You'll never guess who I ran into this morning."

Vincent didn't need to guess. He knew. Olivia Breaux. The few hours of sleep he had gotten had been full of Olivia. Her black eyes, her midnight hair, her full lips.

He refused to play Beau's game though. Without a word, he turned to the table where a map of the parish drawn by their great-great grandfather sat. A clear sheet lay on top of it for protection and so they could mark the areas they had been without marking the map.

"Olivia Breaux," Beau said. "Damn, Vincent, she looks hotter than ever. Didn't you have a thing for her in school?"

Vincent picked up the black pencil and marked the areas

he had searched the night before. "I'm going to head out shortly and check the southeast side of the bayou. There are some gator nests there so the creature shouldn't be anywhere near that, but I want to check anyway."

"Olivia," Beau persisted.

"That's nice," Vincent responded. "It's about time she returned to her grandmother. Maria is a good woman."

Beau grunted. "Is that really all you have to say? Isn't it time for your weekly visit to Maria?"

Vincent straightened and faced his brother. "Do you really need to ask? Look at Christian. If you need a reminder about our lives, think back to Dad when he found Mom. That's what our family endures. Do you want that? Because I sure as hell don't."

"We need sons and daughters to carry on the family business." The smile was gone as a serious note filled his voice.

Vincent knew all too well about having to carry on the family name, but he was weary of it all. "The Chiassons have protected this parish for over three hundred years, and in all that time we're scorned and disparaged. Is that what you want for your children?"

"I want children. I want a wife, a family. I want more than what I have now."

Vincent set down his coffee. "Then take it, Beau."

"Because you won't?"

"Because I can't. I won't go through what Dad did. I

won't have children and put them through what we went through growing up."

Beau cracked two eggs at once into a bowl before tossing the shells into the garbage. He grabbed two more. "Mom went out hunting with us. She knew what could happen. So did Dad. I won't allow my wife to hunt."

"Good luck with that," Lincoln said as he walked into the kitchen from outside. He went to the sink and began to wash the grease off his hands. He dried his hands and looked from Beau to Vincent as he pulled up the sides of his long hair to secure it at the back of his head with a piece of leather. "Both generators are fixed now."

"Good. There's already a hurricane headed to Florida," Vincent said, his mind still on what Beau had said.

Lincoln was glaring at him when Christian walked in, his arms loaded with weapons. "Damn. You've been busy."

Vincent and Lincoln exchanged a look as Christian laid out the various weapons on the dining room table that hadn't been used for a meal since the night their parents died.

"It'll kill tonight," Christian said. He lifted his favorite weapon, the crossbow, and met Vincent's gaze. "You know it will."

Lincoln ran a thumb over the edge of his axe and smiled as blood formed. "Not if we have any say in it."

"We searched all of yesterday and last night and didn't

find its lair," Beau pointed out. "How are we to get the drop on it tonight?"

Vincent pointed to a spot on the map. "I lost the beast here. That's where I'm going to start."

Christian leaned over and looked at the map. "That's the Breaux place."

"Olivia," Beau said.

Vincent nodded woodenly. "She was outside last night. The creature saw her. I thought it might attack, but then it just disappeared."

"Well, hell," Lincoln stated angrily. "How did the damn thing just disappear again?"

Christian threw a thick book down atop the table. "I think I know."

Vincent gazed at the leather-bound book that held all the creatures that the Chiasson's had killed through the decades. It also listed how to kill certain beasts, and just what might have brought them to the parish.

"Start reading," Beau said as he turned back to the stove.

Vincent placed his hand on the book. Atop the leather was the Chiasson family crest that dated all the way back to France where their family originated.

As children they had poured over the entries learning all they could while their parents hunted. Once they were old enough, their father taught them how to code the beasts and how to add pages to the books.

"I've been updating the book ever since…that night," Christian said.

Vincent nodded in approval. "That's good. It needed to be done."

There was a hiss behind them as Beau dumped the eggs into the pan. Vincent opened the book to a random page in the middle to find a detailed drawing of a banshee.

"What did you find, runt?" Lincoln asked Christian.

"I think someone is summoning this thing."

Vincent jerked his hand away from the book and took a step back. The last time a creature had been summoned was when their parents had been killed. It was their mother who had figured out the summoning. That night, she had been killed. Their father had gone to confront who he thought was responsible. And within hours, both their parents were dead.

Vincent had been the one to find their father. He had also been the one to tell his siblings. That night had left a wound inside him that still bled.

Whoever killed his parents was back to their old tricks again. This time they wouldn't get away with it. Vincent didn't care how long it took, but he would kill whoever it was.

That's the only thing that would heal him. And bring closure to his siblings.

"I knew they would come back," Lincoln said, hatred dripping from his lips. "I've waited years for a piece of them."

Beau flipped the omelet over. "Stand in line, dickhead."

Vincent lifted his gaze to Christian. "What else did you find?"

Christian's brow furrowed. "Y'all aren't going to like it."

"Spit it out," Lincoln demanded.

Christian locked gazes with Vincent. "Mom thought the person was targeting our family, our friends, to kill. I think it's happening again."

FOUR

No!

The word exploded in Vincent's head, but he didn't say it. His three brothers were all talking at once after Christian's announcement. All he could do was thank God that Riley was nowhere near Louisiana at this point.

"Vincent," Lincoln said.

It snapped him out of his thoughts. None of them lived that night like he had, and they all knew it. He swallowed and leaned his hands on the table as he closed his eyes, wishing he could close out the past as easily.

"Evil was here eleven years ago. It infested the bayou until people were scared to venture out once night fell. Linc and I hunted with Mom and Dad while you two stayed with Riley."

Christian nodded as he pulled out a chair and sat. "I

remember it all. I was so pissed that I couldn't go with y'all, but Dad wanted me here to guard the house."

"There are times I wish I hadn't seen what I did," Lincoln confessed.

It was the first time Vincent had heard such words from his brother. "I wish you hadn't either."

"Riley was asleep," Beau said. "I had just looked in on her when I heard Dad. I ran out onto the porch and saw…"

Vincent knew why he couldn't finish. None of them could. Not even him, and he had been with his father when they found his mother.

She had been brutally beaten before something clawed her and then ripped her heart from her chest. After all these years, Vincent could still hear his father's cry of grief and anger, he could still see his father rocking his mother against his chest as tears fell.

Then the rage had taken his father.

Vincent had done his best to keep up with him. He had known the evil could take both his parents that night, but he hadn't been quick enough.

"It's not your fault," Lincoln said as if sensing where Vincent's mind had been.

Beau cut into the omelet and took a bite. "You came back to us. Without you, the state would've sent us into foster care."

"If this thing is back, the only target that's come close to us is Molly," Vincent said, changing the subject. He couldn't stand to think back to that night.

Beau cleared his throat. "That's not exactly true. The first victim—Lindsey—I had asked out. She was new in town."

"Why didn't you say something sooner?" Vincent demanded as anger began to spread inside him. "We could have connected the dots sooner if you had."

He then looked at Lincoln. "What about Breanne, the second victim. Did you know her?"

"We hooked up every now and again. We were friends with benefits."

Vincent grabbed the plate with the omelet and threw it against the wall. He hadn't felt this anger in eleven years. There was nothing more to say to his brothers, not when he was this infuriated.

He stormed out to clear his head and try to figure out who was after his family. And just why they had waited eleven years to finish what they started.

Olivia was so startled by the sound of her cell phone ringing that she fell off the couch. She grappled for the phone that had fallen with her and hastily answered before she looked at the caller ID.

"You sound groggy. Did I wake you?" Ava Ledet asked.

Olivia leaned against the cushion and laughed. "Actually,

you did. I didn't sleep much last night, and I thought to just lay down and chill."

"I guess you were sleepier than you realized."

"Obviously." Olivia climbed back on the couch and tried to push aside the butterflies wreaking havoc in her stomach. "I didn't expect to hear from you so soon."

Ava covered the phone as she spoke to someone else. "Sorry. My assistant had a question. Yeah, nothing to worry about. I wanted to check in and see how you were doing."

"That's not what attorneys normally do, is it?"

Ava chuckled, the sound rich and seductive. "No, but then I don't consider myself a normal attorney. You were a wreck the last time I saw you."

"Wow. Thanks for putting it so mildly." It was no wonder Olivia liked Ava so well. The woman put it all out there, but in a way that you adored her for.

"I'm not one of those women who have lots of girlfriends. Well, to be honest, I don't really have any. I'm more of a loner, which works well with being a workaholic. It's weird, but as soon as you walked into my office I felt as if I'd known you my whole life. As if we had always been friends."

Olivia smiled as she leaned her head back against the cushion. "I felt the same. I had a lot of friends at one time, and yet the more we talked, the more I realized none of those women had really been my friend."

"Great. So now you don't think I'm some kind of freak or anything."

"I broke down in your office, Ava. I let some buttlick sway me so that he committed a crime and framed me. I'm the freak."

Ava made a sound through the phone. "Not even close, hon. I do have some news about Calvin."

That made Olivia sit up straighter. "What?"

"You know your company had cameras all over, right? Well, I got a court order to obtain the times that the computer says you were stealing the funds."

Olivia rubbed her eyes. "Why didn't the company do that when I said it was Calvin?"

"I think that's exactly what they were doing when I arrived today with the order. I'm still waiting to get the footage from them. They have until five. Oh, and look. That's just five minutes from now." There was a commotion through the phone. "Gotta go. I'll call you as soon as I know something."

The phone went dead before Olivia could respond. She set down her phone and ran her hands through her hair. It had come loose from the ponytail.

With a yawn, she rose and walked to the bathroom where she stared at herself in the mirror. There was nothing special about her black hair, black eyes, and dark skin so common in the Cajun culture. At just five-foot-two, she was on the short side, and top heavy.

Her only redeeming feature was her eyelashes—they were long and lush. At least she didn't have to get extensions like so many of her co-workers.

"As if that matters now," she muttered.

She pulled out her ponytail and let her hair fall down to the middle of her back. With a huff, she blew the long, slanted bangs out of her eyes.

Maybe she should go out with Sean. It might be good to move on with her life as her grandmother said. At the thought of her grandmother, she realized she had been gone all day.

Olivia walked back into the living room and looked through a window. Her grandmother's truck wasn't in the driveway. It wasn't until she checked her phone that she saw the message waiting.

She let out a sigh of relief when she heard her grandmother's message saying she was going to stay with Grace that night since Grace wasn't feeling well.

That meant Olivia had the entire house to herself. She had longed for such things as a kid. Now, she didn't relish the prospect of being alone.

Two hours passed as she flipped through channels, catching bits of shows and the news. At seven she finally fixed a sandwich and popped in *Horrible Bosses*. She was shocked to find her grandmother even had that movie, but she was glad since she needed a good laugh.

By ten, Olivia couldn't stand to have the TV on anymore.

She grabbed a beer and walked out onto the porch to inhale the sultry night air. The heat of the day still lingered long after the moon rose.

So many nights had been spent sitting at the end of the dock with friends imagining their futures. In all her dreams, her life had never turned out like the one she led.

She hadn't expected to live a glamorous life in front of the cameras, but she had thought to be a successful accountant, wife, and mother. The only part of that she had gotten was the accounting degree.

Even her job hadn't been as prestigious as she had wanted. Working for one of the top companies in Dallas had paid well, however. She thought she was about to get the next step in her dream—wife.

Calvin dashed all of that in a heartbeat.

Now there was a chance she could go to jail. Over something she didn't do. Olivia trusted Ava to help her, but she wished she was still in Dallas to be right there through it all.

All but ten thousand dollars of her savings had been used remaining in Dallas for as long as she had. At least she had a home to return to.

She looked longingly at the water. After the night before, she wasn't going out there alone. Whether it was her imagination or not, it had been a creepy experience.

Goosebumps rose up all along her skin as she felt something behind her. She had been alone on the porch, she was sure of it. And yet, she knew without a doubt that someone—something—was with her.

She turned around to see a dark, hairy shape come out of the shadows and slam her into the side of the porch. Olivia fell heavily, unable to move her limbs.

Her eyes couldn't focus on the thing that had hit her. She tried to call out for help. The...thing...loomed in front of her as she blinked to try and see it clearly.

There was a low growl as it grabbed her arm. She winced when something cut her, but it paid her no heed as it began to drag her to the porch door.

She could feel herself falling into the blackness. Olivia fought it, instinctively knowing that her life was on the line. Dimly, she heard someone shout.

The grip on her arm tightened, and she felt something warm and wet slide down her arm. Suddenly, it released her so that her head once more banged on the wooden porch.

"Shit!" a male voice growled.

She heard the squeak of the porch door as it was thrown open. Large hands, tender and soothing, smoothed back the hair from her face. "Olivia? Olivia, can you hear me?"

She forced open her eyes long enough to see a familiar face. He had hair so dark a brown it was almost black. It brushed the tops of his shoulders with a soft wave that begged to be touched.

His face was hard and rugged. A dose of handsome that gave him a dangerous air with a scar that ran across his right cheek. She was snagged by his bright, brilliant blue eyes ringed with navy.

Vincent was protecting her just as she had always wanted.

Perhaps she had hit her head too hard. Vincent would never be here.

"Olivia," he whispered.

Was it her imagination, or had there been a bit of longing in his voice?

A tearing sound pulled her from the darkness. She opened her eyes again as he gently lifted her arm. The pain pulled her out of unconsciousness enough to realize she was hurt, and it really was Vincent with her.

Olivia looked at her arm, but all she could see was red. Was that blood? Her blood?

She was mesmerized by how Vincent diligently wrapped her arm and tied the black bandage that looked suspiciously like his tee shirt.

Olivia blinked as the fog of her head cleared even more. His hand was on her forehead pushing back her hair again. A frown marred his forehead.

She had the insane urge to smooth it away and run her hands over his sun-bronzed skin. This was the Chiasson she had silently coveted, the Chiasson that had never looked at her.

"You're eyes are clearing," he said.

She tried to swallow, to wet her dry mouth, so she could ask what had happened.

"Answers later. First, we need to get you to safety."

Olivia wasn't sure if she could stand, but she shouldn't have worried because Vincent gathered her against him. She rested her head against his shoulder and closed her eyes. The rest of her fear melted away.

It had taken long enough, but she was finally in Vincent Chiasson's arms.

CHAPTER
FIVE

Vincent gently laid Olivia on the couch and checked the bandage on her arm. The cuts weren't deep enough to require stitches, but the fact that she had been injured, that he hadn't gotten to her in time, made him furious.

He touched her hair again, as he had yearned to do years ago. He couldn't seem to stop himself. It was like cool silk running through his fingers. The length boggled his mind, as did the thickness.

Unable to help himself, he ran the pads of his fingers over her high cheekbones down to her full lips. His body stirred, heat flaming his blood and desire engulfed him, as if it hadn't been nine years since the last time he had seen her.

Vincent recalled with crystal clarity the night he truly noticed her. He had been with his parents when they told

Maria that her son and his wife had been killed by a demon. Olivia had walked out onto the porch still half asleep with that magnificent hair of hers mused, her luscious curves on display in her tiny tank top and shorts, and he had fallen instantly under her spell.

"I'm going after it," Christian said as he started for the door.

"No!" Vincent bellowed as he jumped to his feet, forgetting that Olivia had drifted off to sleep. He wiped his hand down his face when his three brothers turned to him. "No," he repeated in a calmer tone.

A muscle flexed in Christian's jaw. "You might be the eldest, but that doesn't mean you can tell me what to do."

"I refuse to find another member of my family dead," Vincent said. It would likely shatter him if he did. It had taken everything he had to put that dreaded night eleven years ago behind him. And he almost hadn't succeeded.

Lincoln leaned against the kitchen counter. "Listen to him, Christian. Please."

"We had it," Beau said. "It was right there. We could have gone after it."

Lincoln's face contorted in anger. "Gone after it? Was I the only one to see it *disappear* right before our eyes?"

"No," Christian grudgingly admitted.

Beau paced the space between the kitchen and the dining area. "I can't just wait around for someone else to be killed.

Most of the things we hunt pose a danger, and few get a chance to actually hurt people."

"Why did it target Olivia?" Lincoln asked.

Vincent glanced at her. "I don't know. I tracked the beast here last night, but that's all."

"I was the one who spoke to her this morning," Beau said.

Christian slapped his hands on his legs. "Does that mean we can't talk to anyone for fear that they'll end up dead?"

"We already keep to ourselves. What else does this thing want?" Lincoln asked.

Vincent scratched his jaw as he considered his brothers' words. "We looked through that entire book of our family's, and nothing in there could just disappear as this creature does. It knows things it couldn't possibly."

"Which means someone is controlling it," Beau said with a grin.

"Ah, Vin," Christian said slowly.

Vincent looked to see his brother jerk his chin to the couch. Vincent turned his head to find Olivia's black eyes open and trained on him.

"We'll patrol the area," Lincoln said as the three of them filed out of the house.

Olivia grabbed her head as she tried to sit up. Vincent helped ease her into a sitting position. It brought him close to her, touching her again. It was unimaginable torture.

For so long he pushed aside the needs of his body, but

with Olivia, he couldn't. He wanted her, needed her. *Craved* her. It burned through him so hotly he could hardly pull breath into his lungs.

He thought he was safe from that driving, reckless desire for her when she left. But now she was back and looking more beautiful and tempting than ever.

"What happened?" she asked in that husky voice of hers.

Vincent had to move away. He couldn't think straight being so near her and wanting to have a taste of her lips. He walked to the fridge and opened it to grab a bottle of water.

"Vincent," she urged. "Tell me."

He looked around the kitchen. "Where is the aspirin?"

"Bathroom," she said and pointed down the hall.

Most everyone living in the parish knew what the Chiasson's did, but Maria had kept the true cause of Olivia's parent's deaths from her. Which meant Olivia might not know his family protected the parish by hunting supernatural creatures.

If she didn't know, he wasn't going to be the one to enlighten her.

He found the aspirin and dumped two in his hand before he walked back to Olivia. He handed the pills and water to her. "This will help with the headache."

The look in her gaze was fierce as she popped the pills in her mouth and drank the water to swallow them. "Spit out whatever you're trying your damnedest not to tell me."

"Where is Maria?"

"Maman is at Grace's house. Why?"

Vincent sat in the chair next to the couch and glanced out the window. "Did you see what attacked you?"

"Yes." She visibly swallowed. "Well. Sort of. It was hairy and dark. It came out of the shadows. I know I was alone on the porch, and then...it was just there. You were hunting it, weren't you?"

Damn. So she did know what his family did. Vincent was disappointed. Not that he stood a chance with someone like Olivia, but for just a moment, he would have liked to pretend.

He nodded. "It could have killed you right then, but it didn't. It looked to be dragging you off. Did it say anything?"

"Not at all. It slammed my head against the wood before I could run away. I need to call Maman. It could be after her, and she shouldn't come home."

Vincent covered her hand before she grabbed her cell phone. "I don't think the creature was after Maria."

"You think it was after me?" Olivia's black eyes went wide. "I just got back. How could it be after me?"

"I'm afraid it has to do with my family. Beau spoke with you this morning."

"Wow. So who did your family piss off?"

She pulled her hand away, and Vincent tried not to be upset. He stood and walked to the door to look out the glass. His brothers were staying close to the house while still patrolling. "I don't know who is after us. This goes back years. I'm sorry you got pulled into this. Perhaps you should return to Dallas."

"I can't."

No explanation, nothing. Vincent looked at her over his shoulder and saw her studying the water bottle as if it held the answers to the universe.

"Well, you can't remain here."

She stood quickly and swayed. Vincent was next to her in a heartbeat, his arms wrapped around her waist to steady her. He urged her back down, and then lifted her feet to put them on the couch so that she was reclining again.

"You should remain lying down for a bit longer," he said, stopping himself from touching her face as he was about to do.

She had her hand on her forehead as she leveled her gaze at him. "I know you want to hunt this thing, but please don't leave me alone."

No one had ever asked a Chiasson—much less him—to stay. It felt as if the sun had shone directly on him after eons of winter. Vincent had to remind himself it was only because she was scared and nothing more.

She had made her life away from Lyons Point, away from him. There was no kind of future there, and he needed to keep remembering that.

"We'll be staying until dawn. After that, you and Maria need to think about leaving town for awhile."

A small smile turned up her lips as she closed her eyes. "You know my grandmother. That's not going to happen."

The door opened and Lincoln walked inside. "We have a problem, Vin."

Vincent pulled his gaze from Olivia and went to his brother. "What is it?"

"We found tracks."

"Where?"

Lincoln paused. "Everywhere. It's like the beast is circling the house waiting to get to her, and yet we can't see it."

If it could disappear and reappear at will, Vincent didn't know how to fight it. He fingered the hilt of his machete at his thigh as his mind ran through different scenarios.

"What makes you think this thing will stop at sunrise?" Olivia asked into the silence.

Lincoln leaned around him and said, "It has every other night. Why should tonight be any different?"

"Because it didn't get its prey," Vincent said as realization hit him. He shifted his gaze to Olivia to see fear cloud her features.

Something slammed into the back of the house. Olivia jerked as Vincent rushed to her side to protect her while Lincoln ran to the back of the house. Outside, Vincent could hear both Beau and Christian shouting at each other.

The second hit came from the front of the house near the porch.

Vincent unsheathed his machete just as Lincoln came back into the living room. Olivia rose from the couch and stood behind him, her hands on his waist.

Everything grew quiet, including Beau and Christian and the profusion of insects outside. The stillness was eerie, sending warning bells clanging in Vincent's head.

Olivia screamed as the lights flickered and something materialized in the kitchen, only to disappear almost immediately.

That's all it took for Vincent to grab her and head to the door. Lincoln fell in step behind them, a Bowie knife in each hand.

Vincent let out a two-toned whistle to signal his brothers as they stepped onto the porch. Christian was the first to appear, his crossbow at his shoulder and aimed. Beau was right behind him with the sawed-off double-barreled shotgun.

As soon as Olivia's foot touched the wood of the porch there was a loud growl and the creature came out of the corner of the porch for her.

Vincent yanked Olivia against him, turning his back to the creature. He winced as he felt something slash his back. The grunts and shouts behind him told Vincent that his brothers had the beast cornered.

It was going to be over. Olivia was going to be safe.

Which meant he had no reason to be with her.

Regret surged within him. How he hated himself for it,

too. Olivia's safety was more important than the stark need roaring through him.

He reveled in the feel of his arms around her, of how her body molded to his. Of how she clung to him. He bit back a groan at the feel of her breasts pressed against his chest.

"Son of a bitch!" Christian bellowed.

Lincoln touched Vincent's arm. "It's gone, Vin. We didn't get it."

Vincent slowly pulled his head back, letting his cheek rub against Olivia's. Her mouth was inches from his, and her full lips were parted.

He made himself look into her eyes, thinking it would cool is ardor. Instead, it was adding gas to the flame when he saw desire reflected in her black depths.

Her hand on his chest flexed, and he found his arms tensing, holding her closer. His balls tightened when her tongue peeked out to lick her lips.

His head dipped, ready to kiss her, when Lincoln said his name.

Vincent wanted to punch him. He turned to give Lincoln a piece of his mind when he felt his back pull. That's when he remembered the creature's claws had gotten him.

"Vincent, you're hurt," Olivia said.

He shrugged it off. The slashes hurt, but it wasn't the first time he had been cut hunting a creature—nor would it be the last.

Vincent was about to tell Olivia that when something caught his eye in the board at the corner of the house. He ran his thumb over the Hoodoo symbol.

"Well, Maria. I didn't expect this," he said aloud.

CHAPTER
SIX

Olivia barely had time to register what Vincent said before she was surrounded by all four Chiasson brothers and marched to her car.

Vincent got behind the wheel with Lincoln taking the passenger seat. Olivia was squished between Christian and Beau in the back. No one said a word as Vincent spun out the wheels in his hurry to leave.

Olivia looked back as they drove off, and she could have sworn she saw something step from the shadows of the house. She shivered as she turned back to the front.

"My grandmother doesn't practice Hoodoo," she stated, because she felt someone had to say it.

Vincent met her gaze in the rearview mirror, but it was Lincoln who said, "You've been away a long time. Do you really know what's going on in Maria's life?"

"My grandmother is devout Catholic, just as your family is."

Beau grabbed the headrest in front of him as they bounced along the road. "The fact is, Olivia, that someone marked your house with that symbol. I think it was meant to keep evil out."

"But evil got in. That creature showed up in the kitchen," Lincoln said.

Vincent jerked the wheel to miss a raccoon. "It didn't stay. It flashed in, and now that I think about it, it might have been trying to get Olivia out of the house."

"So I was safer there?" she asked and rolled her eyes.

Christian grabbed her seatbelt and strapped her in. "You'll be safer with us. That thing wanted you, and it isn't going to stop until it has you."

"I'm screwed then." Just what she wanted to hear. Her professional life was falling apart, and now, apparently, so was her private life.

Beau rested his shotgun over his legs. "Not where we're taking you."

"And that is?"

"Home," Vincent said.

Home. He couldn't mean... Oh, God, he did. They were taking her to their home. As far as she knew, few people had ever seen the Chiasson house. It was even deeper in the bayou than her grandmother's.

Olivia remained silent as Vincent wound them through

back roads she hadn't even known were there. She worried her little car wouldn't make it over some parts, but Vincent managed to get them through each time.

She leaned forward when she spotted the drive that was lined on either side with massive live oak trees. As impressive as the trees were, it was the house that took her breath away.

The two-story white house was the picture of a plantation home. The huge columns, the porches—upper and lower—wrapping all the way around the house, and black shutters.

Olivia was still staring at the house when Christian unbuckled her seatbelt and Beau pulled her out of the car. She was ushered into the house quickly.

Once the door was closed behind them, all four brothers let out a sigh of relief. Olivia gapped at the splendor before her. The wood floors were dark and had rugs of various sizes and colors placed throughout. The staircase was front and center as it curved to the second floor.

The walls were painted a soft gray and the crown molding was thick and ornate. A round table sat in the foyer with an array of pictures of the family.

She wanted to explore every inch of the house. How could something so grand have been in her town and she not know about it?

Olivia walked around the table and started for the stairs,

only vaguely aware that Beau, Christian, and Lincoln went off to different parts of the first floor.

"How's your head?"

She stopped, her eyes closing at the deep timber of Vincent's voice. The house forgotten, her body trembled as she recalled the hard press of his muscles, the heady scent of him when he had yanked her against him.

And then when he had looked down at her. Her stomach quivered just remembering how his bright blue eyes had filled with desire.

She had thought he would kiss her back at her house. For just a moment, the desire, the yearning, had burned bright in his gaze and on his face.

And then just like that, it was gone.

"It's better," she answered.

"And your arm? I'll need to check the bandages."

She bit her lip as she thought about his hands on her skin again. Around Vincent all she could think about was him. On her.

In her.

Thrusting hard and fast, slow and deep.

She nearly moaned at the thought. How was it that he could inspire such erotic thoughts? No other man had ever affected her this way.

"Olivia?"

She jerked open her eyes to find him standing in front of

her. He was frowning, searching her face as if he could determine what was wrong.

"Your face is flushed."

So was so much more of her, but she wasn't going to tell him. "It's just all the excitement. How am I safe here?"

"The house is warded against...well, everything. No evil can penetrate these walls. Most can't even get on our land."

She was duly impressed. Olivia rubbed her hands along her arms and gave a shake of her head. "I need to call my grandmother. She'll be worried."

"One of us will see to that," he said and motioned her to follow him.

With nothing else to do, Olivia did just that. She found herself in a large kitchen with a map spread out on the breakfast table.

"We've been hunting this thing for a week," Vincent said as he stared down at the map. "It's killed three women already."

"What?" Olivia hadn't heard any of this. Then again, she hadn't been in town long enough to learn the gossip, nor had she seen any of the papers.

Vincent's look turned stony. "All three were connected to us somehow, whether being asked out by one of us, a friends-with-benefits arrangement, or even just a phone call."

"Yep. You already said you think it was because Beau spoke with me today."

His hesitation made fear snake down her spine, but it was the look of regret that made her take a step back.

"You felt something last night on the pier," he said.

Olivia realized two things in that moment: Vincent had seen her, and so had the creature.

She nodded weakly. "I knew something was there. I felt it."

"I was tracking it. It stopped near your house. That's when I looked away long enough to spot you, and then it was gone."

Olivia pulled out a chair and practically fell on it. "You knew it was coming for me."

"Which was the only reason it didn't get you tonight." He waved his hand at the map. "We've searched this entire bayou and the surrounding areas to no avail. We can't find this thing."

Her grandmother had never had anything negative to say about the Chiassons. Olivia had graduated with Lincoln, but he hadn't paid her any attention. In fact, the Chiassons were usually never around for any school functions or parties.

Now she understood why.

Vincent ran a hand through his dark hair. "My family has been hunting since our ancestor followed a creature to Nova Scotia from France, and then from Nova Scotia to here."

Now she understood why they kept themselves apart from others. Few would believe what they did, and the others that did would want to keep their distance just in case.

"Thank you for tonight. You saved me."

He shrugged, almost as if he wasn't used to the praise. Olivia rose and moved to stand beside him. She gazed at the map seeing the three X's where she surmised the victims had been found.

"We've never brought anyone into our home," he said.

She looked at him, surprised by his words. "Then I should thank you again."

His hand brushed hers, sending chills racing along her skin at the contact. She had been in his arms, molded to his body, and yet so simple a touch could turn her to mush.

She hungered for more.

Breathing became difficult when she was once more caught in the web of desire. It tightened around them, pulling them closer—urging them deeper.

She lifted her face as Vincent lowered his. Their gazes clashed, tangled. She feared where this was going, feared how desperately she needed his touch.

Some might say it was the trauma she had been through that night, but Olivia knew differently. She had always felt this way toward Vincent. She just hadn't been this close to see how far it might go.

Beau stepped into the kitchen and said, "The three of us are going hunting. You've...ah...got things covered here I see."

"Go," Vincent growled.

Olivia shivered, not from his tone, but from the raw need in his gaze. No one had ever looked at her with such longing, such fire before.

It wasn't long before the house grew quiet, leaving her alone with Vincent. Would he finally kiss her?

"I'll see to your wound now," he said and turned away.

Olivia was crushed. So much for that kiss. She held out her arm as he unwrapped the part of his shirt he had torn off and set about cleaning the wound before he wrapped it in clean gauze.

"Your turn," she said when he finished.

He hesitated for just a second before he jerked off his torn and bloodied black tee. She bit her lip when she saw the scars that covered his body, and he would have four new ones to add to it.

The slashes from the creature went deep, gorging the skin. "You need to go the hospital for stitches."

Vincent was shaking his head before she finished talking. "Take the jar I just used on you. Spread the contents liberally over the wounds."

Olivia looked at the simple jar. "What's in the jar?"

"Herbs to heal us. We can't exactly go to the ER every time we have a run-in with the creatures. Our ancestors came up with ways for us to take care of things here."

Olivia set about following his instructions until all four

slashes were cleaned. She taped a piece of gauze over it and stepped back to survey her work.

"Thanks. Time for you to go to bed," he said without even looking at her.

As if she could sleep now. She was being chased by a creature that could disappear at will, learned that her grandmother's house was protected by Hoodoo, and discovered that the rumors about the Chiassons were true. Not to mention she had come close—twice—to kissing Vincent.

Sleep was the last thing on her mind.

"Isn't there something else I can do to help you? I can cook or clean or—"

"You'd be in the way. Follow me. I'll show you to a room."

Olivia stomped after him. "I'm not tired. Need I remind you that this thing is after me?"

He was halfway up the stairs when he turned around and walked back to her. "Need I remind you that we hunt these things?"

"I want to help."

"No." He pivoted and walked back up the stairs.

"I want to be useful."

In an instant, he was before her again. "And I don't want you to die!"

The impact of his words went right through her. They held a deeper meaning. She saw it there in his eyes right before it was replaced with that glowing flame of desire again.

"I won't."

"No, you won't," he said, before he claimed her lips.

CHAPTER

SEVEN

VINCENT ALLOWED himself one taste of her. That's all he was going to take. Then their lips met. The desire that had been riding him erupted into a firestorm of need.

He pulled back, startled by the intensity of longing. Olivia's eyes reflected his surprise—and hunger.

It was a mistake to give in, a mistake to allow himself to think he could hold Olivia Breaux in his arms and not pay the consequences later.

Yet, even as those thoughts ran through his mind, he slid his hand into the thick tresses at her neck and yanked her against him for another kiss.

Desire licked at him, urging him onward. Their kiss was fierce, fiery. Passion sizzled between them, scorching them with the promise of pleasure.

There was only one thought in Vincent's mind—to claim Olivia as his.

If only for one night.

He ended the kiss and lifted her in his arms while he waited for her to put a stop to their encounter. Instead, she looped her arm around him and smiled.

Vincent took the stairs three at a time. He strode down the hallway and shouldered open his door before kicking it shut as he carried her into his room.

All the while, her hands had been caressing his chest and shoulders. It drove him mad with need. The feel of her hands on him, stroking him, was more than he could take. His chest heaved, his blood burned.

He slowly released her legs and let her slide down his body. Somehow Vincent stood still so she could continue her exploration.

"So many scars," she said softly. "So much pain."

She didn't know the half of it, and yet with her touch, he couldn't seem to recall anything other than his desire. He closed his eyes and gritted his teeth when her hands went to the waist of his jeans.

A moan exploded from him as her hand ran over his aching cock through his jeans. His eyes flew open to see her looking down at the hard length of him.

Didn't she know she was pushing him to the edge of reason? Didn't she know how desperately he needed to fill her?

Vincent could wait no more. He grabbed the hem of her shirt and roughly pulled it over her head. She unbuttoned her jeans and began to push them down her hips when he took her mouth again.

She was out of her pants in record time. Then both of their hands fumbled with getting his jeans off. Vincent couldn't remember ever getting out of his clothes so quickly, but then again, he hadn't had Olivia in his arms.

His hand caressed her back while he tightened his hold on her. With a twist of his fingers, he had her bra unhooked. She pulled back long enough to take it off and fling it aside.

Her smile enchanted him, mesmerized him. Captivated him.

He watched, his breath caught in his throat, as she stepped out of his arms and slowly removed her black lace panties. Vincent feasted his eyes on the beauty before him.

"You're exquisite." It's the only word that could come close to describing her.

Her skin, tinged a constant bronze, was flawless. Her glorious curves—from her full breasts to her small waist and flared hips—made his cock jump in anticipation.

A smile formed on his face when the dark bud of a nipple tightened under his gaze. Her chest heaved as she watched him with hooded eyes.

Vincent caressed her hip, then around to her shapely bum and squeezed. A soft moan passed through her lips. Her arms wound around his neck, bringing their bodies together.

He ground his cock against her, wringing a groan from both of them.

He hissed in a breath when her fingers delved into his hair and her nails lightly scoured his scalp.

"Please, Vincent. Please, don't make me wait for you any longer."

Her whispered plea was his undoing. He walked her to his bed and fell upon it, taking her with him. They came together as one, their lips seeking, their hands learning.

Vincent cupped her breast and squeezed. He thumbed her nipple, causing her to jerk her hips against him. If he was only going to have one night with Olivia, he wanted her screaming his name, the night burned in her memory.

He slid down her body to take a taut nipple in his mouth. While his tongue teased the tiny bud, he cupped her sex and felt the moisture of her arousal.

He dipped a finger inside her and heard her moan as her hips rose against him. His thumb found her clit and began to circle it, slowly at first, increasing the harder he sucked at her nipple.

Her nails dug into his arms, her back arched off the bed, and her moans turned into soft cries. He continued his assault until he felt her body tighten.

Olivia wanted to scream when Vincent abruptly ceased and moved down until his mouth was between her legs. She shook her head. There was no way she was going to let him have all the fun.

After all, she had barely gotten to explore that hard, amazingly ripped body of his. She wanted more time to explore him, to learn what drove him wild.

She scrambled up and motioned to him with her finger. His blue gaze narrowed, but his smile said he was game. He crawled toward her. When he got even with her, she shoved him onto his back. Olivia paused and looked at him, waiting to see if his injuries hurt. His smile and nod indicated he was fine.

Her gaze raked over his chiseled abdomen to his narrow hips. Muscles bunched, waiting and ready. She splayed both hands on his chest and smoothed them over every valley and ridge of his muscles.

Just out of reach was his cock. She drew her hands closer and closer to his arousal, watching it jump each time. His length begged to be touched.

Olivia straddled his chest, putting her back to him as she took his rod in hand. She wrapped her fingers around him and stroked up and down his impressive length.

His moan brought a smile to her lips. She leaned down and brought the tip of his arousal into her mouth. His fingers clenched at her hips. A moment later and it was her turn to moan when his tongue flicked over her clit.

She took him deeper in her mouth, letting her hands rub his length and his sac. It was hard for her to concentrate since his tongue was doing amazing things to her, sending her closer and closer to the edge of her climax once again.

Would he let her fall this time? Or would he pull back again?

She trembled as he pushed a finger inside her while he tongued her clit. When the second finger entered her, she sucked him harder. If she was going to be brought to the edge, so was he.

Olivia was suddenly thrown onto her back and Vincent loomed over her. Her legs were held wide and his cock brushed her sex. She urged him closer, needing to feel him inside her.

His gaze held hers as he slowly entered her, stretching her, filling her. She moaned, hungry for more.

He began to move, leisurely at first, but steadily building. She wrapped her legs around him and lifted her hips to meet his thrusts, sending him deeper inside her.

VINCENT'S ARMS shook as he held himself over Olivia. She was a beautiful sight to behold with her black hair against his white sheets and her mouth open on a scream.

As soon as her legs wrapped around him, he wanted to bury himself deep within her. He tried to hold back, but she refused to let him. The harder he thrust, the more pleasure spread over her face and the louder her cries came.

This time when he felt her body tighten he didn't stop her. Vincent was awestruck by the sight of her flushed skin as the climax struck. She screamed his name, her body jerking with the force of the pleasure.

Vincent didn't relent. He ruthlessly pounded her until her cries grew faint. Only then did he pull out long enough to flip her onto her stomach.

He ran a hand over her smooth ass and pulled her to the edge of the bed so that her legs hung off. With one thrust, he entered her.

She moaned, her fingers digging into the sheets. He held her hips and filled her again and again, harder, deeper. To his shock, she began to move with him.

And it sent him spiraling out of control, the orgasm so forceful that it took his breath. He pulled out of her at the last minute and spilled his seed on her back.

Vincent grabbed a discarded shirt and wiped away the remnants of his climax. He started to turn away when Olivia grabbed his hand.

He looked into her black eyes and saw only satisfaction reflected there. Tossing the shirt aside, he climbed into bed and lay on his back. A moment later and she snuggled against him.

Vincent put one hand behind his head, the other he

wrapped around Olivia. He stared at the ceiling, wondering how he could have another night with her.

"I never thought I'd get to kiss you," she said.

He glanced down at her with a frown. "What?"

"It was well known that the Chiassons were hard to catch. Some girls said each of y'all had girlfriends in other parishes. I used to do all sorts of things to try and get you to notice me."

"I noticed you," he confessed.

Olivia leaned up on her elbow. "You did? I had no idea."

"Take a look around. How could any of us bring a girlfriend into this? We couldn't. So, we didn't."

She returned to his chest. "Sounds like a lonely life."

"At times it is."

"And now? What happens between us next?"

Vincent took a deep breath and slowly released it. "We'll find whatever is after you and end it."

"That's not what I meant."

He knew that, but he couldn't tell her what she wanted to hear. Nor would he lie to her. It was better to ignore the question all together.

"I see," she murmured.

Vincent clenched his jaw. It wasn't the first time he hated the life he'd been born into. Someone had to do it. He just wished it didn't always have to be their family.

His father and ancestors had managed to find love, but with it had come devastating loss. Every male Chiasson had lost his wife. Not all had been killed by the very beings the Chiasson's hunted, but many of them had. His mother included.

"Will you live your life alone then?" Olivia asked.

Vincent shrugged and opened his eyes. "Most likely. Christian and Beau will carry on the Chiasson name. Lincoln probably will as well."

"But not you."

It wasn't a question, and he didn't treat it as such. "I have my reasons."

"Because of your parent's deaths?" She tapped his chest with a finger. "It didn't take much to put two and two together. The story around town was that your parents died in a boating accident, but I gather it was one of these things you hunt."

He nodded, unable to voice the words.

"I'm so sorry, Vincent." She tightened her arm across his chest in a half hug. "I lost my parents as well."

"You don't remember me being there, do you?"

There was a beat of silence before she rose up to look at him. "At Maman's? Yes, you were there when they came to tell her about my parent's car accident."

He waited, knowing she was smart enough now to put it together. Would she hate him for keeping the truth from her all this time? He wouldn't blame her if she did.

"Oh, God," she said as she jerked upright. "My parents didn't die in a car accident, did they?"

Vincent sat up and tucked her hair behind her ear so he could see her face. "They happened to be in the wrong place at the wrong time. The demon didn't target them. It ran from us and headed straight to the road where your parents were on their way to dinner."

Her eyes swam with tears. "Did you kill the demon?"

"That night before we notified Maria."

"I'm glad."

EIGHT

ALL THESE YEARS she had thought her parents died in a car accident. In a way they did, but not by running off the road from a blown tire as she had been told.

Then there were the Hoodoo symbols on her grandmother's house. So many secrets. What else was being kept hidden from her?

She turned her gaze to Vincent, who watched her carefully. "What is it about our parish that brings these creatures?"

The relief on Vincent's face was plain to see. He leaned back against the headboard. "I asked my father that same question when I was eight years old. The truth is that the creatures are everywhere. We're one of the few families throughout the States who protect an area."

"There are more families like yours?" She couldn't

imagine there being anyone like the Chiassons, with their vivid blue eyes and warrior attitude.

"A few."

When his eyes dropped to her chest, Olivia realized she was still naked. Her breast swelled and her nipples puckered under his gaze.

She swallowed loudly and gathered the sheet in her hand. Vincent looked at her as if she might shatter at any moment. And she just might after everything she had witnessed and learned that night.

How could she not believe it though? The stories of strange sightings had made the rounds through the small town often. Olivia herself had heard peculiar sounds late at night, but her grandmother had told her it was just the animals of the bayou.

Olivia leaned into Vincent's hand when he cupped her cheek. She wished they had all night to themselves, but there was something dark and dangerous after her.

"I wish my life was different," he said, a small frown line marring his forehead. "I wish I had asked you out years ago. I wish...for so many things."

He was telling her that they didn't have a future, that what happened between them wouldn't happen again. Olivia hadn't been looking for a relationship, but she had never expected to end up in Vincent Chiasson's arms.

She pulled his hand from her face and smiled. "I've been out in the world, and I've seen what it had to offer. I thought

I had found the man to be my husband, but it turns out what I was looking for was right here at home."

"Olivia, no," he said and rose from the bed. "Don't do this. I don't want to hurt you, but I can't be in any kind of relationship."

It took her a minute to realize why he was pulling away. "You're afraid."

He paused in the process of pulling on his jeans. "I'm not scared to give my heart to someone."

"No. You're scared of losing someone." How could she not have seen it before? He kept a wall between him and the world, a protection from the wickedness that invaded his life.

Vincent fastened his jeans and grabbed a shirt from his closet before he pulled it on over his head. "I care about you. Because of that I won't subject you to what every Chiasson woman endures."

"The love of their men."

His face hardened. "Death. Most by the hands of the creatures we hunt."

She opened her mouth to reply, but he left the room before she could. For several seconds, Olivia stared at the doorway hoping he would return.

When he didn't, she dressed and ran her hands through her hair before she stepped into the hallway. Only to draw up short when she spotted Lincoln nonchalantly leaning against the wall.

He pushed away and slowly walked to her. "Vincent is a complicated person. He's stubborn as hell, and he thinks he has to shoulder everything himself."

"He won't ever let me in, will he?"

"That's the thing, Olivia. He did let you in. That's why he's pushing you away so hard. Vincent hides many things, but the one thing he could never hide was his fascination with you. He got drunk the night you left Lyons Point."

Olivia's mind reeled with the news. "He never even looked at me before tonight."

"Oh, he looked. Always. We followed you home many late nights just to make sure you arrived safely."

Was that why she had never been afraid in the bayou? Did she know that someone watched over her? Thinking back, she remembered her grandmother often looking into the trees after Olivia got home.

"Does my grandmother know what y'all did?"

Lincoln nodded and gathered his long dark hair at the nape of his neck to tie it off. "She knew it was Vincent who looked out for you."

"Why didn't he ever say anything? If he only knew the outrageous things I did to get his attention."

"Our parents died on the same day, but the hours between when our father found our mother and his death has stayed with Vin. We were both there, but he saw much more than I did. Though I can still remember the sound of our father's yell of grief. That's what keeps Vincent from telling you of his love."

That drew Olivia up short. Lincoln smiled sadly as she gawked at him.

"You didn't expect that, did you? Vincent won't admit it to anyone, but he does love you. Why else would he look in on Maria every week and ask about you? Why else would he follow you home every night before you left? Why else would he think to save you first rather than kill the creature we've been hunting? Why else would he bring a woman to our home—and his bed—for the first time?"

With each of Lincoln's questions, more arose in her head. She remained in the hallway long after he walked away. Vincent had admitted to her that he cared, but love?

Then again, who was she to think she knew Vincent? Lincoln knew him better than anyone.

Olivia made her way back downstairs. She glanced in a doorway as she passed by and halted when she saw Vincent with his back to her. He stared at a picture of his parents that hung over the mantel.

There was only one light on, and it came from a large desk off to his right piled with books and papers. To his left were bookshelves stuffed to the brim with books.

Movement caught her eye and she spotted Lincoln as he came to stand next to Vincent. Olivia knew she should let them know she was there, but she wasn't sure what to say to Vincent, especially after the bombshell Lincoln had dropped.

She was deciding on whether to stay or go to the kitchen when Lincoln said, "You're a fool if you let her go."

"Leave it alone," Vincent said dangerously.

Olivia stepped to the side against the wall so they wouldn't see her. Eavesdropping was bad, and yet, she couldn't make her feet move away.

"Olivia has finally returned, and you've given in to your desire for her," Lincoln stated. "If you let her walk out of your life, you'll spend the rest of it miserable."

Vincent blew out a long breath. "You don't know that."

"You've had a taste of her. Tell me that you could forget her, and I'll drop the issue now."

Olivia squeezed her eyes closed hoping that she had made some kind of impression on Vincent. She strained her ears to hear.

"I couldn't forget her if I tried," he admitted, his voice low and full of pain.

"Then hold on to her, Vin."

"I can't."

Olivia frowned as Lincoln let out a slew of curses. She might be hurt by Vincent's words, but all it did was make her want to fight for him. She had dreamed of finding the perfect man for her, but it wasn't until she had been held in his arms, kissed by his lips, and loved so tenderly that Olivia knew her perfect man was none other than Vincent Chiasson.

"You figured out something," Lincoln said, drawing her out of her thoughts.

"The creature that killed our parents simply vanished once they were dead. Now, eleven years later, it's returned and has been focusing on any woman connected to us. I do believe someone has a vendetta against our family, and they won't be happy until all of us are dead."

"Then why haven't they attacked us? Why kill people we know?"

"Because they want to hurt us first."

"Shit," Lincoln cursed. "And once we're dead, Riley will return home and be an easy target."

"The Chiasson's will be wiped out. Leaving the parish open to all sorts of evil."

Olivia had heard enough. She darted into the kitchen and found the phone. It might be almost two in the morning, but she knew her grandmother would answer her cell phone.

Her grandmother answered on the second ring, "Hello?"

"Maman," Olivia said and faced the doorway so she could see when someone walked in. "I'm sorry to wake you, but it's an emergency."

"Olivia?" she asked, her voice rising. "I thought you might be occupied with Vincent. What are you doing calling me?"

"I'll tell you all about it later. Suffice it to say that they saved me tonight."

"Lincoln phoned earlier to tell me. I still can't believe something came after you."

She sighed wearily. "Maman, you know everyone in this parish. Who do you know that would have a grudge against the Chiassons?"

"Sha, you shouldn't get mixed up in that."

"I wasn't given a choice, since I was attacked simply because I happened to speak to Beau at the store."

Her grandmother let loose a string of Cajun French that was mumbled too low for Olivia to comprehend. "Once you start digging, sha, you're liable not to like what you find."

"You mean like the Hoodoo symbols on the house?"

"Exactly like that," her grandmother grumbled. "I know the things that are out there, Olivia. I did what I had to do to protect you and myself."

Olivia rubbed her neck. "I can understand that. Right now we need to stop whoever is after Vincent and his brothers. They've already killed three girls. I was almost the fourth, and I seriously doubt they'll give up so easily on seeing me dead."

"I won't lose you," her grandmother vowed solemnly through the phone.

"Then tell me what you know."

There was a long pause, and then her grandmother said, "When Vincent's father chose Yvonne as his wife, she wasn't the only woman he had been dating. Once married, however, he was faithful, no matter how many times others tried to lure him away from Yvonne."

"Who was the other woman he dated?"

"Years went by, and no matter the rumors, Yvonne and Bran remained happy and devoted to each other. They brought four sons and a daughter into the world all while keeping the parish safe."

Olivia drew in a calming breath. "Who was the woman?"

Instead of answering, her grandmother asked, "Did Vincent tell you about your parents?"

"Yes."

"I should've done that years ago, but when you moved away I didn't see the point."

Olivia looked down at her thumb to see her nail broken to the quick. She pulled off the rest of the nail and toyed with it. "Did you know that Vincent—"

"Walked you home all the time? Yes. I also know of his love for you. Whether you've known it or not, you've held a good man's heart in your hands."

Olivia let the nail drop to the floor. "I know it now."

"What are you going to do about it?"

"Well, I'm not walking away, if that's what you're thinking."

She could practically see her grandmother's smile through the phone as she said, "That's my girl. We Breauxes are fighters."

"Yes, we are."

"The woman you need to look for is Patricia Hebert."

Olivia nearly dropped the phone.

"Listen to me carefully, sha," her grandmother said. "There have long been stories of Pat's practicing a mixture of Voodoo and witchcraft. She's powerful. Powerful enough to call forth a golem. The boys are going to have their hands full."

Her eyes grew wide as understanding dawned just as Vincent and Lincoln walked into the kitchen.

CHAPTER

NINE

VINCENT SAW the shocked look on Olivia's face and was at her side in an instant. "What is it?"

She held the phone out to him. "My grandmother wants to talk to you."

He took the receiver and put it to his ear. "Maria?"

"My granddaughter is in your hands," Maria said. "You've always watched over her. Don't stop now. I can't lose her as I lost my son and daughter-in-law. Do I have your word, Vincent Chiasson?"

"You do," he answered without hesitation.

"I knew I could count on you. Olivia called looking for information. I think you're going to be interested. All I'll tell you is to be careful, and try your best to keep Olivia out of it."

The line went dead before he could respond. Vincent replaced the receiver in its holder.

"Did she give you an earful?" Lincoln asked with a smirk.

Vincent looked from his brother to Olivia. Beau and Christian were still patrolling the edge of their property. He ran a hand over his jaw as he thought of Maria's words. "Linc, get Beau and Christian. They need to be here."

Lincoln immediately turned on his heel and opened the back door where he let out a shrill whistle that would have their brothers making their way back to the house.

Olivia looked anywhere but at him, and yet Vincent couldn't take his eyes off her. He knew the taste of her kiss, her skin, her essence. He knew what it felt like to have her come apart around him, to bury himself deep within her.

He thought he could be content with what he had been given, but he wanted so much more.

Beau and Christian came through the doorway together. "What's going on?" Christian asked.

Vincent nodded to Olivia. "It seems she might have discovered something."

"I didn't do anything," she hurried to say. "Since Maman knows everyone, I thought she might have an idea of who would want to hurt y'all. So I asked her."

Vincent's heart missed a beat. The only way Olivia would know that was if she had been listening to his conversation with Lincoln. Which meant...she had heard everything.

No wonder she couldn't look at him.

Lincoln threw him a nasty look before he turned to Olivia. "I gather Miss Maria had an answer."

Olivia woodenly nodded. Whoever it was shocked her. Vincent wasn't surprised. She didn't know the darker side of people. She had seen only the light, only the good. It's where she belonged.

She blinked her large eyes and fiddled with a broken nail. "Did any of you know that your father had been seeing another woman alongside your mother before he chose her?"

"That's the first I heard of that," Beau said.

Lincoln shrugged when Olivia looked at him.

As soon as Olivia's gaze touched him, Vincent shook his head. "I never heard either of my parents mention it."

"It seems that the woman wasn't at all happy when she wasn't chosen. She made it her mission to try and lure your father away from your mother, and when that didn't work, she spread rumors that he was unfaithful. Your parents remained together through it all."

Christian's rage was palpable as he stood with his hands fisted by his side. "Who is this woman, and why did she wait until after we were grown to take our parents?"

"You'd have to ask her," Olivia said.

Vincent walked to her side and squatted beside her. "Who is it, Olivia? Who killed my parents and the three girls? Who is trying to kill you?"

"She's trying to hurt all of you as well," Olivia said.

He took her hands in his and felt how icy they were. He rubbed his hands over hers to try and warm her. "The sooner we know who it is, the sooner we can confront her."

"I don't want you to. Maman believes she's used a mixture of Voodoo and witchcraft to summon a golem."

"Fuck!" Lincoln said as he slammed his hand on the table. "A damn golem? Is that what we've been chasing?"

Beau pulled their family book to him and flipped through the pages. "There was only a vague reference to a golem in here. It's rare, Vin, and requires a tremendous amount of power, just as Olivia said."

"Do we even have anything to kill it?" Christian asked.

Lincoln grunted. "You can't kill a golem. Don't you ever read, Christian? We have to kill the one who summoned it, the one who controls it."

Beau nodded as he ran his hand along the passage he was reading. "That's right. That's what our great-great-great-great-great grandfather says, anyway."

Vincent and Olivia didn't look away from each other while his brothers were talking. It was just a short time ago he had Olivia's body bared before him as he learned her curves and kissed her silky skin.

"Who is it?" he asked again.

She licked her lips. "If I tell you, you'll go after her. You didn't hear Maman's voice. There was a thread of fear in it that I've never heard before."

"Olivia. This is what we do. Can't you understand now why there can't be anything between us? You wouldn't want me to do my job, and I would be too worried about protecting you to do what I need to."

Her shoulders drooped as if all hope had left her. "Patricia Hebert."

Vincent thought he had been prepared for whatever name Olivia would give him, but he was stunned. Pat had always gone out of her way to speak to the Chiassons when others wouldn't. She'd had a rough life after Sean's father died when he was just two.

Pat had never remarried, preferring to remain in the parish alone and dedicated to Sean.

"We'd know if she was practicing Voodoo or witchcraft," Beau said into the deafening silence of the kitchen. "That kind of magic calls to the most evil of paranormal creatures."

Lincoln cracked his knuckles. "I say we go have a little chat with her and clear up a few things. Namely that she call off the golem."

Vincent looked down at his and Olivia's hands as his brothers filed out of the house. He stood and was surprised when Olivia threw herself against him. His arms wrapped around her of their own accord. For several seconds he simply held her, feeling the tremors running through her.

It was Olivia who pulled back and looked up at him with a solemn black gaze. "I respect what you and your family do. I don't want you to go because Patricia and the golem will try to kill you. I can't live without you in this world, Vincent Chiasson. So, I don't care what you have to do, but you come back to me."

His heart pounded in his chest. Never had he dared to

hope that she might care for him. He might have planned to live his life alone, but he couldn't now. "Only if you promise not to leave this house."

When she eagerly nodded in acceptance, Vincent bent his head for a quick, hard kiss. It was all that he would allow himself.

He started for the door when Olivia called, "Hurry back. We've got some talking to do."

Vincent stepped out of the house and joined his brothers. They knew what they were hunting, and they knew who controlled it.

Christian rested his crossbow on his shoulder. "Let's get this over with. I'm starving, and Beau promised to cook crawfish étouffée."

"Yum," Lincoln said with a lick of his lips. "Incentive enough for me."

Beau finished loading his gun and snapped it closed. "Consider it done."

Vincent looked at all three of them. "This is the thing that killed our parents. This is the woman whose jealousy made her take our parents from us too soon. We all want a piece of her for that. We weren't the only family affected by Patricia's delusions. Let's remember that when it comes time to kill her."

Olivia found a deck of cards and began to play solitaire. She went through several games before she put away the cards and explored the house.

It was huge, and the brothers had made it their own. What was once a back parlor was now a media room complete with theatre seating and a 72" flat screen.

On the other side of the house, Olivia found a workout room with all sorts of training equipment. One of the walls was covered by glass that protected a selection of weapons any military would be impressed with.

Besides the kitchen and study, she also found a formal dining room and a room off the front of the house that was so feminine and formal that it must have been their mother's.

Olivia made her way back upstairs and discovered eight bedrooms in all. Four were used by the guys, and there was another set the farthest away from their rooms that was covered with posters from movies, TV shows, and bands.

"Riley's," Olivia said with a smile.

The other three bedrooms were empty, as if they were waiting to find their occupants.

Olivia was on her way back downstairs when she heard the telephone ringing. She ran to the kitchen, skidding on the rug as she dove for the receiver.

"Hello?" she answered breathlessly.

"Olivia? Olivia, is that you?" said a male voice.

She couldn't quite place where she knew the voice, but

the fact he was calling from her grandmother's phone made her heart pound against her ribs. "Yes? Who is this?"

"It's Sean Hebert, Olivia. I'm sorry to be the one to tell you this, but there's been an accident. Your grandmother was on her way home when a drunk driver hit her."

The room tilted around Olivia. No. She had lost too much. "Is she all right?"

"They've taken her to the hospital in Crowley."

She needed to get to her grandmother, regardless of the promise she gave Vincent. He would understand. "I'll be there shortly," she said and hung up the phone.

Olivia grabbed her keys that Vincent had tossed onto the counter earlier and rushed from the house. Her hands were shaking so bad that it took three tries just to get the keys in the ignition.

As soon as the car roared to life, Olivia threw it in drive. All she could think about was her grandmother being hurt and alone and confused at the hospital. That only made her drive faster over the bumpy terrain.

With her hands squeezing the wheel, she sped over the worn path Vincent had called a road. She could see the lights up ahead on the main road. Once she reached that then she could really fly.

One moment she was driving, and the next something slammed into her car, shattering the glass. She screamed as the vehicle began to roll.

She had no idea how many times her car rolled until it

finally came to a stop upside down. Her head pounded from when it slammed against her door.

Olivia moaned and tried to unbuckle her seatbelt. Blood from the many cuts on her hand from the glass made her fingers slippery so she couldn't press the lever. Tears welled, not from her injuries, but because of her grandmother.

It was the low growl that took her breath. She looked around trying to find the source, when she caught sight of thick, hairy legs right next to her.

She bit back a scream and turned her head away when the driver's side door was ripped off and tossed aside like a kid would toss a toy.

A massive hand with long claws reached for her. Olivia leaned as far as she could as her tears fell freely now. If only she would have done as Vincent asked.

The golem's hand latched onto her seatbelt and ripped. Olivia screamed as she fell.

CHAPTER

TEN

OLIVIA OPENED her eyes to see a fire. Grass itched her cheek and a mosquito was happily sucking on her shoulder. She tried to swat the mosquito away when she found her hands tied.

"A precaution. I'm sure you understand."

She stilled, her blood turning to ice as she recognized Sean Hebert's voice. Olivia lifted her head to find him sitting on the opposite side of the fire, making what looked like a doll out of straw.

"What are you doing, Sean? You're a sheriff's deputy." Maybe if she could reason with him he would let her go. It was a long shot, but what did she have to lose?

He ignored her and focused on the doll. "I was so excited when you came back to town. You were cute in school, but damn, you turned into a fine-looking woman, Olivia."

A glance around showed a house about a hundred yards away while the bayou was behind her. She tugged at her bindings, hopeful that she might get a hand free.

"You came here once," Sean said as he looked up at her with an overly bright smile. "Our senior year; I had the party at Christmas."

So they were at Patricia Hebert's house. Was Sean helping his mother commit the murders? How had Patricia convinced her son—a cop—to kill?

"I remember," she said, to keep him talking.

"I kissed you that night."

She winced as her bonds seemed to tighten the more she struggled. "You kissed a lot of girls that night."

"True. I had my pick of girls."

"You always have." Wasn't she supposed to make him feel good? It would be so much easier to tell him what a complete nutter he was.

He stopped working and cocked his head at her. "Except for you. Why didn't you accept my invitation yesterday?"

"Is that why you're doing this? Because I didn't agree to go out with you? I also didn't say no, idiot."

His answer was a low, rumbling laugh. Words she couldn't understand tumbled from his lips as he held the straw doll against the fire.

A sickening feeling rushed through Olivia. They had gotten it wrong. It wasn't Patricia who was controlling the golem this time.

It was Sean.

"WHAT THE FUCK?" Lincoln whispered.

Vincent was glad someone could voice what he couldn't. He was too infuriated to do more than glare at Sean Hebert. Vincent didn't know whether he wanted to save Olivia or shake her senseless for going back on her word.

Christian peered closer through the weeds. "Is that blood on Olivia?"

"Yes," Vincent said through clenched teeth.

This was exactly what he hadn't wanted. He didn't want to be put in a position where his first concern was Olivia, not killing the very thing that could hurt her.

He rubbed his temple in an effort to shut out the part of him that bellowed for him to rush to her side and protect her. He had to be smart, had to remember everything his father had taught him.

"We've got your back," Beau said.

Lincoln met his gaze and gave a single nod. "You get Olivia. We'll get Sean."

"Y'all are forgetting the golem is here," Vincent said.

He had felt the creature's eyes on them since they first arrived from the bayou.

"I guess Patricia passed the torch on to Sean," Christian said.

"You didn't say yes!" Sean yelled as he stood up and scowled at Olivia. "Why couldn't you just say yes?! You would've been spared this! But you had to go and talk to those damn Chiassons!"

Olivia laughed, causing Vincent to blow out a harsh breath. "Jealousy? You've killed because you're jealous of the Chiasson brothers?" she asked.

Vincent motioned for Beau and Lincoln to circle back around to the bayou and look for the golem. He then sent Christian near the house.

"Breanne fucked everyone except me," Sean said, spittle flying in his rage. "She told me that after she'd had Lincoln she would settle for nothing else."

Olivia looked bored. "You think you're the only one to be turned down? You're pathetic. What about Lindsey?"

Sean wiped his mouth with the back of his hand. "I simply couldn't let a single Chiasson find any kind of happiness. My mother felt the same about Yvonne. How she hated Yvonne. Even after she had the golem kill both Bran and Yvonne it still didn't lessen her hatred."

"But it made you hate the Chiassons, right?"

Vincent was amazed that Olivia could be so calm in such a situation. He was barely holding it together, and he was only watching.

"What about my grandmother?" Olivia asked. "Did you hurt her?"

Sean sat back down and petted the straw doll. Vincent recognized it as a Voodoo doll, but just who was it for?

"Not yet," Sean said.

"What's that mean?" Olivia demanded as she squirmed until she had her legs underneath her and she sat up. "Where is she?"

The smile Sean gave her was pure evil. "She'll be fine as long as you remain with me. This doll will ensure it."

"With you?" Olivia choked.

"As my wife, of course."

Vincent had heard enough. He stood and walked from the shadows. As soon as Sean spotted him, he leapt to his feet.

"Let her go, Sean," Vincent said.

Sean shook his head with a laugh. "She's mine. You'll never take her from me."

Behind him, Vincent heard that low growl a second before the golem appeared. He ducked and rolled as claws swiped at his head, then came up on his feet.

Vincent wanted to be the one to kill Sean and the golem, but he wanted Olivia safe more. He let his brothers attack Sean as he hurried to Olivia's side.

He had just started to cut her bonds when the golem hit him, sending Vincent flying through the air. He landed with a bone-jarring thud. It dazed him, making the world spin every time he opened his eyes.

"Vincent!" Olivia screamed.

He pushed aside his pain and climbed to his feet, using a tree to steady himself. Vincent shook his head to clear it and saw that Sean now had Olivia next to him with the golem behind him.

"You'll never win," Vincent told Sean.

Sean spread his arms wide. "I've already won, Vincent. Look around. I'm revered and sought after while people turn away from everyone with the Chiasson name."

Vincent saw Lincoln hiding in the brush behind Sean. With a slight nod, Vincent gave him the go ahead. "You'll never have Olivia. She's mine."

Sean's face mottled with rage. He opened his mouth, but no words came. His face fell with incomprehension. The straw doll fell from his fingers.

The golem let out a howl of outrage and lunged at Lincoln. Olivia ducked as Vincent unsheathed the machete and prepared to throw it at the creature.

Just before it reached Lincoln with its teeth bared and claws raised, it disappeared.

For long moments, no one moved.

"That was too damn close," Lincoln said with a laugh as he walked from the tree.

Beau and Christian came out of their hiding spots and walked straight to Lincoln. Vincent couldn't stay away from Olivia another second. He cut her bonds and pulled her against him.

"I was so scared," she whispered.

He tightened his hold. "I never knew it. You were brave."

"He tricked me. He said Maman had been in a wreck and was on the way to the hospital. It's the only reason I left the house," she said hurriedly.

"It's all right." He closed his eyes, thankful that it had all worked out.

Vincent opened his eyes and all the blood drained from his body when he saw the golem reappear behind his brothers. He shoved Olivia away from him and looked at the house.

At the backdoor was Patricia Hebert, her deadly gaze directed at Lincoln.

"Linc," Vincent shouted as he took off toward the house.

He didn't wait to see if his brothers reacted. He knew they would. With his machete still in hand, he lifted it over his head and let it fly with deadly accuracy.

Patricia had been so intent on killing Lincoln that she had forgotten about him. She turned her surprised gaze to him now and pointed a finger at him as blood ran down the front of her body from where the machete embedded in her heart.

"Your time will come," she said.

"Oh, shut up," Maria scoffed as she shoved Patricia off the steps.

Olivia rushed past him with her arms out. "Maman!"

Vincent sighed and watched Olivia and Maria embrace,

both talking at the same time. He smiled, because he knew his life had changed the moment he took Olivia to his bed.

"What now?" Lincoln asked as he walked up.

Christian slapped at a mosquito. "Food."

"You need to learn to cook for yourself," Beau grumbled as he walked away.

"Why?" Christian asked and followed him. "You do a good job."

Lincoln smiled at Vincent. "What are you going to do about her?"

"The only thing I can do. Keep her by my side."

Lincoln slapped him on the back. "Good choice. I'll see you at home."

Vincent turned back to see Olivia standing in front of him. She was covered in blood and grass, but she was still the most beautiful thing he had ever seen. "Are you hurt?"

"Nothing that Maman's herbs can't cure. Did you mean it?" she demanded.

He frowned as he tried to figure out what she was talking about. "Mean what?"

"That I was yours?"

Vincent glanced at the stars and nodded. "Yes. You've been in my heart since you were seventeen standing on Maria's porch. I've run from my feelings for you. I don't want to do it anymore."

"Good," she said smartly. "Because you'd lose. We Breauxes are fighters. We always get what we want."

He pulled her against him. "And what is it you want?"

"You, Vincent Chiasson. I want you."

He rested his forehead on hers. "You have me, heart and soul, Olivia. I love you."

"I think I've loved you for years and didn't realize it until I came home."

Maria cleared her throat behind them. "Now that you two have things finally figured out, can we get out of here? I'm being eaten alive by mosquitoes."

EPILOGUE

A week later...

OLIVIA PULLED out of Vincent's arms to grab her cell phone on the nightstand. She yawned and accepted the call. "Ava, how are things?"

"Going very well. I think you're going to be extremely happy with what I've found."

Olivia smiled when Vincent snuggled against her back. "Well? Don't leave me in suspense."

"Holbert and Dobbs have dropped the charges against you once I proved that you were nowhere near your computer and that Calvin was always in the Accounting Department during those episodes. They've also offered you your old job back."

"I'll pass," Olivia said without hesitation.

"Hmm," Ava said with a smile in her voice. "Do I detect a note of happiness?"

Olivia laughed. "That you do."

"I'm happy for you. I'm almost sad your case is over."

"We're having a big party in a few weeks. Come down and let me say thanks in person. Besides, I need to settle up our bill."

Ava chuckled. "Hon, I just might take you up on that offer. Bye for now!"

Olivia put down the phone and curled back against Vincent. "I think we need to make sure we have enough food for Ava."

"I gather that everything got worked out and you won't be going to jail?" Vincent asked with a smile.

She playfully punched him in the side. "That's right. She cleared me just as I knew she would. Calvin will get his due."

"Damn straight he will. If he doesn't, I'll have to make a trip to Dallas to deliver it myself."

How had she gotten through life without Vincent? She couldn't believe everything had worked out as it had. She had thought her life was over when she drove back to Lyons Point a week earlier.

Now she had the man of her dreams and a future that would be filled with heat and passion. As well as danger.

"Are you prepared for a life with me?" Vincent asked.

Olivia leaned up to meet his gaze. "As I've told you every day for a week, my answer is yes. I know it won't be easy. I know I'll have nights where I'm up worrying or tending to your wounds, but I'd rather have that than not have you at all."

"You are an amazing woman Olivia Breaux. I don't deserve you."

"Oh, but you do. Let me show you," she said as she straddled his hips and kissed him.

A CHIASSON NOVEL
WILD
DREAM
DONNA GRANT
NEW YORK TIMES BESTSELLING AUTHOR

CHAPTER
ONE

Lafayette Regional Airport
July

Ava Ledet stepped off the private jet and smiled when her gaze landed on Olivia Breaux with her dark hair pulled back in a ponytail and her black eyes crinkled at the corners as she smiled. Olivia pushed off the truck she had been leaning against and ran to her.

"I can't believe you're finally here," Olivia said as she enveloped Ava in a hug.

Ava wasn't a touchy-feely type person, but Olivia never gave her a choice. In the short time they had worked together, Ava felt as if she had found her first true friend.

She returned Olivia's hug, genuinely happy to see her. "I'm sorry I'm so late."

Olivia stepped back and raised her brow at the private jet. "Flying in style though, aren't you?"

"Company jet. They allow us to use it every now and again."

"Your law firm must really bring in the big bucks."

Ava didn't respond to the comment. Instead, she turned to the co-pilot who held out her bag. "Thanks, Jim."

Jim gave her a wink and entered the plane. Olivia hooked her arm with Ava's while turning her to the truck.

Olivia leaned in and whispered, "He's cute."

"I suppose." She glanced over her shoulder to see Jim's tall form bend to enter the plane. He looked at her, his hazel eyes holding hers a moment before he disappeared inside.

"You suppose," Olivia repeated in surprise. "Ava, he's a hunk."

Ava grinned and opened the door to the truck where she tossed her bag. "All right. I admit it. I'm not blind. I've seen his cute ass. But I'm not looking for a guy. I'm too busy with work to even dream about going on a date, much less actually going on said date."

Not to mention there was her past, the same past she had returned to Louisiana to face.

When Olivia didn't respond, Ava looked up to see her black eyes watching her thoughtfully. Ava had seen that look before, though not from Olivia. It had come from her mother.

Ava got into the passenger seat and strapped on her seat belt. Just being in Louisiana was more difficult than she had expected, but she could handle it. She'd made a name for herself in Dallas as one of the best attorneys in the city. If she could handle courtrooms, juries, and judges, she could handle the part of her life that had nearly ruined everything.

Olivia cleared her throat as she climbed into the truck. "It's not that far of a drive, but I'm starving and the boys will only wait so long before they dive into the food."

Ava laughed, grateful that Olivia talked of something so mundane. She looked around the interior of the Chevy truck. "The last time I saw you, you were driving a car. Is this yours?"

"Yep." Olivia's face scrunched as she drove away from the airfield. "I was in a bit of an accident and needed a new vehicle. In this area, it's better to have a truck."

Ava looked at Olivia to see a happiness about her that hadn't been there before. "You've changed. I guess we can say that your man has something to do with that."

Even though Ava had gotten the lawsuit against Olivia dismissed the month before, they still talked often. It hadn't taken Olivia long to spill the beans on Vincent who had swept her off her feet. Ava was happy for her friend. In her world, all she ever heard about were divorces. So it was nice to see that love did exist.

For some.

"Yes," Olivia said dreamily. "Vin is...well, he's amazing."

"He has to have one flaw."

Olivia merely smiled and cut her eyes to Ava.

Ava laughed. "I really want to meet him now."

"How long has it been since you've been to Louisiana?" Olivia asked.

The smile dropped from Ava's face, and she hastily looked out her window so Olivia wouldn't see. "It seems a lifetime ago. I was thirteen when we left. The day after Christmas."

"Fourteen years? That is a long time."

Ava stared out the window, but it wasn't the rice fields she saw. It was a flood of memories from a happier time—a time before her world was ripped apart.

"Are you all right?"

Ava roughly shoved aside the hated memories and threw a smile at Olivia. "Of course."

Olivia's frown remained in place. "For a lawyer, you're a terrible liar."

"Why did the party get moved from your grandmother's?" she asked, hoping Olivia would let her change the subject. The one thing Ava never did was talk about her past.

Olivia paused as she turned off the paved road. "Maman loves to cook for people, but Vin convinced her to use his kitchen. It's easily twice the size of Maman's. Needless to say, he only had to say that once before she jumped at the chance."

It was only a little later that the truck turned onto a drive lined by massive live oak trees dripping with thick moss and through the trees there were clusters of crepe myrtles drenched in bright pink, white, red, and pale pink blooms.

"My God. This is gorgeous," Ava said as she leaned forward to get a better look at the trees.

There was a smile on Olivia's face. "Wait until you see the house."

No sooner had the words left Olivia's mouth than Ava spotted the white plantation house. She felt as if she had stepped back in time, that the busy world she knew was gone, vanished—never to be seen again. And part of her enjoyed the thought of that.

Olivia parked the truck at the side of the house behind others and got out. Ava closed her mouth and opened the door to slide to the ground. She went to grab her bag when a large hand wrapped around the handles.

Startled, she jerked her head to the side to find a tall man with a red tee she could see every rippling muscle through, and short, dark hair. He flashed her a smile, but it was his bright blue eyes that arrested her.

"Thanks, Christian," Olivia said. "Christian, this is Ava Ledet. Ava, this is one of Vincent's brothers, Christian."

Christian gallantly took her hand. "Nice to finally meet you, Ava. Olivia has told us so much about you."

Ava hadn't realized until that moment how she missed the Cajun accent. She was forced to tear her gaze away from Christian when Olivia turned her around so that Ava got a good look at the backyard. The bayou was about two hundred feet from the house. The grass was a rich green while the live oaks and cypress tree leaves were a darker green. The sun hung in a cloudless sky, and the water of the bayou appeared fathomless.

"Take a deep breath and prepare," Olivia whispered.

Ava glanced at her, unsure of what she meant. Until her gaze landed on the men under the covered deck of the house. It was almost as if she had stepped into the cover of Hunk Daily. Every man there was supremely gorgeous.

Her lungs seized when she spotted one of the men leaning casually against a thick post next to the grill with a beer in hand. He had long dark hair that fell to his shoulders. The top half was pulled away from his face and held at the back of his head with a leather strap.

His white V-neck tee molded to his muscular body and wide shoulders, and his dark denim jeans hung low on trim hips. As spectacular as his body was, it was his face that kept drawing her gaze.

He had a square jaw and chin with dark brows that slashed over his eyes. She was too far away to see his eyes, but she had a suspicion they were brilliant blue. His lips were wide, inviting. He smiled easily, making the corners of his eyes crinkle.

In a word, he was striking.

Before Ava could mentally get her feet underneath her, she and Olivia reached the deck. That's when she noticed the many fans hanging from the ceiling that kept the air moving and the occupants cool.

The man at the barreled grill closed the lid and smiled seductively at Olivia before he walked to her. Ava couldn't help but smile while she watched Vincent pull Olivia into his arms and kiss her languidly.

Ava looked away and found her gaze snagged by the intense blue eyes of the man she had been drooling over just seconds before. They stared at each other for several moments. She was drawn to him, like an invisible string connected them and tugged her to him.

He didn't push away from the post and walk to greet her, and Ava was both glad and perturbed that he didn't. She wanted to know his name and to get a closer look at his face. Then she reminded herself that she hadn't come to Louisiana to find a man. She had come because she wanted to see Olivia, but also because she had something to do.

There was no time for a dalliance of *any* kind.

It was really too bad. Whoever the man was, he left her breathless, unbalanced.

Lustful.

Perspiration dampened her skin, and it had nothing to do with the heat. Her mouth was dry and she throbbed low in her stomach. If he could do that with just a look, what would he do to her with a kiss? Or...more? Part of Ava desperately wanted to find out.

"Vincent Chiasson, don't you let that meat burn," a

petite woman with silver hair pulled back in a bun chastised from the door of the back porch. She wiped her hands on her apron as she smiled at Olivia. "Sha, you're back. And you must be Ava. My, aren't you a pretty one."

"Maman, Vincent knows what he's doing," Olivia said, even as Vincent hurried back to the grill.

Ava's ears were filled with a rushing noise as black dots edged her vision. Chiasson. Olivia's grandmother had said Chiasson. It couldn't be possible.

"Ava?" Olivia asked and touched her arm.

She swallowed and took a step to the side. *Breathe. Just open your lungs and breathe, dammit.* "I'm fine."

"It's the heat," Maria said. "Get her inside to cool off."

Suddenly, a bottle of beer was shoved in her hands. "This should do the trick," Christian said and walked her to a chair under one of the fans.

Olivia pulled a chair next to her and peered at her closely. "You look as pale as death."

She felt it as well. How did she not know Vincent's last name was Chiasson? Hadn't it come up in conversations with Olivia? No. She would have remembered, because that name was burned, seared in her memory.

"I'm fine." Ava forced the words past her lips and lifted the beer to her mouth. She hated beer, but right now an adult beverage was an adult beverage. And she needed a lot of alcohol. An entire store still wouldn't take the edge off.

Olivia blew out a breath. "All right. Then let me make the

introductions. You already met Christian. The hunk who kissed me is Vincent."

Ava looked toward the grill to find Vincent smiling at them. She gave a nod of her head.

"Next up is Lincoln, the brooding one next to my man."

So the hunk had a name. Lincoln. His blue eyes were the exact color as both Christian's and Vincent's. Ava once more found herself ensnared in his gaze. Lincoln lifted his beer in a salute to her and promptly turned away to answer his cell phone.

"The lazy bum in the hammock is Beau. Normally he's in the kitchen. He's an amazing cook, but Maman promptly shooed him out this morning," Olivia said with a laugh.

Beau lifted his head long enough for Ava to see the same vivid blue eyes the rest of the Chiasson clan had. His hair wasn't near as long as Vincent's and Lincoln's, but the semi-long length looked good on him. "Nice to have you here, Ava."

The entire scene was surreal. It was bad enough that she was back in Louisiana, but just down the road from where she grew up. To make the situation even more bizarre, she was in the Chiasson home. As a guest.

There was no way she could pull off what she wanted to do. It was all too much. All around her were the sounds of the bayou, the smell of nature at its finest. At one time it had been her life's blood.

The Cajun accent of the people, the sounds of zydeco

music playing in the background, the smell of spices from the food. It brought back a deluge of memories that threatened to drown her.

Somehow she got through the next thirty minutes as Vincent finished cooking the meat. Ava plastered a smile on her face as they all sat around the table outside laden with food made by Maria. She ate the delicious meal and savored every bite. Because she knew the idealistic scene was about to be shattered.

CHAPTER

TWO

LINCOLN WANTED to forget the haunting beauty that was Ava Ledet, with her long, wavy auburn hair and unusual amber eyes. She walked fluidly, almost as if she glided upon air.

She had the look of a city girl, but there was something in the way that she gazed longingly at the bayou. Then there was her creamy skin accentuated by her black shirt that molded to her pert breasts and tight white pants.

Lincoln watched her help Olivia clear the table and bit back a moan when she bent over and he got a view of her breasts as her collar dipped.

"She's very pretty," Beau said as he walked up and handed Lincoln a beer.

"Yep."

Pretty was like calling the Grand Canyon a hole in the ground. Ava was...enthralling, spellbinding. Captivating.

She was calm and easy going now, but he would wager his best knives that she had a temper to go with that hair of hers. Her face was that of an angel with her high cheekbones and wide, expressive eyes. But her sensual mouth and tempting curves hinted at a sexier side that Lincoln itched to bring out of her.

"Are you laying claim, because I'm definitely interested," Beau said.

Lincoln paused with his beer raised to his lips and slanted a glare at his youngest brother.

Beau chuckled and shook his head. "I get the point, Linc. Stop with the look. By the way, who called earlier? You looked upset."

Shit. How could he have forgotten about Solomon's call? As his gaze once more snagged on Ava, he knew exactly why he had forgotten.

"Is it bad?" Beau asked.

"Bad enough. I can't exactly tell the family with Ava here."

Beau rubbed his jaw. "Christian brought her bag into the house. Is she staying?"

"I hope to hell not." For several reasons. The main one being that Lincoln didn't think he could keep his distance from her.

Beau nudged him with his elbow. "You need to tell Vin that."

Lincoln waited for Olivia to take Ava down to the water

before he made his way to the house. Maria was sitting on the porch as he walked up.

"A fine meal, Maria. Thank you."

She smiled, a knowing look in her dark eyes. "Don't think I didn't see you looking at Ava as if she was the finest dessert served up on a platter for you. She was looking at you as well, boo."

Lincoln didn't even try to lie to the old woman. She might not be family yet, but he had known Maria since his birth. After their parents' deaths, she had looked out for all five of the Chiasson children—or as much as they would let her—despite raising her own granddaughter.

"Ava's a looker, but she's just visiting."

"For now," Maria said shrewdly. "You don't know what the future holds, Linc. Remember that."

"Yes, ma'am." He had a grin on his face when he walked into the house that lasted until he reached the office doorway. He didn't have to search to know that Vin was in the office.

Lincoln walked straight to the office and found Vincent writing in the family journal that listed all the paranormal beings the family had killed through the years, and how to kill them.

Vincent looked up and stopped writing. "What is it?"

"I got a call from New Orleans."

That's all that needed to be said for Vin to lay down his pen. "Get the others."

"Ava is here."

A muscle twitched in Vincent's jaw. "It's that bad?"

"Unfortunately."

"Can it wait for Olivia, Maria, and Ava to return to Maria's?"

Lincoln shook his head. "It's an emergency."

Vincent ran a hand down his face. "Get the others."

Lincoln turned on his heel and quickly found Beau and Christian in the kitchen. The three walked back to the office to join Vin. Beau lounged on the loveseat while Christian sat on the edge of the chair, his elbows on his knees.

Lincoln leaned a hip on the edge of the desk so he could see everyone. "I received a call from New Orleans. There's a bit of a problem that they've asked for our help with."

"We never turn away family," Vincent said.

Christian laced his fingers together. "They're cousins. It's a no brainer. When do we go?"

"We don't." Lincoln set down his beer. "Solomon said that Kane is on his way here."

Beau jerked into a sitting position. "The next full moon is a day away. What the hell is Kane doing traveling now?"

"It seems our cousin doesn't know how not to piss off a Voodoo priestess."

Vincent let out a long sigh. "Not again."

"We can't handle this with Ava here."

"Afraid I'll learn your Chiasson secrets?" Ava's voice said from behind him.

Lincoln stilled, her voice going through him like a blade. He slowly straightened and moved to the wall so he could see the doorway. And her. Ava and Olivia stood in the entry of the double doors no one had thought to close.

There had been something in Ava's voice, almost a hint of fury.

"I was coming to tell you that we're headed to Maman's," Olivia told Vincent.

Vin stood and leaned his hands on the desk. "Ava, please forgive us. There is some family business that we like to keep private."

"You mean how your family hunts the supernatural?" she said offhandedly. "I used to live in this area. I know about the Chiasson family."

There was more to her story, Lincoln was sure of it. And he wanted to know what it was. "Olivia said you left as a child. I doubt you knew very much."

Her amber gaze swung to him. Her smile was cold and laced with such anger that her eyes burned with it. "When I was twelve my father lost his half-brother in an accident. At least that's what the papers called it, but my father suspected something else. So, he began to look into it. For the next six months he researched the paranormal. Ultimately, it led him to the Chiassons."

"Oh, God," Olivia whispered, her eyes wide as she stared at Ava. "That's why you looked faint when you learned the family name."

Lincoln's mind raced with the people his parents had brought into the house, trying to place Ava's father.

"My father began hunting the creatures. It became his obsession. He quit his job, would sleep all day, but the worst was when he left. He walked out on his wife and daughter. To hunt the supernatural."

"Jack," Lincoln said as he finally remembered. "Jack Ledet was your father."

Lincoln recalled how much Jack had spoken of his family. He was obsessed with killing the supernatural—but to protect his wife and daughter. There was no way he would have just walked out on them. Lincoln may have only been in his early teens, but his father had taught them all to recognize good men when they saw one. Jack was a good man.

"Where is he?" Ava asked.

Lincoln frowned and looked at Vin. Vin shrugged his shoulders.

"We've not seen Jack in years," Vincent said. "We assumed he returned home and was finished with hunting."

"Assumed." Ava pinned him with a withering look. "Did it not occur to one of you that one of those *creatures* might have gotten him?"

Lincoln shook his head and stepped forward so that Ava would look at him. "The last time we saw Jack was years ago. We finished a hunt, and he shared breakfast with us before he started back home. We all thought he finally had enough of the life."

He wanted to help Ava locate Jack, but he couldn't do anything until the full moon had passed and Kane had gotten out of his mess.

"I'll take Ava and Maman now," Olivia said.

Lincoln didn't want Ava to go, but by the look of her, she needed to get away from the Chiassons. Vincent walked Olivia out, and Lincoln found himself standing at the door watching them get into the truck and drive away.

Vincent walked back into the house and closed the door. He let out a long sigh as all four brothers stood in the large foyer. "Well, that was a surprise."

"I feel sorry for her," Christian said.

Beau swirled the last bit of his beer in the bottle. "It seems we've got two issues to deal with now. I for one want to help Ava find her father. I was pretty young, but I remember Jack."

Christian nodded. "Riley used to sit on his lap."

Lincoln missed his sister, but as the youngest of the clan —and the only girl—Riley deserved something more than the Chiasson family business, which was why she was in Austin at the University of Texas.

"One thing at a time," Vincent stated. "First, let's get this business with Kane sorted out. What does Solomon want us to do?"

"What do you think with a full moon coming?" Lincoln said testily.

Christian walked away, toward the kitchen. "If we're going to argue, I need fortified with some of that chocolate cake Maria made."

Beau made a dash through the dining room to beat Christian to it, while Vincent and Lincoln leisurely walked to the kitchen. When they reached it, both Beau and Christian were eating a piece of cake.

Lincoln pulled one of the chairs at the table out and turned it around so that he straddled it, his arms resting on the back. "The Voodoo priestess has altered Kane's curse. He'll forget he's really human while in wolf form. He'll kill indiscriminately."

"He really fucked up this time," Beau said.

Vincent remained standing and began to pace. "Will the cage we have hold him?"

"If he gets here in time," Lincoln answered. "That was another of Solomon's worries. There were those trying to prevent Kane from leaving New Orleans. Solomon, Myles, and Court got him out, but they don't think it'll stop there. The people know he's coming to us."

A horrified expression crossed Christian's face as he swallowed the last of his cake. "Why would they want to keep Kane in New Orleans?"

"To punish him," Vincent said. He stopped and heaved out a breath.

Lincoln nodded. "Vin is right. When the dawn comes, he'll see what he's done. It's likely to destroy him."

"What did Kane do to be punished so severely?" Beau asked.

"Solomon didn't provide that information, and I didn't ask. I figure Kane will tell us the entire tale when he gets here."

"If he gets here," Vincent said.

Lincoln glanced at his watch. "Solomon called two hours ago. It takes three to get here by car from New Orleans, but Kane is on foot. He'll come through the bayous and stay off main highways since he's being followed."

"We need to get ready then. Kane could arrive at any time," Christian said.

Vin rested his hands on the back of a chair. "I've got a bad feeling that he won't get here until tomorrow night. When he's already shifted. Before we can get him into the cage."

"That means we'll need to be on patrol starting tonight," Beau said. "We alert everyone we can. Those we can't we keep an eye on."

Vincent and Beau filed out of the kitchen. Lincoln stood and pushed the chair under the table. He turned and found Christian blocking his way.

"We're going to need you fully in this."

Lincoln frowned and crossed his arms over his chest. "When have I ever *not* been fully involved?"

"Never. Then again, Ava Ledet didn't walk into your life until today. The others may not see it, but I do, Linc."

"See what, exactly?" He thought he'd been doing a hell of a job keeping his desire hidden.

Christian raised a dark brow. "Your desire to protect her. That could get her—and you—killed."

"Not going to happen."

"Focus on her once Kane is in the cage. Until then, do us all a favor and forget her."

If only it were that easy.

CHAPTER

THREE

Ava was so lost in her memories of that night her father left and never returned that she didn't realize they had reached their destination until Maria patted her on the shoulder.

"Come inside, sha," she said and exited from the back passenger door.

Ava got out of the truck and grabbed her bag. She closed the door and sighed before she turned and faced Olivia. "If I'd have known it was the Chiassons you were involved with, I wouldn't have come."

"Then it's a good thing it never got brought up before today." Olivia smiled softly. "You have every right to your anger, but I don't believe you're mad at Vincent or any of the other Chiassons."

"I'm angry at what they did that lured my father away. I'm furious that he got involved with the hunting, and I'm sad that his half-brother was killed by something so awful. But, you're right. It's my father I'm really irate at. He left us."

"You don't know that for sure," Olivia pointed out. "You heard the guys. Your father was always talking about you and your mother. The hunting he did was to keep you safe. A man like that doesn't walk out on his family."

"Then where has he been the last fourteen years?" Ava was so tired of wondering that same question.

Olivia took her bag and wrapped an arm around her shoulders while leading her to the house. "Hopefully we'll find out. It's why you really came, isn't it?"

Ava nodded and looked at the white house. They walked around to the side where she spotted a long dock that went all the way out to the bayou. Like most other houses in the area, it had a screened in porch that overlooked the water.

They climbed the steps, walked through the porch, and into the quaint house. Maria made use of every inch of space, but the house had a relaxed feel.

Ava felt right at home instantly. It also helped that Olivia and Maria took care of her. Olivia put her bag in a back room, and Maria motioned her to one of the plush chairs in what was obviously the living room.

The house, built almost a hundred years earlier, had an open living area to optimize air flow. Ava had no sooner taken a seat than Maria put a mug in her hands.

"It's coffee milk. It always made Olivia feel better," she said with a wink.

Ava smiled and drank the coffee that was more milk than anything, but it did exactly what Maria wanted it to do—made her relax.

When Olivia joined them, Maria handed her a cup. All three sipped for a while before Olivia lowered her mug. "You said you and your mother remained for a year before y'all left. What happened?"

Ava remembered that night as if it happened yesterday. "It was the day after Christmas. Mom got a job anywhere she could. At one point, she worked three jobs just to pay the bills and put food on the table. Every morning I woke thinking that I would see my father. I knew the week of Christmas that something was going to happen. Mom kept counting money she had put away and boxing things."

"She was getting ready to take you away," Maria said.

"Yes." Ava hadn't realized that at the time though. "It wasn't until the morning after Christmas that I saw the resignation on her face mixed with determination. She told me to get my stuff. She had stayed up all night packing away everything. In six hours, everything was in boxes and we were on our way to Texas. I cried the whole way. The last bit of hope I had that my father might return disappeared somewhere on I-10."

"Your mother must have had her reasons for leaving. She needed a fresh start is my guess," Maria said.

Olivia lifted one shoulder. "I don't know. To take Jack's

daughter away? What if he returned that night and had no idea where to find them?"

"That's the same thing I told Mom," Ava said. "Her response was that he'd had a year to find his way home and he hadn't, which meant he didn't want us."

Maria shook her silver head and got to her feet. "That's a tough one. I'm going to Grace's for a while and leave you young girls alone. Don't get into too much trouble," she said as she grabbed her purse and walked out of the house.

Ava looked at Olivia and shared a laugh.

Olivia set aside her mug and reached for her laptop. "I've been thinking. There has to be some kind of record of your father. These days, people can't sneeze without it showing up somewhere."

Ava swallowed, suddenly overcome with emotion. "I've done a little searching on my own, but that was in Dallas. I even hired a private investigator for a little while."

"What did he find?"

"Nothing. That's why I came. I knew if there was a chance to find my father, it was with me in Louisiana."

"Then we'll find him," Olivia said with a reassuring smile.

AFTER TWO HOURS of searching online and Olivia making some calls, Ava had to get out of the house. And she knew exactly where she wanted to go.

"Can I borrow the keys to your truck?"

Olivia didn't hesitate to toss them to her. "Sure. Want me to come with you?"

"Not this time. I need to be alone for a little bit."

Olivia stood and walked with Ava to the door. "I'm not trying to be nosey, but can you tell me where you're going? I ask because I know what my man and his family hunt, and night is coming soon."

"I'm going to the house where I grew up."

"In Lafayette?"

"On the outskirts. I won't be gone long."

Olivia gave her a hug. "Keep your cell near. And call when you're on your way back."

"Will do," Ava promised and walked out of the house.

She drew in a deep breath once she was in the truck. Seeing her old house was something she had to do—no matter how painful it was.

LINCOLN HID in a clump of cypress trees and surveyed the expanse of bayou around him. He was thankful it didn't get dark until well after eight. That gave them more time to search for Kane in the light.

All of their friends had been notified to remain inside for

the night, and a few had even offered to help keep a lookout for Kane.

It had been years since he or his brothers had seen their family in New Orleans. That branch tended to keep to themselves, not that he blamed them. He would do the same if a Voodoo priestess had cursed their entire family to be werewolves.

Lincoln looked at the setting sun. They had another twenty minutes of good light at best before twilight hit and that eerie time between light and dark descended. Most people didn't realize that was the most dangerous time to be out.

He nudged a snapping turtle out of the way as he moved to a different location. The fading sun glinted off the eyes of a large gator resting on the banks, his gaze trained on Lincoln.

"Don't even try it," he warned the gator. "I'm after something else entirely this night, but if you push me, I'll take you home for dinner."

The problem was, the Chiassons couldn't kill Kane. He was family, and on his way to them for help. It wasn't Kane's fault he was being tracked by a relentless group determined to see him kill.

Lincoln was of half a mind to track the fuckers, bind them together, and let Kane have at them. It's what they deserved for detaining him just so he could kill some innocent person.

His mind immediately went to Ava. He knew she was safe with Olivia. Then there was Vincent, who had set up watch near Olivia as well. Ava was more than protected. Still, Lincoln couldn't stop the knot of doubt in his gut. He wanted to see her with his own eyes, to know with unwavering certainty that she was all right.

But that wasn't going to happen. He had to trust Olivia and Vincent.

Lincoln paused, the water rippling slightly around him as he spotted something moving in the brush ahead of him on the shoreline. He slowly withdrew both of his bowie knifes and waited.

With him on the outskirts of Crowley, he had a good chance of being the one to encounter Kane or the group after his cousin. The full moon didn't technically begin until the next night, but anyone who hunted werewolves knew the day before and the day after a full moon they would also shift.

The lower the sun sank, the higher the moon rose. It was going to be tricky to get Kane in the cage before nightfall. And Lincoln couldn't rely on his brothers for help. Everyone was dispersed in a wide range for maximum opportunity to find Kane.

But that also left them exposed. Which was going to be a complete bitch when night hit.

The bush rustled again. Lincoln tightened his grip on his knives and waited. A moment later a raccoon ambled out and rose up on his hind legs as it chatted at him angrily. A second later and it ran off.

Lincoln let out a breath and just happened to look down in time to see the water move around his legs. He spun around in time to see the gator disappear beneath the water not five feet from him.

"Fuck me," he murmured.

A second gator slid into the water off to his left.

"Fuck me sideways," he hissed.

Lincoln wasted no time in getting out of the bayou. Once he was on land, both alligators swam away. Damn, but he hated full moons. The animals went crazy.

He looked at the sky and grimaced when he caught sight of the sunset. Everything was drenched in gold, including the water. It was a magnificent sight. It was also an omen of bad things to come.

All Lincoln could hope for was that Kane was the only thing they would have to hunt during this full moon. If not, things were going to get hairy.

It was the quiet of the bayou and the way sound bounced over the water that allowed him to hear the shouts of agitation and fear. Lincoln sheathed his knives in the holsters strapped to his legs and took off running in the direction of the yells.

Lincoln dodged low hanging branches and the deepest parts of the bayous. He jumped fences, raced over private property, and took every shortcut he knew. When he scaled the last wooden fence and jumped over the side, he looked up to find Christian standing over Paul Boudreaux, who was on the ground, unmoving.

"Glad you got here," Christian told him while never taking his eyes off a large shadow in front of him where his crossbow was aimed.

Lincoln slowly straightened and pulled out his weapons. "Is it Kane?"

"I don't know. I arrived to find Paul right there and spotted something large moving off. Hard to tell in this damn twilight just what it is." Christian sighed. "I think its Kane."

"Let's hope it is. I don't want to be hunting something else as well."

Lincoln took a quick survey of the area. It was dense with tall pines and giant live oaks. Perfect hiding area for anything. It could come at them from above or any of the numerous shadows.

All in all, it was a sucky night.

Lincoln motioned to get Christian's attention. He pointed to Christian and told him to stay put before he pointed to himself and used his hand to tell him that he was going to go behind it. Christian gave a nod of understanding.

Lincoln carefully, silently, put one foot in front of the other and slowly walked around the large shadow. When he was behind it, he heard the unmistakable growl of a werewolf just before he leapt out of the shadow at him.

CHAPTER
FOUR

Ava knew seeing her old home was going to be a bit like getting kicked in the stomach, but knowing it and experiencing it were two different things. For several long minutes she merely sat in the truck, pulled along the side of the road in the neighborhood, and stared at the house. When she lived in the house it had been painted yellow with white trim. Now it was a sand color with navy trim. Shutters had been added to the outside of the windows in the same navy.

That wasn't the only difference in the small house. Her mother's rose bed had been ripped up, replaced with crepe myrtles and day lilies. The stone path she had helped her father put down from the rock-lined drive was also gone. In its place was a concrete path that matched the concrete drive.

There were no more tears to shed. Ava had given all she

had years ago, but that didn't stop the sadness from descending. Her parents had been happy there once.

The three of them had been happy—before it all fell apart.

If she was ever going to move on with her life and shut the door to her past, she had to find her father. No matter how long it took, no matter what she had to do, she had to know where he was.

Ava sank lower in the truck when the door opened to the house and a young couple came out and got in their SUV. Ava waited until they drove away before she peeked her head up. She was about to start the truck when she looked at the house again. After waiting until the taillights of the SUV were out of sight, she got out of the truck and stood in the street.

The neighborhood had grown a lot in fourteen years, but that's not what she had come to see. Her feet felt stuck in concrete as she walked to the other side of the road and stood before the yard she used to play in.

It was several minutes before she got up the nerve to step upon the grass. It was more than strange standing in the yard. She had remembered it to be so much bigger. Then again, everything was big to a kid.

She smiled as she recalled her father teaching her to ride her bike along the street. She remembered the Halloweens they would walk the neighborhood for candy, and the celebrations during Mardi Gras.

Those were the memories she wanted to hold on to, not the one of the last night her father left.

When she pulled herself out of her memories, she was surprised to discover dark had fully descended. Olivia was going to be worried. Ava turned back to the truck and palmed her cell phone from her back pocket.

She had only gotten three steps and pressed Olivia's name to dial before she was attacked from behind. The phone went flying through the air to land with a *thunk* on the road. A man held her arms at her sides from behind her while another came at her from the front.

Ava kicked out both legs and connected with her frontal attacker. As soon as both feet were on the ground, she threw back her head, slamming it against her attacker. He released her with a savage curse. Ava turned and gave him a sideways kick in the jaw that sent him sprawling to the ground.

She started to run to the truck when two more men rushed her. Every bit of her training in martial arts was used.

They were trying to grab her, which made it easy for her to block them and deliver swift kicks and punches. It wasn't until they changed tactics and began to hit back that she had to quickly change her own strategy.

She knocked another down and faced her last two opponents when something slammed into her from behind.

"Linc! Damn you. Wake up!"

Lincoln winced and batted at the hands shaking him. "Enough, dammit."

"Then you should've woken," Christian said, but released him.

Lincoln gingerly sat up. "What the hell happened?"

"Kane, that's what."

Lincoln found his knives and sheathed them once more. "He didn't hurt me."

Christian snorted derisively. "Really? I'd say knocking you on your ass, lights-out, hurt you."

"He didn't attack either of us, little brother. Nor did he rip Paul to shreds. I think that's a good sign."

No sooner had the words left his mouth than the unnatural howl of a werewolf split the air.

Christian's lips thinned. "If he was in his own mind, he'd know better than to do that."

"He's moved on. So should we," Lincoln said as he got to his feet. "Let's get Paul and get going."

Lincoln carried Paul over his shoulder, Christian in the lead with his crossbow.

"Maria's place is closest," Christian said as he turned right instead of left.

Lincoln wasn't about to argue. Paul was heavy, and they still had to catch Kane. At this rate, it was only a matter of time before Kane killed someone.

By the time the lights from Maria's house came into

view, sweat coated Lincoln and ran down his back and into his eyes. There was no need to call out to Vincent. He would see them soon enough and come to the house to find out what happened.

Christian let out a bird-like whistle that had Olivia at the porch door in seconds. When she spotted them, she opened the door and motioned them inside before rushing to the house door and flinging it open.

"Is he injured?" she asked.

Christian shook his head. "Just knocked out."

Olivia pointed to the couch and told Lincoln, "Lay him there."

"Where's Maria? Paul could use her herbs when he wakes," Lincoln said.

"She's with Grace," Olivia said. "I called her after Vin stopped by to tell me what was going on with Kane, so she'll stay at Grace's all night."

Christian stood in the doorway of the house. "That's probably for the best. When's the last time you talked to Vin?"

"Hours ago, when he told me he'd be out there guarding this area."

Lincoln gratefully accepted the glass of water Olivia handed him as he looked around the house waiting for a glimpse of Ava. It wasn't as if there were many places for her to hide.

"She's not here," Olivia said.

Lincoln jerked his head to her. "What?"

Christian let out a string of curses as he stepped out onto the porch.

Lincoln had thought Ava was safe with Olivia. She should have been. "Why did you let her go?"

Her black eyes narrowed on him. "I didn't know about Kane until after she had left. That's because none of y'all bothered to tell me until hours later."

Lincoln closed his eyes as he envisioned all sorts of things happening to Ava. She might know of the supernatural and that his family hunted the creatures, but she hadn't been around those beings or know how to defend herself.

"I've been calling her," Olivia said in a strangled voice.

Lincoln looked up to see her haggard expression for the first time. He felt like an ass for blaming her. "Where did she go?"

"Her old house near Lafayette."

She could be anywhere. Lincoln rubbed the back of his neck. That knot that he felt earlier doubled. He'd known then something was wrong. He shouldn't have ignored his instincts.

"Linc?" Vincent said from the doorway.

Lincoln walked to the kitchen sink and turned on the water. He splashed his face a couple of times before he turned off the water and walked out of the house.

"Linc!" Vincent called.

"I've got to find her. Kane didn't hurt us, but I think he's beyond that now. He'll rip her to shreds."

"Lincoln."

He whirled to face his elder brother. "Don't you dare try and stop me, Vin."

"Be careful."

Lincoln glanced at the ground, all his anger disappearing at the concern in Vin's voice. "I'll do my best."

Christian walked up then. "You find Ava. We'll track Kane."

They were better when they all worked together, but Lincoln knew the need to find Kane was imperative. "Once I get Ava back here with Olivia, I'll catch up with you."

"A sound plan," Vincent said.

Christian grinned mischievously. "Just don't get your ass knocked out again. I won't be there to wake you."

"Won't be an issue since I don't have to look out for you," he teased in return.

The smiled dropped, because they all knew how quickly life could be taken with what they did.

"Come home to us," Vincent ordered.

It was the same order their mother had told their father whenever he went hunting. "Make sure Beau has something good cooking. I'm already hungry."

"I can come with you," Christian offered.

Lincoln shook his head. "Vin will need both you and

Beau to track Kane. Kane is quick and viciously strong. Make sure none of you get bit."

"Ditto," Vincent said. "Having one branch of the family as werewolves is plenty."

Lincoln turned on his heel and walked into the darkness. Ava's life could be on the line, and he'd be damned if he wouldn't be there to find her.

Ava woke and immediately grabbed her head. It felt as if a million little men were inside beating on drums. She groaned and sat up. Through the pain in her head she wondered why she felt grass and leaves beneath her hand. Her heart beat a slow sickening beat when she looked around to find herself in the middle of a field, Olivia's truck nowhere in sight.

She climbed to her feet and felt the bruises from her fight with the jackasses who had jumped her. But why? Why had they taken her out here?

She looked to her left and saw more open field. To her right was a clump of trees. From the light of the nearly full moon she could make out the cypress trees, which meant she was close to water.

The bayou was beyond those trees. Water moccasins, gators, snapping turtles, and all other kinds of animals awaited her in that direction. But the trees could offer her some protection. More than the open field could.

Ava took a step to the trees, looking around constantly. She had no weapons nor a cell phone to call Olivia. She was truly on her own, and she was terrified.

She had an awful sense of direction. Not to mention it had been years since she had been in the area, so she had no idea which way to go to find a road, or even a house. She could be walking for days if she went the wrong way.

Ava let out a sigh when she reached the trees. She leaned on one and rested her head against the bark. It was going to be the longest night of her life.

The mosquitoes were relentless in their desire to suck her blood. Every rustle of leaves or the sound of the water moving made her jump. Ava had no idea how long she sat at the base of the tree before the bayou went deathly silent. Not even the buzz of a mosquito broke it.

That's when she knew something was out there hunting her, stalking her.

Ava used the tree to get to her feet. Her heart hammered in her chest when she heard a low, rumbling growl that sounded like a wolf.

But she knew there were no wolves in Louisiana. That meant...it was something else entirely.

If she hadn't been so frightened, she would've broke down.

She heard a twig snap to her left. Her head swung around to see something large moving in the shadows.

Suddenly a hand wrapped over her mouth. "Don't move."

Ava about fainted when she heard Lincoln's voice. The relief in knowing she wasn't alone was profound. Then the realization that there was something supernatural out there sent her into a panic.

"Easy," Lincoln whispered near her ear. "That's my cousin stalking us. I'm not going to let him hurt you, but I also can't kill him."

Ava turned her head to look at him and see if he had completely lost his mind. Their lives were at stake.

"We're going to have to make a run for it," he said as his blue eyes met hers. "Now!"

CHAPTER

FIVE

IT HAD BEEN pure luck that Lincoln stumbled across Ava. He was crossing the field when he happened to see someone out of the corner of his eye. He had been coming to warn them to get home when he spotted auburn hair in the moonlight. The terror, the panic that gripped him was indefinable.

He held her hand tight and pulled her after him as they crashed through the bayou.

Lincoln glanced behind him and saw Kane's huge werewolf form gaining ground. They were nothing but bait out in the open, and the only way to stop a werewolf was with silver.

And that silver would kill Kane.

There was only one place they could go to be safe. If they could make it in time.

"Faster!" Lincoln shouted as Ava stumbled, but quickly gained her feet.

Her amber eyes were wild with fear. Sweat made strands of her hair stick to her neck. She clung to his hand with a firm grip. She didn't scream, didn't ask what was after them. She just kept running.

Lincoln kept them out of the water because it would slow them down and allow Kane to catch up. Remaining on land was making them take the long way around as well as draining them of energy.

It had been years since Lincoln had been to the site, and he prayed he remembered exactly where it was. He happened to see a white cross painted on a tree as they ran past, which gave him hope.

"Just a little farther, Ava," he urged.

They didn't slow, but Kane increased his speed as if he knew they were about to reach a place he couldn't go. Lincoln withdrew a knife and pushed Ava harder. The site was just a hundred yards ahead, but at the rate Kane was gaining on them they would never make it. Lincoln waited until they were closer before he shoved Ava ahead of him.

"Stay by the oak with the cross!" he shouted.

He turned to confront Kane only to have a large paw slam into him.

Ava kept running, hoping she would see an oak with a cross on it. She practically ran into it when she tripped over something and reached out to remain upright. That's when she saw the silver cross hanging from a limb, dangling in the middle of the tree where the giant limbs branched out into all different directions.

She turned to find Lincoln and sucked in a breath when she got her first look at what had been chasing them. It was a wolf, with black fur, on steroids. It was easily three times the size of a normal wolf.

Its yellow eyes appeared to see everything, and the sheer size of the paws were large enough to take off a man's head. But it was the teeth she saw when it lifted its lips and growled that made her heart miss a beat.

The beast circled Lincoln, who was on the ground. The fact he was moving kept her focused. Ava took a half step away from the tree.

That small movement focused the wolf's gaze on her. He stared at her as if sizing up his next meal. Ava had never been so frightened in her life, but she had to give Lincoln enough time to get to the tree.

She took another step, and she could have sworn the wolf smiled in anticipation. Her courage was waning fast, and she wasn't sure how much longer she could continue. A quick look at Lincoln showed him watching her with bewilderment. He blinked and looked at the wolf before he rolled toward her a couple of times and then jumped to his feet.

The wolf went nuts at that point, pawing the ground and growling while chomping its jaws furiously as its growls grew deeper and angrier.

Ava rushed to Lincoln and threw her arms around him. It was only because of him that she was alive. That beast would have torn her to shreds.

"We're safe now," Lincoln whispered, but she noticed he held her just as tight as she held him.

He pulled back and took her face between his hands. He turned her face one way and then another. "Are you hurt? Did Kane scratch you?"

"No," she whispered, her chest still heaving from the mad dash to the tree.

Lincoln's hands softened and his gaze lowered to her lips. Ava knew she should push him away, but after coming so close to death, she needed to feel something. Which is why she didn't turn away when his head lowered to hers. Lincoln's lips were soft, insistent, as he kissed her. His hands delved into her hair, holding her firmly.

But it was the moan that rumbled in his chest that made her shiver with anticipation.

Need burned through her as she stepped closer to him. The kiss deepened while desire flared unchecked. Ava was ready to give in to him—until the wolf snapped its jaws, jerking her out of her haze of desire.

Ava ended the kiss and stepped away from Lincoln. He

slowly dropped his hands to his sides but didn't take his eyes from her. While her heart hammered and her body ached for more of his kisses, he stood calm and firm.

It was only the fire in his bright blue eyes that told her he was fighting the passion inside him.

Ava swallowed and looked away. Lincoln might be hotter than any guy she had ever seen, and his kisses might send her body into overload...but he was a hunter. She refused to go through that again.

"Tell me how a tree with a cross can keep us safe?"

He took a step closer and tilted her chin up with his finger until she was looking at him. "Listen carefully, Ava. We're on holy ground. As long as we remain here, you won't be hurt. Understand?"

She nodded. "That's a big wolf."

"Werewolf," he corrected. He dropped his hands and let out a sigh as he glanced at the creature. "He's also my cousin."

She remembered him saying something about family when they were running, but she was too intent on remaining alive to have thought much about it at the time. "Family?"

"A branch in New Orleans. They're the LaRues. The first Chiasson that came to Louisiana didn't come alone. He brought his brother. And his sister."

"Ah."

"That's Kane," Lincoln said and pointed to the black

werewolf. "A couple of hundred years ago the LaRues brought the wrath of a Voodoo priestess upon them. She cursed their family to be werewolves until the end of time."

"They must have really pissed her off."

"I don't even know what they did, truth be told. It's not something they talk about. Even with family."

Ava looked at Kane, who was pacing an invisible barrier that seemed to go into the bayou, since the wolf went to the edge of the water and all the way around the oak to the water again. "Why would Kane travel, knowing he would turn?"

"When werewolves turn, they know what's going on. They remember who they are. When the LaRues shift, they make sure to kill deer or cattle. Never humans."

Ava raised a brow. "Want to remind him of that?"

Lincoln walked to the oak and slid down the tree until he was seated on the ground. "That's the thing. It seems my cousin didn't learn anything from his relatives. Kane managed to piss off another priestess. She altered his curse so that when he shifted he would forget he was human and kill whatever—or whoever—crossed his path."

"He didn't kill you."

"No," Lincoln said thoughtfully. "He didn't."

Ava shivered despite the hot night as she recalled the way the wolf seemed to zero in on her. "He would have killed me."

"Why the hell were you in that field?"

"I was attacked. The men came out of nowhere," she said and wrapped her arms around herself.

"You shouldn't have been alone."

Ava glared at him, no matter that his Cajun accent made her blood heat. "I'll have you know it took five of them to take me. I know how to defend myself. I took down several before they got the upper hand."

Lincoln's slow smile made her stomach flutter with...was that excitement and pleasure? God, she hoped not. It was already bad enough that she was insanely attracted to him. The last thing she wanted was to seek his approval. On anything.

"Did you get a look at the men?"

"No." And she should have. "They were in all black, and they were intent on taking me no matter what. When I woke, I was in the middle of that field."

Lincoln smoothed down a few strands of hair that had come loose from his queue at the back of his head. "It's pure luck that I saw you at all. Had I gone a different route, I wouldn't have."

Ava glanced at the werewolf—Kane—to see him staring at her while he paced. "Where is your vehicle?"

"I was on foot."

"What? Why in the world would you be on foot? It's quicker to go anywhere by car."

"Perhaps," he drawled. "But had I been in my truck on the road miles from where you were, I wouldn't have spotted you."

"Oh." She found herself looking at the immense paws of the werewolf.

"Besides, I can cross more of the land on foot if I'm tracking something than if I was in a vehicle."

"Looks like you found Kane."

"I wasn't tracking him. I was coming for you."

Ava's gaze jerked to his. He had been out looking for her. She couldn't remember the last time someone had thought of her. She had been on her own for so long she had forgotten what it was like to have someone worry about her.

It was uncomfortable to have Lincoln's direct gaze on her as if he knew the turmoil she was in. Ava swallowed and said, "I lost my cell phone. Do you have yours so we can call Olivia or your brothers to get us?"

"No. We don't carry phones on our hunts. The sound of a ringer could get us killed."

"How are we to get away?" She wouldn't panic. She wouldn't panic.

"We can't."

She was panicking.

Ava turned away, her mind racing with everything that had happened. She needed to put some distance between her and Lincoln.

One moment she was on her feet walking, and then next she saw a blur of black fur and white fangs before she was on her back, Lincoln leaning over her with a murderous expression.

"Are you trying to get yourself killed?" he ground out.

Ava blinked, unsure what had happened. Then her mind stopped working at all at the feel of Lincoln's weight atop her. Before she could wonder at her body's instant—and traitorous—response, Lincoln jumped off her and grabbed a stick.

Ava sat up and watched him jab the end of the stick in the ground and begin to draw a line in the ground. All the while the wolf pawed the dirt and growled.

Lincoln threw down the stick and grabbed her upper arm. He yanked her up and dragged her to the line in the ground. "Don't go outside this line unless you want to be Kane's next meal. As you almost were just now."

Ava followed the line to see it made a large square around the live oak about twelve feet by twelve. The werewolf stayed just on the other side of the line.

She turned to look at Lincoln. "Thanks for saving me. Again."

He kept his back to her as he stared out over the bayou. Not that she blamed him. She had nearly ended her own life. Not on purpose. It wasn't as if she knew where the barrier was. If she hadn't been so worried about being alone with him she wouldn't have made such a dumbass move.

Nope. The blame was squarely on her shoulders.

Ava walked to the oak and sat at its base. The night had turned into a nightmare, and she just wanted it to be over.

The problem was, she feared that if she and Lincoln did survive it, she wouldn't be able to stay away from Lincoln and his sexy, soul-stirring kisses.

CHAPTER

SIX

Lincoln thought he had experienced dread before, but that was before he saw Kane lunge for Ava. For a split second, Lincoln feared he wouldn't reach her in time. He still wasn't sure how he had gotten to her before Kane. Yet, somehow he had. Lincoln closed his eyes and tried to calm his racing heart.

If something happened to Ava, it was on his conscience. He was the one who was supposed to keep her safe. The first thing he should have done was mark the ground so she would know how far she could go.

Instead what had he done? Kiss her. And what a kiss it had been. He could still taste her, still feel the warmth of her body against his.

He wanted more of her. Needed more of her.

Just as Christian had warned him, Lincoln had to focus

on keeping them alive and not on the many ways he wanted to strip away her clothes and make love to her.

Lincoln looked at Kane to find his cousin's yellow werewolf gaze focused with intensity on Ava. If Kane didn't remember who he was, why hadn't he clawed or bitten him when Lincoln had faced him? Why had Kane merely knocked him to the ground and fixated on Ava?

That was twice that night that Kane had let him live. Not that Lincoln was complaining, but it didn't make sense. Something about the entire situation didn't add up, no matter how he tried to look at it.

Lincoln squatted on the balls of his feet and considered their options. With Kane seemingly obsessed with Ava, and with Kane's speed and power, they wouldn't get one foot off holy ground before they were attacked.

Not even the bayous would be safe under a full moon. All animals—supernatural and not—were affected by the full moon. Their only possibility for continued life was to remain on holy ground until dawn.

Lincoln looked over his shoulder at Ava to find her asleep. He rushed to her when she began to tilt to the side, getting to her just before she fell. He sat beside her and propped her against his shoulder. She sighed and sagged against him while Kane sat, his gaze still on Ava.

"What are you doing, Kane?"

The werewolf briefly looked at him.

"Why are you after Ava?" Lincoln whispered.

Lincoln looked at the sky. It was still several hours before dawn.

OLIVIA PACED THE FLOOR. She dialed Ava's number again, hoping against hope, that her friend would answer this time. Instead of ringing, it went directly to voice mail.

She halted and stared at the phone. If it went directly to voice mail, then that meant someone had turned off Ava's phone. And that wasn't good news at all.

Olivia sank onto a chair and closed her eyes. Ava knew what it was that the Chiassons did. She understood the things that were out there. There was no way that she would knowingly put herself in danger.

No matter how Olivia looked at it, it didn't appear good for Ava. But if anyone could find her, she knew Lincoln could. Olivia just prayed that it was before something awful happened.

LINCOLN'S EYES snapped open when he heard the faint whistle. His brothers had found them. Lincoln let out a sign of relief and looked at Kane. His cousin hadn't moved. His ears swiveled, indicating that he too heard the noise, but he didn't turn his gaze away from Ava.

"Be careful," Lincoln said into the night to his brothers. "Kane is gone for now."

Kane lifted his snout and sniffed the air. He knew others were out there, but instead of going after them as Lincoln expected, he remained.

His brothers wouldn't make any undue noise, which meant no talking. The same didn't apply to Lincoln since he was on holy ground.

"Kane is focused on Ava. He knows you're out there."

Lincoln smiled when he saw a canoe coming toward him in the water. He started to rise when Beau held up his hand. Lincoln frowned. What were his brothers up to?

Beau stopped paddling while he was still in deep water. Kane growled low, but didn't go after him.

"We got another call from Solomon," Beau said softly, the water allowing his voice to reach Lincoln.

An uneasy feeling filled Lincoln. "What did he say?"

Beau set the paddle across his lap. "They managed to catch the priestess. With a little...prompting...from Solomon and his brothers, she imparted a little more information about what she had done to Kane."

Lincoln glanced down at Ava. Her deep, even breaths indicated she was still asleep, and Lincoln had never been more grateful. He looked back at Beau and waited for his brother to continue. The fact that Beau hesitated told Lincoln the news was going to be worse than he had hoped.

"Kane thinks he came here to get away from New Orleans

and the threat of killing. He has no idea the priestess sent him."

"For us?" Lincoln asked. "Because he's had two chances to kill me and hasn't."

"No. He was given a target."

Lincoln's heart stopped. He knew exactly who that target was—Ava. But why? As far as he knew, this was Ava's first time back to Louisiana since she left as a teenager. Why would a Voodoo priestess have targeted her?

It was an answer he would find once dawn arrived. He vowed then and there that he would be the one to protect Ava.

"There's more," Beau said.

"How much more can there be?" Lincoln asked. "Kane is after Ava. Do we know why?"

Beau shook his head. "Linc, if Kane kills a human, he'll remain a werewolf forever. Or until he's killed."

The hits just kept coming. Damn. "Did Solomon kill that priestess?" Lincoln asked through clenched teeth.

"They're keeping her alive in the hope that they can...*persuade*...her to lift the curse."

Lincoln blew out a deep breath. "We'll talk to Kane when dawn hits and find out why he was sent after Ava."

"That won't be possible."

Lincoln shook his head. "That bitch couldn't have done anything else."

"She made it so that Kane would remain a werewolf for

the entire cycle of the full moon. He won't shift back to human at dawn, Linc."

"Then how in the hell am I supposed to get Ava back home?"

"You can't. Kane will follow her through Hell itself if he has to. You have to stay on holy ground." Beau tossed a bag from the canoe onto shore. "There are some supplies. One of us will be nearby watching. We'll return with more supplies."

"Ava said she was attacked by five men. See what you can find out about them. I want a chance at the assholes."

Beau's smile was full of wickedness. "Only if I get a go at them as well."

Lincoln gave a nod to his brother and watched as Beau turned the canoe around and paddled away. Anger simmered within Lincoln. If Solomon and the others didn't kill that priestess, he was going to go to New Orleans himself and do it.

He wasn't looking forward to explaining to Ava that they would be spending two more nights—and days—there. Ava was a city girl. She might know how to defend herself, but he didn't see her as the camping type.

Two nights. Alone.

With Ava.

How the hell would he be able to keep his hands off her? Especially when she used him as a pillow? It was going to be the longest forty-eight hours of his life.

CHAPTER
SEVEN

Ava woke to the worst crick in her neck. She grabbed her neck and opened her eyes to see the bayou. Shit on toast. It hadn't been a dream. She really had been attacked by a group of men clad in all black, chased by a werewolf, and...kissed by Lincoln Chiasson.

In that instant, she realized the cushioning for her head was none other than Lincoln himself. Her stomach fluttered at the knowledge that she had spent hours against him.

All those hard muscles.

All that warm skin.

All that sexy goodness.

Ava slowly sat up to find Lincoln looking at her with a grim expression. "What? Did I snore?"

One side of his lips lifted in a half smile. "Only once or twice."

164

Oh, God. Was he joking? Ava sincerely hoped so. She stretched her neck and discreetly checked her mouth to make sure she hadn't drooled in her sleep.

The sky was lightening by the minute. Ava couldn't wait to get back to Olivia's to have a hot shower, food, and at least three pots of coffee. She looked to her right where the wolf had been. When she didn't see him, she looked to her left expecting to see the werewolf gone and a man in its place.

Instead, she found the black werewolf still staring at her.

"It's dawn," she said, shaken to her core.

Lincoln's chin touched his chest as he sat forward. "My brothers came last night."

"And they didn't help us?" She scooted away from Lincoln, as apprehension iced her veins. "What's going on, Lincoln. I have to know."

"I let you sleep, because you were exhausted." He lifted his head while taking a deep breath and met her gaze. "We won't be going anywhere for a few days."

"A few days?" she repeated, wondering how she sounded so calm when her heart pounded against her ribs. Ava searched his face to see if he was joking, but it only took another glance at Kane to comprehend the truth of Lincoln's words. She licked her lips. "What happened?"

"Solomon and the rest of the LaRues caught the priestess in New Orleans. With a bit of LaRue persuasion, she told them a bit more about the curse she put on Kane."

It didn't take much for her to guess what it was. "Instead

of reverting back to human form at dawn, I gather the priestess made it so that Kane will stay a werewolf until the full moon cycle is done."

"That's part of it." Lincoln got to his feet and walked to the edge of the bayou. "If Kane kills a human while in werewolf form, he'll remain a werewolf forever."

"That's...a bit extreme. This woman must be a real piece of work."

"Most don't understand that messing with Voodoo is not a good idea. Infuriating a priestess is even worse."

Ava ran her fingers through her hair in an effort to detangle the strands. She gazed at Lincoln's back, wondering what he was thinking and wishing like hell that she could see his face. "Why do I get the feeling there's more?"

"Did you have any dealings with anyone in New Orleans?"

She considered his words for a minute. "There's a law firm there we were working with, but that's the extent of my association with New Orleans."

"What about your mother?"

Ava chuckled. "My mother doesn't even like to say Louisiana, much less get anywhere near the border. Trust me, she doesn't have anything to do with anyone in New Orleans. Why are you asking?"

Lincoln faced her. The look of regret and frustration caused her stomach to clench in dread. "The priestess sent Kane after you," Lincoln said.

Ava shook her head. "There must be some kind of mistake."

"None. Twice I encountered Kane last night, and neither time did he harm me. Both times he could have. One of my brothers and a friend also had a run in with Kane, and both of them came out of it alive and unhurt. I was there when Kane was chasing you last night. He wanted you."

"No."

"Stand up. Walk around," Lincoln urged.

It took Ava a full minute before her legs were steady enough to hold her. She thought Kane was big last night, but in the light of day he was massive. And frightening.

Her gaze was on Kane, and there was no denying the way his eyes narrowed when she stood. He rose up on his paws, the light from the sun soaking into his midnight coat. His lips peeled back to show fangs that were thicker and sharper than she had first thought.

Ava walked toward Lincoln, and Kane was in step with her. When she retraced her steps, he followed.

She was so screwed.

"See how his eyes watch you, see how he looks at nothing but you. Then tell me he wasn't sent for you," Lincoln demanded.

"I don't know why." She began to shake. She had held out hope for dawn, that once the sunlight arrived she could leave the awful night behind and get on with her life.

Lincoln was beside her in an instant. He grabbed her arms and turned her to him. "What about a client?"

"I'm not a prosecutor. I help people like Olivia."

"Then it could be someone you went after while helping a client."

"I suppose. I'd have to look through my files to know for sure."

That's when she noticed his hair was down. The long, chocolate strands hung around his face and to his shoulders just begging to be touched. He raked a hand through his hair in frustration.

"There has to be a connection between you and the priestess. She wouldn't have just pulled your name out of thin air," Lincoln said. "And she knew you would be here. How?"

Ava shrugged when he looked at her. "I didn't share my plans with anyone. Not even my coworkers. All they know is that I'm taking some vacation time."

"Olivia said you came on a private jet. Did you have to tell your company where you were headed?"

"I told them it was a short flight. I did have to let the pilots know so the flight plan could be registered."

Lincoln's lips flattened. "That's how the priestess knew. She managed to get them to give her the information."

Ava was happy she hadn't tried to make a move on the co-pilot. "It still doesn't explain why she has focused on me."

"We likely won't know that until we confront her."

Ava lifted her brows at that. "You want to go to New Orleans?"

"Definitely. However, I don't see that happening for a few days. I'd like to know the answers now. Convincing Solomon to bring the priestess here might be more difficult than getting away from Kane."

That reminded Ava that they were stranded for two days. "What are we going to do about food?"

Lincoln pointed to a bag. "Beau brought it last night. They'll return with more food."

Ava shifted feet. "What about...other things?"

A smile flashed before Lincoln turned away. "I'll be on the other side of the oak. It's all the privacy I can give you."

She waited until he had disappeared behind the tree before she went to the water. She knelt beside it and splashed some on her face. It took her two tries before she was able to pull her white shirt over her head.

It was stained and dirty, but she didn't care about the shirt. It was the way her body ached that concerned her. She looked down at her legs to see the cuts and bruises from her and Lincoln's dash through the woods.

Ava then twisted to try and see her back and right side. She bit her lip when she spotted the edge of a bruise that was already black. It felt like the bruise covered most of her right side.

"What the hell?"

She looked up to find Lincoln staring at her with a

mixture of fury and shock. Ava shrugged. "I told you I had a run in with those men."

"How many times did they hit you?"

"Not half as many times as they tried."

He walked to her and squatted beside her. "That looks bad. Where else does it hurt?"

"Back of my head."

She closed her eyes when his hands gently pushed her head down and moved her hair. His touch was light, tender. So at odds with the harsh curse words that tumbled from his lips a second later.

"That bad, huh?" she said as she opened her eyes.

"You've got a pretty big bump. This is where they must have hit you to knock you out."

"That explains the pain." She held her shirt against her chest to hide her breasts. Being around Lincoln made her yearn for him, but it had been years since a man had seen her naked.

His fingers trailed down her spine alluringly, making goose bumps rise over her skin. "Where else?" he whispered.

Ava gathered her shirt at her breasts and let him see the left side of her ribs. She hadn't needed to look there to know she would have a bruise. It hurt to breathe deeply.

Once more Lincoln's fingers lightly touched her skin. His gaze locked with hers. He was so close she could see the ice-blue ring around his eyes.

"Why didn't you tell me last night?" he asked softly.

"I was being chased by a werewolf."

He smiled seductively. "You are some kind of woman, Ava Ledet."

That kind of compliment coming from a man like Lincoln was high praise indeed. As much as she wanted to kiss him again, she knew it would be the biggest kind of mistake to get involved with him.

He would always put hunting above anything else. It was in his blood, in his very DNA. She had already been left once. She refused to put herself in that kind of place again.

No matter how much her body burned for him.

Ava turned away before she did something stupid and kissed him again. She stood and turned her back to him while she put her shirt on.

She reached for the bag of food only to look up and see that Lincoln already had it in hand, holding it out to her. When had he stood, much less moved to get the bag? Did he hold supernatural powers as well?

"Eat," he told her. "There's plenty, with more coming."

Ava took the bag and pulled out an apple and a bottle of water. She downed the water first and quickly ate the apple. As she ate, she remembered she hadn't had any food since the day before at lunch. No wonder she felt as if she could eat the entire menu of her favorite Italian restaurant. Twice.

While she munched on a bag of pretzels and a cheese stick, Lincoln found a bag of jerky. She tried not to stare at him, but she couldn't help it. It was only the safety of the holy ground that allowed her mind from going on overload about the werewolf after her. But that gave her mind—and her body—something else to focus on. Lincoln.

How many more times could she find the strength to pull away?

How many more times would she want to?

The fact was, she didn't want to. She wanted to tackle him to the ground and run her hands over his rippling muscles, to feel the strength of him, the power.

If she wasn't very, very careful, she would fall into the trap that was Lincoln Chiasson. She would become her mother, waiting every dawn to see if he would return. Even as a child it had been a horrible existence. How much worse would it be as his lover?

Ten times worse? Fifty? A hundred?

She should never have returned to Louisiana. If her father didn't want to be found, then she shouldn't be looking for him. What had it gotten her? Being chased by a werewolf and on the radar of a Voodoo priestess for who knew what reason.

And being attracted to the exact kind of man that she had never wanted to find.

"Why did you pull away?"

She stilled, the water bottle halfway to her mouth, and looked at Lincoln. She didn't need to ask what he was talking about, because it was still in her mind. His gaze was on the bayou, giving her the impression that he didn't care about her answer. But he did.

Ava lowered the bottle. "Because I refuse to live like my mother did."

There was a beat of silence before Lincoln's head swiveled to her. "You base everything on what happened to you fourteen years ago? After taking on those five men and holding it together last night while Kane chased us, I didn't take you for a woman frightened of anything."

She was more afraid than he could possibly imagine. Because with Lincoln, she could see herself doing anything just to be in his arms.

EIGHT

THE DAY CRAWLED BY, each minute feeling like an eternity. Ava kept her distance from Lincoln, preferring to remain sitting against the oak. Not because she worried he might try to kiss her again, but because she worried *she* would kiss *him*.

She knew when his eyes were on her. Her entire body warmed, as if anticipating his touch. As if eagerly awaiting his caress.

And always there was Kane.

The werewolf only took his eyes off of her long enough to get a drink, and then he was back to watching her. Between Lincoln and Kane, her nerves were rubbed raw.

The hours of silence also grated on her. It was past noon, and she couldn't go another minute without conversation. She picked at her nails and glanced at Lincoln, who walked the perimeter of the holy ground.

"If Kane remains here, then he won't kill a human. That part of the curse will be broken."

Lincoln looked at her as he continued walking. "That would be a nice thought, but that's not how a curse from a Voodoo priestess works. If he gets past this full moon, it will happen again, and again, and again, and again. Until the unthinkable happens, and he kills a human."

"Oh." How stupid of her to think there was a bright spot in an otherwise shitty incident.

"I wish you were right. We all do. It's just not how things work."

"My naivety is showing."

Lincoln stopped and tilted his head to the side as he regarded her. "Not naivety. Your optimism, your hopefulness. We...I...forget that sometimes. It's refreshing."

"Perhaps, but without you, I'd be dead, and your cousin condemned to a horrible life."

Lincoln turned his blue eyes to Kane. "He wouldn't live long. Between us and his family, he would be put down quickly."

The easy way he said it told Ava that he must have done something similar before. And yet, there was sadness in his gaze. He didn't enjoy what he had to do, but he did it as a necessity to protect those around him.

"Was my father a good hunter?" she asked.

Lincoln grinned as he squatted and picked up a stick that he broke in half. "Not at first, but he was a fast learner. He soaked up every bit of knowledge my father imparted. I remember the first time we took Jack with us. He hesitated for only a moment. After that, he never paused again. His aim was always true. He was so good that my father began to take him regularly with us."

"Where did he go, Lincoln? Why would he leave us?"

"I don't believe he did." Lincoln turned his head to her. "Every night before we left the house while my mother was kissing all of us goodbye, he was off in the corner looking at a picture of you and your mother. I don't recall a single time of him mentioning your name. He always called you his sweet pea."

Ava smiled at the reminder. "It was his favorite name for me."

"He didn't leave you, Ava. Something happened to him."

All those years of her hating her father made tears cloud her eyes. Instead of stroking her hate, she should have been looking for him.

"I wish we'd have known," Lincoln said. "We could've looked for him."

"After all these years, my chances of finding him are pretty slim, aren't they?"

"Yes. I'd like nothing better than to sugar coat things for you, but I won't."

Ava looked at her clenched hands. "I appreciate that."

"I'll help you look when Kane is back in his normal form."

Her gaze lifted to Lincoln. His blue eyes were clear and locked on her. "You would do that for me?"

"I would do a great many things for you."

The double meaning of his words didn't go unnoticed. Ava shifted under the heat of his eyes. Her body—the treacherous thing—responded instantly.

She might have walked away once, but she wouldn't be able to do it a second time. Lincoln was like a magnet, pulling her toward him, silently urging her to give in. If he knew how precariously she teetered on the edge, he most likely would press his advantage. And part of her wished like hell that he would.

She feared giving in to her desires for him.

But she feared walking away even more.

A whistle broke their focus. Ava was the first to look away. She heard Lincoln sigh as he straightened and turned to the water.

Ava closed her eyes and silently berated herself. Lincoln was a force to be reckoned with, a man who would demand everything of her. He would consume her body, mind, and soul. He would require her love and claim her as his.

She shivered in eagerness.

All the men she knew were metrosexual. None were aggressive or as in control as Lincoln. He was the type of man who would do *anything* to protect his family.

He was the type of man who would give her heaven in his bed.

The type of man who would give unconditional love.

The type of man who would make the woman he loved his entire world.

That was a man she hadn't thought existed except in movies and books. Yet, he stood right in front of her.

Ava looked around him to see a canoe coming toward them. She spotted Christian and jumped to her feet to stand beside Lincoln. Christian smiled at her as he drew closer. His gaze darted to the left where Ava saw Kane out of the corner of her eye. She forced her lips to turn into a smile.

"How are you?" Christian asked her.

Ava nodded. "I'm holding it together."

"She's doing well," Lincoln said. "What did you find out about the men?"

Christian's smile widened. "I'd like to say they'll be waiting for you when this is finished, but Beau and I couldn't seem to stop ourselves. We were giving them a right fine beating when one mumbled something and all five fell to the ground. Dead."

"Well, shit," Lincoln mumbled.

Ava looked between Christian and Lincoln. "What men? Are you talking about the men who attacked me?"

"Yes," Lincoln said without looking at her. "The priestess made sure to have a plan if they were caught."

Christian nodded grimly. "They took a beating from someone."

"That would be Ava," Lincoln stated.

Ava shifted under Christian's pleased gaze. "I'm impressed," he said.

"She didn't come away unscathed. We need something for her bruises and scrapes, and probably some aspirin for that knot on the back of her head."

Christian nodded quickly. "I'll make to bring that soon. Olivia packed enough food for a dozen people," he said as he threw another bag at them.

Lincoln grabbed it out of the air, set it down and opened it. Ava looked back at Christian. "You didn't happen to pack a bed or a TV in there, did you?"

"Not this time," Christian said with a wink. "I'll try to sneak them in the next time."

Ava waved as Christian turned the canoe around and drifted away. How she wished she could be on that boat, but that would be putting so many people in danger, because Kane wouldn't stop until he had her.

"Stop thinking about Kane getting you," Lincoln said, breaking into her thoughts.

She looked to find him standing again. "A mind reader, huh?"

"Nope. Just easy to read the emotions on your face. I'll get you out of this, Ava."

"This time. What about the next full moon? Or the one after that? Will I live the rest of my life on holy ground during full moons?"

"We'll find a way to end this."

"Do Voodoo priestesses reverse their curses often?" she asked skeptically. But she already knew the answer.

"We Chiasson's and LaRue's can be very convincing."

"It's not just my life. It's everyone else's that gets in the way of Kane killing me. And let's not forget Kane. He didn't ask for this curse, and I'm sure he wouldn't want to be a werewolf forever or have his family hunt him down."

"We'll figure it out," Lincoln said again.

She placed her hand on his jaw, the scrape of whiskers prickling her palm. "Such conviction."

"You act surprised by it."

If he only knew the type of men she worked with. They were good attorneys, but she doubted a single one of them could do what Lincoln did. "I believe you would do everything you could to save both Kane and me. What would be the cost to you?"

"I'm willing to pay it."

"I'm not willing to let you. Your family needs you."

He covered her hand with his. "It's not your decision to make."

"I could step off this holy land and end it now."

Lincoln's brow furrowed deeply. "You would do that to yourself and Kane?"

"I'm saying I could. Not that I will."

"So, you'll consider ending your own life but not kissing me again?"

The pain in his eyes was too much for her. Ava threw her

arms around his neck and pulled his head down. His lips moved over hers with skill and passion that set her ablaze.

This kiss was intense, savage in the need that pushed both of them. He backed her to the tree and pressed his body against hers. She moaned at the feel of his arousal. He wrapped her hair around his fist and held her head as he plundered her mouth. He robbed her of thought, deprived her of breath.

And she wanted more.

"Tell me you don't want this," he said as he kissed down her neck. "Tell me you don't want me."

"I can't." She clung to him, her body raging with a fire that only Lincoln could put out. "I won't."

He held her head between his hands. Her lids lifted, only to find his gaze pinning hers. "Try to deny it again, and I'll kiss you until you remember."

"Promise."

Desire flared in his bright blue eyes. "Fuck, yes."

"Stop talking and kiss me," Ava demanded as she yanked his head back down.

No sooner had their lips met than Kane began to growl and snapped his huge jaws. Ava had forgotten about Kane and the threat to her life in those few precious moments in Lincoln's arms.

Lincoln chuckled as he backed away from her. "I don't think my dear cousin is at all happy with what we were doing."

Ava looked down at herself to see the sweat and grime. She couldn't let Lincoln have sex with her looking like this. It wasn't just the dirt, she was pretty sure she smelled.

"What did I just promise you?" Lincoln threatened.

Ava motioned at herself with her hands. "Look at me! I'm disgusting. We'll have to wait."

"Wait?" Lincoln asked with a raised brow. "Because of a little dirt?"

"I smell."

He threw back his head and laughed. "In case you haven't noticed, I do, too."

"I can't smell you, and you look good covered in sweat." Too damn good, actually. It should be against the law for a man to look that hot while she felt so repulsive.

That seductive grin of his was back. "I look good, huh?"

"You know you do."

"Our lives could end tonight. Do you really want to wait?" he asked as he closed the distance between them again.

Ava pushed his long, dark hair out of his face. "We're not in danger as long as we're on holy land, right?"

"I'm going to make you pay for that," he said as he nipped her ear.

"Promise."

He put her hand on his thick cock. "Fuck yes."

CHAPTER

NINE

LINCOLN COULDN'T STOP LOOKING at Ava. She had devoured two of the roast beef sandwiches, three bags of chips, a bottle of water, and a soda Olivia had packed.

"What?" she asked as she reached for some chocolate chip cookies. "I like to eat."

"I'm not complaining."

"Ah," she said after swallowing a bite. "You're used to the women who eat like birds. That's never been me. I like food. A lot."

Lincoln wasn't sure how he was going to keep his hands off her for another two nights. She was temptation and enticement, persuasion and fascination. She aroused him to the point of no return only to infuriate him in the next second. She kept him on his toes and in a constant state of arousal.

Ava was a seductress, an enchantress.

A siren.

And he prayed she never left his life.

"Christian's back," she said.

Lincoln looked over his shoulder to see Christian in the canoe, but he had someone else with him. Lincoln jumped to his feet when he recognized Solomon.

"Who is that?" Ava whispered when she came to stand beside him.

"The eldest LaRue, Solomon."

Ava dusted off her hands. "I thought you said it would be difficult to get him here."

"I thought it would since he also turns on a full moon."

She leaned closer. "Please tell me this Voodoo bitchress hasn't sent another after me."

Lincoln grinned at her. "I doubt it." His grin faded when his gaze met Solomon's. "But it can't be good that he's here."

Kane, who had generally ignored Beau and Christian when they came, began to growl in warning, his fur standing on end as he stared at Solomon.

"He recognizes another werewolf," Lincoln explained.

"Great. I'm all giddy," she said sarcastically.

Solomon looked at Kane with the same blue eyes that Lincoln and his brothers had. That was the only similarity between their families. The LaRue's had varying shades of blond hair. Solomon's was a dark blond with strands of brown.

"He looks intimidating," Ava said.

"We hunt in the bayous. They hunt in New Orleans. It's a different beast all together."

Lincoln nodded in greeting to Solomon. "Kane isn't thrilled you're here."

"I'm not happy to be here," Solomon stated flatly. "I had to come. For Kane. And for you."

Lincoln glanced at Christian who merely shrugged in response. It wasn't good news they brought then. Lincoln jerked his head to Ava. "This is Ava Ledet, who your brother is trying to kill."

"Ledet," Solomon repeated.

Lincoln took a step closer to the water. He didn't like the way Solomon was looking at Ava as if she were a morsel he wanted to sample.

"Are you any kin to Jack Ledet?" Solomon asked.

Lincoln held Ava back when she leaned forward. She glanced at him, but quickly answered Solomon. "Yes. Do you know him?"

"It all makes sense now," Solomon said, more to himself than the rest of them.

Lincoln inhaled deeply and gathered his control. "It might be helpful if you shared it with the rest of us."

"He happened to kill Delphine's niece who had wandered close to here years ago."

"Who is Delphine?" Ava asked.

Solomon looked at his brother again. "The Voodoo

priestess. She discovered it was Jack who killed her niece, and she sent her people after him."

Lincoln wrapped an arm around Ava as she sagged against him. She might have learned where her father was, but that didn't mean it would be a happy reunion.

"That's where he's been? With that woman?" Ava asked, her voice breaking with emotion.

Solomon looked at Ava before shifting his eyes to Lincoln. "For a time. She's a cunning bitch. She must have learned he had a daughter. That's why she used Kane. She wants revenge."

"You came all the way here to tell us that?" Lincoln wasn't buying that for an instant.

"I came for Kane. The only one who can go up against him is another werewolf. You need me."

Lincoln knew it was true. Now that they understood why Ava was targeted they could focus on fixing it. "What's the plan?"

Solomon's smile was cold and calculating. "We wait for the moon. I'll...occupy...Kane. Your brothers will get you and Ava to the house."

"Won't Kane still come after me?" Ava asked.

Lincoln faced Ava and turned her to look at him. "Solomon will ensure that Kane is fighting him all night."

"Even if Kane tracks you to the house, he won't be able to get to you," Christian said. "It's also holy ground."

Ava's shoulders relaxed instantly. "And how soon can we do this?"

"It's not going to be as easy as it sounds," Lincoln warned her. "It's going to take a lot for Kane to be distracted from you. Solomon is putting his own life in danger. He might be a werewolf, but they can still be killed, just like any other supernatural creature."

"I understand," Ava replied.

Lincoln looked at Christian in time to catch a stuffed backpack. He grunted as he caught the bag and glared at Christian.

His brother merely smiled. "Ava, Olivia packed a change of clothes for you. There is also some aspirin and other things for you."

"What did she pack me?" Lincoln asked.

Christian's smile grew mischievous. "She didn't mention you."

"I'm wounded," Lincoln teased to help lighten the mood for Ava. "I'm going to be her favorite brother-in-law."

Christian rolled his eyes. "As if."

"It's time Vin found someone to carry on the Chiasson name," Solomon said, instantly bringing down the mood.

Lincoln tossed aside the backpack.

"When are you going to take that step?" Christian asked Solomon.

"Not for a long while yet. I'm hoping one of my other brothers does it for me. Women are a hindrance."

Christian shook his head and put his paddle back in the bayou. "Look for us when the moon rises. Remember, Linc, you're not completely alone out here."

"What did he mean by that?" Ava asked as they watched them drift away.

Lincoln looked around, wondering who was watching them, Vincent or Beau. "My brothers are taking shifts keeping an eye on us far enough away so as not to draw Kane's attention."

"In other words, we're being watched?" she asked, her eyes wide with mortification.

"We kissed. They saw it."

"Is that so?" she asked saucily.

Damn, but Lincoln couldn't wait to get her alone to show her just how she tied him in knots.

And what he proposed to do about it.

Ava was grateful that Olivia packed a pair of cargo pants in the backpack. That, along with the aspirin, the cream for her bruises, and the ponytail holder to get her hair off her neck had gone a long way to improving her mood.

If the morning had gone slowly, it was nothing compared to the time dragging through the rest of the afternoon. She didn't think the sun would ever set. It was worse than when she was a little kid waiting anxiously for Christmas morning to see what Santa had brought her.

"Will the canoe come on shore? Or will we need to swim out?" she asked.

He shrugged as he stood with his arms crossed over his chest staring at Kane. "Won't know until they get here and we see how Kane reacts to Solomon."

"Right, right." Was she ever nervous. It was worse than running from Kane that first night. "What happens if Kane doesn't go after Solomon?"

"Then we don't leave."

She hated how calm Lincoln was being. She was being eaten alive by the mosquitoes, and years had been taken off her life by Kane scaring her.

Ava wished she hadn't eaten that last fig tart. Her nerves were so shaken that her stomach rolled. If she could fight off five men, she could keep her food down.

"My God, does the sun never go down?" she said in exasperation.

"Look at the sunset, Ava."

"I have been."

"No. Really look at it," Lincoln said. He was beside her in an instant, turning her toward the setting sun. "Look at the colors. Tell me if you've ever seen anything so beautiful."

She had to admit the colors were breathtaking. Deep red to orange to pale pink, all with a hint of gold added in. She had been so anxious about the coming night that she had forgotten to enjoy the life in front of her.

Lincoln hadn't though. Was that because there were few nights he wasn't out risking his life?

"I can't remember the last sunset I saw. I'm normally so busy with work that I don't pay attention."

"Perhaps you work too much."

She snorted. "That's an understatement of the year."

"Do you like your job?"

"I like helping people as I did Olivia. The money is an added bonus."

"Do you always see yourself in Dallas?"

Ava knew what he was asking. She couldn't give him the answer he was looking for, but she wasn't sure she could return to Dallas as if nothing had happened. "It's where my life is."

"Of course."

They watched the sun dip below the horizon and the vibrant colors in the sky fade to gray and then black, all without uttering another word.

Ava jumped when Kane let out a howl. The full moon shed its bright light upon the ground, and Kane was responding to it. In the distance, another howl sounded. Solomon. Ava wasn't sure she wanted to be anywhere near two werewolves.

"Solomon will know who you are," Lincoln said. "He won't attack you."

"Are you so sure of that?" Ava couldn't shake the way he had stared at her when he discovered who she was. She didn't know why she was more frightened than ever, she just was. "Are you so sure he wouldn't come out here to help his brother kill me if it meant the curse would be lifted from Kane? You would do it for your brothers."

Lincoln started to deny her claim. Then he closed his mouth and let out a long sigh. "Shit. I hadn't thought of that. He's family."

"And that's his brother," she said and pointed to Kane. "What wouldn't you do for your brothers?"

"There's nothing I wouldn't do for them."

"And Solomon? Don't you think he feels the same way?"

Lincoln ran a hand down his face and turned away to pace a few steps before he faced her once more. "We're taught at an early age that family means everything. We hunt to protect the people of this parish, but family comes first. Solomon was taught the same."

She really hated being right. "We won't know if Solomon is helping Kane or not until I start to go for the canoe."

"Then we don't go. We stay right here."

Ava took his hand. "Do you trust your brothers to help get us to the house?"

"I trust them with my life."

"Then let's give it a go."

"Ava," he began.

She held up a finger to his lips. "You know these bayous, Lincoln. I trust you with my life."

A low growl came from the darkness opposite Kane. Ava watched as Kane's fur stood on end again. Her head swiveled in time to see another wolf, this one silver, step from the shadows.

It had begun.

CHAPTER

TEN

Lincoln wanted to call the entire thing off. He was no longer sure of Solomon's intentions. There was a chance Ava would never make it to the house. It was a long way to Chiasson land.

Solomon walked around the oak along the barrier in werewolf form, his silver coat almost glowing in the moonlight. The closer he got, the louder Kane's growls. Solomon's big silver head turned to him. Lincoln met his yellow eyes before Solomon issued his own warning growl to Kane.

What would he do for his brothers? Everything. And Lincoln knew damn sure Solomon felt the same.

Lincoln took Ava's hand. The tension between Solomon and Kane was escalating at a rapid rate. Any minute now they would begin to fight, and holy ground or not, Lincoln wanted Ava far from them.

There was a flash of light in the darkness over the bayou. Lincoln's gaze jerked to it and found Christian in the canoe hiding behind a crop of cypress trees. Lincoln backed Ava to the edge of the water. They had barely taken two steps when Kane launched himself at Solomon. The growls and general sounds of fighting filled the night like an explosion.

"Go," Lincoln softly urged Ava.

Ava stepped into the water and Christian paddled furiously to them. To their left another form came out of the shadows. Lincoln let out a sigh when he recognized Vincent. His brother moved to Ava's other side and the three of them walked deeper into the water.

As soon as Christian was near enough, Lincoln lifted Ava in the canoe and got in behind her at the rear. They both picked up paddles and helped Christian turn the canoe around.

"Hurry," Vin whispered and gave them a push.

The water was like glass, and they glided over it effortlessly. As they rounded the crop of trees, Lincoln looked back to see the wolves still fighting.

"Beau is waiting up ahead," Christian whispered over his shoulder. "Vin will also go around and set up in case Kane gives chase."

"And Solomon."

Christian's silence told Lincoln they too had doubts on

Solomon. Lincoln put his energy into getting home. He put his oar in the water and steered them around submerged trees and shallow water while Christian and Ava paddled.

The oars barely made a sound as they sliced through the water. None of them spoke. Until the howl of a wolf cut through the night.

Lincoln set his jaw. If he had to, he would kill both Kane and Solomon. He had vowed to keep Ava safe, and that's what he would do.

A second howl, this one longer and deeper, sounded near them. Solomon and Kane were no longer fighting. The question was, who was closer to them?

"Faster," Christian urged in a whisper.

A shrill cry of pain sounded from one of the wolves. Lincoln paid it little heed. His gaze was ahead of them, looking for the bend in the bayou that would signal Chiasson land. It wasn't that much farther. Just another half mile or so.

The waters of the bayou were deeper in this end. Too deep for a werewolf to try and take them, but there was one place they could. It was called the Bridge, although it wasn't man-made. The waters created it in the bayou long ago. There was a slim area of water between two outcroppings of land where only one canoe could fit.

If even one werewolf was there, it spelled doom for Ava. It was a death trap. Lincoln's only other choice was to pull over and try their luck on land. With as fast as the wolves ran, they stood a better chance on the water.

Thanks to the light of the moon and its reflection off the water, Lincoln spotted the Bridge ahead. The crashing through the brush on either side of them said the weres had caught them. As they drifted closer to the Bridge, Lincoln pulled his oar from the water. Christian did the same and raised his crossbow.

"They're your family," Ava said softly to Christian.

"And they're trying to kill you," he replied.

Lincoln hated how torn he was. He didn't want to kill, but he refused to allow them to end Ava's life.

Ava shifted to look at him over her shoulder. "You'll never forgive yourself if you kill your family. I'm an outsider here, Lincoln. A nobody. That's your family."

Lincoln's attention was pulled away when he saw Solomon's silver fur out of the corner of his eye. He ground his teeth together when Solomon calmly walked out onto one side of the Bridge and looked across to the other.

"Son of a bitch," Christian murmured angrily.

Ava shook her head at Lincoln. "No."

To the right, Lincoln spotted a dark mass moving through the trees. Kane. He would bunch them in. Which of the LaRue brothers would attack first? Lincoln could already guess their plan. While one attacked and he and Christian fended them off, the other would claim Ava.

It was simple and flawless, especially with the power and size of the wolves.

There was just one tiny catch—they forgot who they were going up against.

Christian caught his gaze and gave him a small nod. Beau and Vincent were out there, waiting. Lincoln lowered his paddle back into the water to steer them directly at the narrow slit of water.

Ava gripped the oar, her eyes locked on Solomon. Fear kept her muscles tight, preventing her from moving, which was exactly what Lincoln wanted.

The distance to the Bridge grew shorter and shorter. Solomon's large head turned in their direction. Family didn't turn against family. But if Solomon and Kane wanted to go after someone the Chiasson's were protecting, then all bets were off.

Lincoln and his brothers might not be able to shift into werewolves, but they weren't lacking in surprises and skill. The LaRue's were going to learn a thing or two about them.

They were ten feet from the Bridge when Kane burst through the trees and skidded to a stop on his outcropping. He barked and growled, his huge claws pawing the ground.

Solomon took a step closer to the edge, but paused before he set down his paw. Christian cursed when Solomon took a step back. Lincoln could guess that his brothers had set some kind of trap on either side of the Bridge. Somehow Solomon had sensed it.

Lincoln's adrenaline spiked, his muscles tensed, and his mind focused. He was a hunter. He had saved countless people from the evils that infested the parish. He wasn't about to let Ava down. He reached down and palmed one of his bowie knifes. There was silver in the blade, not pure silver. It would be enough to slow the weres down and for Christian to get Ava to their land.

Lincoln readied to spring as they came even with the Bridge. Solomon let out a growl right before he leapt over their trap into the air.

Ava screamed, the sound swallowed by Kane's growling. Lincoln dove to cover Ava. Any moment he would feel claws and fangs, except...there was nothing.

He turned his head to see Solomon had jumped over them and was fighting Kane once again. Lincoln sat back and grabbed his oar, which had fallen overboard. "Get moving!"

Christian didn't hesitate. He set the crossbow in his lap and furiously paddled past the Bridge. Lincoln placed a hand on Ava's back. She was still bent forward, her body shaking. He couldn't wait to hold her in his arms and taste her lips again, but that wouldn't happen until they were on Chiasson land.

He sheathed his knife and joined in paddling them forward. Lincoln glanced back at the wolves just once. It was a vicious fight. He saw blood on Solomon's fur. Whether it was Solomon's or Kane's, Lincoln didn't know.

Another three hundred yards and Christian jumped out

of the canoe and pulled it on shore. Lincoln tossed aside his oar and lifted Ava out of the boat. He set her on her feet and turned her to face him.

"You're on holy ground again," he told her.

Her eyes were wide, but she nodded. "I thought I was going to die."

"And I told you I wasn't going to allow that to happen."

"Ava!" Olivia shouted as she ran from the house.

Lincoln released Ava as Olivia wrapped an arm around her and steered her to the house. He watched them go, amazed that they had made it unscathed.

"Close call," Vin said as he and Beau walked up.

Beau glared at the wolves still fighting. "I want to know how Solomon knew we had a trap set for him."

"It doesn't matter now," Lincoln said as weariness set in. "He kept his word."

Christian nodded. "Agreed. But it isn't over. Solomon will need to get Kane into the cage."

"I'll stay on lookout," Beau said.

Vincent slapped a hand on Lincoln's shoulder as they turned toward the stone building. The building was partially over the bayou on stilts and was the only part of Chiasson land that wasn't blessed, allowing them to hold supernatural creatures when needed. "Almost done, brother."

Lincoln glanced at the house. He couldn't leave Kane out there to hurt someone, but it was hard not to follow Ava inside the house and just hold her. Never in all his years of helping his family and friends had he ever been so afraid. Afraid that he would fail Ava, afraid that he wouldn't get Ava to safety, but more than anything, he was afraid that she would die.

When they reached the building, he walked inside and leaned against a wall before he bent over, his hands braced on his knees.

"Linc?" Christian called.

Lincoln squeezed his eyes closed. "She almost died."

"But she didn't," Vincent said calmly.

Lincoln heard a chain rattle and knew Vincent was getting the cage ready for Kane's arrival.

"You did everything right," Christian said.

Lincoln straightened and raked his hair out of his sweat-soaked face. "Anything could have gone wrong. I...my God, the fear won't lesson."

"And it never will," Vincent stated.

Lincoln met the gaze of his older brother and realized the truth of his words. "How do you do it?"

"With difficulty."

"Have you ever thought of just letting Olivia go?"

"Many times."

Christian scrunched up his face. "What are you two idjits talking about?"

"Love," Vincent said with a smile.

Christian backed away, lifting his crossbow to rest

casually on his shoulder. "Oh, hell no. I want no part of that. I thought Vin had lost his mind, but I understood it because he's always had a thing for Olivia. But you, too, Linc?"

Lincoln threw up his hands in defeat before letting them fall to his sides. "I didn't go looking for it, little brother. She walked into my life, and I had to have her. There was no thinking, just...acting on a driving need, an overwhelming hunger to hold her in my arms."

"You two are bat-shit crazy to let women into your lives with what we do," Christian said as he positioned himself at the open door to look out.

Vincent flung wide the sliding cage door. "The Chiasson name must live on."

"Good luck with that," Christian said sardonically.

Lincoln exchanged a look with Vincent before he turned his head to Christian. "Why are you so against falling for a woman?"

"I might not have witnessed Dad finding Mom, but I heard his bellow, heard the anguish and the agony when he found her dead body. I'll spare myself that, thank you very much."

"You don't think you could keep your woman safe?"

Christian snorted. "I think eventually the things we hunt will take us all."

Before Lincoln or Vincent could respond to his remark, they heard Beau's shout from outside. Christian aimed his crossbow through the tall steel doors on rollers.

Lincoln and Vincent used the ladders on the walls to climb on top of the cage. Solomon was the first to burst into the building with Kane right on his heels.

Solomon turned and lunged at Kane. The wolves circled each other until Solomon had one of the cages behind Kane. He attacked again, backing Kane into the enclosure. When he was fully inside, Lincoln threw the door closed.

The iron and silver mixture of the cage would keep Kane locked away until the full moon had finished its cycle.

Vincent smiled at Lincoln as he snapped the lock in place. Lincoln looked down at Solomon and was surprised to find the eldest LaRue stood next to the second cage.

"You don't have to," Lincoln said.

The silver wolf simply regarded him with yellow eyes. Lincoln jumped to the ground and walked to Solomon. The werewolf was so large he stood almost eye to eye with him.

"Thank you," Lincoln said. "I owe you a debt. Call it in anytime. I'll be there."

"We all will," Vincent said as he joined Lincoln beside Solomon.

Solomon nodded his head in understanding. It was Vincent who opened the cage. Solomon went to the back and lay down on his side.

"We'll be back at dawn," Christian said.

Vincent locked the cage and walked out behind Christian. Lincoln remained for a moment and turned to Kane. The wolf was near rabid in his attempt to get out. It was horrific to watch, and he couldn't imagine what Solomon was going through observing his brother.

Lincoln glanced at the silver wolf. Solomon was watching Kane silently, and most likely would all night. The duties of both families kept them apart, but Lincoln understood the bond of blood. No matter what, Solomon would be there for Kane, just as Lincoln was there for his brothers and Riley.

And Ava.

He turned on his heel and closed and locked the door behind him. Lincoln faced the house and lifted his gaze to the second floor. Ava was waiting.

CHAPTER
ELEVEN

Ava showered and got into clean clothes. After all she had been through she should be exhausted, and yet she couldn't sit still. She paced the floor of the bedroom waiting for Lincoln. Every creak of the stairs brought her to peek out the door to see if it was him.

She was more nervous than she had been when interviewing at her law firm for a job. She wrung her hands, her mind going over every scene she could think of with Lincoln. She could just come out and tell him she wanted him. Or she could wait for him to make the move.

Or she could...

Her heart missed a beat when she recognized the sound of his footsteps coming up the stairs. He walked the opposite way of her room, to his. Olivia had made a point in telling Ava where Lincoln's room was.

The sound of his door closing made her jump. Most of her life she had sat on the sidelines or buried herself in studying or work. This trip to Louisiana, back to the beginning, had reset things.

She wasn't the same woman who had gotten off that jet. She thought differently, felt differently. Acted differently.

Lincoln dared her to face her feelings for him. He pushed her to experience the fire between them, and he let loose a raging need within her for him that would never diminish.

Ava refused to wake up the next morning with any more regret. No longer would she push people away and keep them at a distance. She had discovered something precious and rare in the bayous, and she couldn't—*wouldn't*—let it go.

She opened her door and stepped into the hallway. For just a moment she hesitated, long enough to square her shoulders. Normally, she would have some kind of plan in place of what she would say, but with Lincoln, he kept her spinning about so that she couldn't think straight.

When she reached his door, she heard the water from the shower. Instead of knocking, she tested the handle and found it unlocked. Ava walked inside and quietly shut the door behind her. The bathroom door was ajar, steam rolling out in waves. Her footsteps were quiet on the rugs and wood floors.

Her heart was hammering, but not in fear—in excitement. In anticipation.

In yearning.

She took in the scene of him through the shower doors when she reached the doorway. Ava stopped and smiled while watching the water slice over his thick muscles and tanned skin. Suddenly his movements stopped, and his head jerked to her. His smile was inviting and daring. Ava pushed down her shorts as he opened the shower door.

She jerked off the rest of her clothes and hurried to him. His large hand closed around her arm to pull her against him. He spun her around and pressed her against the cool tile.

"What took you so long?" he asked.

Ava laughed and wound her arms around his neck. "Close the shower door and kiss me."

"Yes, ma'am," he replied with a wide smile as he reached behind him to close the glass door. "I thought you'd be asking for more."

"Oh, believe me, I want so very much more."

"Really?" he asked and ground his hard cock against her. "How much?"

"Everything you have."

"No more running?"

"No more running."

The conversation ended as he took her mouth in a scorching, searing kiss. Her fingers delved into the long locks of his hair as he deepened the kiss. Her skin sizzled from the heat of the water and the feel of his hard body. She groaned when he slid a hand between them and cupped her breast, stroking his thumb over her already rigid nipple.

Ava clung to him as he kissed down her body before kneeling before her. She looked down at him to see his bright blue eyes filled with desire. She couldn't believe she had found someone like Lincoln, or that she had almost let him go. That wasn't a mistake she was going to make again.

His hands stroked over her stomach and hips before caressing down her legs. He leaned forward and kissed the inside of each thigh. She gasped, her hands slapping against the tile in a futile attempt to remain standing as his tongue licked her sex.

"Lincoln," she whispered in mindless need when his tongue found her clit and began to tease it mercilessly.

Her body was already on fire for him, and it didn't take long to send her to the edge of an orgasm. Without his grip on her hips, she would be a puddle on the floor.

He licked, he laved. He tantalized, he aroused.

He stirred, he seduced.

Ava was barreling toward her climax when he pulled away. She cried out, needing the release only he could give her.

His body covered hers again. She opened her eyes to see him watching her. The need, the longing she saw in his blue depths made her stomach flip. He wanted to claim her, and

Ava wanted to be claimed by him, to have his brand on her so everyone would know that she was his…and he was hers.

As soon as he bent and palmed the back of her thighs, Ava grabbed his shoulders. He lifted her, keeping her legs wide, until he was standing straight.

He glanced down and smiled. Ava didn't have a chance since he lowered her, allowing her back to slide down the tiles. The thick, blunt head of his arousal brushed against her sex. She squeezed her legs in a vain effort to try and wrap them around his hips, but he held her steady.

The feel of him entering her, slowly, caused the breath to lock in her lungs. Ava sank her nails into his skin as he stretched her, whispering her name as he did.

He released her legs so she could wrap them around his waist. The desire was undeniable, the decadence unquestionable.

The pleasure blissful.

She kissed him, letting her hands roam over his back. The feel of his muscles bunching and shifting as he thrust inside her only heightened her senses.

LINCOLN COULDN'T HOLD her tight enough, couldn't get close enough to her. Need rode him hard, but so did the hunger to imprint himself on her in a way that she could never forget him.

Or think of walking away.

He thrust deep within her, in time with their kissing. Her tight, slick walls pushed him closer and closer to the edge of oblivion.

No woman had ever wrapped him in such knots before, but it only made him want to keep her by his side. She was smart and stubborn, beautiful and tenacious. She was the woman for him, and he was prepared to do whatever it took to convince her of that.

Lincoln turned them so that the water sloshed her back. She ended the kiss and opened her eyes. He could drown in her amber eyes.

She leaned her head back to wet her auburn locks as he pumped inside her. The way she tilted her hips sent him deeper, making her moan low and deep. When she straightened, she blinked the water out of her eyes and tightened her legs.

The look of sheer unadulterated need shoved him over the edge. He had been holding on with an ironclad control to prolong her pleasure, but she had destroyed it, shattered it all with just a look.

He pushed her against the wall again and increased his tempo to thrust harder, deeper. Her soft moans turned into cries of pleasure.

AVA COULD FEEL the tightening low in her belly, could feel the tension building as Lincoln took her higher and higher. She let herself go, gave up every ounce of herself to him. The look of pure satisfaction in his beautiful blue eyes, his long dark hair slicked to his head was an image she would always hold within her.

The world exploded in a bright light when the orgasm hit. It carried her high, swept her deep. And it mended her broken world.

She was coming down from the high when Lincoln shouted her name and buried his head in her neck. Ava held him tight as he pulled out of her before he climaxed.

For long minutes they remained locked in each other's arms, the hot water cascading on them. When he lifted his head, Ava smiled and wondered how she could survive another day without Lincoln in her life.

He kissed her softly, gently, as he released her legs until she stood before him. Without a word, he grabbed the bar of soap and began to wash his seed from her stomach.

When he finished, Ava took the soap and washed him from head to toe, lingering over the impressive length of his cock. She reached for the shampoo when the soap had been rinsed from him.

He closed his eyes and smiled contentedly as she washed his hair, allowing her nails to lightly scrape against his scalp. She took her time, because the outside world and all the horrors that waited were kept at bay while they showered.

All too soon the shampoo was rinsed, and Lincoln shut off the water. He opened the door and grabbed a towel. Instead of handing it to her, he began to dry her himself.

Ava's eyes watered. He cared for her as if she were precious to him, as if she mattered as much as she dreamed she could with someone special.

As soon as he finished with her, Ava stepped out of the shower and found another towel. When she turned back, Lincoln stood outside the shower with his arms out waiting on her.

They shared a laugh. Ava never knew drying someone off could be so much fun. He didn't let her finish. Instead, he lifted her in his arms and carried her to bed.

Beneath the covers, they were once again in each other's arms. In the silence she could hear voices below them, but she couldn't make out what they were saying.

"Don't worry. You're safe," Lincoln said.

"Because of you and your family. Thank you."

He kissed her forehead and tightened his arms around her.

"I'm sorry for thinking you had something to do with my father's disappearance. That wasn't fair."

"We were the last to see him. Of course it was fair of you to blame us."

She licked her lips, unable to keep her eyes open another minute. "Do you think he's alive?"

"We'll find out all we can from Solomon. If need be, we'll go to New Orleans."

Now that surprised her. "You would leave your family?"

"For you, yes."

Ava forced open her eyes to look at him. "You're a good man, Lincoln."

"Just don't tell anyone," he replied with a wink.

LINCOLN LET Ava sleep after their endless hours of making love. They had spent over twenty-four hours locked in his room, coming out to grab food before closing themselves back in. He wanted to remain in bed with her, but it was past dawn after the last night of the full moon, and he needed to talk to Solomon. Lincoln dressed and quietly left the room.

He hurried downstairs and rounded the corner to walk into the kitchen where he found his brothers sitting at the table.

"'Bout time you showed your face," Christian grumbled.

Beau mumbled something Lincoln couldn't make out and got to his feet.

Vincent shot Lincoln a knowing smile. Lincoln tried to keep from grinning, but he couldn't. He punched Vin in the arm as he walked past. The morning sun chased away the shadows. A heavy dew had descended the night before, coating the ground with water.

"Ready?" Christian asked, when all four stood on the porch with clothes in hand.

Lincoln was the first to reach the door. He opened it and headed to the stone building, his brothers right behind him.

It was quiet within, and that gave Lincoln pause. He unlocked the sliding door and opened it only wide enough for them to fit through. Vincent clicked on the lights. Kane slept like the dead, but Solomon sat against the metal bars of the cage still staring at his brother.

"It worked," Solomon said. "I had my doubts, but you were right, Vin."

Vincent unlocked his cage. "You can take him home, Solomon. I think Lincoln and Ava will be going with you."

Christian tossed in the clothes to Solomon and checked on Kane's lock. Beau leaned against the wall and used his pocketknife to dig out a splinter in his palm.

Solomon quickly dressed and cut a speculative look at Lincoln. "Bringing Ava to New Orleans isn't a very good idea, cousin."

"Because of this priestess, Delphine?" he asked.

"Exactly. Look what she's done to my family. She wants Ava dead, and she will make sure it's done."

Lincoln fisted his hands. "Over my dead body."

"It might come to that." Solomon shifted his gaze to Christian, then Beau, and finally Vincent. "Is that what the three of you want? To lose your brother to some psycho bitch?"

"No," they replied in unison.

Solomon winced as he pulled the shirt over his head. "I don't want any of your blood on my hands either. Especially not Ava's. I owe her old man. It's because of him that I set some things up before I came here."

"Ah, guys," Beau said as he straightened and looked out the door of the building.

"Right on time," Solomon said with a smile.

Lincoln frowned when Solomon walked out of the cage and past his brothers. They were quick to follow him. Lincoln drew up short when he saw the black Dodge truck. The doors opened and two men stepped out. One with the blue eyes that signaled his blood, and the second man older, the face more wrinkled and the auburn hair liberally laced with white.

"I'll be damned," Beau said with a wide grin. "Jack Ledet."

Solomon waved the two men over. Lincoln couldn't take his eyes off Jack. He walked with a slight limp and wore a patch over his left eye.

"That ugly ass walking with Jack is the youngest of us LaRues, Court," Solomon said.

Court rushed Solomon, lowering his shoulder into his gut and tackling him to the ground. The two brothers were laughing when they got to their feet.

Jack didn't stop until he stood in front of Lincoln. "I hear you're the one who saved my Ava."

"It was all of us," Lincoln answered.

Jack held out his hand. When Lincoln took it, Jack smiled. "I remember you, Linc. The one who sat quietly sharpening his bowie knives. Ava couldn't have been in better hands than with you Chiasson boys. Thank you all."

Lincoln started to answer when a flash of auburn caught his gaze. He looked past Jack's shoulder and saw Ava coming toward him wearing jean shorts, a gray tee, and a brilliant smile.

"She thinks you left her," Lincoln hurried to tell Jack. "Be careful with her."

Jack turned to see what had taken Lincoln's interest. Lincoln knew the instant Ava saw Jack. Her smile faded, and she came to a halt.

"Uh, oh," Christian said and disappeared into the woods.

Jack swiped a hand down over his chin. "She's grown into a stunning woman."

"Daddy?" Ava asked.

Lincoln walked around Jack to her. "Solomon had his brother bring your father."

"What do I say?" she whispered, looking past his shoulder to her father

Lincoln tucked her hair behind her ear. "Tell him what's in your heart."

He started to walk off when she grabbed his hand. Her amber eyes beseeched him. "Stay with me."

Lincoln nodded and walked her to her father. Several

awkward moments passed with Jack blinking away tears before she threw her arms around his neck. Tears slipped down Jack's face as he held her tight.

CHAPTER

TWELVE

"IT ALL WORKED OUT," Vincent said and took a long drink of his beer.

Lincoln sat beside him on the porch and watched Ava and Jack down by the shore. They had been talking for hours. "Has it? Ava has her father. There's no need for her to stick around."

"You were going to take her to New Orleans."

"I was hoping that a little more time with me would help her realize..." Shit. He couldn't even say it.

"What?" Vin pressed.

Lincoln shrugged and propped his foot on a post. "That she might care for me."

"Because you love her."

"A person can't fall in love after a few days," Lincoln said derisively.

Vin gave him a droll look. "This coming from a man who did just that, but I think you fell for her the moment you saw her."

"It's impossible."

"Is it?"

Lincoln set down his beer beside the chair. "Ava has a life in Dallas. She's a successful attorney. What could I possibly offer her?"

"Love."

"A life of fear and worry. Christian has it right. Why put ourselves through it?"

Vincent sat up and rested his forearms on his knees. "She hasn't said she was going back to Texas."

"She hasn't said she was staying either."

"Then give her a chance to make that decision." Vin got to his feet. "Besides, when have you ever given up on something you really wanted? If she's worth it, fight for her, Linc."

Worth it? Of course she was worth it. The problem was, Lincoln wasn't sure he was. She had been put through the wringer. What kind of life was that?

She was used to the city, to comfort and fine things. He could protect her from werewolves, but he wouldn't know the first thing about living in the city, wouldn't know how to be the kind of man she was used to being around.

Fight for her?

He would die for her a thousand times over.

AVA LOOKED ALL over the house for Lincoln. It was Beau who finally told her he was in the building with Kane. Not even that stopped her from going to him.

She walked inside and found him leaning back in a chair and balancing on the two back legs near the far wall next to Kane's cage.

"I've been looking for you," she said and glanced at Kane who was still asleep laying on his side, his back to her in human form.

"How did the talk with your father go?" Lincoln asked.

"Difficult at first, but then better," she said as she stuffed her hands into her front pockets. "He killed Delphine's niece, a vampire, outside our house. It was trying to get in my window. He took the body away to dispose of it, and that's when Delphine's people caught him. They took him to New Orleans where she held him for years."

Lincoln lowered the chair to the floor. "Is that how he lost his eye?"

"Yes. She wanted to kill us, but he wouldn't tell her anything about Mom or me. By the time her people came looking for us, we were gone."

"She found you anyway."

"That was through me. I sent a private investigator looking for my dad. Apparently the PI went to New Orleans and his questions caught Delphine's attention."

Lincoln stood and walked to her. "How did Jack get free of Delphine?"

"Your cousins. They healed him, and he chose to remain with them so as not to lead Delphine to us."

"What happens now?"

So that was why he was acting so weird. He thought she was leaving, and perhaps, for a while, even she had thought that. Until she realized what type of man she would be letting get away.

"That depends," she answered.

He kicked at the leg of the chair. "On what?"

"You."

His gaze lifted to her face. "What about me?"

"If you want me."

The last word hadn't left her mouth before she was against his hard body, his face inches from hers. "Want you? You fool, woman. I love you."

She couldn't form a coherent thought. She had held out hope that he wanted her to stay. It never occurred to her that he might love her.

"Say something," he said and gave her a little shake.

The only thing she could think of was to throw his words back at him. "Took you long enough."

He smiled and lowered his head. Just before his lips

touched hers he said, "Stay, Ava. Stay for me, for us. I'll love you from now to eternity."

The kiss was toe-curling, reminding her of one of the many reasons she couldn't walk away from him. When he ended the kiss, she drew in a shaky breath and smoothed away his long hair from his face. "I'll stay for you, for us, because I love you, Lincoln Chiasson."

EPILOGUE

One month later...

Ava looked around her new office with approval. She had always wanted to start her own practice, and by deciding to remain in Louisiana, it had given her that opportunity.

"Mighty fine digs," Beau said as he and Lincoln finished hanging the last of the pictures.

Ava beamed. "I can't believe I officially open tomorrow."

Christian adjusted the filing cabinet next to the reception area. "Can you really say that after already taking on three clients?"

She shrugged. "It's not as if I could turn them away before I had the office up and running."

"That's my girl," Lincoln said with pride in his voice.

Olivia walked through the front door with a box of files

from the law firm. "These came from Texas. I'll get to work on them tomorrow."

"You have more experience than required to be my receptionist," Ava said.

Olivia gratefully handed the box to Beau, who sat it on the front desk. "You need help, and I need a job. Seems a perfect solution."

Lincoln walked over to her and wrapped an arm around Ava's shoulders. "You two spend so much time together already planning the wedding."

Olivia cut her eyes to him. "I needed help. Since y'all are so adamant about keeping Riley in Texas, of course I turned to Ava."

Ava winked at Olivia. "We might need to take a trip to Austin and pay Riley a visit. I'd love to meet her."

"She'll love you," Lincoln said, though his forehead was furrowed. "But if you go, she'll want to come back with you."

"This is her home," Ava stated. "I tried to stay away, but I eventually returned. So will Riley."

"The hell she will. If I have to go to Austin and find her a husband, she won't be coming back," Christian declared.

Ava and Olivia exchanged a look, deciding it might do the Chiasson boys good not to know about the phone call they received from Riley just the day before. Everyone needed a surprise every now and again.

A CHIASSON NOVEL
WILD
NEED
DONNA GRANT
NEW YORK TIMES BESTSELLING AUTHOR

PROLOGUE

**Algiers, Louisiana, on the outskirts of New Orleans
Six years earlier...**

THE CLEAR, cool October night was shattered with screams.

And blood.

Davena stood in horrified fear as she watched her mother being ripped apart in front of her. There was no attacker for her to see, no one to try and save her mother from. There was only...magic.

"I told her," Delia whispered.

Blood coated every inch of their small living room from cut after cut that appeared on their mother. Through the window, Davena could see the cause of all the horror. She was dressed in all white, her midnight skin cast in an orange glow from the flames she brought to life around her.

In all her seventeen years, Davena had never thought to see her family attacked by Delphine. Her mother kept clear of the Voodoo priestess, so what would make Delphine attack?

Delia grabbed Davena's arm and tried to turn her from the window. "We need to go. Now!"

But Davena couldn't leave. It was their home and their lives being ripped apart. She wiped at a tear and rushed to her mother who now lay still and quiet, her eyes staring blankly up at Davena. She tried to gather her mother against her, but the blood made it impossible to get a hold of her. Davena took her mother's hand instead.

Suddenly, her mother's head turned and her brown eyes locked with Davena. "Run," she whispered with her last breath.

Davena looked up as she heard the crackle of fire. Smoke billowed up from beneath the front door. She quickly covered her head with her arm as all the windows shattered and flames shot high. The fire consumed her mother, and Davena barely got away without being burned. Hands grabbed her from behind and half-dragged, half-carried her into the hall.

Davena looked into her sister's face. Delia's green eyes were wide, and there were tear marks down her cheeks. She had a bag on her shoulder overflowing with clothes. Delia let it drop as she slid down the wall to sit on the floor. "She's not going to let us live. We're going to burn alive, Davena. All the doors are locked with her magic."

They could either remain huddled in fear, or they could fight. Davena was about to head to her room to see about climbing out the window when she remembered her mother had foreseen this day—and a way out.

Davena grabbed Delia's bag. "Get up," she said through the thickening smoke.

Delia coughed, her arm covering her mouth. She climbed to her feet with the help of the wall. "Why?"

"Because we're getting out."

Davena blinked against the smoke stinging her eyes and burning her throat. She desperately wanted to breathe in clean air. Their time was running out. If they didn't hurry, they would never get out.

Fire flared up just as they reached the doorway to their mother's room, as if it knew they were trying to get free. Delia screamed. Davena hastily covered her sister's mouth and put a finger on her lips to urge her to silence.

If Delphine thought they were alive, she wouldn't stop. Ever.

Davena pulled her sister in front of her and then shoved her through the flames. A moment later, she jumped through them herself. The fire singed her skin, the heat crushing. Never in her life had she ever been afraid of anything. Now she was terrified of everything—especially fire.

It destroyed without conscience, killed without consideration. It was judge, jury, and executioner.

And it had its sights set on them.

The room was enveloped with flames. Delia's screams could be heard over the roar of the fire. Davena didn't try to hush her sister again. The screams would help Delphine think they were dying.

Davena focused on shoving aside the dresser to reveal a small door. She managed to slide it a few inches when the flames suddenly fell back. Hesitating, Davena listened and heard the tell-tale squeak of the front door hinges. Delphine wasn't going to let the flames kill them. She was coming for them herself.

Delia was on the floor coughing uncontrollably. Davena shoved the dresser with all her might, her teeth gritted. Suddenly, the dresser slid against the carpet enough that the small door became visible. She let out a relieved sigh at seeing it. Davena had been a small child when her mother had told her about it, and then never brought it up again. Until that moment, Davena thought she had dreamed it.

But her mother was nothing if not prepared.

With tears stinging her eyes from the smoke and her mother's gruesome death, Davena reached for the handle on the door without thinking. She hissed in a breath as the metal burned her skin. It was all she could do to hold in the scream of pain.

Davena pulled her hand back as some of her skin stuck to the handle. She blinked through her rapidly falling tears. There was no time to see to the wound. She snatched a shirt hanging out of Delia's bag and wrapped it around her hand before she reached for the handle again.

It took three tugs, but the door finally gave and flew outward. Davena glanced inside and saw nothing but cobwebs and a tunnel. It was their only chance at freedom—and life.

She grabbed Delia and shoved her through the door. Her sister landed on her hands and turned her head around to look back. Davena hesitated in the door as the light from the fire illuminated Delia. The terror that found them that night would be with them for the rest of their lives.

That second of hesitation was all Davena allowed them before she stepped into the tunnel and closed the door behind her. They crawled through the tiny, dense space for over fifty feet with no end in sight. The air was oppressive and sweltering, but at least they were no longer in danger of burning to death.

She was glad she couldn't see what was around her, because she was certain it wasn't just the ground that her hands kept touching. Her right hand throbbed in time with her heart from the burn. Later, she would have to see to it, and no doubt it would be impossible to use for a while, and would scar, but how could she complain about that when she had her life?

Davena didn't know how far they had crawled. The silence was as eerie as the flames. Just when she thought she couldn't go anymore, she heard the faint trickle of water.

"Do you hear that?" Delia whispered.

Davena swallowed hard as she recognized the drainage ditch the tunnel led them to. "We made it."

Delia gave a soft whoop and stood suddenly, her foot splashing in the water. "We actually did it!"

Davena climbed out of the tunnel and wiped her good hand on her filthy jeans. She and her sister were both covered in sweat and dirt, their faces stained black with smoke, but they were alive. Davena sucked in mouthfuls of clean, fresh air and looked to the night sky that was red-orange with the flames from their home.

"She'll find the tunnel," Delia said and motioned to the tunnel. "You know it."

Davena adjusted the bag on her shoulder. "She'll burn the house until there's nothing but ash. There won't even be bodies to identify."

"I hope you're right. If not, she'll come for us."

"No," Davena said confidently. "We're safe now."

CHAPTER
ONE

Crowley, Louisiana
Present day...

Beau Chiasson was tired and hot. The September sun was brutal on the already roasted earth. The summers were always vicious in the bayou, but this past one had been exceedingly so. The thick, ominous rain clouds teased everyone with the promise of a brief respite from the heat.

He put his truck into park and reached the store just as the first fat drops of rain landed on the windshield. Beau smiled and leaned his head back as he closed his eyes. The sound of the rain was soothing, restful. He didn't know how long he sat there before he opened his eyes and saw the steam rising from the concrete as the rain continued. It was now a steady downpour that would cool the temperatures several degrees.

Out of the corner of his eye, he saw a flash of golden blonde, and immediately his gaze snapped in that direction. Instantly, he sat up and focused. Beau could still recall the first time he saw Davena Arcineaux. It had been just a year before, with the same stormy weather. She had swerved to miss a dog running across the road and landed her car in the ditch.

Beau hadn't helped her that day. Others had been quick to reach her before he could. She had stepped out of her car into the mud and was immediately drenched.

He still wasn't sure if it was the uncertainty he saw in her gaze as she looked around, or the take-charge attitude she had as she got her sister out of the car. Either way, there was definitely something appealing and altogether fascinating about her.

Snapping out of his reverie, his gaze followed Davena as she walked laughing in the rain. Most shielded themselves from getting wet, but not Davena. She welcomed it, eyes bright and lips wide. Her head tilted back to let the rain fall on her face. She remained that way for several seconds before she smoothed her hair out of her face and walked to the doors of the veterinary clinic.

Beau could stare at her all day. It was the same every time he saw her. He gave a rueful shake of his head and opened the truck door to step out into the rain. He shut the door and started to walk away when he glanced back at Davena. He paused when her gaze met his. Even from across the street, he knew the exact color of her eyes—spring green.

They were as bright and enchanting as her laugh.

Davena and her sister kept mostly to themselves, just as the Chiassons did, so Beau had yet to actually talk to her. Not that he would. Why bother getting to know her? The Chiasson name would be carried on through Vincent and Lincoln. That was enough for him and Christian. Especially Christian. If anyone was averse to finding a woman to share life with, it was Christian.

Beau nodded a greeting at Davena before he strode into the store. He tried to forget the way her shirt molded to her breasts, or how her hair looked like spun gold, even wet. He desperately tried to ignore how his body instantly came alive at seeing her.

He grabbed a basket and pulled out his list of the items he needed for dinner. It didn't take him long to get them and start toward the check out. He turned the corner and heard a soft intake of breath right before he collided with someone.

There was a soft, feminine gasp. Immediately, Beau released the basket and grabbed a hold of the person. His hands wrapped around thin arms as he looked down into spring green eyes. He could only stare dumbfounded at Davena. The ends of her blonde hair dripped onto her soaked pink plaid shirt. It was the closest he had ever been to her, and he found it wasn't nearly close enough.

Beau felt a shiver run through her, and even though he knew he should release her, he couldn't. He held her, marveling at her simple beauty.

"I'm sorry," she said, her gaze skating away for a heartbeat. "I wasn't watching where I was going."

He cleared his throat. "It's my fault. I had my head down."

Beau knew he should let go of her, but his fingers refused to loosen their hold. Her skin was warm beneath his palms, and a slight flush stained her cheeks. She was utterly charming without even meaning to be. Beau was thoroughly shocked to discover he wanted to know her, to hear her laugh, to walk with her down the street.

Then he remembered who he was.

He released her and took a step back, instantly missing the feel of her smooth skin. "My apologies."

Beau bent to pick up his basket. He straightened and threw a glance at her over his shoulder. Her guileless eyes watched him. He blew out a breath and started to walk away.

Only to be halted when she said, "I'm Davena Arcineaux. I don't think we've met."

Everything he had learned as a Chiasson, as a protector of the parish, told him to walk away and keep a professional distance. Yet, he found himself turning back to her.

Her oval face with her soft, clear skin was sun-kissed, making her golden locks stand out even more. She tucked her hair behind her ear, giving him a glimpse of her long neck. How he wanted to slide his fingers along the column of her throat and then kiss his way down.

His balls tightened just picturing it in his head. Beau mentally gave himself a shake. "I'm Beau. Beau Chiasson."

"I know," she said with a faint smile.

His gaze locked on her lips. Did she know how appealing she was? Did she have a clue how much he wanted to yank her against him and kiss those luscious lips?

"Everyone knows the Chiassons."

Beau had to get away from her. She was trouble with a capital T. "Is that right?"

"You know it is. I just haven't figured out why everyone all but whispers the Chiasson name."

And there it was. The reason why Beau, like Christian, knew it was better to keep himself apart from any entanglements—no matter how attractive and tempting.

That was the curse of a Chiasson. They kept the bayous safe from supernatural elements, but in turn, they were outcasts. If they dared to marry, it never ended well. Most of the time it was with death—like what happened to his mother.

Still, it didn't stop the ache inside him for someone to share his life with.

"You've been here only a year. I'm sure you'll figure it out soon enough," he said briskly and turned away once more.

The words were like acid on his tongue, but it had been

necessary. For himself and the beautiful and tempting Davena. He wasn't sure he could keep his distance. The words, as well as his brisk tone should make Davena rethink getting to know him.

It was what he wanted. Why then did he feel like shit for doing it?

Beau lengthened his strides to the checkout and set his basket down. Waiting for each item to be scanned and packaged felt like an eternity. He hastily tossed down some money and grabbed the bags as he hurriedly walked from the store.

Once inside his truck, he clutched the steering wheel, closed his eyes, and thought of Davena. Her face materialized in his mind, showcasing every detail. Right down to the flecks of gold in her eyes.

He sighed and snapped his eyes open. The sooner he forgot about her the better. Distance was his friend at the moment. Beau started the truck and backed away. He pulled out onto the road heading home, but even with music blaring through the speakers, he could still hear Davena's voice in his head.

DAVENA WATCHED BEAU DRIVING AWAY. She hadn't needed anything in the store, and it hadn't been an accident running into him. Well, it had sort of been an accident.

She had been trying to find a way to run into him. Before she knew it, she had been so absorbed in her thoughts of how, that she had done just that. Literally. She had ended up in his arms and looked up into blue eyes so bright and vibrant that it was all she saw. They were penetrating, piercing. It was almost as if he peered into the depths of her soul.

Perhaps it was the whispers around town about the Chiassons that first caught her attention, but once she saw the tall, dark-headed Beau, nothing else mattered. After that, she was always looking for some glimpse of him and hoping that she might get to talk to him one day.

Davena didn't know if it was the secrecy around the Chiasson family, or how others tended to keep their distance from them, but she was curious to know more. It didn't hurt that Beau made her heart skip a beat and her stomach do that fluttery stuff that felt as if she were on a roller coaster.

All of the Chiasson brothers were good looking, but Beau stood out. From what she had seen, he was a little more reserved than the other three brothers. Vincent, the eldest, kept everyone and everything in check. Often by his side was the dark-haired beauty, Olivia. It was rumored that a wedding would soon be coming.

Then there was Lincoln. He was the one who wore the easy smile, the one who was never far from the beautiful flame-haired attorney that had set up a new practice here in town. The love shining between the two was so obvious that Davena wondered why they weren't married yet.

Next up was Christian. He could be seen teasing his family, but with one look, he could stop a person in their tracks. To Davena's knowledge, no woman was attached to either Christian or Beau.

She thought of Beau's deep brown hair with its streaks of bronze from his time in the sun. Her fingers itched to run through the strands, to see if they were as silky as they looked. And the length. She'd always had a thing for guys with long hair. Beau's came to just below his jaw, giving him a devil-may-care appearance.

"Damn, but he's hot," she mumbled to herself.

Davena turned once his silver truck was out of sight. The lone cashier, a thirty-something woman with dirty blonde hair and dark eyes was staring at her with a look of disapproval.

"You'll stay away from those Chiasson boys if you know what's good for you," she stated with a sneer.

"And why is that?" Davena wanted to know why the entire parish was almost half-scared of the Chiasson family. What was it about them? They looked innocent enough.

"Heed my warning," the woman said. "If you want to stay alive, you'll keep your distance from that family. Even the sister was wise enough to leave."

Sister. Beau had a sister? That was the first Davena had heard of it, but then she had been focused on Beau.

Davena didn't bother to respond to the cashier as she walked back out into the rain. As soon as she returned to the veterinary clinic, Delia looked up from the receptionist desk with irritation.

"What?" she asked.

Delia rolled her eyes. "You know what. You went chasing after a guy. We're supposed to be working."

"And why not?" Davena leaned her forearms on the chest high counter and peered over the side to see what Delia was typing. "We've been safe for a year. Delphine thinks we're dead. Everything is fine, and I haven't shown any interest in a guy, unlike you."

"Fine?"

Davena bit back a sigh at the anger and resentment in her sister's voice. It was the same argument they'd had since the night they had run from their home.

"Nothing is *fine*," Delia stated. "Our mother was murdered, and we didn't even get to go to the funeral. Her killer is running around free as a bird."

"You want to try and stop—" Davena paused to look around the office and then whispered, "Delphine?"

Delia met her gaze. "We could try."

Davena couldn't hold back a laugh. "You're insane. We have nothing to fight against her magic."

The door opened with the next client before Delia could say more in response. Davena hurried to the back, thankful that the conversation was over. She wasn't fool enough to think Delia would drop it entirely, though.

Davena stopped in front of the cages filled with dogs and cats. The dogs, tails wagging, came to the front looking for some attention. Most of the cats remained asleep, while a couple deigned to crack open an eye at her, stretch, and then slip a paw through the bars to get her notice.

She lavished affection on each of them. She had always been partial to animals, so it had been fortunate that a position had been open at the animal clinic. Even more opportune was the fact that the doctor paid her in cash. It had taken a few months, but as soon as the receptionist left, Davena was able to get Delia hired on, as well.

It wasn't that Delia needed someone to watch her all the time, but she didn't always think things through. She wanted revenge for what happened to their mother. So did Davena, but she understood that to go up against a Voodoo priestess as powerful as Delphine meant certain death.

She wasn't ready to die. There was still so much of her life in front of her that may or may not include a husband and a family.

But to Delia, the only thing that mattered was killing Delphine.

With Delia working at the vet's, Davena could watch her somewhat. Her free time was severely cut down, which allowed Davena to sleep better at night, as well.

"Davena!" Delia shouted from the front

She gave the cat she had been petting one more scratch beneath his chin before she returned to her job. Davena opened the door and smiled at the elderly woman with her overweight dog. "Let me get Boomer weighed in," she said and lifted the chunky Maltese.

Even as she spoke soothing words to the dog, Davena couldn't stop her thoughts from drifting to Beau Chiasson with his captivating eyes and gentle touch.

CHAPTER

TWO

Beau had just finished chopping the onion and bell pepper and moved on to the garlic when the back door opened and Vincent walked in. Beau glanced up at his eldest brother, noting the smile that was a constant on his face of late.

It hadn't been so long ago that Vincent had thought to live his life alone. Then Olivia returned to Lyons Point, and everything changed.

"It's all set for tonight," Vin said as he pulled out a chair and sat at the table.

Beau nodded. "Which area do I have?"

"I thought we'd all stay together this time."

Beau stopped chopping and turned his head to Vincent. "Since when? We cover more ground when we split up."

"That's a fact, and we've all been pretty lucky in keeping

our injuries to a minimum. I think we should be more careful now, though."

"Ah." Beau understood all too well that this was about Olivia and Ava.

Vincent's forehead creased. "What's that supposed to mean?"

"It doesn't mean anything."

"Spit it out, runt." Though Vincent's words were said in jest, his tone had taken a hard note.

Beau set down his knife and faced him. "It means, that you're thinking has shifted from protecting the parish to protecting Olivia, just as Lincoln is now thinking the same about Ava. Don't get me wrong, I like Olivia and Ava, and I understand."

"But," Vin urged.

Beau looked around the kitchen, remembering when they were children how they would all pile in there and watch their mother cook while their father readied his weapons for the night.

He swallowed and shoved aside the memory. "But nothing has changed for me, or Christian. The house and land are more protected than any other place for thousands of miles. If you and Linc want to stick close to your women, then do it. I still think we should split up."

"Just last week we killed that swamp monster, and that took all four of us. If we hadn't all been together, it could've killed whoever stumbled upon it."

"I know." Beau watched his brother, waiting to see what he would say next.

Vincent let out a deep breath and placed his hands on the table before he pushed to his feet. "Are you trying to get yourself killed?"

"No. We have a job to do. Isn't that what you told us when Mom and Dad were killed? Didn't we all step in and do our parts? That's all I'm trying to do now."

"We took risks. Too goddamn many risks!" Vincent shouted. "I don't want to bury another member of my family, Beau. Can't you see that?"

Anger Beau didn't even know had been bubbling within him exploded. "And I don't want any more people to needlessly die like Olivia's parents because we were grouped together over worry that one of us might get hurt!"

"That's enough. Both of you," came Christian's calm voice from the door.

Beau glanced toward the door to find Lincoln standing beside Christian. They walked further into the kitchen, with Lincoln leaning against the wall after he stepped into the room, and Christian moving to the stove to see what was cooking.

Lincoln fingered the hilt of one of his Bowie knives strapped to his leg. "Both of you are right. We tried to tell you that, but the shouting was out of control."

"I'm surprised Olivia and Ava didn't come running in here," Christian said with a chuckle.

Vincent ran a hand through his long, dark hair and sat back down. "I just want to keep the family I have."

"We all do," Lincoln said, his blue eyes briefly meeting Beau's.

Beau turned back around and picked up his knife. He began to dice the garlic and felt Christian's gaze. He shot a glance at his brother and raised a brow. "What?"

"What's really bothering you?"

He wouldn't—couldn't—tell them about Davena. Vincent and Lincoln would encourage him, because if they could find women who understood what they did, then so could he.

The fact was, he wanted them to push him into going to her. It was that and that alone that kept him quiet. Both Olivia's and Ava's life had been in danger, and luckily both Vin and Linc had been able to save them.

But what if they hadn't?

Beau knew it would've completely destroyed both of his brothers. They were strong, determined men, but their hearts belonged to their women. If those women were killed...it would end them.

Their mother's murder had shattered their father. His grief had made him reckless, and that's what got him killed the same night. In one fell swoop, the five Chiasson children had become orphans. Beau told the others he didn't remember much of that night because he had been protecting their sister, Riley, but he remembered every second of it.

Love was so powerful it could do amazing things. Losing that kind of love, however, could obliterate someone as it had their father.

"Beau?" Lincoln called.

He swallowed and moved the diced garlic into the pan with the olive oil and onion to sauté. "I'm fine."

"Bullshit," Christian said.

Vincent's hand hit the table with a slap. "You can't fool us."

"True," Lincoln said. "You might as well tell us. We'll be on your ass until you do."

Beau dumped the chopped chicken breast into the pot. "Any word from our cousins? Was that bitch of a priestess taken care of?"

There was a stretch of silence, and Beau knew that behind him his brothers were looking at each other trying to determine whether to let him change the subject or not.

"Solomon called," Vin said. "They released Delphine after she vowed to leave Ava and Jack alone."

Lincoln gave a shake of his head. "I'm most grateful for that, but they could've had her reverse the curse upon the LaRue line."

"They've been werewolves for so long they probably didn't think it mattered," Christian said.

Beau snorted derisively. "I saw the way Solomon acted with Kane. It matters. They want the curse gone."

"They're making do hunting in and around New Orleans just as we do," Vincent said. "We survive, and so do they."

"Speaking of surviving," Christian said. "Instead of all of us staying together or separating, let's pair up."

Beau stirred the food and let his brothers sort out who was going where. It wasn't long before Ava and Olivia came down and joined the conversation.

It made him cognizant of the fact that so very much had changed. The last time female laughter had been in the house it had been Riley's. God, how he missed his sister, but he agreed with Vincent that she needed to be as far from Lyons Point as possible.

Out of all of them, Riley had a chance at a normal life, and all four brothers were going to see that she got it. She made no secret of her anger at not being able to return home, but Vin came up with valid reasons to keep her in Austin as she finished her degree.

"It's odd, isn't it?" Christian said as he leaned against the counter near Beau.

"What's odd?"

"This," Christian said with a jerk of his chin to the table where the two couples sat.

Beau glanced over his shoulder and shrugged. "Mom and Dad would be happy."

"Without a doubt. As much as I like the girls, I think we might want to think of moving out."

Beau met Christian's gaze and nodded. "I've been thinking the same thing lately. I feel like the third wheel most of the time. They want their privacy, and I think they do things because we're around."

"I know they do," Christian replied with a grin. "They'd rather be having sex than watching movies with us."

Beau chuckled and elbowed Christian in the arm. "Both Vin and Linc will argue that we remain. They'll say there are enough rooms."

"There are enough rooms, but that still doesn't make it right."

"Nor does living in sin, as Maria puts it," Beau said, smiling as he thought of Olivia's grandmother.

Christian's smile widened. "Maria is getting her wedding to plan. It's still a few months off yet though."

"I'd just as soon elope than plan something big if it were me." As soon as the words left his mouth, Beau regretted them.

Christian's brow rose as he regarded him. "Is that so? Who are you considering?"

"No one. I was just making a statement."

"You lie for shit, Beau. You've been thinking about it."

He shot Christian a withering look. "Of course I have, dumbass. It's all Olivia and Ava can talk about, and when they aren't talking about it, Vincent and Lincoln are. I bet any day Linc proposes to Ava. Then there will be two weddings being planned."

"Just kill me now," Christian said sarcastically as he dropped his head back to look at the ceiling. "Do you know I couldn't sit down in the media room the other night because of all the wedding magazines and notebooks? There were color swatches everywhere."

"Hell, I didn't even know what a swatch was until Ava brought them to Olivia and patiently explained them to me. In minute detail," Beau said with a sigh.

Christian grunted as he folded his arms across his chest. "Remember when we didn't have to worry about watching those chick flicks or having room for our beer in the fridge because of their vitamin water?"

Beau wondered if Davena liked beer. Then he grew angry because he shouldn't care what she liked or didn't like. She wasn't part of his life and never would be.

"You're doing it again," Christian said.

"What?"

"Scowling."

Beau opened his mouth to argue the point when he realized he was doing just that. He relaxed his face and concentrated on the meal.

Christian walked to the fridge and pulled out two beers. He opened them and handed one to Beau. "Who is she?"

"There isn't anyone."

"Remember when I said you lie for shit? You're doing that again."

"Don't you have someone else to bother?"

Christian smiled before he took a long drag of the beer. "Nope. Out with it."

Beau wanted to tell him about Davena. Christian would be the voice of reason, the voice that set him straight on removing her from consideration for his future. Yet he didn't.

"I realized today that you were right."

"Holy shit," Christian said and took a step back in mock surprise. "It's only taken twenty-some odd years to hear that from you. As your older brother, I can say I'm proud of you," he said and put his hand on Beau's shoulder.

Beau jerked away from him and frowned. "You're a dick."

"Among other things." Christian took another drink of beer. "What was I right about?"

"Not being...encumbered," Beau said and nodded his head to the table.

"Ah," Christian said, his eyes growing big as realization set in. "Honestly, I was worried that you'd fall in with their thinking."

Beau shook his head. "You don't have to worry about me."

"Is that so? If that's your thinking, why are you so angry? Could it be that there is someone, but you just don't want to give in because you're afraid?"

Beau glared at Christian.

"You're right to be afraid, little brother," Christian said, all the teasing gone from his voice. "Death follows this family close. You bring a woman into the fold, you're ushering her toward a grim reaper."

THREE

Davena sighed in frustration and plopped her head back on the pillow twice, still unable to get comfortable. The rain had been steady for two straight days, putting everyone in an irritable mood. She gave up trying to sleep and opened her eyes. The porch light shining through the blinds only added to her annoyance. It didn't help that it was her night on the couch while Delia got the bed.

Why she ever agreed to that deal, she'd never know. The furnished house had been all they could afford—all they could *still* afford. She had thought they'd share the bed, but Delia had refused, stating they needed their space.

Davena rolled her eyes as she remembered that conversation. It hadn't been a pretty one. Davena had given in because it was the first time Delia had found a place herself. Usually, it was Davena searching for a decent—if not cheap—place for them.

Nothing had been easy since the night their mother was killed. They had left Algiers with barely thirty dollars. It had been Delia's money, which was somehow how she became the one responsible for their finances.

Davena had trusted her, because even though money had been tight, they had eaten and had a roof over their heads through the years. There may not have been nights out at the movies or even to a restaurant, but when fighting for your life, none of that seemed to matter.

She threw an arm over her head as she did a quick calculation of what the two of them had been bringing in together for the past few months from work, minus rent, groceries, and their few bills. That's when she realized they should be sitting pretty well.

They were the best jobs they'd had in years. They were making more money now than they ever had, so why then did Delia tell her they had no money to rent a movie that night?

Davena threw off the blanket and sat up. It was true, Delia had been acting strange lately, but that had been the case ever since they came to the small town. Davena had chalked it up to them not moving on after a few months, but now that she looked back and pieced everything together, it was apparent Delia was up to something.

"Great. Just freaking great," Davena said and ran her hands through her ruler straight hair.

She rose from the couch and padded across the wood floors, careful to walk around the creaky boards, to the closed door of the bedroom. There was no bright light showing through the bottom of the door, but neither was it as dark as it should be with the lights out.

Davena put her ear to the door and heard a faint mumbling. Without a doubt, she knew Delia had lit candles. Her heart rate accelerated as she realized her sister was chanting. And chanting meant magic.

A sound from the front of the house had her spinning around. Goosebumps rose along her arm as her heart pounded against her ribs. There was something outside.

She glanced over her shoulder at the door and briefly considered alerting Delia, until she gathered that it could be Delia summoning something.

"I'm going to stuff one of those candles up your ass, Delia," she whispered to herself.

Davena retraced her steps until she stood before the wide window in the living room. She parted the blinds and saw nothing. A laugh erupted from her as she started to step back.

That's when her gaze caught on a shape across the street dressed all in white.

Davena jerked back, tripping over the coffee table in her haste. A scream lodged in her throat as the world went black.

BEAU CAME AWAKE INSTANTLY, his body covered in sweat and smoke clogging his throat. He shoved aside the sheet and swung his legs over the side of the bed. For long moments, he sat in the quiet of his room trying to determine what caused him to wake so suddenly with an odd—and persistent—feeling of impending doom.

He ran his hands down his face and glanced at the clock. It wasn't yet dawn. He managed to get only three hours of sleep. There would be no returning to dreamland for him. Whatever woke him, wanted him up for a reason. Beau never doubted the signs his body and mind gave him. They had saved his ass on numerous occasions.

Beau looked out his window to see another gray day ahead. The rain was still as steady as the day before. It had made hunting in the bayous the night before miserable. He rose and took a quick shower, not bothering to shave. He was dressed in jeans, pulling a tee over his head as he walked barefoot down the stairs to the kitchen.

The house was quiet as a tomb, but in a few hours it would be filled with laughter and conversation. It was the silent hours that Beau enjoyed the most. He was usually the first to wake, but the silence wasn't what set him on edge. It was the gnawing, distressing feeling that grew by the minute.

He poured a glass of orange juice and walked to the back

door. With a flick of his wrist, he unlocked the door and swung it open. He stood in the doorway, his hand on the jam as he looked out past the screened porch to the bayou beyond.

There was something out there. It was waiting, plotting. The question was, who was it after? The normal consensus would be any of the Chiassons, but this time, Beau thought it could be someone else.

The squeak of a rocker had his gaze jerking to the left to see Maria, her long silver hair pulled back in a bun, slowly rocking, her eyes on the bayou.

"I couldn't sleep," she said. "It woke me."

Beau frowned but remained silent. Maria wasn't just Olivia's grandmother, she had learned how to protect herself and her family by using spells and markings from other cultures. By dabbling into that world, Maria had learned... certain things. He didn't speak as he waited for her to say more. She practiced Hoodoo, and that in itself made her a woman worth listening to.

"It's out there, Beau. It's coming for someone, but I don't know who." She swung her dark gaze to him. "Whatever it is, it's going to touch this family."

"They always do, Maria," he said. "It happens when we hunt them."

She was shaking her head before he finished. "No. It's going to take a life. A Chiasson life, unless it's stopped."

Beau glanced up, thinking of his brothers, Olivia, and

Ava. Then there was Riley. She might not be in Louisiana, but she was still a Chiasson. "The threat is here only?"

"Yes." Maria's face was lined with worry. "Riley is safe. It's everyone else I'm worried about. Especially my Olivia."

"Vin won't let anything happen to her."

Maria smiled sadly. "He may not be able to stop this force. I don't even know if I can. It's...powerful."

Beau licked his lips and stepped out onto the covered porch. The screen surrounding them kept them from being swarmed by mosquitos. "Is this the first time you've felt something like this?"

"Once before. It was here for a very brief time, and gone before I could try to discover what it was. Now, it appears it's here to stay."

"What kind of creature is it?"

She drew in a deep breath and looked back at the bayou. "There are many types of supernatural things out in the world, Beau Chiasson. Don't narrow your thoughts to a creature."

He finished his OJ and sat in the chair next to her. "What do you think it is?"

"I don't have a clue. Not yet, at least. I've been trying to determine what it is since I woke."

"Olivia is going to have your hide when she discovers you got out in this weather."

Maria laughed softly. "She's the last of my family. She can get angry at me all she wants as long as she lives."

Beau wondered how Vin and Linc were going to take the news. It made him infinitely glad he didn't have a woman to worry about.

No sooner had that thought ran through his head than an image of Davena popped up. He swallowed and turned his head away from Maria. He wished he knew if Davena was safe. It wasn't as if he could call her and check without completely freaking her out.

"I hear there is someone in town asking about you," Maria said.

Beau shrugged. "People are always wanting to know stories about our family."

"Do you have mud in your ears?" she asked testily.

Beau swung his head to her to find her steely gaze on him. He sat back, waiting for her to continue.

"I said you," Maria said. "Who do you think would be asking about you?"

He knew. Davena. Beau didn't so much as whisper her name, but Maria's smile said she knew exactly who it was.

"She's a pretty thing. So is her sister, but Davena is much friendlier than Delia. Grace saw Davena ask several people before she approached Grace."

Beau didn't bother to hide his grimace. Grace and Maria had been best friends since both were young girls. Just as Maria had looked after the Chiasson siblings after their parents' deaths, Grace had done the same. Which meant there was no telling what Grace told Davena.

"Don't worry," Maria said. "Grace didn't tell her much, other than you were single and could use a good woman."

Beau dropped his head back and closed his eyes. Was this what it was like to have grandparents or eccentric aunts who liked to meddle?

Her cold fingers clamped around his wrist, turning his attention to her. Maria's eyes were once more filled with distress. "We have to find out what's here. I can't lose Olivia."

He could see her panic rising. She had tried to change the subject by talking about Davena, but whatever woke the both of them had a strong hold on her.

"You said it would touch this family," Beau said slowly as he thought through all she'd said. "But it isn't after us right now. I gather it will come for us when we try to stop it."

Maria nodded, her eyes blinking quickly. "That's my feelings on it. You've felt it too, haven't you?"

"Yes," he admitted with a slight nod. "It woke me."

"What did you see? What did you feel?"

He briefly closed his eyes and thought back to when he first woke. "I didn't see anything. It was just a feeling of trepidation. Like something ominous was coming. And smoke."

"Smoke?" Maria repeated with a deep frown. "I wish we had time, but I think it's already here."

Beau covered Maria's hand with his. "We'll find it."

"I don't want to worry Olivia."

"Vincent needs to know. So do Lincoln and Christian. I have to tell them so we can start looking for this thing."

Maria released him, pulling her hand from his and sat back with a sigh. "Grace is at my house. My place is more protected than hers. She'll remain with me until this thing is caught and ended."

"You're powerful in your own right, Maria. Don't forget that."

"I'm not forgetting it, but this is more powerful than me and Grace combined."

The fact that Maria wasn't just worried but frightened was telling. "What should I be looking for?"

"Death. And magic."

CHAPTER

FOUR

DAVENA WOKE ON THE COUCH. She blinked and stared at the small TV across from her. She stretched as she rolled onto her back and immediately winced. She stilled, recalling the previous night. Had it all been a dream? It had to be. Otherwise, how would she have gotten back onto the couch? And yet, her shoulder blade was sore.

The coffee table. Her gaze went to the table to see nothing out of order. She remembered tripping over it, she remembered falling, and then...nothing.

Davena slowly sat up and looked around. A glance at the clock hanging on the wall above the TV said it was just after six. The sun couldn't penetrate the thick rain clouds fully, only lightening the room enough for her to see without turning on a lamp.

She shoved her hair out of her face, and had to quickly

bite back a yelp of pain. Davena fisted her hands and waited until the worst of it had passed. Then she rose and walked to the bathroom where she flipped on the light and tilted her head to the side as she carefully moved her hair.

The bump was barely visible on her temple, but the bruising was evident, as was the small cut. There was no blood, nor had she woken up on the floor as she should have.

"What the hell is going on?" she asked her reflection.

Davena braced her hands on the edge of the sink and swallowed past the sudden nausea that threatened, which had nothing to do with her injury. Only one other time had she felt such dread. Less than a week later her mother had been murdered.

She broke out into a cold sweat and began to shake. Gagging, she rushed to the toilet, tears falling as she tried not to be sick.

Their life had been good in Crowley. It was a small city surrounded by even smaller towns. She and Delia were making good money and had remained longer than their customary six months. Davena had thought they were through moving.

Her legs buckled, dropping her to her knees as she rested her cheek against the cool porcelain seat. She didn't know how long she stayed that way before the tears finally dried up and the worst of the nausea passed.

Davena wiped her face and straightened. She was going to have to find some way to tell Delia it was time to get moving. They were only two hours from the Texas border. Perhaps it was time they left Louisiana again. They had spent time in Mississippi and Arkansas. It was always tough to convince Delia to leave Louisiana, but she would do it. Then make sure they never returned.

She climbed to her feet and walked back to the living room. Davena inspected the coffee table to see a chip on one edge. She touched it, and the entire table rocked.

Just as she had thought. She hadn't just tripped, she had broken the thing. Someone had cleaned up the entire incident so she'd think she was losing her mind.

Davena's head turned to the bedroom door. Delia was up to something, but Davena had a hard time believing her sister would allow her to believe she was going insane. Delia was many things, but not manipulative. At least, she hadn't been.

She walked to the front door and checked the locks. All were in place. Same with the back door and all the windows Davena could get to. The bedroom door opened just as she finished checking the window over the kitchen sink. Davena whirled around, her head pounding at the quick action.

"Morning," Delia said with a yawn. She shuffled into the kitchen in her bare feet and clicked on the coffee pot before making her way to the bathroom and turning on the shower.

Davena pulled out a chair at the tiny kitchen table that only sat two and dropped her head into her hands. They had two hours before they had to be in to work. That was two hours she had to convince Delia to leave Louisiana.

The smell of the coffee brewing filled the small house. As soon as it finished, Davena poured herself a cup and contemplated what to do. One more day wouldn't hurt them. They could turn in their notices at work and be gone by the next day.

By the time Delia walked out of the bathroom in her robe with a towel wrapped around her head, Davena had it all figured out.

"You're going to be late," Delia said as she poured her coffee with four heaping spoonfuls of sugar.

"Let's leave."

Delia threw her an exasperated look. "Very funny. I thought you were happy here."

"I am. I was. I just think it's time to move on. We've stayed longer than we've ever stayed before."

Delia shrugged and faced her as she blew on her coffee. "It's been six years, sis. Delphine didn't come after us in all that time. She's not going to come after us now, because she thinks we're dead."

"Did you pick me up last night after I fell?"

"Pick you up?" Delia's forehead furrowed. "What is going on with you? You fell? Are you all right?"

Davena waved away her words and rose to set her empty cup next to the sink. "Yeah, I'm fine. I'm just getting antsy to leave."

"I'm not going."

"What?" she asked, her head whipping around to her sister. "We've always stayed together."

"It's been six fucking years!"

"Don't say that word. Mom hated it."

"Fuck. Fuck. Fuck!" Delia yelled. "Mom is dead, and I'm an adult. I can say whatever I want."

Davena could only stare after Delia as she stormed away, the door slamming after her. They may not share a bed, but they shared a closet and clothes.

She stomped after her sister, throwing open the door and causing Delia to gasp as she turned from the closet, a shirt in hand. "Finished with your temper tantrum? You'd think you were the younger sister."

"Puh-leeze," Delia said with a roll of her eyes. "Ten months separate us. You think you've got it all under control, but the truth is, you're always grasping at straws. There's no control, Davena, but you've never realized that."

Now she was more confused than ever. "Control? What the hell are you talking about?"

"You want to control every aspect of our lives from where we live to how long we stay somewhere."

"Oh, no you don't." Davena began to shake she was so angry. "I distinctly remember leaving many places behind because you were ready before I was. How many decent places have we left? That one in Mississippi was a good place, and the job at the deli was really good."

Delia barked with laughter and yanked the towel off her head, her wet, dark-blonde hair spilling to her shoulders. "Louisiana is our home."

"It's where Delphine lives. God!" she yelled and glanced helplessly at the ceiling. "You're just like Mom. She knew the threat was there, but she remained, taunting Delphine with it until Delphine killed her. And you want to remain in the same state with a Voodoo priestess who wants us dead?"

"You don't get it, do you?"

"Obviously not," she replied sarcastically. "Explain it."

Delia crossed her arms over her chest and cocked her hip out. "I'm going to make Delphine pay for what she did to Mom and what she's put us through these last six years."

Davena shook her head in regret. "What have you done, Delia?"

"Nothing. Yet. But I will. I'll get strong enough, and I'll face Delphine."

Davena put her hand to her forehead and closed her eyes. "Mom didn't teach us any of the spells, because she didn't want us involved."

"I followed her many nights while you were out running around with your friends in New Orleans."

Davena dropped her hand to her side and stared dumbfounded at her sister. "Please, no. Mom went out of her way to help those who had been cursed with Voodoo. She began it before we were born, and she tried to get out of it after us. She couldn't. Dad was killed as a warning, which is why she spent many, many years away from it all."

"She helped them in secret," Delia said, a smirk on her face. "Mom told you she was out of it, but she wasn't."

Davena's stomach began to churn again. "I knew she helped those in deep. It wasn't in her nature to turn away someone suffering."

"The spells she learned while practicing Voodoo are what allowed her to do that," Delia said. "I want to do the same."

"You want to use those spells to kill Delphine. How is that any different than what Delphine did to Mom and Dad? You'll be a murderer."

"I'm following in Mom's footsteps. Someone has to. It isn't going to be you," she said with a scathing look.

Davena was taken aback. "Following in her footsteps, my ass. Mom helped people. She would protect us, and the house, but she never harmed anyone—not even Delphine. How is that doing what Mom did?"

"I'll help people once I kill Delphine."

Davena slapped her hands on her legs in frustration. "Do you hear yourself? Do you even know what you're saying?"

"Yep. I'm saying I'm staying here. You can do whatever you want," Delia said and turned on the blow-dryer before putting her back to her.

Davena gave up and went to take her shower. The entire time she was bathing, the bad feeling festered in her belly until she was sick with it. There wasn't another word shared between her and Delia the rest of the morning, or on the drive into work. Delia opened the car door before the vehicle was in park and jumped out, practically bounding into work with a bright smile.

Davena shut off the engine and remained in the car. Her mood matched the gray sky. It was Friday, which meant they closed at two. Hopefully by then she could decide what to do.

The thought of leaving Delia behind didn't seem right, and yet she knew they couldn't remain in Crowley. Something bad was going to happen, of that Davena was certain.

She had ignored the warnings until the last minute before, and then her mother had pushed her words aside. Hours later, their mother was dead, and they were running for their lives.

Davena looked down at her right hand where the skin was puckered on her palm from the burn she sustained while trying to get the door opened. The scar ran horizontally across her palm, a constant reminder of how quickly life could be changed.

She was so tired of trying to keep going. So many times she wanted to fall down and curl up in a ball, to pretend that life didn't suck major moose dick. The fact was, life did suck the big one.

Not once had she allowed herself to fall apart. That had

been Delia, and one of them had to stay strong. Only once had she come close to losing it. Somehow, she had pulled herself together and carried on. Had it not been for Delia, Davena knew she would've never made it as far as she had. It was her sister that kept her focused.

She wanted to believe that Delia was right and that six years were long enough for Delphine to forget them. But Davena knew how vengeful the priestess could be. She had seen the evidence when the people would come to her mom for help.

It would be a cold day in Hell before Delphine ever forgot them.

CHAPTER

FIVE

T HE HUSH that fell around the kitchen table was deafening. Beau let Maria do all the explaining of what was going on. He didn't volunteer what he had experienced that morning yet.

Vincent put his arm on the back of Olivia's chair and touched her as he looked at Maria. "And you have no idea what it could be?"

"No," Maria said.

Lincoln rubbed his forehead, his face already lined with worry. "We need it narrowed down some. Is it a ghost? A demon? A creature?"

Maria slid her dark gaze to Lincoln. "How many times do you know what you'll be hunting when you leave this house?"

"Maman's right," Olivia said. "It doesn't matter what it is. It's just another supernatural problem we have to solve."

"We?" Vin said with a raise of his brows. "Oh no, sweetheart. It's a problem my brothers and I have. You and Ava aren't going to leave this house."

Ava lifted her amber gaze to Lincoln. "I thought the entire Chiasson property was warded and protected like the house."

"It is," Lincoln said as he took hold of her hand and squeezed it. "The house is safe. We need y'all to remain inside."

"Don't leave unless one of us tells you to," Vincent told Olivia.

She rolled her eyes. "Oh, come on, babe. You've got to let that go. I thought Maman was in the hospital. How was I to know that creep was responsible for all those deaths?"

"That's the point," Christian said as he leaned back in his chair. "The only people you can trust are in this house."

Beau watched the way the two couples looked at each other before he turned his head away. If his brothers didn't have Olivia and Ava, they would be facing the growing threat differently. They would be heading out now to look for it, not worrying about whether the girls were safe.

Like he was worrying about Davena.

He looked back at the group to find Christian's gaze on him. Beau shoved his hair out of his face and got to his feet.

"The women will be safe here. Let's get out there and find whatever this is."

"Night is the best time for hunting," Christian said.

Lincoln grunted. "Most of the time, but if it's a human we're after, we can find them in the day."

Maria pushed the chair away from the table and stood. She walked to her purse and reached for her keys when Olivia rose so quickly she knocked her chair over.

"Maman, where are you going?"

Maria smiled softly. "Back to my house. As I said earlier, Grace is waiting for me."

"Vincent can bring Grace here. Make Maman stay, Vin."

Vincent stood beside Olivia and pulled her against his side. "Your grandmother is a grown woman. I can't make her stay."

"Damn right," Maria mumbled, the smile gone.

Olivia jerked her head to Vincent. "But you can make me stay?"

"We both will," Maria stated in a no-nonsense voice.

Olivia harrumphed and flattened her lips as she glared at her grandmother.

Maria gave a small nod. "Now that that's settled, I'll expect to hear from y'all later. Grace and I will remain at the house, safely ensconced inside."

She then opened her arms, and Olivia flew into them. They shared a lasting embrace before Maria turned to Ava.

Ava hugged Maria tightly, soft words falling from Maria's lips.

Beau and Christian remained behind as the two couples walked Maria to her vehicle. It was still raining, though the rain had diminished to a drizzle.

"I'm going to take a drive around to see if I can find anything. Want to tag along?" Christian asked.

Beau knew the driving would eventually take them into Crowley. That would put him too close to Davena for his peace of mind. "I'll pass."

"I don't know who you're trying to stay away from, but it won't work. It never does."

"Don't have a clue what you're talking about," Beau said as he pushed open the screen door and walked off the porch.

It didn't matter that he was getting wet. He had spent the last few days soaked, and today wouldn't be any different. Beau looped his thumbs in his belt loops and gazed out over the bayou.

No matter how he tried, he couldn't determine what the threat was. More unsettling, was the fact that he had felt something. Maria sensing something he could understand since she practiced Hoodoo, but not him.

"Thank goodness Maria knows Hoodoo, huh?" Lincoln said as he came to stand beside him.

Beau nodded. Voodoo was a religion, but Hoodoo was a practice of magic that combined some elements of Voodoo. There were instances where Hoodoo was used to combat

Voodoo curses. Sometimes they worked. Sometimes they didn't.

"Voodoo isn't to be trifled with," Lincoln said and pulled his long hair back at the base of his neck before he wrapped a piece of leather around it and tied it off.

Beau swept his arm across their view. "We live in Louisiana, Linc. That's like saying a gator shouldn't be teased. It's common sense, even for those who don't live near those practicing the religion."

"Ah, but we've both seen how the Voodoo religion has profited from tourists when we've been in New Orleans. They sell spells, Voodoo dolls, and anything else they can think of."

"I know." Beau had never cared to be near those shops. Some sold fake items, but there were a handful of stores that sold the real things.

Lincoln crossed his arms over his chest and blew out a long breath. "You've been peculiar all morning. Want to tell me what's going on?"

"No." Beau dropped his chin to his chest and kicked at the wet grass. "Maria wasn't the only one who felt something."

There was a heartbeat of silence before Lincoln pushed at his shoulder so they faced each other. "What the hell? And you didn't say anything?"

"Why?" Beau said with a shrug. "Maria's explanation was good enough. There was no need to add mine."

"Did Christian hit you and addle your brains? Of course there's a need," Lincoln said peevishly. Then he mumbled, "Damn fool."

Beau rolled his eyes. As the youngest of the brothers, he was constantly being picked on. Not even Riley was teased as mercilessly as he was, and she was the youngest of them all. But she was the only girl, and for some reason that made her different.

"Enough of that shit," Beau said, his patience at an end.

Lincoln threw up his hands. "Fine, but you're going to tell me everything."

"There isn't much to tell. I woke up with a feeling of dread twisting my stomach. I came downstairs and found Maria."

Lincoln gave a shake of his head and looked at the house. "Beau, not a single Chiasson has ever had those kinds of things happen to them. We aren't psychics or seers or anything of the sort."

"I know," Beau said wearily. It wasn't anything he hadn't already told himself, but there was no doubt in what he had felt—was still feeling.

"For both you and Maria to feel something..." Lincoln trailed off and hung his head as he put his hands on his hips. "We need to be extra careful. I'm worried like I've never been worried before."

"Ava and Olivia will be safe. We'll remain in two groups

to watch each other's back. Christian wants to drive around. I'm going to go out into the bayou."

"I'll go with you," Lincoln said and lifted his head. "We live dangerously every day, but I get the feeling that whatever is here is infinitely more treacherous."

"It's not after us right now, but based on what Maria sensed, we'll find it and get in its way."

Lincoln snorted. "That's when it'll come for us."

"Yeah," Beau said weakly.

Lincoln faced the house as Vincent and Christian joined them. "The Chiasson land has always been a refuge against the things we hunt."

"Your point?" Vin asked.

Beau knew what Lincoln was going to say, and he knew how much it was going to cost both of his brothers.

"Aww shit," Christian mumbled and slapped his hand on his leg.

Linc cleared his throat. "If Maria is right and this thing does come after us, I won't lead it back to Ava or Olivia. I don't want any of us to return here once we figure out what it is."

Vincent opened his mouth to argue, and then stopped. He briefly squeezed his eyes closed and nodded. "You think it's that powerful?"

Lincoln glanced at Beau. "I do. Beau felt something, as well. It was enough to hear it from Maria, but Beau too? I don't want to take any chances, no matter how well we think the house and land are warded."

"Before y'all jump my ass, there was no need to tell you anything. Maria's senses were more targeted than my ominous feeling," Beau explained.

"Shit for brains," Christian said with a wry twist of his lips.

Vin scowled. "I don't care what you thought. You should've told us."

"He's done it now," Lincoln said. "Let's leave it and move on to the next step. I'm going to head out into the bayou with Beau."

Christian scrubbed a hand along the top of his head to ruffle his short dark locks. "I'm going to drive around."

"I'll join you then," Vin said. "We remain together. We don't normally take our cell phones out on hunts, but I think we need to this time. Keep them on vibrate, but at least we'll be able to get ahold of each other if necessary."

Beau gave a nod. "Agreed."

"One more thing," Linc said. "We don't tell the girls we might not be coming back until this is over."

Vin made a sound at the back of his throat. "You don't have to tell me twice. I'd rather explain to Olivia after it's all over than argue with her now. Besides, we might not find anything today."

Christian slapped Vincent on the back. "Better you than me, bro."

Lincoln shoved Christian, causing him to slip on the slight incline leading up to the house. With the wet grass, he went face down with a loud grunt.

Vincent kicked Christian's legs out from underneath him when he tried to get to his feet. Beau joined in the laughter, and waited until Christian was up on his hands before he pushed down on Christian's back, causing him to face plant again.

"I'm going to kick y'all's asses!" Christian bellowed.

The three ran to the house with Christian right on their heels. To some, it might seem odd for them to be joking around when circumstances were so dire, but they had to relieve their emotions somehow so they could face the danger.

They came to a screeching halt in the kitchen when they found all their weapons laid out on the table with the girls packing food and provisions.

Vincent and Lincoln went to their women while Christian kicked off his muddy boots and headed upstairs to change. That left Beau once more unsure of where he stood or what he wanted.

He didn't want the added weight of someone else to watch over and worry about. His family was more than enough. Nor did he want to anxiously await the day his wife would be taken from him in the most heinous way.

In that regard, he wholeheartedly sided with Christian.

Yet, no amount of rational thought could stop the need

to share his life with someone. To curl up in bed with a woman, and talk about the day or the future. To wake up with her every morning in amazement that someone had chosen him.

As he watched his brothers sharing whispered words with their women, Beau wanted it more than ever.

And he knew who he wanted—Davena.

CHAPTER

SIX

BEAU STOOD knee-deep in the bayou and wiped the sweat from his brow with the back of his hand. The rain halted an hour into their search of the bayou. With the clouds moving fast, the sun was baking them, making the heat oppressive.

He started forward when he caught sight of a snapping turtle swimming across his path. It was a big one, measuring nearly two feet long. Once the turtle was past, Beau continued onward. Lincoln was off to his left searching, and unfortunately, nothing had been found by either of them in the four hours they had been out.

Every few minutes, Beau cursed himself for not going into town with Christian. He might have caught a glimpse of Davena, which would have calmed him some. Maybe. Hell, he wasn't sure of anything anymore. Not since that encounter with her. She was on his mind constantly, and that could get him killed in his line of work.

He didn't know how Vin and Linc did it. It might help his brothers knowing their women were safe on Chiasson land. He didn't have that. Davena was out in town with danger closing in.

If they only knew who they needed to protect.

It would also help if they knew *what* they were after.

The crickets were singing loudly, as were the birds. All the animals of the bayou were out in the sunshine after days of rain.

He worked his way forward, searching for the tiniest hint of paranormal. It wasn't easy in the murky water, and the longer he went without discovering anything, the more frustrated he became.

Lincoln let out a three-tone whistle. Beau jerked his head to his brother and saw Linc motion him toward an outcropping of land. Beau didn't need to be told twice. He waded forward, careful of where he placed his feet. Lincoln was already there when he stepped out of the water.

Lincoln pulled off his rubber boots and wiggled his toes. "My toes are going to become webbed if we keep this up."

Beau chuckled and sank down on a fallen log next to his brother and removed the pack from his back. He pulled off one boot, then the next before he yanked off his wet socks and slapped them on the tree next to him. "Tell me about it."

"At least the girls packed us extra socks." Lincoln shook

his head as he laughed. "Extra socks. Do you know how many times I walked around all day with wet ones?"

"Yep. All our lives."

"Exactly, but what does my Ava think of? Dry socks." Lincoln looked up at the sun and closed his eyes. "How is it that women think of those things, but we don't?"

"You're the one with a woman. You should know."

Beau knew it was the wrong thing to say the moment Lincoln looked at him with his penetrating gaze. Beau wanted to groan in annoyance. He might have gotten away with saying that to Vincent, but Linc looked deeper, listened harder, saw more.

Lincoln rubbed his chin silently for a moment. "Are you really going to follow Christian in his absurd quest to remain alone?"

"Why not? You and Vin have everything covered. Both of you will have children to carry on the Chiasson name."

"Do you really think that's what our parents wanted? For just two of their children to carry on?"

Beau shrugged and dug his toes into the damp earth. "Riley will also have children. Fortunately, she and her offspring will be far away from this life."

"You won't hear me arguing about that." Lincoln leaned his forearms on his knees. "But do you really want to be alone? Don't think about what we do or how we live. You're talking about spending decades by yourself instead of with someone else."

"I can't think about a future without considering what we do and how we live. We didn't even have normal high school years, Linc. Not a single one of us went to college, except for Riley, and only because we forced her to go. What kind of normal is there for us?"

"Are you worried about a woman accepting what you do? Ava and Olivia understand things."

Beau sighed and shook his head. "Olivia grew up here. She had already heard the stories about our family, and she knew we were different. Ava, damn, Linc. You were fortunate there. She was born here, and her father was already in our line of work."

"You're a fool if you think that made things easier," Lincoln said with a wry twist of his lips.

Beau shrugged and watched as a young crane tried to fly, only to land awkwardly on a branch just a foot above the water. A moment later, a gator sprang up out of the bayou, his jaws snapping around the crane before he fell back into the water.

"It's not that I want to be alone," Beau finally said. "It's just...I don't want a woman to see how we live. I don't want to have to justify things, or talk her into this way of life."

"If she loves you, it won't matter."

"Bullshit. It matters. You think Ava likes you going out every night? You think she likes the worry involved, wondering which night you'll come home badly wounded? Or if you'll die?"

"That's life, Beau. Anyone's life. You think it's any different for those who commute into work? Each time they get into a vehicle could be their last."

Beau gave him a droll look. "You're actually going to compare driving to what we do?"

"No." Lincoln made a sound at the back of his throat, his forehead furrowed and his eyes filled with growing anger. "You know I'm not. I'm trying to prove a point that life itself is full of dangers. You think the innocents that die around here don't know there is danger out in the world?"

"I know."

"Do you really, little brother? Because I'm not so sure. If there's someone you want, go get her. You deserve happiness. Hell, we all do. It took me a long time to realize that."

Beau unzipped his pack and pulled out a bottle of water. He drank deeply before he glanced at Lincoln. "I know I won't survive having someone taken from me the way Mom was taken from Dad."

"Who says that's going to happen?"

"The odds are stacked against us with our lifestyle. You can't expect to keep Ava locked in the house all the time. And what about your children? They're going to want to get out and see friends. How are you going to protect them?"

"Mom and Dad protected us. I'll do the same."

Beau had no doubt Lincoln would go to extremes for his

family. Any of them would. "I know you mean well, but when faced with what we do, it's better that I remain alone."

Lincoln took a sandwich out of his pack and unwrapped it before taking a bite. "One day you'll find someone who will change your mind," he said around the food.

Beau didn't bother telling him that had already happened.

Christian pulled the truck to a stop and turned off the ignition. He sat with his hands on the steering wheel, his gaze out the windshield.

"What's going on?" Vincent asked from the passenger seat.

"I think someone has caught Beau's interest. I thought he might want to come into town with me, but he was quick to decline. Too damn quick."

Vincent opened the door to let in some air and turned his head to Christian. "He was acting peculiar this morning. I chalked it up to him waking with that odd feeling."

"It's more than that. He won't admit it, but I think there's someone."

"Who?"

"That's the question. Let's take a walk around Crowley and see who we run into that could be a candidate."

Vincent laughed. "He's so going to kick your ass when he finds out."

"Don't you mean our asses?" Christian asked as he got out of the truck and shut the door.

"Hey," Vincent said with his hands raised as he came around the back of the truck. "I'm just along for the ride."

"Yeah. No one around here believes that shit," Christian said, lacing his words with heavy sarcasm.

Vincent playfully shoved him as they walked down the street. The smile Christian wore faded as he looked around with his trained eye. The usually smiling, friendly folks kept their gazes on the ground and their footsteps quick as they went about their business.

"I was really hoping Maria and Beau were wrong," Vin said from beside him as they came to a stop. "But from what I'm seeing, there's no doubt something is stirring."

"There's only one reason for people to change so suddenly."

Vin ran his hands through his long hair. "Yeah. Evil. They may not recognize who it is or where it's coming from, but they sense it."

"Most of what we hunt never affects any of the people unless they're targeted. It looks like Maria had cause to be afraid."

Vincent nudged him and walked a little further down the street. They encountered short tempers, rude stares, and hateful words.

"Vampire?" Vincent asked.

Christian shook his head. "People sense them, but it doesn't cause them to act like this."

"A demon could."

"Yep, except I've not seen anything else to point to a demon or possession. It could be a poltergeist."

Vincent gave a rueful shake of his head. "In a small town like this? We would've already heard about it."

"Why do I get the feeling this is going to be something we've not tangled with before?" Christian asked.

"It may call for some time pouring over the Chiasson journal."

Christian nodded a greeting at an elderly couple as they passed. The journal was a record of every supernatural being the Chiasson family had ever encountered, its strengths, its weaknesses, its habitat, and how to kill it.

As a young child, Christian had often snuck downstairs and poured over the journal with a flashlight under his father's desk. A large portion of it had kept him up many nights afterward, afraid to go to sleep.

It wasn't every child that grew up knowing there really could be monsters under the bed. The only thing that did get him to sleep was knowing that nothing could ever penetrate the house and get him or his siblings while they were inside.

"I'd hoped having a look around would give us some kind of clue. We've driven for hours down dirt roads and rice fields, and there are only so many times you can drive up and down the roads in Crowley before someone gets suspicious."

Vincent reached a corner and waited for the stoplight to turn red before he crossed the street. Christian was beside him, his curiosity spiked as to what might have caught his brother's attention.

Then he realized the reason when Vincent walked to the small office Ava used for her law practice. Vincent unlocked the door and strode inside. It took the two of them just a moment to do a quick search to make sure no one had been there.

"What did you think to find?" Christian asked.

Vin shrugged and fiddled with the keys. "Nothing. I just wanted a look around. Lincoln would've come here first."

"Yeah, he would've," Christian said with a nod. "Ava can remotely access her computer here, so I've no doubt she's working from the house."

Vin looked around once more. "Let's head out and see if Linc and Beau found anything."

Christian was the first out of the office. He turned and watched Vincent lock up. "Since we've not heard from either of them, I'm betting they came up as empty-handed as us."

"Most likely," Vincent said and pocketed the keys.

They turned as one, and Christian's gaze snagged on a woman with straight blonde hair that just skimmed her shoulders. She got into an old Dodge car and drove off.

"What is it?" Vin asked.

"The town's newest occupants. We might want to look into them. There were two sisters that moved into Crowley about a year ago," he said.

Vin shrugged. "We do occasionally get people who actually want to move into the parish. Crowley is a decent city and very close to all the smaller towns."

"Whatever," he said and waved away Vincent's words. "What do we know about the sisters?"

CHAPTER

SEVEN

"HAVE YOU LOST YOUR DAMNED MIND?" Lincoln asked Christian. "Those two sisters aren't the newest people to move into the area. What about that weird family who bought the old Richard rice farm? If you want to look into anyone, that's who I place my vote for. Have you seen their two kids?" Lincoln shuddered. "Right out of a Stephen King novel."

Beau looked around the table at the empty dishes pushed aside from the evening meal as they talked. Just as Vincent had predicted, they had found nothing during their search. Beau had yet to say anything, but what was there to say? He also wanted to know more about the Arcineaux sisters. The fact that it had nothing to do with whatever they were hunting didn't need to be stated.

"Fine," Christian said. "We look into everyone new."

Olivia set down her glass of lemonade. "Need I remind

you, Christian, that it wasn't a new member of the area that killed your parents or those women a few months ago? It wasn't new people who came after me, either."

"She's got a point," Vincent said.

Christian looked away from the table. "We can't look into everyone."

"No," Ava said. "Trust your instincts. If the sisters and that family stand out, then look into them both. There's no reason Olivia and I can't do some digging. We're pretty handy with computers."

Olivia's eyes brightened. "Yes! I need something to do."

"Beau?" Vincent said. "What are your thoughts?"

Beau threw up his hands and then let them fall to his thighs. "Ava's idea sounds like a good one."

"You don't have an opinion?" Christian asked with a roll of his eyes. "There's something wrong."

"Nothing's wrong," Beau hurried to say.

Lincoln's blue gaze was once more on him, and no matter how hard he tried, Beau couldn't hold it. Beau pushed his chair back and walked to the fridge. He pulled out a bowl and set it on the table in front of everyone. "I made banana pudding for dessert."

He walked out of the kitchen and straight into the office. He sat behind the desk and opened the laptop. Once his fingers were on the keyboard, however, he couldn't manage to type anything. It seemed wrong for him to dig into Davena's past. She hadn't done anything amiss in her time in Crowley, but there was no doubt he would find something if he looked. Everyone had something in their past they regretted and wanted forgotten.

If he went searching, he *would* find something. What if it was something that led the others to believe she and her sister were the ones in danger? What if he told Davena what he did, and they were wrong about her and her sister? What if the Arcineaux sisters weren't, in fact, the ones being targeted?

What if she decided she never wanted to have anything to do with him?

Beau's phone vibrated in an S.O.S. signal. It was Riley's code that she had programmed in all four of their phones so they would always know when she called.

"Hey, squirt," Beau answered.

"Hey!"

He sat back, instantly on alert at the false happiness in her voice. "What's up?"

"Apparently not my boobs," she said sarcastically. "Do you know they don't stay perky all that long?"

"Riley," he said with a sigh. "I don't need to know about that stuff."

"Who else do I talk to about it? It's not as if I have sisters," she complained.

He pinched the bridge of his nose with his thumb and forefinger. "You're about to get a sister-in-law in Olivia, and I don't think it'll be much longer before you can call Ava that, as well."

"I know, and I adore both of them. We talk almost every day."

Beau's eyes snapped open. He knew without asking that neither Lincoln nor Vincent knew how often Riley and their women spoke. Riley had always been outnumbered in their family, but suddenly, her side was gaining.

She laughed through the phone. "Now that's got you worried, doesn't it?"

He stretched out his legs and crossed them at the ankle. "You didn't call to talk about your boobs or to shock me."

"I sure didn't. Damn, but you're perceptive."

Beau couldn't help but smile. Since he and Riley had been the youngest, they got left together a lot. It had brought them closer, and if there was ever a problem, she normally came to Beau first.

"You might as well just tell me instead of hem-hawing around."

Instead of the loud, dramatic sigh he was expecting, there was silence. A thread of fear raced through him.

"You aren't in trouble are you?"

"No, no," she hurried to answer. "I want to come home."

He almost wished she were in trouble. It would be easier to handle than telling her she couldn't come home. "Your deal with Vincent was that you remain in Austin and get your degree from the University of Texas."

"LSU is closer. Can't I transfer there?"

"Look, squirt, you know I want you home. You also know why we all agreed to send you away."

"It's not fair, Beau. I'm a grown woman. I can make my own decisions."

This was what they had all dreaded. When Riley told them to kiss off and did what she wanted. Beau knew it would one day come, but Vincent believed Riley would do what he wanted for the sake of the family.

"Finish the semester—"

"I'm finished with my summer classes," she interrupted.

Beau looked at the computer screen, the cursor waiting for him to type in his search. "Finish the fall semester. I'll convince Vin to let you come home for Christmas, and we can talk to him then."

"Thanks, Beau."

He frowned when he heard the sadness in her voice. "Is it really so bad up there?"

"I've got friends. I've even gone on a few dates. Austin is nice, but it isn't home."

"Be safe, squirt. You know we love you."

"Love ya, too," she said and ended the call.

Beau set aside the phone and sat up, ready to type in his search when his gaze landed on all three of his brothers in the doorway. His gaze shifted to the couch as Ava and Olivia waved at him. When had they all come into the office? Was he that preoccupied with Davena and Riley that he hadn't noticed?

He really was going to have to get his own place. He desperately needed his own time.

"How is Riley?" Christian asked.

Beau met Vincent's gaze. "She wants to come home."

"We gathered that," Vin said tightly.

Lincoln walked into the office and sank into the chair near the desk. "I think her coming home for Christmas is a great idea. It's been a few years since we've seen her."

"Which I warned you wasn't a good idea," Beau added. "I told you to let her return on her breaks, Vin."

"It's for her own good," Vincent said.

Olivia raised a brow at him. "Careful, babe. That might come back on you soon."

Beau narrowed his gaze on the girls, who exchanged a look. They knew something. He would bet his LP collection on it. With as often as they spoke with Riley, no doubt all three had formed some kind of plan.

He bit back a smile. Beau really couldn't wait to see how everything all played out. No doubt it would be a doozy for sure.

"I thought y'all were eating dessert," Beau said.

Lincoln shrugged. "We figured you were doing some research, so we thought we'd come and help."

That was the thickest load of crap Beau had ever heard. If

he weren't careful, they would discover his interests lay with one Davena Arcineaux.

"What did you find?" Christian asked.

Beau glanced at the blank screen. "I haven't even started."

"I have," Ava said.

Every eye in the room focused on her. She pushed up her reading glasses and adjusted herself on the couch. "I typed in Delia Arcineaux and found an obituary for six years ago."

"Where?" Vincent asked.

Ava glanced up. "A small town called Algiers, right outside of New Orleans."

"That means nothing," Christian said. "It's common for criminals to find names in obits and use them."

"Is it common for Davena Arcineaux to have an obituary on the same day? To have died the same day as her sister?" Ava asked.

Beau felt that knot in his stomach tighten. "How did they die?"

Ava pulled off her glasses and looked up at him. "A fire. The mother, Babette Arcineaux, was suspected of being killed in the same fire."

Fire. There had been smoke in his dream. Or at least he had thought he smelled smoke when he woke.

"There's no mother with them," Olivia said.

Lincoln shifted lower in the chair. "It could be just like Christian said. Two women looking for a change of pace find an obituary with the names of two young sisters and take them."

Ava set her glasses aside on the couch. "Except that Davena was seventeen at the time, and Delia eighteen when they died. That matches the Davena and Delia here."

"Were there only three bodies found in the burned house?" Vincent asked.

"There were no bodies," Ava said. "The fire was so intense there was nothing left to identify. The house was reduced to ashes. When the girls and the mother weren't located, everyone assumed they were in the house."

"What if they weren't?" Olivia said.

Christian walked to the fireplace and put his back to the mantel. "You mean, what if they weren't ever in the house? Why not just tell the authorities where they were?"

"Because they couldn't," Beau said.

Silence lengthened, each lost in thought.

It was Lincoln who broke the quiet. "Has the mother been seen?"

Ava put her glasses back on and punched the keyboard some more. Another ten minutes went by before she gave a shake of her head. "Nothing. None of her credit cards have been used, and no money has been withdrawn from her bank account."

"The mother could've been in the house," Olivia said. "She might really be dead."

Vincent walked to the couch and sat on the arm next to Olivia. "It's a possibility."

"That leaves the only reason the girls wouldn't step forward to let others know they weren't dead. They're running from someone," Christian said.

"Or some*thing*," Beau added.

Lincoln sat up and leaned forward. "Ava, do a search on that new family now. Last name Dumas. Father's name is Frank, mother's is Liz."

While everyone was focused on Ava, Beau quietly punched in Davena's name and New Orleans and searched. In a blink, links and photos popped up on the page.

Staring at him was a photo of Davena her freshman year of high school in a cheerleader uniform at a football game. Her green eyes were clear and innocent, and though the ones he had looked into a few days ago were older and warier, they were still the same eyes that matched the same smile, and the same golden hair.

She and her sister hadn't stolen the names. They were Davena and Delia Arcineaux. He suddenly wanted to know what they were hiding from. More than anything, he wanted to be the one to help her.

Idiot. You want to save her so you can bring her into your life and the Chiasson family business? She's better off left on her own.

There was no denying the truth of it. He would help her if she and her sister were the ones in danger, but he would keep his distance.

"There's no record of Frank and Liz Dumas or their children anywhere," Ava said. She looked up at all of them. "They seem to have appeared out of thin air."

Christian crossed his arms over his chest. "Witness Protection Program, perhaps?"

"As if," Lincoln said. "We found our culprits. The Arcineaux sisters are intriguing, but it's the Dumas family we need to dig deeper on."

"I agree," Vincent said.

Christian rolled his eyes. "Fine."

Beau exited his search and shut the laptop. "Where do we start?"

CHAPTER

EIGHT

Davena sat against the headboard with her knees hugging her chest. Delia hadn't said two words to her the entire day, and no matter how she tried, Delia wouldn't relent. If anyone should be upset, it should be her, not Delia. Davena glanced over the side of the bed to where her bag was packed. Everything she owned was in that bag.

If asked six years ago if she could live without her iPod, makeup, clothes, and dozens of friends, she'd have said never. After that one life-changing night, she discovered what the important things were.

It wasn't makeup, hairstyles, or clothes. It was money and food and having a safe place to rest her head. She had gone from wearing designer clothes to digging through restaurant garbage for food.

Her iPod, laptop, and even her cell phone were forgotten.

No longer did she spend twenty dollars on one meal. Instead, she and Delia made twenty last several days between the two of them.

It brought home what the essentials were—and what was wasteful. Did she dream of walking into a mall and spending the day shopping? Often. She knew her clothes weren't the latest styles, but they were clean and in good condition. It was a rare event when she and Delia would stop off at Goodwill and rummage through the clothes others had so easily discarded—some still with price tags on them.

Makeup was an indulgent extravagance she only allowed herself a small portion of. Blush, eyeliner, and mascara. As for her hair, there wasn't much she could do with it anyway.

She used to spend hours trying to get it to curl, spending her mother's money on products and tools to get just the right hairstyle. Now, Davena let it go to its natural state—board straight.

A sigh escaped as she rested her chin on her knees. Her body vibrated with the need to leave the area, but she couldn't seem to make herself walk away from her sister. As angry as Delia made her more often than not, they were the only family each of them had.

Leave? She couldn't do it. Whatever might be coming for them, they would face it together.

Davena lifted the covers and settled on her back. Her gaze locked on the ceiling, but it wasn't the square tiles she saw, it was bright blue eyes and chin length dark hair.

"Beau Chiasson," she whispered.

She discreetly asked around about the Chiassons, trying not to let anyone know it was Beau she was interested in. Somehow everyone seemed to know. If they didn't outright guess it was Beau, they made it clear that Vincent and Lincoln were taken.

What was really odd was how they were so protective of the Chiassons, and yet, they seemed to fear them, as well. It reminded Davena of how the people of Algiers had treated her mother.

At least there was no fear of the Chiassons practicing Voodoo or Hoodoo. That thought brought a smile to her face. They may still be in the bayous of Louisiana, but there was no one attempting Voodoo in Crowley.

Davena touched the wound on her head. It was still tender, the bruise turning a nasty shade of blue-black. The smile disappeared as she remembered what had made her urge Delia to leave. How long did they have? A few weeks? One week? A day? Something was coming for them, whether it was Delphine herself or one of her lackeys, Davena and Delia weren't long for this world.

What did she have to lose going after Beau? If he didn't want her, she would have lost nothing. If he did…then it was a small piece of pleasure in an otherwise hellish world. Only a fool would let something like that pass.

And her mother hadn't raised a fool.

Deciding to do it was one thing, and actually carrying

through with her plan to kiss Beau was something altogether different. Impending death, however, put things into perspective.

She had been fool enough to believe she would be able to lead an ordinary life, regardless of who her mother was. And her dear mother had allowed that belief to grow. The truth was that there was nothing normal or typical about them.

The last time she kissed a boy was the night her mother had died. Her boyfriend of more than a year had taken her on a date, except they hadn't gone to a restaurant. They had ended up on the banks of the Mississippi River where she had given him her virginity.

There had been one other instance during the past years where a man had pursued her. Davena had been so lonely that she had almost stayed with him. Where she kept her distance from men, Delia was the opposite. She would find one she was interested in, get him into bed, and then promptly ignore him the next day. It was her flippant attitude that had guys continuing to come after her.

Their mother's murder, and their close call with death had changed both sisters drastically. Neither was who they had been. The scars they bore were hidden within them. They were deeper, longer than the one on Davena's palm.

She fisted her scarred hand and rolled onto her side. Her gaze went to the door where she saw lights coming from the living room. She almost got up and tried to talk to Delia again, but she was tired of arguing. A good night's sleep would clear her mind.

Davena closed her eyes hoping for sleep. All she found were fantasies revolving around her and Beau.

BEAU WAITED until he knew everyone had taken his or her beds and the house was quiet before he pulled his laptop from beneath his bed and quickly did a search for Davena again. He knew it wasn't a good sign that he couldn't get enough of her.

If he couldn't have Davena, the next best thing was a picture. He clicked on the images, scrolling through each one where she was wearing a brilliant smile. A few she was by herself. More often than not, she was with other girls, and some she was with a boy. He wore a letterman jacket and had short blond hair.

There wasn't a single picture of her newer than six years ago. It was like she dropped off the face of the earth. He couldn't help but wonder who had killed her mother. That's when he remembered that there was someone who might know more about the event. He reached for his cell phone and held it in his hand as he debated on whether to place the call or not.

He shoved aside his reservations and quickly dialed. With the phone to his ear, he listened to it ring once, twice.

On the third ring a deep voice answered over loud music, "It better be important for you to interrupt the plans I had tonight."

"She'll wait," Beau said with a smile.

The laugh was boisterous as the music faded with Court walking out of the pub he and his brothers owned called Gator Bait. "What can I do for you, cousin?"

Beau licked his lips. "Court, I need you to remember back six years ago."

"I'll try. What's this about?"

"A fire that burned a house and the women inside to ash. It was in Algiers."

There was a pregnant pause before Beau heard Court's loud sigh. "Ah, fuck. I wish I could forget that night. That was Babette Arcineaux's house. She and her daughters were killed."

Beau removed the computer from his lap and swung his legs over the side of the bed. "Was the fire an accident?"

"Not even close. Babette was a good woman. Unfortunately, she acquired a powerful enemy."

"Who?"

"Delphine."

Beau briefly closed his eyes. "The same Delphine that cursed Kane?"

"The very bitch," Court said, hatred dripping from his voice. "Why are you asking about something that happened six years ago? Does this involve Ava? Delphine swore to leave her alone."

"No," Beau hurried to explain. "Ava is doing fine so no need to worry her father. Delphine hasn't bothered her since y'all took care of things in New Orleans."

"What is family for? Besides, Delphine sent my brother after Ava."

"How is Kane?" Beau asked.

"He's…Kane. It isn't easy for any of us to deal with our curse. You'd think being a werewolf would have its advantages, but not so much."

"I'm sorry the LaRue's are dealing with that."

"It's not like you were the one to piss off a Voodoo priestess," Court joked. "Now, back to the Arcineaux's. Why do you want to know?"

Damn. Beau had hoped Court would let it drop. He should've known his cousin wouldn't let up so easily. "Are you sure the daughters died?"

"There was nothing left of the house, and neither Babette nor her girls were seen again. Everyone assumed they died. You found the girls, didn't you?"

"Maybe."

Court lowered his voice to a whisper. "Beau, if you have them, keep them safe. Delphine might still be after them."

"Why? What did the sisters do?"

"Isn't it enough that they have such a powerful enemy? Trust me, cousin, you don't want to get on Delphine's bad side. She never forgets or forgives. She holds a grudge forever, and revenge is second nature. All the Chiassons are already on her radar for interfering last time."

Beau wiped a hand down his face. "Yeah. After what she did to Kane, Ava, and Jack, I'm beginning to see that."

"Do we need to come down there?"

"No," he said firmly. "We've got something weird going on, and we think we've pinpointed a young family that could either be responsible or on the receiving end."

Court chuckled dryly. "Ah, but the Arcineaux girls caught your attention. How did you piece it together? What name are they using?"

"Their own. They've been here for a little over a year."

"And you thought they could be in danger? No doubt they are. They have been since the night of their mother's death. As long as Delphine doesn't know they're alive, they'll be fine. I'd have thought they would be long gone from Louisiana though."

Beau did, as well. What kept them in the state and so close to someone as dangerous as Delphine? "Look, if you don't hear from any of us over the next few days, one of you might want to come check on things."

"Sounds like you've got something big in town. What is it?"

"I don't know." Beau rested his head in his hand. "Olivia's grandmother was here this morning after being woken by something."

"She's the one who practices Hoodoo, right?"

Beau nodded, and then said, "Yep. She got into it years ago when she had her own child. The thing is, Court, I woke up with a bad feeling, as well. And I smelled...smoke."

"Smoke?"

"That's not all. I just had a really bad feeling that grew as the day went on, but Maria had more information to impart. She said whatever is coming isn't here for us, but that we'll try to stop it and it'll turn its attention to us. She said that it would come for us, and that someone was going to be hurt."

"Shit. Maybe we should make another trip to Lyons Point."

"I wouldn't mind the help, but y'all have your own problems. Just in case, if I haven't called to update you, check in on us."

"Will do. Tell me, are the sisters as pretty as they used to be?" Court asked.

Beau could hear the smile in his voice. "I suppose."

"You really need to work on your lying, cuz. Delia was pretty, but I always suspected it would be Davena who ended up being the beauty of the two. So, which one is the looker?"

"Davena." Beau hadn't had to think twice about it.

"I knew it."

Beau sat up and cleared his throat. "Thanks for the information."

"Anytime. Watch yourself, Beau."

"Same to you, Court."

He disconnected the call and set aside his phone. Beau leaned back against the headboard and settled his laptop back in place as he typed Babette Arcineaux in the search engine.

CHAPTER

NINE

Davena woke feeling rested and ready for a Saturday off. She didn't wake Delia as she tiptoed into the bathroom. She took her time in the shower, letting the hot water beat on her tense shoulder muscles. What she wouldn't do for a massage. It seemed like the most self-indulgent thing she could do for herself. It was also too pricey for her to even consider.

By the time Davena dried off and combed her hair, she was determined to put their argument behind them. She belted her robe and stepped out of the bathroom.

"Good morning," she called cheerfully as she went to turn on the coffee pot.

The next thing she was going to splurge on was a coffee pot with a programmable timer so the coffee would be waiting for them when they woke. As soon as the coffee began to brew, she drew in a deep breath and turned to the couch. It was empty, but that was nothing odd. Delia had always been an earlier riser.

Davena didn't think anything of it, thinking Delia went down the street to pet the horses. Davena decided to make some breakfast as she waited. That's when she determined it was time both she and her sister did something fun for themselves. And today was just the day.

She finished the eggs and gave a shout to Delia that breakfast was ready in case she was outside. Davena tucked her wet hair behind her ear and hurried to the metal shelves against the wall. She grabbed an old leather-bound book they had found at a flea market.

The pages had been half burned from a fire, and ruined from the water, but it was perfect for them. She had hollowed out the center to put their money in since they were never in one place long enough for a bank. Davena flipped open the cover and stared in disbelief. Every cent of their money was gone. Only a folded piece of paper remained.

Her hands shook as she pulled out the note. Discarding the book, Davena opened the note. She immediately recognized Delia's looping, whimsical handwriting. The note was simple. It read:

DAVENA —

It's for the best. Let me go.

D.

The note fell from her numb fingers as her ears began to ring. It was all a dream. It had to be. She and Delia made a pact never to leave the other. Ever.

"No," she mumbled, her eyes jerking to the window.

In her haste to get to the window, Davena tripped over her feet that felt encased in concrete. She fell against the blinds awkwardly.

"Dammit!" she yelled while trying to open the blinds so she could see out.

Her heart was thudding in her chest when she finally got them open and saw the empty space in front of the house where their car was always parked.

Not only had Delia left with all their money, but she had taken the car as well. What was Davena supposed to do? She had nothing with which to pay the rent on Monday or for food. How was she going to go into work without a vehicle?

Her knees buckled and she fell to the ground, resting the side of her face against the wall. With no idea of where Delia could have gone, Davena didn't know where to begin looking. The questions rushing through her mind were so many and so loud, that she let herself zone out.

She didn't know how long the buzzing went on until she finally noticed it. Davena blinked, looking to the kitchen table where the pager the veterinarian gave them for emergency calls bounced around as it continued to vibrate.

Davena suddenly had a purpose. She climbed to her feet and walked to the table. 911 flashed on the screen when she answered it, which meant an animal had been brought in for an emergency. With nothing else to do, Davena rushed into the bedroom and threw on some clothes. She ran back into the kitchen, turned off the coffee pot, quickly made a sandwich out of the eggs she had cooked, and grabbed the house keys on her way out.

She ate as she walked into town. It was only a few miles, but what would take them only a couple of minutes by car, would take her much longer on foot. Running wasn't an option since she was eating, and she had to eat since she had no idea when she would be able to replenish the food. She knew what it was like to miss day's worth of meals, and she wasn't going to turn away food just because she wasn't hungry.

Incredulity over what Delia had done turned to fury, and then resentment.

She was about a mile from the house when a car slowed beside her and the window rolled down. Davena glanced over and saw it was the sheriff's department.

"Hello, ma'am," said the man with a tip of his hat as the car drove alongside her.

Davena stopped and forced a smile as she faced him. "Good morning, sheriff."

"I'm just a deputy with the sheriff's department, ma'am.

My name is Marshall Ducet. I'm new to the area, so I mean no disrespect by asking if you need anything?"

She looked into his gray eyes. His black hair was short and held a wave to it. He had an easy, charming smile that she bet normally put people at ease. Young and handsome, Davena knew if he weren't already taken, he would be soon.

"Deputy, would it be too much trouble to ask for a ride? My sister has taken the car, and Dr. Hebert has an emergency."

"The vet?" Marshall asked with a small frown. "Of course. Get in."

Davena started to grab the handle of the back passenger door when he laughed. She looked up, and he motioned her to come around to the front. She gladly rushed to the front passenger seat and got into the car.

After she buckled her seatbelt, she looked over at him to find him staring at her. "Oh. My apologies. It's been a… difficult morning. I'm Davena."

"What an unusual name. Do you have a last name to go with that?" he asked as he pressed on the accelerator.

She had given her name so many times over the last few years, but now she found herself hesitating. Davena decided to take another approach. If he thought her nervous, she knew he would continue to press her. "Must you know details of everyone who sits up here with you?" she asked with a grin.

He smiled and glanced at her. "I'm just curious. I come

from a big city, so this is a change for me. I want to get to know everyone."

"You will soon enough."

"Are you a veterinarian yourself?"

It was Davena's turn to laugh. "No, though I do love animals. I help out in the office."

Thankfully, they pulled up to the clinic then. There were only two vehicles there. A tan heavy-duty truck that belonged to Dr. Hebert, and an older dark green Suburban.

"I appreciate the ride," Davena said and opened the door.

"My pleasure. Good luck in there," Marshall said with a nod.

Davena closed the door behind her and briefly watched him drive away before she ran into the clinic.

BEAU SMELLED THE SMOKE AGAIN. It was heavier, clinging to him. He couldn't take a breath, couldn't see. The smoke wrapped around him as if alive. He swatted at it, but he couldn't get free. It wound up his legs to his waist, clinging to him until he couldn't move. He tilted back his head in an effort to keep it out of his face, but there was no escaping it.

He was held immobile. Through the smoke, he could see a female dressed in white. No matter how hard he looked, he couldn't make out her face. Then the smoke took him to the ground and seeped into his mouth and nose and into his lungs. It was killing him, choking him.

Beau's eyes snapped open as he jerked upright in bed. Once more, he was drenched with sweat. He sucked in huge mouthfuls of air and hastily glanced around to make sure there was no smoke.

His door suddenly burst open as all three brothers bounded into his room. Lincoln was the first in, his boxers barely pulled over his hips while Vincent's hair stuck up at odd angles as he began to search the room.

Beau watched them both with a mixture of annoyance and amusement. Christian was the only one who seemed to have things together. He leaned, fully dressed, against the doorway and cocked a brow.

"What the hell is going on?" Beau finally asked.

Vincent stood up from looking under the bed and raked his hair back. "What's wrong? You're the one who shouted."

"Yep," Lincoln said as he checked the connecting bathroom.

Beau remembered the dream clear as day, but he hadn't shouted. He had wanted to, but had been unable to do it.

"What happened?" Christian asked.

With all three of them staring at him, Beau knew he wouldn't get out of it unless he told them the truth. "It was a dream."

"A dream?" Vin repeated, skepticism thickening his voice.

Beau sighed and tossed off the damp sheet. He shoved

Vincent out of the way and hastily stripped the sheets from the bed. That would make two days in a row with clean sheets. "Yes, a dream," he answered crossly.

Lincoln grabbed one of the pillows and pulled it out of its case. "What was the dream?"

Beau paused and closed his eyes as he recalled it with perfect clarity. "Smoke. It came for me like it was alive." He opened his eyes and looked at each of his brothers before he said, "It came to kill me."

"This could be what Maria meant," Christian said.

Vincent sank onto the mattress and shook his head. "What about that feeling you had yesterday, Beau? Do you still have it?"

He wanted to lie to Vin and tell him that it was gone, but that would put everyone in danger. "It's worse."

"Well, hell," Christian said. "What now?"

Lincoln ruffled Christian's hair. "We do what we do."

"Everyone meet downstairs in ten minutes. We need to find out more about the Dumas family."

Beau waited until everyone left his room before he dropped his head. It wasn't just the smoke. Whoever had been in his dream was who controlled the smoke. She was the one meant to do harm, she was the one they needed to find.

If only he could've seen her face. The only thing discernible had been the fact she was female and dressed in all white. He couldn't tell his brothers that. It wasn't enough to go on.

DAVENA PUT her hands on the small of her back and stretched. A car had hit the German shepherd, but luckily its owner had been close and able to bring the dog in for surgery.

With Delia nowhere around, Davena had to stay with the dog until Sunday when Dr. Hebert came in to relieve her. She checked on the dog again before going to the kennels and taking one dog at a time outside.

She walked outside, surprised to find that night had already fallen. It had been well after noon before the surgery had been completed, and a few hours after that before either her or the doctor had been able to take a few moments and get something to eat.

The Pomeranian she was walking kept barking at something across the street. Davena peered into the darkness, but she couldn't see into the shadows.

"Just pee already," she urged the dog.

The small strip of grass left the animals little room to do their business. The dog growled and began to turn in circles before barking again, this time incessantly. Davena had no choice but to pick the dog up and try to quiet it. As she held it close, she could feel the animal shaking uncontrollably.

She looked from the dog to the shadows where he was

still staring. Fear ripped through her. She clutched the dog, ready to bolt, when something ran out of the shadows and beneath the next streetlight.

"A raccoon. It was only a raccoon," she said with a laugh. The fear should've dissipated, but it didn't. It grew.

Davena turned and quickened her pace even as she walked back into the building. Not that it could keep her safe. Nothing would be able to keep her safe now.

CHAPTER
TEN

"THERE'S NOT a goddamn thing out here," Christian said, not bothering to whisper.

Vincent shot him a withering look. "They're the most likely ones. We agreed."

"That's a crock of shit. We three voted, Beau just nodded. He doesn't believe this Dumas family is our target."

Beau wanted to slam his fist into Christian's nose. "That's not true. I agreed that this family could be the target. Ava's connections found a lot of good evidence that pointed to them."

"Tell the truth, Beau," Linc said. "If it were up to you, would we be staking out the Dumas family tonight?"

Beau looked at the ground and blew out a breath. "No."

"Son of a bitch," Vincent mumbled as he turned his head away.

"I'm not going against you, Vin," Beau said hastily. "I don't know if I think it's Davena Arcineaux because it is, or because…"

Shit. He couldn't even say the words aloud.

"He finds her interesting," Lincoln supplied for him.

Vincent met his gaze and nodded in understanding. "All right. You and Christian go into town and check on the Arcineaux sisters. Lincoln and I'll stay here."

Christian slapped Beau on the back and started across the field toward his truck. Beau looked at Vincent and Lincoln, unable to explain his need to get to Davena. He started to thank them, when a feeling of such hatred and evil rushed through him that it brought him to his knees. It clutched at his stomach, knotting it until he knew without a doubt that it wasn't the Dumas family they should be watching.

Beau looked up as his brothers grabbed him. "Davena," he said through clenched teeth.

"Christian!" Vincent bellowed.

Beau saw Christian run full tilt across the field to the truck while Vincent and Lincoln were on either side of him helping him walk.

"What is it?" Vincent asked.

Beau knew every moment they wasted was a second Davena and her sister were closer to death. "That feeling is back."

"It's not the Dumas family. I can hear the kids laughing all the way out here," Lincoln stated.

Christian's truck roared to life and came barreling toward them only to slide to a stop next to them. Beau was shoved in the front seat, and Vincent and Lincoln got into the back.

"Hurry," Vincent said and grabbed the back of Christian's seat.

Christian floored the accelerator, bouncing them over the land until they rejoined the road. He sped down the road going over a hundred. "We've got company," Christian said.

Beau turned around and saw the flashing red and blue lights of the police. "Get me as close as you can."

"We don't even know where she lives," Lincoln said.

That was a mistake on Beau's part. He'd known she could be the target, but he'd been so intent on keeping his distance that he had failed to get the details. "I'll find her."

"I'm coming with you," Vincent said.

On the outskirts of town, Christian jerked the wheel and sent the truck into a spin. Beau opened the door and rolled out, landing hard on his shoulder on the concrete.

"Fuck," he muttered and jumped to his feet, his double-barrel sawed-off shotgun in hand.

Vincent ran past him. "Hurry!"

Beau gritted through the pain in his stomach and his shoulder, and followed him into the shadows just as the sheriff's car pulled up behind Christian. There wasn't time to watch and see if his brothers could talk themselves out of going to jail.

"Which way?" Vin asked.

Beau looked first one way and then the other. "I don't have any idea."

"Start with what you do know."

"She works at the animal clinic." Beau fisted his hand in frustration.

Vincent grabbed him to keep him still. "Your feeling told you it was Davena and her sister, right?"

"Yes," Beau said hesitantly.

"Then trust that feeling to lead you to her now. For some reason the two of you are linked."

"Or it's just that we're both going to die by the same hand." Beau grimaced and turned away when he saw the look on Vincent's face.

Vincent unsheathed his machete. "You're not going to die. No one is going to die tonight."

"Then explain how I know these things?" Beau asked as he looked at Vin.

"I can't." His voice was calmer, composed. Vincent was once more in control of his emotions. "Find her, Beau."

Beau knew it was pointless. The knot in his stomach grew more and more painful, a warning that time was running out. He thought of her sexy voice and her amazing smile. What an idiot he was not to have touched her hair when he'd had the chance.

"It's no use," Beau said.

Vincent parted his lips to talk when a scream rent the air. Both turned in the direction of the sound and took off running. Beau prayed it wasn't Davena, and that they weren't too late.

They rounded the corner and saw a woman with her hand at her throat. "She just disappeared," she told the man beside her. "Right in front of me!"

Beau exchanged a look with Vin and hid his shotgun against his other leg as they walked past. Only three blocks up was the animal clinic.

"Looks like we're on the right track," Vincent said.

"Looks that way."

"We'll get there in time."

Beau was beginning to doubt it.

DAVENA LOOKED at the whining yellow lab. He pawed at the kennel door, his big gold eyes silently beseeching her. The last thing she wanted to do was go outside. It was silly to think that walls could keep her alive, but it was a lot like thinking if she kept her eyes closed, the monsters in her closet would never get her.

She even managed to remember a few of her mother's spells, not that it did her any good. She hadn't practiced in years, and without the practice, the spells wouldn't work.

Death was death, no matter how it happened or when. She could remain in the clinic and take the chance that the animals were killed along with her, or she could go outside and face it.

Davena rested her forehead on the kennel. "I was going to get my hair done today," she told the lab. "I was also going to go to the Chiassons and find Beau. I'm not sure exactly what I was going to do once I was there, but I was going to do it today."

The dog cocked his head at her and whined again.

"All right," she said and grabbed a leash from the hook. She opened the kennel door and snapped the leash to his collar.

Davena gave him a good rub before she walked him to the door. On the way out, she checked on the shepherd to make sure he was still all right. With her hand on the knob of the back door, Davena hesitated a moment, and then cautiously opened it. Nothing jumped out at her. She barely had time to let her shoulders sag before the lab pushed his head through the opening and raced outside.

She caught the edge of the door with her fingertip and managed to swing it closed as she followed the dog. He went to the grass and lifted his leg against the lone tree. Her gaze scanned the area around her. The darkness concealed too much. It made her jumpy and edgy.

The lab finished and lifted his ears as he looked behind him. Davena turned, her blood turning to ice as she expected to see Delphine appear in front of her. She bit back a scream when she saw the all-white clothes come out of the darkness. The dog jerked the leash out of her grasp as he raced to the figure.

Davena stood in shock as the dog sat in front of the person, tail wagging. She frowned and looked closer. That's when she realized it wasn't Delphine, it was her sister.

"Delia," she said, unsure of whether to be angry or relieved.

"It's me," her sister said and walked to her.

Davena started to speak, then stopped since she didn't know what to ask first.

"I had to," Delia said.

Davena rolled her eyes. "Had to what?"

"I had to do this. I had to prepare, and in order to do that, I had to leave you last night. It's going to end tonight for good."

"I hate riddles, Delia. Just tell me."

Delia smiled in triumph, her gaze over Davena's shoulder. She pointed. "Look for yourself."

Davena didn't want to turn around because she was afraid she knew exactly who was there. She slowly turned, and caught sight of Delphine herself, still looking as young and beautiful as she had six years before.

"Everything is going to be all right," Delia said as she came to stand beside Davena. "Trust me."

"Trust you?" Davena asked in bewilderment.

Delia's brown gaze met hers. "I can do what our mother couldn't. I'm going to kill Delphine."

Davena reached for her sister, only to be thrown backward. She hit the side of the clinic, her head banging against the brick. The lab was by her side licking her face and nudging her with his cold, wet nose.

She opened her eyes, but everything was blurry. Unable to focus on anything, she patted the dog until she found his collar, and then the leash. With the building to steady her, she got to her feet and managed to find the back door. "Get inside," she told the lab, closing it behind him.

Davena turned around so fast that everything began to spin. She reached out for the building to steady her, but only grasped air. She could feel herself tilting, falling.

Suddenly, strong hands steadied her, pulling her against a thickly muscled chest. "What hurts?" asked a rich, smooth voice she recognized instantly.

She looked up into Beau's intense blue gaze. "You're here. How is that possible?"

"Later. What hurts?" he asked again, his voice rough as if he were keeping something tightly leashed.

"My head. Delia threw me against the building."

His big hands gently smoothed back her hair. "My brother is going to get you out of here."

"No," she said with a shake of her head that she instantly regretted. "Delia's in trouble. I can't leave her."

"She's up against someone she can't handle," said another male voice as he stepped closer.

Davena recognized the eldest Chiasson brother, Vincent. "I can't leave her."

A muscle ticked in Beau's jaw as he simply stared. "If you stay, you could die."

"It's my sister. Would you leave one of your brothers?"

Beau gave a single shake of his head. "Never."

"Let's get Delia then," Vincent said.

Davena placed her hands on Beau's chest, feeling the heat of him through her palms. He took a breath, expanding his chest and causing his muscles to move beneath her hands. "It won't matter where you take us. Delphine knows we're here. Nothing will stop her now."

"So everyone keeps telling me," Beau said angrily.

Vincent's gaze narrowed on Beau. "Who precisely?"

Beau shrugged. "I might have called Court."

Vincent mumbled something in Cajun beneath his breath and peered around the edge of the building. "It's now or never."

"Go," Davena said and tried to push him away. "This isn't your fight."

Beau's blue eyes flashed dangerously. "How very wrong you are."

Davena wanted to stay with him, to see if he might lean down and kiss her. That would have been the easy thing to do. Instead, she stepped out of his arms. She could see clearly once again, and she would stand by her sister and face the bitch that murdered their mother.

She saw Beau's frown as he tried to figure what she was about. Davena took that second and rushed around the building in time to see Delia and Delphine face off. Delia was chanting, preparing a spell. She had only just begun, when Delphine lifted a hand in front of her and cupped the air. She then spread her fingers flat.

That same gnawing fear clawed at Davena that had been with her for days. She kept running toward Delia, even as Delia began to scream as she bent over. Davena was steps away when her sister burst into flames.

CHAPTER

ELEVEN

BEAU GRABBED Davena before the flames could touch her skin
and dragged her away.

"Nooooo!" she screamed, fighting him to get free.

He held Davena with one arm, her back against his chest,
while his other hand lifted the shotgun to aim it at Delphine.
The priestess merely smiled at him, her face alight with
exhilaration. The smoke that was drifting skyward suddenly
shifted toward him.

Vincent knocked his gun down. "Don't be a fool."

Beau pulled his gaze from Delphine to focus on his
brother. "I could end this."

"You'll get killed," Vin stated through clenched teeth.

Beau winced when one of Davena's feet connected with
his shin. Delia's screams ceased. She fell to her knees, the
flames so thick that he could no longer make out her

features. The sound of quickly approaching footsteps had Beau shifting to aim his gun behind him. Vincent had his machete ready as he faced the oncoming threat.

They both lowered their weapons when they saw Christian and Lincoln. It was the man in a police uniform that came up behind them that caused worry.

Beau pulled his full attention back to Davena who was doing her damnedest to get free. A couple of times she nearly succeeded. "Stop," he whispered urgently in Davena's ear. "Her attention is focused on Delia right now, not you."

That just fueled Davena to fight him harder.

"What the fuck?" the sheriff's deputy asked as he rushed past them to Delia.

He tried to reach through the flames to Delia, but she fell to the side. "Get some water!"

One moment Beau was holding Davena, and the next he was flat on his back, the wind knocked out of him. He blinked and shook his head. When he looked up, he found his brothers and the deputy laid out as well. Only Davena remained on her feet.

He rose up on his elbow and watched as she walked to Delia. With words tumbling hurriedly from her lips, Davena put out the fire. Beau looked across the street to find Delphine's victorious smile gone, replaced with a look of utter incredulity.

"Did Davena just do that?" Christian whispered from beside him.

Beau nodded as he jumped to his feet and slowly started toward Davena. He still had his shotgun, not that it would do any good against Delphine or even Davena. He halted behind Davena as she knelt beside Delia and took her sister's hand.

"Everything is going to be all right," Davena said.

Beau breathed through his mouth as the stench of burnt flesh reached him. He glanced at Delia to see there was no clothing, skin, or hair left.

"Let me go," Delia croaked.

Davena shook her head. "I'm going to make you better."

"You want to keep me in this kind of pain?" Delia asked brokenly.

"No, I'm—"

"You stopped the flames. Let them finish," Delia said hoarsely. "Please."

Beau's gaze latched onto Delphine. The Voodoo priestess wasn't done, but he didn't know if she would attack Davena that night or if she would wait.

"I love you, Delia," Davena said and rolled back onto the balls of her feet before standing.

As soon as she released Delia's hands, the flames returned. He stood beside Davena as she watched her sister burn, the life draining from her until nothing was left but a shell. The moment Delia's life ended, Delphine turned and vanished. But it wasn't the end. Things had just begun.

"What the hell just happened here?" demanded the deputy once he was on his feet.

"A shit storm," Christian answered.

Beau wanted to offer comfort to Davena, but he didn't know if it would be welcome. She looked so forlorn, standing there silently staring at her sister. There were no tears, just an absence of hope.

He finally gave in and wrapped an arm around her shoulders. When she didn't shrug him off, he stepped closer so their bodies touched. "I'm sorry."

"Beau," Vincent called.

He looked over his shoulder at his brothers to find the deputy staring at Davena. Beau nodded and turned Davena around to face them. She didn't fight him, didn't utter a word. He bent and glanced at her to see her gaze vacant.

"She's in shock," Lincoln said.

Christian snorted. "Hell, I think we all are."

"Someone tell me what just happened before I arrest you all," demanded the deputy.

Beau looked him over. He was well built, and wore his gun like a man who knew how to use it and wouldn't hesitate to do so. His black hair was kept short and combed back, and his wild gaze said he was on the edge of losing it all.

"Magic," Beau finally said. "You witnessed a powerful Voodoo priestess exact her revenge."

Lincoln cleared his throat. "Deputy Marshall Ducet, let me introduce my elder brother Vincent, and my youngest brother, Beau. The woman on his arm is—"

"Davena Arcineaux," Marshall interrupted in a calmer voice. "I gave her a ride to work this morning."

Beau tightened his hold on Davena. There was much about her he didn't know, but he wanted that to change.

"Voodoo," Marshall said and shook his head as he looked at the ground. "I left New Orleans to get away from that shit."

The brothers exchanged looks. It was Vincent who asked, "You were a cop in New Orleans?"

"For over seven years," Marshall said.

There was more to Marshall's story, but Beau was concerned with Davena right then. "We need to get off the streets and get Davena to the house."

"Agreed," Vincent said.

Christian looked at Marshall. "I wouldn't stay out here alone. She saw you with us."

The deputy shrugged. "I don't much care. Get out of here, all of you," he said as he looked around at them. "I'll get this cleaned up."

Beau didn't have to be told twice. He walked Davena to Christian's truck. He put her in the middle of the back seat and climbed in beside her. Lincoln sat on her other side, and as soon as Vincent shut his door, Christian drove them home.

They rode in silence, with each of his brothers casting furtive glances at Davena. To Beau's surprise, she reached over and took his hand. He wasn't sure she was even aware of it. She needed comfort from whoever would give it. And he was most willing to give it.

When they reached the house, Davena was still glassy-eyed from shock. Beau didn't ask, just gathered her in his arms and walked her inside the house. Ava and Olivia met them at the door, their questions coming all at once. Fortunately, Lincoln and Vincent were there to answer them.

Beau took Davena into the office and laid her on the couch. He took the throw off the back of the couch and draped it over her. Then he squatted beside her. He stopped himself from stroking a lock of her golden hair.

"You're safe here," he said, hoping she heard him.

He stood and sat in the chair next to the couch. The last thing he wanted was for her to come out of her shock and find herself alone in a strange house. Not to mention he wanted to be with her in any way that he could.

"How is she?" Olivia asked in a whisper from the doorway.

Beau shrugged helplessly. "Not good."

"I'll make some coffee. I have a feeling we're all going to need it."

Beau propped his elbow on the arm of the chair and dropped his head into his hand. He squeezed his eyes closed. Delphine had found the sisters. That was surprising enough, but not nearly so much as knowing that Delia tried to go up against the priestess with Hoodoo.

Then there was Davena. She was infinitely more

powerful than her sister. She had shown that tonight by putting out Delphine's flames and knocking all of them on their asses. Why then didn't the sisters attack Delphine as one?

The minutes ticked by as the voices from the kitchen drifted into the room. His family was keeping their voices down, but he knew they were talking about the night's events. It wouldn't be long before they would want his take on things.

"I couldn't stop her," Davena suddenly said into the quiet.

Beau's eyes snapped open and he lifted his head to look at her. After a brief hesitation, he leaned forward so he could see her face. "Delphine can't be stopped."

"Delia. I couldn't stop Delia." Her voice was soft, grief filling every syllable.

Beau blew out a breath, unsure of what to say. "You're not responsible for her decisions."

"I should've known she would try something."

He was thinking of how to reply, when her hand reached out for his. Beau didn't hesitate to slide his fingers into hers.

"Tell me how you came to be there," she asked.

She might be looking at the empty fireplace, but he knew she could see his every move. Beau licked his lips. "The Chiassons have been protecting this parish for generations from the supernatural."

Her gaze snapped to his, a small frown forming between her eyes. "So you knew Delphine was here?"

"No," he hurried to say. "We knew something was here, but we didn't know what or who."

"Yet you were there tonight. It wasn't by accident."

Beau paused. He hadn't liked explaining what had been happening to him with his family. He certainly wasn't keen on sharing it with Davena.

"Tell her," Lincoln said from the doorway.

Davena looked from Beau to Lincoln and then slowly sat up, removing her hand from his. Then her gaze came back to Beau. "Tell me what?"

Beau fisted the hand that had held hers, hating how much he missed the contact, and slowly sat back. "I had a feeling it was you."

"It was far from a feeling," Lincoln said and walked into the room. "He's had dreams of smoke. Tonight, while we were watching someone else, he doubled over in pain, telling us we had to get to you."

Beau couldn't stand Davena's troubled eyes on him. He rose and walked to the desk on the other side of the room. How was it he had to put distance between them while needing to have her close?

"How is that possible?" Davena asked.

Lincoln said, "I thought you might tell us."

Beau kept his back to her, afraid he couldn't look at her again and not touch her. And if he got close enough to touch her, he wasn't sure if he could keep from pulling her close and kissing her. Here he was thinking of her lips and tasting her when she was dealing with the death of her sister and the arrival of Delphine. If she knew his thoughts, she would never let him near again.

"I don't know," she finally answered.

A sound from the doorway drew his gaze. Beau found the rest of his family standing there waiting. It was Olivia who walked into the room with a mug of coffee that she set on the coffee table.

"I thought you might need that," Olivia told Davena.

Beau turned just enough to see Davena. She eyed the coffee and then looked at Olivia. "I could use something much stronger, actually."

"We've got that, too," Christian said as he moved to the cabinet near the desk and poured a glass of bourbon. His eyes briefly met Beau's.

Unable to help himself, Beau turned around and let his gaze settle on Davena. Her blonde hair fell like gold around her shoulders. She kept her legs tucked against her and used the throw like a shield.

Her hands shook a little as she took the proffered liquor from Christian. She took two sips before she let out a wobbly breath and met his stare. "You know what happened in Algiers, don't you?"

Beau nodded. "You and Delia were safe all this time. Why draw Delphine out now?"

"I didn't. Delia did." Davena looked down at her hands. "I knew something bad was coming. I even knew it was Delphine, but Delia didn't want to leave."

Ava took the chair Beau had vacated and laid a comforting hand on Davena's arm. There was no need for words. The action said it all.

Beau walked to the desk and leaned against it. "Do you know what you did tonight?"

"Did?" Davena asked, her gaze jerking to him.

"You stopped Delphine's fire."

CHAPTER

TWELVE

IT WASN'T POSSIBLE. Davena wasn't powerful enough to even think about going up against someone like Delphine. She looked into Beau's fierce blue eyes and wished he were still beside her. His warmth and comfort were all that kept her from losing herself.

"You're mistaken." She took a large swallow of the bourbon and felt it burn down her throat and settle warmly in her stomach. "I don't have that kind of ability. My mother, perhaps."

"And Delia?" Vincent asked.

Just thinking about her sister brought an ache to her chest. She wanted to cry for all the years her sister had lost, but no tears would come. Davena grinned ruefully. "She thought she did, but she didn't. Our mother didn't want either of us involved in what she did."

"Which was what, exactly?" Christian asked.

When she heard Beau's growl directed at his brother for such a question, it eased some of the numbness gripping her. She knew it had been Beau who came to her and placed his arm around her, who walked her to the truck, and who carried her inside the house. He had stayed with her, silent and patient.

"My mother got into the Voodoo religion when she was thirteen," Davena said as she studied the gold liquid in her glass. "She had an affinity for the…other side of the religion. Soon, others were coming to her for spells and dolls. It wasn't until she met my father when she was eighteen that something changed. She never told us what, but she backed away from the religion."

Lincoln rubbed his hand over his jaw, his palm scratching along his whiskers. "I gather there were those upset by her move."

"I guess." Davena shrugged. "She didn't like to talk about it. It was part of her past we knew never to speak of while growing up. A year later, when she was nineteen, she married my father and got out of Voodoo altogether. Yet people still came to her for help. That's how she turned to Hoodoo. Some of her friends were being cursed because of their connection to her. She didn't think that was fair, so she found a way to counter it."

"Brave woman," Beau said.

Everyone else in the room was forgotten as she looked at

him. How she wanted to run her hands through his hair and draw him close. She imagined he would kiss like he lived—softly at first, and then full throttle. "She was. She put her very life on the line every day. She saved a lot of people in the process."

"Did things change when you and Delia were born?" Ava asked.

Davena stiffened as she remembered it wasn't just her and Beau. "Not really. My father owned a restaurant in the French Quarter, and mother went on as she was, bringing in a little extra money in the process. That continued until I was four. I don't know why things changed that summer, but they did. It began when my father was killed in an alley outside his restaurant. He was found with his throat slit, and Voodoo markings painted in white all around him."

"It was a warning," Christian said.

"One my mother heeded in her own way. She stopped being so blatant about helping those who had been cursed, and took over the restaurant. Delia and I forgot all about the spells being practiced in our kitchen and became like every other little girl."

Davena took another long drink, coughing as it made her eyes water with the burn. She blinked away the moisture and tried not to stare at Beau. Still, he drew her gaze like a horse to water. She didn't know what it was, but she had to know him. It felt like...destiny. Fate even.

Abruptly, Beau walked to her and took the now empty

glass as he sat on the coffee table. She was caught in his magnetic blue gaze. He asked, "Then what happened?"

"For thirteen years, nothing. We knew our mother would occasionally help someone by meeting them at the back of the restaurant, but she kept that very hush-hush. Delia had graduated a few months before, and I had just started my senior year. Mom began to act strangely, telling us to make sure no one was following us. I knew something was going to happen."

He set the glass beside him, never taking his eyes from her. "How?"

"A feeling. It began simply as a niggling that I promptly forgot. Every day it grew worse until it was knotted in my stomach. Mom thought someone had hexed me. She made me and Delia a mojo bag to carry around for protection."

"It wasn't a hex."

She shook her head. "Delphine is known all around New Orleans. I'd seen her multiple times, and knew she was someone not to be messed with. That night, before Mom was killed, I knew it was Delphine who would show up."

"Did you and Delia try to stop Delphine then?" Ava asked.

Davena couldn't stop the laugh that bubbled forth. She covered her mouth and briefly closed her eyes before she gave a quick shake of her head. "No. Our mother taught us a few things for safety, but she told us not to get involved with any of it. I didn't, but I didn't know Delia had been following her for years and memorizing spells."

Beau took her right hand and spread her fingers. His gaze dropped to her mouth before his eyes lowered to her palm. "You got this that night."

"Mom tried to counter Delphine, but Delphine was too powerful."

The memories of that night mixed with recent ones, and she shivered at how similar her mother and sister acted as the fire consumed them. It was Beau's thumb slowly rubbing circles on her palm that slowed her breathing. She was transfixed, watching his thumb stroke over the burned portion of her palm to the normal skin. When she dared to look at him, she was struck by a blatant, deliberate desire.

Davena swallowed, her heart racing for an entirely new reason now.

"How did you get out?" Christian asked.

His words shattered the daze she was in, and she looked away, only to have her gaze skate right back to Beau. "The house began to burn with the unholy fire Delphine created. Our mother knew something could attack at the house, so she dug a tunnel that led underground from her bedroom to the drainage ditch nearby. I grabbed the door that hid the tunnel, forgetting the metal handle would be hot."

"But you got out," Vincent said. "That in itself is a miracle."

"You should've gone to the authorities."

The new voice had every head turning to the doorway where Davena saw Deputy Ducet standing with his hat in his hands.

"You've overstepped, man," Christian said as he started toward Marshall.

Vincent interceded and stepped between the two. He put a hand to Christian's chest before he faced the deputy. "I agree with my brother. The polite thing to have done would've been to knock."

"I did," Marshall said and shifted his weight to his other foot. His eyes landed on Davena. "I was one of the officers who scoured your house for remains. We all thought you were dead."

She remained where she was because Beau still held her hand. His gaze urged her to stay as she was, to trust him. He had promised she was safe there, and for some reason she believed him.

"State your business, deputy," Beau said.

Marshall licked his lips. "Miss Arcineaux, your sister has been taken to the county morgue. I didn't think you wanted any more attention on this, so her death has been ruled an accident."

"How did you pull that off?" Lincoln asked.

Marshall turned his cowboy hat around in his hands. "The sheriff has been ready to retire for three years, and the other deputies are either so new they don't know their ass from a hole in the ground, or so old they don't give a shit anymore. With my time in New Orleans, they take my word for things. Not to mention, as soon as I mentioned the Chiasson name, they forgot all about it."

Olivia harrumphed. "I don't know whether to be grateful or angry that we have such men patrolling the streets."

"Sweetheart, why do you think we hunt?" Vin asked with a wink that made Olivia grin.

Ava stood and smiled at Marshall. "I'm sure you could use a cup of coffee, deputy. Let's give Davena a few minutes."

Davena smiled appreciatively at Ava as everyone filed out of the room. Everyone, that is, except for Beau. Now that they were alone, she had a hard time keeping eye contact.

"Do you want to be alone?" he asked.

"No," she answered quickly. Then she met his gaze and said in a steady voice, "No."

"You are safe here. This house is warded, blessed, and spelled. Nothing can come in."

"Our house was the same, and Delphine didn't have to come inside to kill my mother."

Beau sighed and looked down at her scar. He ran his thumb along the scar again. "We've had a recent dealing with Delphine. We'll figure this out."

"What you should do is throw me out and forget you ever knew me. If not, she'll come for you."

"Let her."

Davena's stomach fluttered as if a thousand butterflies had taken flight. Before her sat the man she had intended to come here and see that night. Nothing had gone as planned, and yet somehow, she still ended up in his arms. But she wanted more.

Her eyes lowered to his wide lips. She had watched her sister die, and knew that Delphine would be coming for her soon. No longer would fear hold her back. If she didn't take what was before her, she would die without ever knowing the feel of Beau's lips on hers.

Davena leaned forward and took her free hand to rest it on his cheek. His brilliant blue eyes darkened as desire flared. It was the boost to her courage that she needed. Her fingers trailed along his jawline to lips that were as soft as velvet.

"I was going to come here tonight," she confessed with a little smile. "I don't know what I would've said or how I would have gotten your interest."

"You've always had my interest."

The truth shone in his eyes. Davena slid her fingers into the hair at his temples and then down the strands that ended at his chin. "I don't know what tomorrow holds, and right now I don't care."

Before she could think twice about it, she leaned forward and gently placed her lips on his. She began to pull back, only to have him roughly haul her against his chest. Her arms wound around his neck for balance as she ended up fully in his lap. His gaze met hers for an instant before his lips took hers. He captured, he seized.

He claimed.

And Davena gloried in every wonderful moment of it.

His hands splayed on her back, holding her firmly against him while his head tilted to the side. His kiss was electric. Then he changed everything by deepening the kiss, a moan rumbling from his chest as she eagerly opened for him.

Davena had never experienced anything so thrilling, so stirring. She felt alive for the first time in six years. The world and all her problems melted away. She let her hands roam over his thick shoulders, marveling at the strength she felt beneath her palms. His thin, black shirt only accentuated his finely honed body.

Desire, thick and needy, blossomed within her. It tightened low in her belly, as the kiss grew fiery and frantic. A wordless, urgent hunger had taken both of them, refusing to let go.

Her breath stopped when he caressed her back, his hands stopping at her side with his thumb grazing the bottom of her breast. He ended the kiss and looked at her with those incredible blue eyes of his.

Then he cupped her breast and ran his thumb over her nipple.

CHAPTER

THIRTEEN

BEAU WAS FOCUSED on the woman in his arms. It might have been Davena that kissed him, but there was no turning back for him now. He'd had a taste of her, and he had to have more. Her spring green eyes were dilated as she stared at him. Her lips were parted and wet from their kisses. Her breathing ragged, her pulse jumping wildly at the base of her throat.

The feel of her nipple beneath his palm through her shirt and bra about did him in. It was all he could do not to toss her on the couch and rip her clothes from her body before he thrust inside her.

He had felt desire before, but nothing came close to the all-consuming craving that burned within him for Davena. There was nothing that could pull him away from her, nothing that could make him release her.

Nothing that could ever wipe out the taste of her kiss.

Beau massaged her breast, his balls tightening when a soft moan fell from her lips. It was wrong for a woman to be so beautiful and tempting. How was he expected to string together rational thoughts? He was only a man, after all.

He was so engrossed with Davena that he almost didn't hear the squeak in the wood floors as someone approached. Here he was, sitting with her across his lap stealing kisses and touches like he was still in high school.

There was no time for an explanation. Beau quickly set her back on the couch and jumped up to stand in front of the hearth. He kept his back to the door so no one would see his arousal.

"Marshall is leaving," Vincent said from the door.

When Davena didn't respond, Beau glanced at his brother over his shoulder. "You filled him in then?"

"On us?" Vin asked. "Of course. We've always kept the local law enforcement apprised of what we do, you know that."

Beau knew a lot of things, but he couldn't seem to make his brain function correctly. "Right."

"Is everything all right?" Vin asked suspiciously.

"It's fine," Beau and Davena said in unison.

Vincent snorted loudly. "Right. That was convincing."

Beau let out a sigh when Vincent walked away. He turned to Davena. Even now it was difficult to keep his distance.

"The animals," she suddenly said. Her face filled with

distress. "I've got to stay with them. One dog was in surgery. I can't believe I forgot about them."

A problem. Beau was good at solving problems. Plus, it gave him something to focus on rather than Davena and the need clawing at him. "I'll take care of it."

He started for the door when she rose and walked with him into the foyer were Marshall stood with the rest of the family. The sheriff's deputy turned his attention to them.

"I left New Orleans because most of the cops turned a blind eye to Delphine," Marshall told Davena. "The other half was paid off as only someone like Delphine could do. The few of us who wanted to do honest work couldn't. Like with what happened to your mother."

Davena crossed her arms over her chest. "One man can't expect to change a city."

"I came here expecting it to be different." Marshall looked around and smiled ruefully. "I guess it is. I never knew there were those like the Chiassons around."

Christian smiled crookedly. "Do you remember any LaRue's in New Orleans?"

Marshall's lips flattened. "Yes. Why?"

"They're our cousins," Lincoln said. "And they do what we do."

"Then they need to do a better job of it," Marshall said. He put his hat on and nodded to the women. "Good night all."

Beau waited until the door closed behind the deputy before he said, "I'm heading out too."

There was a lengthy stretch of silence as every eye turned to him. Finally, it was Lincoln who asked, "Why?"

"I need to go to the animal clinic. Davena was supposed to stay there all night and watch over the animals. She's not leaving the house."

Vincent widened his stance and looked from Davena to Beau. "This is the safest place for Davena. I don't think it's a good idea for you to be out there either."

"Someone has to be there until the doc arrives at seven," Davena said. "I can't have those animals left alone. As I told Beau, it doesn't matter where I am or how safe it is. Delphine will come for me whenever she wants."

Christian threw his keys up in the air and caught them. "I'll go."

"Dammit, Christian," Vincent said angrily.

Beau held up a hand to quiet everyone. "He goes or I do, because if we don't, Davena will."

Davena nodded in agreement.

Without another word, Christian turned on his heel and walked out the back door. Beau wasn't sure if he should be relieved that he stayed behind, or concerned about how he was going to get through the rest of the night.

"There's food in the kitchen," Olivia said. "Beau made the best banana pudding I've ever had. There is still some chicken left, as well."

Ava scrunched up her nose. "Actually, Christian and Marshall finished off both."

"I can fix her whatever she wants," Beau said.

Davena cocked her head at him. "You cook?"

"He's the best around," Lincoln said.

Vincent nodded. "He does the lion's share of the cooking around here. He's got a gift."

"Is that so?" Davena said, a small smile playing at her lips. "Thank you for the offer, but I don't think I could eat."

Beau inhaled and looked at the stairs. "I'm sure you want to rest."

"I thought we'd put her in Riley's room," Ava said.

Olivia came to stand next to Davena. "We'll take her up now and show her around."

Beau watched the three of them ascend the stairs, his gaze locked on Davena's hips as they swayed side to side.

"You are so screwed," Vincent said as he came to stand on Beau's left.

Lincoln moved to Beau's right. "Actually, he won't be tonight."

Beau rolled his eyes as his brothers laughed at the joke. "Y'all are fucking hilarious."

Davena was ashamed. She knew she should be overcome with sadness after Delia's death, but all she could think about was Beau.

She walked next to Ava and Olivia as they pointed out each of the rooms upstairs in the old plantation house. She was the last to walk into the room kept for the lone female Chiasson. The white, iron bed was set against the far wall with a large floral print comforter in bright pink.

The room held several boxes stacked against one wall, but it was sparse other than a table next to the bed with a lamp and a picture frame. Davena walked to the table and sat on the bed as she lifted the frame.

She smiled at the picture that was about twenty years old, judging by the young faces and the style of clothes. She looked at all five Chiasson children surrounding their parents, the smiles wide and infectious.

Davena easily picked out Beau despite all the siblings having the same dark hair and blue eyes. It wasn't a matter of narrowing it down. It was the way Beau smiled. It was warm and welcoming with a hint of waywardness.

It was a smile she had seen herself.

"They were a close family," Olivia said.

Ava sat beside Davena. "Olivia knew them from growing up here, but I only knew their reputation within the parish. They're still close, despite what happened to their parents."

"What happened?" Davena was intrigued. Besides, it would take her mind off of Beau and Delia.

Olivia sat on the opposite side of the bed and rested her arm on the tall footboard. "They were murdered on the same night by a woman who lusted after their father."

"That's horrible," Davena said and shifted to see both women. "How long ago was that?"

"A week after that picture was taken," Ava replied softly.

Davena glanced back at the picture. "Worlds can crumble in an instant, can't they?"

"Both mine and Ava's did. Then our men found us," Olivia said with a bright grin.

Ava winked at Davena. "Just as Beau found you."

Beau. She licked her lips, still feeling his on hers. His kisses had literally curled her toes. She hadn't been able to remember her name, but the one thing she knew with certainty was that she wanted to kiss him forever.

"Once Delphine decides to come for you, nothing will change her mind," Davena said.

Ava shrugged one shoulder. "She was after me, but the LaRues managed to change her mind."

Davena studied Ava closely, trying to determine how much to tell her. "I've never heard of her giving up on someone unless there was a trade made."

"Trade?" Olivia repeated, frowning.

"A trade that was worth it to Delphine," Davena explained. "If she was out to kill someone, then someone would have to know the whereabouts of an individual she sought, or offer something else of similar value."

The two women exchanged a look as Ava's face grew pale. "They told me Delphine released me after they captured her."

"Captured Delphine? No one captures her unless she wants to be caught." Davena wasn't trying to start trouble, but everyone needed to understand the danger Delphine posed.

Olivia rubbed her hand up and down Ava's arm. "We don't know who lied, so don't get angry yet. It could be that Delphine was playing everyone."

"She does that well enough," Davena said.

Ava took in a shaky breath. "So you've had several dealings with her?"

"A few," Davena replied. "She is a mainstay in the French Quarter. She's famous and greatly feared. Those who practice the Voodoo religion worship her for her great powers. She always knows a person's weakness. That's how she gets so many to do as she wants."

"So you've never met her personally?" Olivia asked.

Davena replaced the frame and rose to look out the window. A scene of tranquil beauty met her gaze as she looked out over the moon-drenched bayou. "There were a couple of instances where I spoke with her. Not even my mother knew. Once, I was twelve. I walked out of school waiting on Delia and there Delphine was."

"What did she want?" Ava asked.

Davena fingered the lace curtains. "I don't know. She

asked me silly questions like how I did in school and if I was happy. She freaked me out so much that I walked away while she continued to ask questions."

"And the next time?" Olivia asked.

She faced the bed, her hands resting on the windowsill. "I was sixteen. I'd been out late with friends and walking home. One moment my friends were talking, and the next they were on the ground unconscious. This time she asked if I was practicing my magic."

Ava blinked in shock. "Magic? I mean, I know what the guys said they saw you do tonight, but does that mean you know magic?"

"No," Davena said quickly. "I don't know how I did what I did tonight. I wanted to go to Delia, and I wanted the fire to stop. Somehow, both happened."

Olivia fluffed the pillows on the bed. "She took an interest in you. Did she do the same to Delia?"

"Not that I knew of, and Delia would've said something. She so desperately wanted to follow in our mother's footsteps," Davena said, remembering it all as if it just happened yesterday.

"What will you do now?"

Davena looked around the room. "As beautiful as this plantation is, I can't stay here."

CHAPTER

FOURTEEN

BEAU STARED at the stove for a long time. Whenever he was troubled, he had always found solace in cooking. That night was the exception.

His body had yet to cool from his kisses with Davena, and knowing she would be sleeping down the hall from him wasn't making things any easier. But it was the knowledge that they hadn't seen the last of Delphine that turned the knot in his stomach tighter.

A glance at the clock showed he had been standing in the kitchen for almost two hours. Everyone else had long since found their beds. Beau didn't want to walk up the stairs because it would put him too close to Davena.

She should have time to herself after losing her sister, not be pawed at by the likes of him. Beau couldn't believe he had groped her so. She had wanted a kiss, and he had taken things much further. If she were interested in him before, she certainly wouldn't be anymore. Perhaps it was for the best. Allowing anyone close was setting himself up for hurt later down the road.

He fisted his hand, the weight of her breast still fresh in his memory. She wasn't just beautiful, she was a fighter, a woman who never gave up. She was tenacious, steadfast, faithful, and trustworthy.

Davena had survived the worst kinds of travesty—twice—and still resolutely faced the world with her shoulders back and chin held high. He didn't know how she did it. His parents' deaths had nearly destroyed him and the family. Looking back, it was his siblings that kept him going.

That, he and Davena had in common, at least.

A sound coming from the study had Beau turning around and silently walking out of the kitchen. He sidestepped the creaking floorboard and stopped beside the open doorway of the office. A lamp on the far side of the room chased away the dark, and the desk light had been turned on, granting him enough light to see who was in the study. He spotted Davena near the sideboard that held all the liquor. She took a long drink of bourbon before setting the glass down.

Her head turned to the side, just now noticing that she was no longer alone. "I thought I was the only one up."

"I never went up to bed." Beau stepped into the room and leaned back against the doorjamb. "Can't sleep either?"

Her glorious mane of golden hair shifted along her back

as she shook her head. "Every time I close my eyes, I see Delia in flames or lying burnt on the ground. I want to cry, but I can't."

"It'll come."

She chuckled dryly. "Will it? I can't feel anything. I'm numb, and I fear I'll remain that way until Delphine finally comes for me." Davena turned slowly to the side and looked at him. "It won't be here, though. I don't want her evil touching this place. You have a good thing here with your family."

"This land and this house were built and protected to help people like you."

"Like my mother helped people?" She twisted her lips in a rueful smile. "Take it from me, Beau. You don't want any part of that."

He glanced around the room, thinking back to his early years when he had played in there just to be near his father while he poured over the journal. "Do we really have a choice? Ever since the first Chiasson came to this parish, we've been protecting the people from the supernatural, whether it's ghosts, demons, creatures, or magic. We've saved a lot of people."

"And lost family."

"Yes," he answered after a short pause. "It's the price we pay for the hunting that we do."

She turned the glass in her hand, gazing down at it.

"Despite the tragedies, Vincent and Lincoln have found women to call their own. What about the rest of you?"

"Christian won't. He refuses. Riley? She's being kept away from this, so I'm sure she will find someone, as well."

Davena's gaze lifted to his. "And you?"

A day ago he'd have said he agreed with Christian, but now, he was no longer sure of anything. "I don't know."

"Because you haven't found anyone?"

"Because I don't want to give my heart to someone only to have them taken away."

She looked away, taking a quick drink and then licking her lips. "I see."

"No, you don't."

Her gaze skated back to his. "Tell me then."

Beau hesitated, unsure of what he was doing. "I thought I would be all right alone. I was prepared for it. I just wasn't prepared for you. I don't want you close, but it's where I need you."

For long moments, their gazes held. Beau anxiously waited for her to respond, to say something, anything, after he put out a statement like that. Finally, she set down her glass and pushed away from the sideboard. She closed the distance between them, stopping a few paces away from him.

"I have a hole inside me," she said softly. "It's growing by the minute. I haven't felt anything since I saw the flames take Delia, except when I was in your arms. I don't want to be alone tonight. I don't want to think of what happened or what is coming. I want…you."

Beau reached out, cupped her cheek, and slid his hand into her hair, the silky strands gliding through his fingers. He understood all too well what she was going through—and what she wanted.

He stepped closer, pulling her against him as he did. Her spring green eyes drew him in until he was engulfed in all that was Davena. Her lips parted, drawing his gaze. His head dipped and he took her mouth. He tried to be gentle, to go slow, but at the first touch of their lips, her arms snaked around his neck. With her body molded to his, the passion erupted like a firestorm.

Beau held her tightly against him. He kissed her fiercely, brutally. All the while, her hands clawed at his shirt, ripping it in her efforts to take it off.

He pulled back long enough to remove the garment. With chests heaving, he paused before he kissed her again and felt something break apart inside him when she smiled. His hands rested on her hips and stroked upward until he reached the hem of her shirt. He slipped his fingers beneath it to touch her stomach.

Beau couldn't wait to strip her slowly of clothes, but that fantasy shattered when she jerked off her shirt and shimmied out of her jeans. In a matter of seconds, she stood before him in nothing but her yellow panties and bra.

Her smile mixed with the blatant desire shining in her eyes, and Beau forgot all about his fantasy. He hastily removed his jeans and yanked her to him. Then, with a twist of his fingers, he released her bra. The straps sagged on her shoulders, causing her grin to widen. She carelessly discarded it over her shoulder.

With nothing separating them other than the silk of her panties, Beau slowly ran his hand up her back. It brought her against him, pressing her breasts to his chest.

The passion was explosive, the desire sizzling. Each kiss brought them higher, closer. Her skin was satin, her touch scorching.

He turned her against the wall and kissed down her neck to her chest. Beau stopped long enough to suckle on each nipple, flicking his tongue over the tiny buds until she was gasping and her hips rocked against him.

Only then did he continue his kisses down her stomach and over her hips, tugging her panties down as he did, until he reached the golden curls nestled between her legs. He lifted one of her legs and draped it over his shoulder. Then he licked her. She cried out, her fingers tightening in his hair. But he didn't stop. He licked, he laved.

THE TASTE of her essence was everything he'd known it would be and more. It wasn't enough to have her on his tongue, he wanted to feel her as well. With his tongue intent on her clitoris, he slid a finger inside her.

~

Davena clung to him as her body shivered with his every touch. Heat filled her until her veins ran with it. Her hips rocked in time with his tongue teasing her.

Her eyes closed as the pleasure became too much. She could feel her body rising to the climax, knew it was there waiting. He spread her legs wider, opening her more to his mouth so he could learn every inch of her.

Then his fingers began to explore her, working her into a frenzy. She slammed her hands on the wall in an attempt to stay upright.

The bliss was intoxicating, the decadence exhilarating.

She was helpless to stop the unrelenting pleasure Beau heaped upon her. She might be powerless, but she'd never felt so safe. It gave her the freedom to open herself to him in ways she never imagined she could—or even knew she wanted to.

The orgasm, when it hit, took her breath. She opened her mouth on a silent scream as she was swept along a tide of unbelievable, incredible ecstasy.

Her knee buckled, but Beau caught her, shifting her until her legs wrapped around his waist. She opened her eyes to see him looking between them. Davena was enraptured as she watched the tip of his engorged cock slip through the folds of her sex and then inside her body.

She bit her lip as he filled her, stretching her. Her nails sank into his shoulders, even as she moaned in pleasure. Sweat glistened over their bodies, allowing them to slide easily against the other.

Beau's strong hands held her steadily as he suddenly turned away from the wall and walked to the couch. Each movement from him made his cock shift inside her, causing her to gasp and groan at the feel of it.

He sat down so that she straddled his hips and kissed her slowly, languidly. They used that time to learn each other. Davena hadn't gotten nearly enough time to look over his amazing body. His muscles were toned and powerful, the sinew molded tightly.

She ran her hands along his chest and over his washboard stomach before caressing the bulging muscles of his arms and shoulders. He abruptly ended the kiss and shifted them so that she was on her back on the couch, with him still inside her. His hands held her arms above her head as his gaze caught and held hers.

Then he began to move his hips. Long, slow strokes that heated her blood soon turned into hard, short thrusts that took her higher and higher.

She locked her ankles around his waist. His eyes darkened and his rhythm quickened. He filled her again and again, harder, deeper.

Davena turned her head into the couch when the scream welled up as her second climax claimed her. Her body pulsated with unending pleasure.

"Davena," Beau whispered.

She looked up to find his face contorted as he jerked, his own orgasm descending.

When he collapsed on her, Davena pulled her hands from his grasp and wound her arms around him, holding him. She knew they had been careless and didn't use protection. It wasn't as if it mattered. She would be dead soon anyway.

He settled against her with his head on her chest. Davena caressed his back with one hand, and leisurely, softly scraped her fingernails against his scalp as she played with his long, dark locks.

She tried to find regret, since it was something she always did, but there wasn't anything she regretted since arriving at the Chiasson plantation. Beau might be strong as an ox with enough bravery and courage to rival a superhero, but he was just as broken and battered as she was.

They were two of a kind.

It was too bad there wouldn't be a future for them.

THE MOONLIGHT DIDN'T PENETRATE the thick branches of the live oak. An owl hooted from one of the many branches, some so heavy they touched the ground. Delphine paid the animal no attention. Her focus was on the plantation where Davena had been brought.

The Chiassons. She had expected that they would interfere, just as their meddling cousins the LaRues often did. Yet, there was something different about one of the Chiassons. It was the way he had looked at Davena, as if he would readily take on the world for her.

Delphine smiled slowly. She would see just how far he would go for Davena.

CHAPTER
FIFTEEN

Beau opened his eyes to find Davena lying on her side facing him, her eyes open. Sometime in the night they had moved to the floor to sleep. His hand rested on her waist while hers lay near his face. She grinned, her eyes crinkling slightly at the corners.

"Did you sleep at all?" he asked.

She shrugged and held the blanket over her breasts. "No. I did try. It wasn't easy with you snoring."

"I would never," he teased, grateful that she didn't seem as weighted down that morning.

The smiles died as they gazed into each other's eyes, desire flaring to life once more. Beau pulled her closer and kissed her softly.

She scraped her fingers along his jaw over his whiskers. "What happens now?"

"Breakfast," he said. "I'll make you anything you want."

"A man who cooks. I could easily get spoiled."

He wanted more than anything to keep her beside him. What an idiot he had been to think he could remain alone. Davena was his. He knew it, but couldn't begin to explain how. "Then let me spoil you."

Davena looked away and sat up, keeping the blanket against her bare breasts. "Is that a good idea? For either of us?"

Beau rolled over and got to his feet. He knew she was pulling away from him, and even though he had fought against her pull, now that he had learned how it felt to have her in his arms, he wasn't ready to let her go without a fight.

He tugged on his jeans and tossed her a smile. "I'll get breakfast started if you want to grab a shower."

"Beau," she said and lifted her gaze to him. "It's a matter of hours before Delphine comes for me."

"We'll pay for Delia's funeral." If he ignored her, she might forget about wanting to put distance between them. Getting her to remain at the house might give him time to make her realize he could keep her safe.

She ran her hands through her long hair and sighed. "Fine. We'll do this your way."

Beau kept his smile in place until he was in the kitchen. Once there, he closed his eyes and knew he was in the biggest fight of his life—two-fold. Not only did he have to contend with Delphine, he had to win Davena. She had come to him easily last night, but only because she expected to die soon.

"And here I thought finding you and the lovely Davena naked would erase that frown."

Beau's eyes snapped open to find Christian at the table with a mug of coffee in one hand and a slice of strawberry cake in the other. "What are you doing back so early?"

"Marshall came by the clinic. We chatted for a bit, and then he called the doc. I've been home for a couple of hours."

"You should've woken me," Beau said crossly as he stalked to the fridge and yanked open the door.

Christian swallowed his bite. "And ruin such a nice picture the two of you made? Not a chance. Tell me you didn't leave her to wake up alone?"

"Of course I didn't," Beau said and threw him a glare over his shoulder. "You're such an ass."

Christian screwed up his face. "Aren't you supposed to be in a glorious mood after a night in a woman's arms? Especially a woman like Davena."

Beau inhaled, and then slowly released it. "I'm making her breakfast."

"Be careful with her, Beau. She'll slip through your fingers if you're not watching. She's used to being on her own."

Christian's words only tightened that niggle of worry at the back of his mind. "She has her sister to bury."

"And a psychopath to stay away from."

Beau grabbed the carton of eggs, milk, and grated cheese. "I don't plan to let her out of my sight again."

DAVENA SMELLED the eggs cooking and briefly thought about remaining, but she knew if she stayed, Delphine would come for her and kill all the Chiassons when she did.

The Chiassons were good people, and Beau...he was the best. He was the kind of man women prayed they would find, the kind of man who could smile and melt the stoutest of hearts.

The kind of man Davena had always yearned for.

The kind of man who needed to stay alive.

Davena slipped out the front door before she changed her mind.

HE WAS A FOOL. A complete and utter fool.

Beau angrily shoved his hair out of his face as he stood in the office, staring down at the perfectly folded blanket that lay on the arm of the couch. A blanket that an hour earlier had been wrapped around Davena's lovely body.

The entire house was being searched for her, but he knew

she was gone. Was it because she didn't trust him? Didn't she know a Chiasson didn't make a promise unless they could deliver on it?

"She's not in the house," Lincoln said as he stormed into the study. "Why did she leave?"

Ava was right on his heels. "You know why. Delphine."

"She said Delphine didn't have to enter the house to get to her," Beau said. "That's why she left. To protect us."

God, why hadn't he realized that sooner? If it had been anyone but Davena he would've comprehended that fact instantly. His mind was in constant turmoil where Davena was concerned.

Beau turned to face his brother and Ava, and spotted the rest walking toward the doorway. He waited until everyone was gathered before he said, "If we're going to save Davena, we need to look for Delphine."

"Right, because that's so easy," Christian said.

Vincent frowned at him. "We know who we're looking for now. It's a small town with few places for her to hide."

"Yeah, but many small communities in which to do it," Lincoln pointed out.

Christian rubbed the back of his neck. "So much for staying away from the house once we found who we were after. She knows now."

Ava lifted a finger to get Beau's attention. "We'll get to that in a moment. What about Davena?"

"She knows I'll come looking for her. She'll stay hidden waiting for Delphine." Which would allow Beau time to find the priestess first if all went according to plan.

Vincent guessed his strategy and shook his head, baffled. "You really think Delphine will talk to you."

"What?" Christian yelled, looking from Vincent to Beau. "Have you lost your fucking mind, Beau?"

Lincoln's smile was sad as he said, "No. He's found his woman."

"I hate to bring this up," Olivia said, a forlorn look on her face. "Maman said someone would get hurt from this family. Beau, if you go looking for Delphine, that could end up being you."

Beau wiped a hand across his mouth. "Possibly."

He walked through the five of them and hurried upstairs to change. The clock had once more been set against them, but this time he knew who he had to save and who he was fighting against. That put the odds in his favor—slightly.

But Chiassons had been winning battles with less for generations. He wasn't going to give up because the odds were stacked against him. That's when a Chiasson excelled.

He dressed in record time, grabbing his shotgun on the way out of his room. When he reached the kitchen to go out the back door, everyone was waiting.

Olivia handed him a backpack with a warm smile. "There's food and water inside."

"As well as bandages and a change of clothes for both you and Davena," Ava added.

Beau drew both women in for a hug. "Thank you."

"Just bring her back," Ava said as Olivia dabbed at her eyes.

Beau then faced his brothers. "I have to do this alone."

"As if we'd allow that," Vincent stated.

Christian slapped him on the back as he walked past him. "We're splitting up and covering your scrawny ass, little brother."

Beau watched him walk out, and a moment later heard the roar of an engine. Beau turned his gaze to Lincoln and Vincent. "Don't interfere in whatever I do."

"We can't promise that," Lincoln said and rubbed his thumb over the hilt of his Bowie knife. "You're our brother."

Vincent gave a small nod. "We'll do our best."

It was all Beau was going to get. He walked out of the house to his truck. Behind the wheel, he sat there for a moment thinking of where he might find Delphine. Then he started the engine and drove away.

He looked in the rearview mirror as he drove down the long crepe myrtle lined drive. The plantation loomed large and white. It had always been his safe haven, and he wanted it to be Davena's.

When he reached the main road, Beau looked left. That would take him toward Crowley, but going right would bring him to Kaplan. There had been rumors recently of Voodoo growing in the town. It seemed like the perfect place to look for Delphine.

Beau turned right. The knot that had been in his stomach for days had let up the previous night, but it was back with a vengeance, and had been since he was in the middle of cooking.

It wasn't long before he reached Kaplan and slowed. There wasn't the normal traffic for a Sunday. Driving the streets wasn't going to get him anywhere. He needed to make himself accessible.

Beau pulled over at the local diner and parked. He glanced at his shotgun. Carrying it wasn't an option, and neither was trying to hide it. Fortunately, he had some throwing knives on him just in case. Not that any of it would matter if Delphine decided to kill him.

He hid his shotgun underneath the seat and got out of the truck. As he closed his door, he spotted Christian's blue truck across the street, and Lincoln's black truck down the street, just coming to a stop.

Beau turned around and came face to face with a man as tall and thickly muscled as an oak. His midnight eyes were emotionless and trained on him.

"Delphine will see you," he said in an eerily deep voice. Then he turned and walked away.

Beau hesitated for a second before he fell in step behind

the big man. Most likely he was walking to his death. At the very least, it was a trap. And yet he kept going.

The small town fell behind them as they crossed rice fields and pastures. Beau could see a copse of trees ahead, and just as he expected, that's where they stopped.

The big man pointed to an overturned bucket for Beau to sit on. Beau looked around at the bare earth. There were bones scattered around a banked fire along with a recently killed copperhead snake.

Beau counted at least ten men and women. Some were hiding behind trees while others sat out in the open staring at him. He rested his arms on his legs and slowly looked around for some sign of Delphine.

Fifteen minutes went by excruciatingly slowly without a single word being spoken. He leaned against the pine behind him and caught a flash of white through the trees.

A moment later Delphine stepped into the clearing. Her skin was a deep umber, her eyes as black as pitch. She wore a white flowing skirt and shirt, and white material was wrapped around her head, hiding her hair.

Beau had only caught a glimpse of her in the dark the night before, so he was wholly unprepared for her exquisite beauty. She wore no makeup, no jewelry, and yet eclipsed everything around her.

"I knew you would come," she said with a small smile.

Beau was taken aback by her lush voice. She wasn't

anything like he'd expected. An old crone perhaps, but not the beauty before him. "How did you know?"

"Because of Davena. You care for her."

"I do." There was no point in trying to lie. "Why do you want to kill her? Just because her mother went against you?"

Delphine's smile widened. "Because she's mine."

CHAPTER
SIXTEEN

Davena sat in the rented house staring off into nothing. The house was particularly quiet without the constant chatter of Delia or the fighting. She kept waiting for her sister to come through the door with some argument about something trivial as she usually did, but Delia didn't come barging in. How could she when she was lying in a cold morgue?

Davena's throat tightened when she thought about the funeral. It wasn't right that Delia wouldn't be buried next to their parents—even though there was already a grave there.

It had been morbid, but Delia had made her sneak into the graveyard three years after their mother was killed to see their graves. Davena had been more interested in saying farewell to her mother, and she hadn't cared that the world thought her and Delia were already dead.

Now Delia would have a second grave, just as she would.

Davena wondered if her death would be as painful as Delia's. She hoped it was quick, but more than that, she prayed that Beau didn't witness it.

She wasn't stupid enough to believe he would let her leave. It wasn't in his genes. He would look for her in the hopes that he could save her. If she had a chance, hopefully she could talk Delphine into not harming the Chiassons.

If she got the chance to talk to Delphine. It was such a huge *if* that it was laughable. Her mother and Delia hadn't had that chance. What made her think she could?

Davena looked down at her hands. She had used magic last night. She realized that while she watched Beau sleep. She hadn't even known she could do it, but spells of Hoodoo from her mother filled her mind without her even trying.

Delia had brought Delphine to town by doing Hoodoo. It only made sense that Delphine would find her if she did the same. Davena stood and closed her eyes as she began to ward the house and those next to it against supernatural fire.

That should be enough to let Delphine know she wasn't hiding. Then Davena went to the drawer in the kitchen that held the knives and pulled out the biggest and two smaller ones. She took them to the table and began to mark them with a Hoodoo symbol to empower them with magic.

She wouldn't hide in the house like her mother, or be fool enough to try and face off against the priestess with her magic like Delia. She stood, hiding the knives in her shorts. No, Davena had another plan altogether.

BEAU KNEW by Delphine's throaty laugh that she found his surprised expression funny. He composed himself quickly. "Yours? How is Davena yours?"

Delphine clasped her hands together in front of her and grinned while she waited for the big male to lift a rather hefty piece of tree trunk from its place on one side of the clearing to set it in front of Beau.

She smiled seductively at the male and then sank gracefully onto the makeshift seat. "I'll tell you all about Davena if you answer me one question."

"Ask," he said, even though he knew it was going to be something he didn't want to answer.

"Would you die for her?"

He thought Delphine might ask if he loved Davena. He hadn't expected the question he got. "She doesn't deserve what has happened to her."

"That's not for you to decide," Delphine said, her black eyes going hard as her smile vanished. "I asked a question. I expect an answer."

The Chiassons were charged with keeping the people of the parish safe—in any way possible. He cared deeply for Davena, so deeply it might even be love. Every night they hunted, the Chiassons put their lives on the line, ready to die to save others. How would dying for Davena be any different?

"I would if I knew she would be free of you," he finally answered.

Delphine inhaled, her chest expanding. "A deal is a deal. You answered my question. Now I will tell you the story that only one other knew—Babette Arcineaux."

Beau waited for her to continue, each second that ticked by with silence grating on his nerves until he wanted to shout with it. That wasn't how to deal with Delphine, however. It took more finesse, more tact.

"Her mother couldn't conceive," Delphine said. "They tried unsuccessfully for years. They couldn't adopt, nor could they afford in vitro fertilization. After years of flaunting her Hoodoo in my face, Babette had the nerve to walk into my place."

He was riveted with the story. Beau couldn't imagine the nerve it took for Babette to see Delphine. "She wanted you to help her conceive," he guessed.

Delphine nodded. "I always knew she would want something from me someday, but it wasn't until she came to me that I knew what it would be."

"You helped her."

"I did." Delphine smiled secretly as she glanced away. "With one condition. I told her she would have more than one child. In exchange for my help, she had to agree that one of the children would be mine to raise in the Voodoo religion to take my place leading my followers someday."

Beau slowly leaned forward. "Davena."

"Davena," she repeated. She reached out her hand and ran her long fingernail over his hand. "There were two spells that night. The first, Babette was witness to and included in. The second occurred long after she left. I gave some of my own power coursing in my veins to one of the children. I thought it might have been Delia."

"Because she was first?"

"She was conceived that very night, but no," Delphine said and caressed languidly up his arm. "It was her desire to know all there was to know of Voodoo and Hoodoo that made me think it was her. Then Davena caught my attention. She didn't care about what her mother did, and yet power filled her so fully she practically shone with it. Why do you think everyone always flocked to her?"

Beau tried to ignore her fingers as they reached his chest and then began to wander downward. "Because she's beautiful and good."

"Did you see how she put out my fire? No one has been able to do that before," Delphine said as she leaned closer. "No one."

"You fear her."

"She is part of me. I don't fear her, I love her. I came for her that night in Algiers, but Babette refused. That's why she died. I didn't know until it was too late that Davena was in there. I could have killed Delia right then, but I let both girls go. For six yeats, I've tracked their every movement."

Beau grabbed her hand right before she reached his cock. He slowly pulled her hand away. "Why come now?"

"Delia all but dared me, and it is past time that Davena takes her place beside me."

"So, you're not here to kill Davena?"

Delphine yanked her hand from his grasp and smiled tightly. "No. However, I am prepared to use any incentive I can to...persuade...her to leave with me."

"You mean you're prepared to kill me and whoever else you need to," Beau guessed.

"I would so hate to end as fine a specimen as you are, Beau Chiasson, but if you don't help me I'll do just that *after* I make you watch while I kill your family. Including your sister."

Beau didn't think he could hate anyone as much as he did Delphine. There wasn't a doubt in his mind that Delphine wouldn't hesitate to do exactly as she claimed. "What do you want me to do?"

"Go to Davena. She wants a battle that I'd like to avoid."

"Can you blame her? She watched you kill her mother and sister, and she knows you killed her father."

Delphine threw back her head and laughed. "I didn't kill her father. That was done in retaliation after one of Babette's Hoodoo spells countering my hex failed. The woman's husband died, so she took Babette's."

"Why not come after you?"

"Everyone knows better."

Beau had come expecting to bargain for Davena's life. Instead, he was going to have to decide whether to convince Davena to go with Delphine to save his family.

Or sacrifice his family for her.

"Davena is at her house. You have a difficult choice," Delphine said as she stood and cupped his face. "I hope you make the right one, *mon cher*."

As one, the rest of the group rose and followed Delphine into the trees, leaving Beau alone. He didn't wait around to see if anyone would come back. He was halfway back to Kaplan when he saw his brothers waiting for him next to a fence. Beau didn't stop as he reached them. Delphine hadn't given him a time limit, but he didn't want to test her.

"So that was Delphine," Linc said as they fell into step beside him.

Beau gave a nod.

Vincent glanced at him. "We didn't get close enough to hear what she said, but she's stunning."

Christian let out a whistle in agreement. "If I didn't know how messed up she was in the head, I'd want her in my bed for a night."

"What did she want?" Lincoln asked.

Beau halted so quickly his brothers had taken several steps ahead of him. They stopped and turned to him. He looked at each of them, and his decision was made. "To make a long story short, Davena has Delphine's power. Babette couldn't have children, so she went to Delphine. The bargain was that one of the children would eventually take Delphine's place."

"Fuck, but that's messed up," Christian said.

Vincent smoothed back the hair in the queue at the base of his neck. "Agreed. So she's not here to kill Davena, but to bring her back to New Orleans?"

Beau grimly nodded. "It's why Babette was killed. Delphine came for Davena that night. She's known all along where the sisters have been."

"And Delia?" Christian asked. "Why kill her?"

"Delphine said Delia called her out, so to speak," Beau explained.

Fury laced Lincoln's face. "And no one can go against her."

"Exactly." Beau let out a long breath. "I have to convince Davena to go with her."

Christian grunted. "The hell you do."

"If I don't, she'll make me watch as all of you die, then she'll kill me."

Vincent's gaze caught his. "Our lives for Davena's."

"Essentially."

Christian shook his head and turned away. "Now do y'all understand why I'll never allow myself to be attached to a woman?"

"Shut up," Lincoln told Christian. He then turned his attention to Beau. "We're not defenseless. We can take care of ourselves."

"Not against the likes of her." Beau flattened his lips as he recalled something Davena had said the night before. "Davena said Delphine never lets something she wants go easily. She hasn't forgotten Ava or Jack, or what our cousins did to her."

Vincent let out a string of curses and began to pace. "They didn't capture her. She let them."

"That's my guess," Beau said.

Christian faced them again, his thumbs hooked in his belt loops. "What are you going to do?"

Beau looked to where his truck was parked, feeling helpless and furious. "I'm going to find Davena."

"We'll come with you," Lincoln said.

Beau stopped him with a hand on his shoulder. "Go home, Linc. You too, Vin. Go to your women. Christian, make sure they get there and stay there."

"You want us to just leave you?" Christian asked.

Beau glanced at the ground. "I don't trust Delphine. You all stand the best chance at the house. I'll feel better knowing all of you are there waiting for me."

"If you don't come home, I'm going to kick your ass," Vin said before dragging him close for a hug.

Beau smiled as Vincent pounded on his back and quickly released him. He said brief farewells to Christian and Lincoln, then headed to his truck.

CHAPTER
SEVENTEEN

Davena found Delia's bag sitting on the bed. Somehow, she knew that Marshall had brought the car back as well as Delia's things. She unzipped the bag and peeked inside. Sitting right on top was a journal. Delia had written in it occasionally during their six years together. It seemed wrong to look inside it, but Davena reached for it anyway.

To read something of her sister's, and have that one last connection, was too great to pass up. So Davena opened it and flipped through the pages chock full of Delia's handwriting. Emotion, thick and choking rose up in Davena when she found the last entry. Davena hastily swallowed and began to read.

September 3rd, Crowley

Davena still hasn't guessed what I have planned, and I'm so thankful for it. I have to do this for her. It's the only way she'll be able to stop looking over her shoulder. I'm hoping with everything that I learned from Mom, it will be enough to take on Delphine.

Even if it isn't, I can't sit back and do nothing anymore. I don't want to leave Davena, but I have to. She's all I have in the world, and it's time I stepped up as the eldest and took care of her as she's always taken care of me.

I just hope she forgives me for leaving. It's the only way I can carry out my plan. If she knows, she'll stop me, and I'm scared enough that I'd probably let her.

If she thinks I've left, it gives me the chance I need. And I know the perfect place to draw Delphine out. It's the animal clinic. It's near water, which will help strengthen what powers I have.

Besides, it's what Mom would've done.

Davena reread the passage three more times, each time more difficult than the last, bringing emotions she didn't want to feel because they frightened her so, overwhelmed her.

She jerked and nearly dropped the journal at the sound of a knock. Davena spun around and hastily walked into the living room. She glanced outside to see a silver truck.

"Beau," she whispered.

How had he found her? It didn't matter. He couldn't be there. She had to get rid of him quickly because he was her weakness.

Davena opened the door, the journal still in hand. His brilliant blue eyes locked on hers, and they held such understanding that a crack formed in the wall around her heart. Her vision swam as tears gathered and swiftly fell down her cheeks. There were no words as Beau stepped inside and drew her against him.

She clung to him, the tears she hadn't been able to shed the night before coming in a torrent. Davena couldn't have stopped them if she tried. All the years of barely surviving, living in fear, and pretending life was better than it was came pouring out.

Beau's strong arms lifted her up and carried her to the couch where he sat down and held her tight. Davena didn't know how long they sat in silence as he let her cry. Even when the tears had dried, she didn't move. She was drained, emotionally and mentally. He moved her hair out of her face and kissed her forehead.

"Marshall brought Delia's things," Davena said finally. "I found her journal."

"Ah," Beau murmured.

Davena squeezed her eyes closed as she felt more tears coming. "The last time we spoke, we argued."

"She loved you, and she knew you loved her. You were family. It's what families do."

"Delphine will come for me today. I don't want you near when it happens."

He took a deep breath and slowly released it. "I'm not leaving."

Davena sat up and looked at him. She sniffed and rubbed her nose that she knew had turned red as it always did when she cried. "I left the plantation to keep this away from you and your family."

"It doesn't matter. Delphine wants it otherwise."

Davena felt the room spin around her. "What?"

"First, I want you to know that I was coming for you regardless."

"Just say it," Davena said nervously. That gnawing, gaping feeling that threatened to swallow her whole was growing bigger by the second. She instinctively knew that whatever Beau was about to say was going to change her world—and not for the better.

He pulled her against him for a quick kiss, and then looked into her eyes. "Tell me you know I was coming for you."

"I knew you would try to find me," she conceded. It was who Beau was. She understood that, which is why she had prayed he wouldn't know where to find her.

His eyes briefly closed. "Delphine isn't coming to kill you, Davena. She's coming to claim you."

"I'm sorry. That sounded like you just said she wasn't going to kill me after she murdered my sister and my parents," Davena said as she slid off Beau's lap.

It bothered her more than she wanted to admit that he didn't try to keep her against him.

He sat forward and ran a hand down his weary face. "Delphine claims she didn't kill your father. She says that one of your mother's clients was seeking revenge when

Babette's counterspell against one of Delphine's hexes didn't work, and because she had lost her husband, she decided to take your mother's."

"And you believe her?"

"She has no reason to lie. She takes credit for every life she's taken."

Davena didn't think her legs could hold her much longer, and it was obvious the surprises were going to keep coming. "Why does she want me?"

"Your mother went to her when she couldn't get pregnant. Delphine agreed to help your mother conceive, but only with the understanding that one of the children would be Delphine's to train in Voodoo to take her spot as priestess one day. Delphine mixed her own power into the spell."

Davena thought of all the times Delphine had sought her out, whether to speak to her or just to watch her. Now she understood Delphine's interest. It sickened her that she was part of someone so evil and that her mother had agreed to such a thing just to have children.

Beau saw her sway, and was on his feet with his arms around her before her legs could give out. He sat her on the sofa beside him, holding her ice-cold hand in his.

On his way to see her, he had thought of a thousand different ways to tell her to go with Delphine in order to save his family. It was the right thing to do because everyone would remain alive.

Then he realized that Davena could be carrying his child. It had been a reckless thing they did, having unprotected sex, but he couldn't find any regret in anything he had done with Davena. The possibility of a child only brought to the forefront the reality that by sending Davena to Delphine, he was going against his family's code.

Then Davena had opened her door. He had seen the remorse and sadness in her spring green eyes, and it had firmed his resolve to help her. His family would take care of themselves. It was his duty to protect Davena at all costs—even if it meant his own life.

"My parents wanted a child so desperately they made a deal with Delphine? What kinds of people do that?"

He didn't know how to answer that because he'd never been in that position. "The fact is, your mother did it. The night your mother died, Delphine had come for you. Babette refused to give you up."

"So Delphine killed her," Davena said. "And nearly killed me and Delia."

"Delphine claims not to have known you were in there initially, but when she found out, she kept the fire from reaching you. She knew you and Delia escaped, but she let you go."

Davena gave a shake of her head. "Why would she do that?"

"She says to give you time, but I suspect there's more to it. She's always known where you were. Delphine was going to come for you soon, but Delia challenged her."

"I'm going to kill that bitch."

Beau gathered her other hand with the first and rubbed his thumb along her knuckles. "You have the power to face her, but I don't want you to."

Her gaze settled on him, anger clearing them of sorrow. "Why?"

"Because I don't want you to die. I care about you, Davena, even though I tried hard not to."

She looked down at their joined hands. "Delphine wanted you to talk me into going with her, didn't she?"

"Yes." Beau wasn't going to lie to her. If Davena was going to make a life-changing decision, she needed to know all there was to know. "I'm not going to though. There has to be another way."

Davena chuckled dryly and looked at him. "There's not. Delphine always gets what she wants. She wants me. If she doesn't get me, she'll kill me and everyone around..." She trailed off, her eyes going wide. "She threatened your family, didn't she?"

This was one thing he wanted to lie about. "It's what people like her do, but we're used to it. My brothers are readying themselves."

"And Ava and Olivia?"

"With my brothers. They're a lot safer than we are."

Davena frowned. "And your sister?"

Beau's gut twisted just thinking about it. He hadn't been able to get ahold of Riley, but he had left several messages. They had believed her safe in Austin, but with her being so far away from any family, there was no one there to help her.

"Oh, God," Davena whispered and hung her head. She sniffed loudly. "Delphine will keep killing unless I go with her. I've lost my sister. There's no reason for you to lose yours."

Beau cupped her face and lifted her chin to look into her eyes. Her golden mane of hair hung around her shoulders, and her eyelashes were still spiky from her tears. "You don't belong with Delphine."

"Your family has been so good to me." She reached up and put her hand atop his. "You protected me, but now it's my turn to protect you."

"Davena, no."

"I won't see you or your family hurt. You see, Beau Chiasson, I care about you, too."

He started to speak when his eyes all of a sudden grew heavy. No matter how he fought, he couldn't stop his lids from closing. That's when he knew Davena was using magic on him. He tried to call her name as his eyes closed.

DAVENA CAREFULLY LAID BEAU back on the couch. She stroked his face and the thick whiskers along his jaw. "I would've shared my life with you. I would have done anything for your love. Stay safe, Beau. You have a full life ahead of you continuing to save those in the parish."

She stood and picked up Delia's journal that had been dropped sometime during their conversation. Davena looked back at Beau sleeping so peacefully. He would be angry when he woke, but she had to do something.

If she hadn't, he would do something foolish like stand with her against Delphine, and she couldn't allow that. She loved him too much for that.

Fresh tears came as she realized that she did love him. Deeply, intently.

Totally.

It was that love that gave her the strength to walk from the house and face her nemesis. There was evil in the bayous, evil that wouldn't stop until she had what she came for.

Davena was going to give Delphine something unexpected, something the Voodoo priestess would never see coming.

EIGHTEEN

BEAU CAME AWAKE after a vicious slap to his face. He jerked upright, his fist swinging.

"Son of a bitch," he heard a male growl angrily.

Beau blinked several times, trying to get his eyes to focus. He was so tired he couldn't form a coherent thought. Somehow he got to his feet, knocking into something heavy, and lifted his fists.

"It might help if you opened your damn eyes."

He frowned because he recognized the voice. It took him a moment, but he finally placed it. Marshall Ducet. What was Marshall doing in Davena's house?

Davena.

Beau's eyes cracked open as clarity hit him like a tidal wave. He wouldn't have fallen asleep on his own. That meant Davena had put him in that state. "Where is she?"

"I don't know," Marshall said as he rubbed his jaw. "You've got a hell of a left hook, even for someone asleep."

Beau plopped back down onto the couch and gave his head a shake to clear it more. "I wasn't sleeping."

"Really? What do you call that?"

"Magic," Beau grumbled. "Why are you here?"

"After your call to find Davena's house, I thought you might want some help."

Right. Beau wasn't fooled. "Who called you?"

Marshall sighed loudly. "I was on my way here when Christian rang. It's a good thing I gave my number to everyone last night. Did Delphine get Davena?"

"No." It was much worse than that. "She went to Delphine so my family would be left alone."

Marshall rested his hand on the butt of his 9mm. "Brave girl."

"Foolish is more like it. We could've thought of something."

"She knows Delphine. Even I know better than to mess with the likes of Delphine."

Beau looked at his watch. "She's been gone about fifteen minutes. Did you see Davena on your way here?"

"No, but she'd likely stay off the roads for just such a thing."

"I know." Beau got to his feet and started for the door. "I've got to stop her."

"Have you ever thought that maybe she's doing the right thing?"

Beau halted with his hand on the doorknob. He looked over his shoulder at the deputy. "I know she's not. She's a good person who doesn't need to be anywhere near Delphine."

"Davena is old enough to make her own decisions."

"I'm not losing her!"

Beau looked away after his outburst and rested his forehead against the door. His nerves were stretched taut, his heart racing with dread and fear.

It was exactly the thing he had never wanted to experience. He'd known how easy it would be to fall for Davena, which is why he hadn't pursued her.

Fate, destiny, or whatever you wanted to call it had put her in his path regardless of what either of them wanted. There had been a part of him missing that he hadn't even realized until she was near and he felt whole. Then it was crystal clear that she was what was lacking.

How did he go through life knowing she was out of his reach? How could he face each day thinking about her learning all of Delphine's ways?

How could he survive without her in his arms?

"You love her."

Beau frowned. "I protect people."

"Especially someone you've fallen in love with," Marshall persisted.

"I know better than to fall in love with anyone."

Marshall chuckled, his boots sounding on the wood floor as he walked closer. "Good luck with that train of thought. Anyone with eyes can see the two of you have something special. Whether it's love now or not, it's extraordinary and shouldn't be carelessly tossed aside."

Beau straightened and looked at him. "I'm so scared of losing her that I don't know what to do."

"Yes you do." Marshall moved him aside and opened the door. "You've been doing this your whole life. You've known what to do this entire time."

Beau looked outside to see the sun shining bright. It seemed wrong to have such a beautiful day when everything was falling apart.

He could wallow in self-pity, or he could remember that he was a Chiasson. Marshall was right. He had been hunting since he was a small boy. The only thing different was that he was older and more experienced at hunting evil.

"I don't know if this will bleed over into the public. You need to get to town."

Marshall walked past him. "Nice try. I'm coming with you."

"The hell you are," Beau said as he stormed out of the house, slamming the door behind him.

"Your family isn't with you, and you're going to need backup."

"Not from someone that doesn't know what's going on."

"Don't forget I lived in New Orleans for years, Beau. I dealt with Delphine and all the other craziness like werewolves, vampires, and witches that abound in that city. I'm not a novice."

Beau looked to the sky for patience before he sighed. Marshall was going to go with him no matter what. Beau could use him to his advantage. "Fine, but you'll have to stay out of sight. If she gets wind that you're there, she'll kill you in an instant."

"I'm interested in living, so I'll stay hidden."

Beau walked to his truck. "I must be out of my mind."

"How do you know where Davena is?"

"I don't, but I know she'll get as far from the city and people as she can. That doesn't leave too many places."

Beau got into his truck and glanced in his rearview mirror to see Marshall already in his own car with the engine started. He started the truck and put it in gear.

"Hold on, Davena. I'm coming."

SWEAT RAN down Davena's face and back. Her thin, turquoise shirt was stuck to her, and her denim shorts only made her hotter. She was squinting painfully in the sun, and the hair sticking to her neck and face was making her itch.

But she ignored all of it as she concentrated on what was to come. If she did have some of Delphine's power within her, then that made her one of a handful who had the ability to stand against the priestess.

A desperate few had dared to stand against Delphine, and every one of them had died. Davena had expected death, but after what Beau imparted, she was willing to bet her very soul that Delphine wouldn't be so hasty to kill her.

Davena swiped at the tears that began. She hadn't been able to shed one yesterday, but today she couldn't stop. She cried for Delia, for the happiness she had found with Beau then lost, and the love she held for him that would never be fulfilled.

She continued walking through the pasture. Davena had lost count of the fences she had climbed over. She was getting further and further from the city, but there were still a few houses nearby.

She walked for another thirty minutes before she stopped and looked around. The nearest house was just a dot on the horizon, and only a few trees were scattered in the field.

Davena went to the nearest tree and sighed once she was under the shade. Now all she had to do was wait.

BEAU SPED down the back roads. He had already been to two of the five places Davena could have gone. The third was just up ahead. He slowed long enough to grab his binoculars and do a quick scan.

His lips flattened when he didn't see a sign of her. Beau tossed aside the binoculars and sped away. The knot he was accustomed to feeling was gone, leaving an empty void once more.

If he didn't find Davena, that emptiness would never be filled again. He would be vacant, hollow the rest of his days. That thought pushed him harder.

He stomped on the accelerator. Marshall was right behind him at all times. With two more spots to check, Beau had to decide which direction to go in when he came to a stop sign. He looked first one way and then the other. If he made the wrong decision, he could lose Davena forever.

Beau slammed his hand down on the steering wheel in frustration. "Come on!" he yelled at himself.

He had known Davena was in trouble, had known exactly where to go to help her. Now that she was in over her head he felt nothing.

"I have to find her," he said and closed his eyes.

It took three tries to clear his head of everything and focus on Davena. He thought of her courage, of the pure energy flowing through her. He thought of her lips and her cries of pleasure as he filled her.

Beau's eyes snapped open. He turned to the left and pushed the truck past a hundred for the next few miles. Then he turned off down a dirt road, his truck bouncing all over the place.

He slammed on the brakes, skidding to a stop when he came to an empty field. By the time he got out of his truck, Marshall was beside him, a rifle in hand. They met at the fence, each man looking over the terrain.

"She's here," Beau said.

Marshall checked the rifle. "There isn't much cover."

"Looks like you're going to have to do some crawling, deputy."

Marshall gave him a droll look. "Don't look so pleased with yourself."

"It might be character building."

"You sound like my drill sergeant."

"Military, huh? Which branch?" Beau asked.

Marshall loaded more bullets into the rifle and then slung the strap over his shoulder. "Marines. Where are you headed?"

"There," Beau said and motioned to a tree off in the distance.

Marshall put his hand atop the fence and leapt over it. "I'll come up on the side."

"Remember, stay hidden," Beau said. "Delphine has a big man with her. He'll most likely be hidden, but he's never far behind."

"I know him," Marshall stated and headed off at a run, bent low.

Beau watched him for a moment before he put both hands on the fence and jumped over it. He landed on the other side and took the most direct path to the tree.

He hadn't seen any sign of Davena, but he trusted his instincts. They hadn't led him wrong about her before. She was somewhere out there waiting for Delphine.

A glance to the right and Beau briefly caught sight of Marshall. He was moving quickly, covering twice as much ground. It gave Beau an idea.

He bent low and started jogging. If Davena saw him before he reached her, she would more than likely do something to stop him, and Beau wasn't going to allow that. He was there to help whether she wanted it or not.

The next time Beau looked for Marshall, he couldn't find the deputy. Beau hoped he was as good as he appeared, because it might well come down to Marshall killing Delphine to end all of this.

When Beau was halfway to the tree he stopped and dropped to his knees. The grass was tall enough to hide him, but wasn't nearly enough cover. He saw movement by the tree and recognized Davena.

The relief left him almost dizzy. He didn't allow himself to celebrate quite yet, though. Just as he was about to continue on, he caught sight of someone else walking toward Davena.

"Delphine," Beau muttered angrily.

CHAPTER

NINETEEN

DAVENA WAS STRANGELY CALM. The serenity that overtook her was almost unnerving. She couldn't pinpoint exactly when it occurred, but it was sometime during her walk that morning.

Perhaps it was because of the certainties she now knew. That she wouldn't let any harm come to Beau or his family. That she wasn't going anywhere with Delphine. That she was willing to die to stop Delphine.

Maybe it was because she felt the power flowing through her, a power she had pretended not to sense for years. That power was formidable and violent.

Whatever the reason, Davena was ready to face her nemesis. So when she caught sight of Delphine coming toward her, she simply closed her eyes and relaxed. She had to calm her mind, to find a place deep within herself to store all of her fears and hopes and dreams.

A place to put her time with Beau and the love that blossomed in her heart.

Because Delphine would use any means necessary to get what she wanted. She would try to hurt anyone connected with Davena, and Delphine would exploit her love for Beau.

Davena couldn't let words anger her or cause her to react quickly. She had to be completely withdrawn from everything and everyone. She had to overlook that her mother had been sliced before her eyes. She had to disregard that Delia had been murdered the day before. And she had to forget all about Beau.

Casting those sweet memories of Beau and the safety his arms provided aside was the hardest thing she had ever done. When the last one was tightly shut away, Davena continued to keep her eyes closed.

She could hear Delphine's steps now, knew she was close. Delphine might be powerful, but she was also predictable. She liked to see the fear in people's eyes. More importantly, she wanted Davena.

That was Delphine's weakness. It would be that weakness that Davena exploited as Delphine had exploited countless others.

Davena let several minutes tick by long after Delphine reached her. She knew the priestess was growing angry, and it was just what Davena wanted. She would be composed while Delphine was anything but.

When Davena finally opened her eyes, Delphine was standing about ten feet from her, just under the shade of the tree. She looked Delphine over in her all-white clothes and couldn't figure out what she had been so afraid of for all those years.

"So," Delphine said in her husky voice. "Beau convinced you. I wondered if he would choose his family or you. Looks like his family means more to him."

Davena remained sitting against the tree as if she weren't facing a powerful Voodoo priestess. "He told me everything."

"Everything? Yes, I suppose he did. Why else would you be here but to protect him?"

Davena smiled. Next, Delphine would threaten Beau if she didn't immediately return to New Orleans with her. Time to shake things up a bit. "I'm here because he told me I have some of you within me."

There was a beat of silence, and a pleased look filled Delphine's black eyes. "That you do, *mon cher*. Without my power and magic, you wouldn't be here now."

"True. I have you to thank, then."

Delphine's eyes narrowed a fraction. "Appreciation? This I didn't expect."

"I'm alive because of you." Davena used the tree and got to her feet. "Did you think I'd be angry because you killed my mother and sister?"

"Yes."

Davena bit back a grin. "I'm not angry. I see now that you were clearing my path so I would see nothing but you."

"Is that so?"

"Yes."

Delphine threw back her head and laughed. "Oh, Davena, you have more of me than I realized. You might have your mother's coloring and your father's eyes, but the rest of you is all me. If I'd known, I'd have taken you when you were just a child."

A thread of fury began to grow, but Davena quickly stamped it out. "Why not have children of your own? Why give me what could have passed to your own child?"

"My ability to have children was taken from me when I was too young to even know what was going on. Do you remember the name Lisette?"

"I know that name well. She was the priestess before you."

"Yes, and she took my ability to have children into herself."

This was a story Davena had never heard. "Why not take it back?"

"That wasn't possible, but I got my revenge."

Davena could well imagine how, but Delphine would expect her to ask nonetheless. "How?"

"I waited until Lisette was in the middle of labor with her third child. I had been brought in to help, along with two others. When it was close to the babe arriving, I brought in her two other children, both girls, and slit their throats as she watched. The women with me held down Lisette's hands as I cut her stomach and pulled the babe from her womb."

"You killed the babe then," Davena guessed.

Delphine's smile grew. "I did. Lisette grew enraged and tried to curse me, but I killed her before she could complete the spell."

"And then you took over."

"I was the youngest priestess ever in New Orleans."

Davena looked away. "You got your revenge and the throne, so to speak. I wouldn't think you'd be giving up your position as priestess anytime soon."

"I won't, but you need to be there to learn from me. The others need to see you, as well."

"You have no intention of turning over your position."

"Of course not. However, to keep others from stepping out of place, I need to pacify them, which means you'll come home with me."

"And if I'm not ready to go to New Orleans yet?" She wasn't about to tell Delphine that she would never return with her.

Delphine's eyes hardened a fraction. "You've had your time, Davena. I gave you all those years as you grew up. These past six you should've been by my side."

"Yeah, about that," she said and smoothed back her hair.

"If you knew where I was at all times, why didn't you come and get me?"

Delphine hesitated a moment too long.

It was Davena's turn to smile. "Ah. You don't want me there, but you've spoken about me to all of your followers for so long that they want me in New Orleans now. You think I'm going to kill you, as you did Lisette, and take over."

"You don't have enough power for that yet."

"Yet," Davena repeated. "And you'll make sure I'm never quite there. You'll keep me under your thumb, to prove to your followers that they need you and only you. Tell me, can you live forever?"

Delphine took a step closer. "I can live far longer than you think."

"I believe you can do a great many things. You kill easily enough, and you are quick to curse and hex anyone you feel might be plotting against you. It must be exhausting."

Davena saw movement behind Delphine and spotted another form in all white. As he drew closer, Davena noticed the man was not only tall, but also hulking.

"That would be Joseph," Delphine said. "He is always near."

Davena still had a few moments alone with Delphine. "What's your plan?"

"You'll come with me, or I'll kill Beau."

"Beau was certainly a nice way to pass the time."

Delphine's head cocked to the side as she asked, "You really think I'll fall for that?"

"If you've watched me all these years, how many times have I ever let a man close? How many have I dated for more than one night?"

"None," she answered sullenly.

"Beau Chiasson is no different from any of the others."

BEAU HATED the uncertainty he felt at Davena's words. He didn't know if she had played him, or if she was pulling one over on Delphine, and he was likely never to know.

He had managed to sneak up close enough before Delphine arrived. Davena had been so intent on her that she hadn't realized he was crawling close enough to the tree to hear her breathing.

The Davena he listened to was in complete control. There was little emotion coming through her voice, and though he couldn't see her from his position, he could only imagine she looked just as calm as she sounded.

"He believes otherwise," Delphine said. "He loves you."

Beau ignored the bite of fire ants on his hand. With one swipe, he raked them off and shifted out of the ant pile while he waited for Davena's response.

"Beau has no such interest in me. It was his way of attempting to allow me time to leave the area. He is dedicated to wiping the parish of people like us. He wants me gone, and you with me."

"You're lying." Delphine finished it off with a small chuckle. "It's so obvious that it's painful."

Beau wasn't sure what Davena's plan was, but he was going to be ready for anything.

"What's painful is you looking for a way to hurt me. You've already done it," Davena said in a soft voice. "You killed my mother and sister. There's no one left for you to threaten."

"I can kill every Chiasson with just a thought."

"Do it," Davena pressed. "All you'll do is send more hunters after you."

Delphine cackled. "You mean the LaRues? They're at my mercy. They may want me dead, but they'll never succeed."

Beau couldn't wait to share the information with his cousins. They would be curious to know that Delphine thought them nothing more than a nuisance.

"Let me save us both some time. You don't want me in New Orleans, and I don't want to be there."

"You're coming with me," Delphine said, and fire rose in a roaring circle around the tree, the flames singeing the branches.

Beau ground his teeth together and stood so that his back was against the tree. The heat from the fire caused him to sweat more. The sweat fell into his eyes, stinging them until they watered.

"Kill me. I don't care," Davena said. "Perhaps I can hurry things along and take you with me."

No sooner had the words left her mouth than the whistle of wind swooped in. The wind swept the flames horizontally until there was a wall of fire spinning around them and rising higher than the tree.

There was no way Marshall would be able to help him now. Regardless, he had to try and kill Delphine. He just hoped Joseph wasn't inside the fire circle with them.

"Impressive," Delphine said.

"If I was trying to impress you, I'd have killed you." Davena moved, stepping on a pinecone.

"Then why the wind and this remarkable wind fire?"

Beau peeked around the tree to see Davena cross her arms over her chest.

"To show you that I have nothing else to lose," Davena replied.

"Is that right?" Delphine asked succinctly.

Beau pressed back against the tree as smoke surrounded him, alive, just as it had been in his dream. It wound around his feet and continued up his legs.

"I'm killing every Chiasson as we're standing here," Delphine continued.

"Lies."

"Is it?"

Beau could stand there and be smothered to death, or he could take his chance while he had it. He shifted, pushing against the smoke, withdrew one of the throwing knives from the belt at his waist, and took aim. The smoke was up to his chest now and moving faster.

If Delphine was right and there was smoke attacking the rest of his family, then everything rested with him. He took a deep breath to block the smoke that was now at his face. He let the knife fly, the blade spinning end over end as it headed toward Delphine.

He fell, the smoke knocking him sideways from behind the tree as he threw a second knife. Delphine used her power to knock the blade meant for her away, but she wasn't able to stop the second, which embedded in Joseph's neck.

The big male fell backwards into the flames, his body engulfed instantly.

Delphine jerked her head to Beau, her eyes filled with hatred.

He glanced at Davena to see her examining the scar on her palm. Just as he thought he might be fighting Delphine alone, Davena's green eyes met his and she winked.

CHAPTER

TWENTY

DAVENA COULDN'T BELIEVE that Beau was there. Her spell should've kept him asleep until just a few minutes ago. Long enough for her to get far enough away that he'd never know where to look.

She was also furious that he was there. The shock at seeing the blade come out of seemingly nowhere had kept her still. Then Beau had appeared. It had been almost comical watching Delphine easily bat away the knife, unaware that a second had been thrown at Joseph.

"I'll kill you for that," Delphine said menacingly to Beau.

That's when Davena saw the smoke covering him. From somewhere in her mind, the spell to stop it appeared. She quickly said the words and watched as it was sucked back into the wall of flames.

Beau sucked in huge mouthfuls of air as he hurriedly

climbed to his feet. Davena reached for one of her hidden knives and stepped between Delphine and Beau, her gaze locked on the priestess. "No, you won't. You're going to leave, and you're going to forget about this parish and everyone in it—including me."

"Not likely, *mon cher*."

"One last chance, Delphine. Leave."

The priestess laughed, a red haze flaring in her eyes. Davena was knocked out of the way as a flash of flames came at her from the circle. She blinked and looked down at Beau. He had been the one to pull her aside, taking the fall as he did. Davena didn't have time to thank him or look for the knife that had been knocked out of her hand. She had to prove her point before they both died.

Davena got to her feet and confronted Delphine. "I did warn you."

"You can't compare to me," Delphine said with an evil grin.

Words filled Davena's mind—Hoodoo and Voodoo alike. It was the knowledge of her mother and the power of Delphine working and mixing together, mingling and blending to form a new power until Davena's entire body hummed with it.

All the while, Delphine was working her own magic, but it couldn't match what was inside Davena. A smile pulled at her lips because she knew she could kill Delphine with merely a thought.

"I'm not a killer," Davena said, more to herself than Delphine.

The priestess smiled coldly. "That's why you're going to lose."

Davena cocked her head, and with a wave of her hand had Delphine hanging in midair. She thought it might be enough to stop whatever Delphine had in mind.

She should've known better.

Beau let out a bellow, his hands on his head as he fell to his knees. The look of excruciating pain on his face was almost enough for her to kill Delphine right then. If she did, how would she ever be able to look at herself in the mirror again, much less face Beau?

Davena turned back to Delphine to see the triumph in her eyes. "Enough."

"No!" Delphine bellowed.

It was the last straw for Davena. She moved Delphine back until the edge of her skirt touched the fire circle. Davena kept the fire from consuming Delphine's clothes, but only just.

Delphine's gaze jerked to her, comprehension dawning that Davena wasn't just a match for her, but more powerful as well. Several seconds ticked by before Beau fell forward on all fours, his head hanging and his breathing coming in great gasps.

Eventually, he looked up and gave a nod. Relief filled her so quickly Davena grew lightheaded. She pulled Delphine away from the fire and extinguished the flames on her skirt, but she kept her hanging in midair.

Beau slowly stood and came to stand beside her. Davena used that time to stop the wind and put out the fire altogether.

She walked closer to Delphine, her chin lifted. "You have two choices. You can push me one more time, in which case I will kill you. You know I have the power to do it."

"And the second?" Delphine asked tightly.

"Leave. Joseph is dead. There's no one to know what really happened other than you. Tell them I'm dead. Tell them I don't have any power. I don't care what you say, but let them know that I will never come to take your place. I make my own destiny."

Delphine's black eyes slid to Beau. "With him?"

"With myself," Davena said. "No more running, no more being afraid. Make your choice, Delphine."

The priestess composed herself, the red fading from her eyes. "I will return to New Orleans."

Davena lowered Delphine back to the ground. She started to walk away when Davena called her name.

"One more thing," Davena said as she moved to stand nose-to-nose with the priestess. "Your anger is with me. Not with the Chiassons, and certainly not with the LaRues or anyone connected with either family. If any of them die under mysterious circumstances or has a curse put on them, I'll be coming for you. I will destroy you and your followers without a second thought or bothering to ask if it was you. Do you understand?"

Fury blazed in Delphine's gaze. "Perfectly."

Davena stepped back and let the priestess walk away. She remained prepared in case Delphine tried anything, and she stayed that way until the priestess was out of sight.

Then Davena sagged against the tree, Beau's arms coming around her to hold her up. She was afraid to look at him, afraid to know that he believed everything she had said to Delphine.

"That was...incredibly sexy," Beau said.

It was so unexpected that a laugh bubbled from Davena. She looked up at him, her throat clogging with emotion when she gazed into his bright blue eyes. "You were here the entire time?"

"Most of it. I arrived before Delphine and hid behind the tree. You were too focused on Delphine to notice."

"Beau, what I said—"

He nodded and interrupted her by saying, "I know."

"You do?"

His smile was slow and heart stopping. "I know you, Davena. I know you care about people and family. I knew you would go as far from the town as you could. And...I know you love me."

She was so stunned that she could only stare blankly at him. How did he know? She hadn't said anything to him about it.

Davena's mind halted when his hand slid to the back of her head and he took her lips in a sensual, savage kiss. Safely ensconced in Beau's embrace, she wrapped her arms around his neck and returned the kiss with fervor.

A new beginning had started for her, one with infinite possibilities.

Someone cleared their throat, breaking them apart. She looked away as soon as her gaze landed on Marshall. Beau chuckled as the two shared smiles.

"You brought Marshall?" Davena asked in surprise.

Marshall grunted, though his smile was wide. "I didn't give him a choice, not that I did much good. That wall of fire thing kept me from seeing anything."

Davena had thought no one would see what she could do. She didn't want to be known as the freak of town. She tried to turn away, but Beau held her still.

"Don't hide what you are." Beau's tone was serious, as was the look on his face.

Marshall slung the rifle over his shoulder. "He's right, Davena. Embrace who you are because I think you'll find you fit in well here."

"As do you, deputy," she said with a grin.

Marshall gave a tip of his hat and turned on his heel. They watched him walk back to his car.

"So," Beau said. "Do you have plans for the night?"

She gave a shake of her head. "No, I'm free."

"What about the rest of your life?"

Davena bit her lip. "You barely know anything about me."

"We're going to remedy that starting tonight. You love me, remember?"

"I do." She licked her lips, suddenly incredibly nervous. Her courage came from the knowledge that Beau wouldn't still be beside her if he didn't care for her, as well. "What about you?"

His eyes twinkled with merriment. "What about me?"

"You know my feelings, but I don't know yours."

"Don't you," he whispered and pulled her tightly against him. "I've not hidden them from our first meeting. I can't, not when it comes to you."

She ran her fingers through his long hair and kissed him. "I've not had any kind of relationship in six years."

"Then we'll take it slow," he whispered. "You get to choose. Just promise you'll never leave. I need you, Davena. I love you."

"And I love you. I don't want to ever be without you."

"I'm a hunter. I'm gone most nights fighting evil."

Davena's heart swelled as she realized what a great man she had. "I'm very good at fighting evil myself, you know."

"Do I ever," he growled and turned them so he had her pinned against the tree.

EPILOGUE

One day later...

BEAU SLAMMED the truck door on Vincent and took Davena's hand. She was laughing along with Ava and Olivia.

"What?" Vincent said as he opened the door and got out of the truck. "All I said was that there was room enough in the house for everyone."

Christian groaned loudly. "For the love of God, Vin, let it go. Everyone wants their privacy, me included. I can't exactly walk around naked anymore."

"See?" Beau said with a hand out toward Christian as he looked between Vincent and Lincoln. "That right there. Yes, the house is plenty big enough, but there's no reason we all have to stay together."

Lincoln was laughing as he held up his hands for

everyone to stop walking and quiet down. "All right. I see both sides. Vincent, you want everyone here, and I see that. However, I also understand Christian's and Beau's sides. They were going to talk to us about moving out before Davena came into the picture, so it's nothing new."

"Riiight," Vincent said grumpily. "You all are ganging up on me. Olivia, are you still on my side?"

"Babe, I'm always on your side." She leaned up to kiss his cheek. "But I think everyone should get to choose."

Ava nodded quickly. "I agree with Olivia."

Vincent threw up his hands in defeat. "Wonderful."

"Wait," Lincoln said. "I wasn't finished."

Christian blew out a frustrated breath.

Lincoln threw him a nasty look. "I get that everyone needs their own space, but I agree with Vincent that everyone should stay here."

Beau laughed and looked down at Davena who wore a bright smile.

"Honey," Ava said. "I hate to tell you this, but that doesn't solve anything."

Lincoln pulled her against his side and slapped her on the ass. "If I could finish."

"By all means," Christian said cantankerously.

"There is plenty of land. Who says we can't build our own homes?" Lincoln suggested.

It was such a good idea that everyone looked around

waiting for an argument. When none was made, Lincoln took a bow. "Thank you, thank you. I'm here all the time."

Christian slapped him on the back of the head. "Jerk off."

Laughter ensued as Lincoln chased Christian around to the back of the house. Everyone else followed in time to see Lincoln tackle him to the ground, then sit on top of him, his hands in the air.

Ava let out a long whistle and clapped. "Yay, baby!"

Beau stopped and frowned. "Do you smell that?"

"Smell what?" Olivia asked as she and Vincent halted beside him.

Davena sniffed the air. "It smells like apple pie."

"It does," Vincent agreed. He looked down at Olivia. "Is Maria here?"

Olivia was shaking her head even as Beau walked through the porch to the back door. Davena was right beside him, and the others were on his heels. He threw open the door and everyone piled into the kitchen.

A whirl of long, dark waves turned and smiled in welcome. "I made Momma's apple pie."

"Riley," Beau said with a shake of his head, but a smile nonetheless.

The shit storm was about to rain down for sure.

A CHIASSON NOVEL

WILD
FLAME
DONNA GRANT
NEW YORK TIMES BESTSELLING AUTHOR

CHAPTER

ONE

September

Nights off were one of his simple pleasures. Christian blew out a breath as he put his truck in park and got out. He looked at the sign on the building that read "Joel's Place."

Normally, he would spend his night off at home, but since the house he shared with his three brothers also had their women, he preferred some time alone.

Christian walked to the bar and opened the door. He was immediately blasted with music and laughter. Stepping inside, he let his gaze wander the place. It might be his night off, but he was a Chiasson, which meant he was always working, since the supernatural never took a day off.

He made his way to the bar and ordered a beer as he continued to survey the people. Ghosts, demons, vampires, witches, werewolves. If they preyed on the innocent, then the Chiassons hunted—and killed—them.

His family had been protecting the parish for generations, and thanks to his brothers finding love, that would continue.

Christian's thoughts went to his sister. Riley. She was the one who was supposed to get out of the life. It's why he and his brothers all agreed to send her away to college.

But they should've paid more attention when she called. Riley was a Chiasson to the core. Stubborn, independent, and determined. She was no longer in Austin, Texas. That fact worried Christian as nothing else could. Riley was smart, strong, and beautiful, but she also had a habit of being at the wrong place at the wrong time.

Their family had enemies. Enemies who had already tried to kill them.

"Hey?" Sherriff Marshall Ducet said as he took the seat next to Christian.

Christian nodded in greeting. "You really come here often?"

"Yeah." Marshall looked around and shrugged. "It's a nice place. No...unwanteds here."

Marshall was a transplant from New Orleans. He left the city to get away from the supernatural, only to land smack in the middle of one of the places in North America that they flocked to.

"Plenty of pretty women," Marshall said, wiggling his eyebrows.

Christian glanced at two women shooting pool who kept eyeing him. They were attractive. Either one would do nicely as his bed partner for the night.

Emphasis on *the night*. Unlike Vincent, Lincoln, and Beau, Christian would do whatever it took to ensure he didn't fall in love.

Ever.

"One for each of us," Marshall said.

Christian snorted. "Find your own. Those two are mine."

"You're a braver man than I if you want to take two women into your bed."

"What's the matter, Marshall? Worried you couldn't please both of them?" Christian asked as he turned his head back to the sheriff.

That's when his gaze was snagged on a vision with pale brown curls that fell past her shoulders. She was wearing a white shirt that showed off her warm copper-brown skin, dipping low enough in the front to get a glimpse of cleavage.

Christian leaned to the side to see her faded jeans and cowboy boots. She waved at someone. Christian quickly followed her line of sight and saw one of the bartenders, the female, return the wave.

Curls smiled, her face lighting up as she walked to a barstool and sat at the corner, giving Christian a perfect view of her.

His body responded instantly, causing his balls to tighten in need. Christian brought his beer to his lips and drank deeply as he took in her oval face and large eyes. The dim lighting of the bar prevented him from seeing the exact shade of her eyes, however.

With her full lips, delicate jaw, stubborn chin, and slender neck, Curls wasn't just pretty—she was intriguing.

"Ah, I see someone has caught your eye," Marshall said.

Christian pulled his gaze away from the woman. "Just checking things out."

"Right. Adding another to your stable?"

Curls was the kind of woman he would want all to himself. No sharing there. "Yep."

Marshall snorted. "Want to play a game of pool?"

"Sure." Christian took another drink of beer and spun around on the stool to follow Marshall.

Marshall racked the balls while Christian set aside his beer and grabbed a cue stick. It was fate that brought Marshall into their lives, but Christian was glad they had someone they could trust in a seat of power.

Few people of the parish actually knew what the Chiassons did, but there were some that joined in a hunt when needed. Though the majority didn't have a clue that his family had saved their hides on multiple occasions, they seemed to realize the Chiassons were dangerous.

Dangerous didn't even begin to cover what they were. What kind of man brought a woman into such a family and the constant threat of death? His brothers might be willing to do it, but not him.

He remembered all too well his mother's murder and his father's death that night all those years ago. It was enough to ensure that Christian remained alone. There was little time to protect everyone. Why would he add a wife and children into the mix?

Only an idiot would do that.

His brothers, obviously, were idiots.

"Any word on Riley?" Marshal asked as he leaned over the pool table to line up his shot.

Christian waited until Marshall broke the balls and two solids went into the hole. "She checked in, but she won't tell us where she's at."

"I can find her."

Christian was tempted to take him up on the offer. He wasn't comfortable not knowing where Riley was, but she was a grown woman. She also knew how to take care of herself. "Not yet. It may come to that."

"She's not with anyone is she?" Marshall asked right before he took his next shot.

Christian narrowed his gaze on the sheriff. "I might like you, Marshall, and that's the only reason I'll give you this one warning to stay away from my sister."

Marshall straightened, grinning, his eyes crinkled at the corners. "Worried she might like me?"

"Yep. Then I'd have to kill you." Christian knew how

beautiful his sister was, but their reputation kept the boys away from her while she still lived in Lyons Point.

Christian didn't want to think about what she had been doing while away. He closed his eyes to try and block out the mental image, but it was already there.

"You could try," Marshall said and ran a hand through his hair.

Christian opened his eyes to stare at the green felt of the pool table. He looked at the balls and bent to line up his shot. That's when his gaze lifted to the bar and Curls.

She had a drink in hand. It wasn't some frilly mixed drink, nor was it a beer. If he had to guess by the glass and color, it was bourbon. Not a drink he expected to see in Curls's hand.

Christian returned his concentration to the pool table. He lined up his cue with the ball and took his shot. The same time Curls laughed. The sound went straight to his cock, causing him to jerk his cue stick right as it made contact with the ball.

He straightened as none of his balls went into pockets. Then he lifted his gaze to Curls and listened to more of her laughter.

Marshall clapped him on the back and leaned in to whisper, "I'm liking your distraction."

No matter how many times Christian tried to concentrate on the game, Curls pulled him away time and again. Three games later, it was obvious he was distracted, since he lost a hundred and fifty dollars to Marshall.

It was after one in the morning, and if Curls hadn't been there, Christian would've already found a bed partner for the night.

But Curls was there.

"Want to go another round?" Marshall asked, laughing.

Christian cut him a dark look. "You've taken enough of my money for the night."

Marshall put away the cue sticks. "Just go talk to her."

"No."

"Why?" he asked in surprise. "You're obviously attracted to her."

Christian raised his beer to Marshall. "Bingo."

They moved back to the bar when others lined up to play pool.

Marshall had a confused look on his face. "Explain this to me. You were ready to bed those two girls earlier—who left disappointed, by the way. But not this one?"

"You're on a roll tonight, Sheriff. Tell me, are you a detective or something?" Christian asked sarcastically.

It was Marshall's turn to glare. "Seriously, Christian. I don't get it."

Christian peeled the label from the beer bottle. "You know what we do. You know the hazards we face daily."

"I do," Marshall agreed with a nod.

"It's a matter of time before one of those monsters get us. My brothers are the biggest kinds of dimwitted fools for bringing the women they love into this messed up life we lead."

Marshall was quiet for a moment. "Your line has to continue."

"Fortunately, it will. Between Vin, Linc, and Beau, I've no doubt there will be many little Chiassons running around soon."

"Riley as well."

Christian shook his head. "Nope. We got her out of this life early enough so that she could lead a normal one. No doubt she'll have children, but they won't be fighting monsters like us."

"You want to be alone?"

Want had nothing to do with it. It was all for his sanity. Christian knew himself well enough to know that if the right kind of woman came along, he would fall in love with her.

He also knew that if he ever did fall in love, if he lost her, it would kill him. He wasn't just saving this unknown woman from a worry-filled life, but himself as well.

"In a house with six people? How the hell can I ever be alone?" Christian joked.

But Marshall didn't smile. "It's not a way to live."

Christian let his fake grin fade. "It's the only way I'm going to."

"Do your brothers know?"

"Yeah. They aren't happy about it, but they've come to terms with it."

Marshall finished his beer and pushed the empty bottle away. "That's messed up on so many levels. I'll see you tomorrow night."

"You're coming out?"

Marshall slid off the stool. "Beau asked if I wanted to help out. If I'm going to live here, I need to know everything."

Christian waved as Marshall walked off. Then his gaze returned to Curls. She was finishing her drink. He watched as she paid and leaned over the bar to hug her friend. Then she was gone.

It was everything Christian could do not to go after her. He was going to make damn sure never to come back to Joel's Place again. Not when there was a chance Curls could be there.

Christian remained for another fifteen minutes, finishing his beer. He declined the offer of a leggy blond and decided to head home.

He walked out of the bar. Christian didn't get halfway to his truck when he caught sight of pale brown curls in the moonlight.

CHAPTER
TWO

"Really?" Ivy Pierce said as she stared at her flat tire.

She had known stopping in at the bar for a drink after work was a bad idea, but Stacy wouldn't accept no for an answer. It wasn't that she didn't have a good time when she was with Stacy, but her friend usually was trying to set her up with some guy.

At least this time Stacy was content with just talk. Ivy shook her head at the tire. The only thing that had gone right the entire week had been her visit with Stacy.

If something could go wrong, it did. Often. This was her second flat in three days. From her air conditioning going out, to breaking her grandmother's dish, to losing her favorite earrings.

She opened her truck and went to get the jack in the

backseat when she remembered her other tire was still being repaired, which meant the spare was already in use.

"Just great," she mumbled.

She was going to have to wait for Stacy to get off work and give her a ride home. Ivy was turning to go back in the bar when dogs began barking behind her. She jumped, whirling around because it had sounded like they were racing toward her.

"Is there a problem?" asked a deep, incredibly sexy voice behind her.

Startled a second time, Ivy turned, her hand on her throat. The man was tall and muscular, based on the fit of his shirt on his arms. But his face was in shadow. She took a step back.

"Forgive me," he said and shifted so that the light on the side of the building shown on his face. "Everything all right?"

Ivy stared at him a full minute, taking in his short dark hair and startlingly handsome face. If you liked the rugged look, which she just discovered she very much did.

She swallowed, recalling that he had asked her two questions. "I've got a flat."

"I can fix it, if you'd like," he offered.

Ivy blew out a frustrated breath. "I fixed the first flat two days ago. The spare is already in use, unfortunately."

"I see." He looked around, a frown forming when the

dogs started barking again. "Two flats so soon? You run over glass or something?"

"No. It's been the week from hell. Everything is going wrong."

"I'm Christian, by the way."

She smiled, unable to help flirting. "I'm Ivy."

"Well, Ivy, you're in a jam. Why don't I call a tow truck for you?"

"No," she said hastily. Too hastily, by his confused look. She licked her lips. "I'll be fine."

"Out here by yourself?"

"I've got a friend coming to help," she lied.

He nodded, looking off in the distance when the barking began again—closer this time. "That's good. When are they coming?"

"In a bit."

"That's not going to be soon enough, Ivy."

She took another step away from him. Then she heard a dog snarl behind her. Ivy turned around, but there was nothing there.

Suddenly, she was yanked against a wall of muscle and turned so that she was pinned between Christian and her car. She could hear the growls and barking of the dogs, but she couldn't see them.

Christian threw something that looked like dirt in the air, and the night went deathly quiet.

"Okay, Ivy, here's the deal. We're going to run to my

truck. It's the gray one parked three away from yours. Get in on the driver's side and scoot over. We're not going to have a lot of time."

"I don't understand."

"I'll explain later," he said in a rush. "Run!"

Ivy scooted away and turned to run. She cut the corner of her car too quickly and jammed her knee into the bumper. Her foot slipped, but she managed to catch herself before she fell.

She heard Christian behind her as well as the jingle of keys. The lights of a dark gray truck flickered as he unlocked the doors. She ran as fast as she could to the door and jerked it open.

"Get in!" Christian bellowed as she struggled to climb in the vehicle and get into the passenger seat.

She fell forward, slamming her face into the passenger door when Christian jumped into the truck and shut the door. Ivy sat up while trying to calm her breathing and her heart.

Something rammed into her side of the truck. She whirled her head around to the window and saw something fogging it up, its breath was so close.

Christian fired up the engine and quickly drove away. Ivy's hands were shaking as she attempted to put on her seatbelt. It took her several tries before it was finally buckled.

She stared straight ahead, her heart hammering in her chest so hard she expected it to burst at any moment.

"Are you all right?" Christian asked as he sped down the roads. "Are you bit? Scratched?"

"N...no," she stammered.

"I didn't figure you for one to make a deal."

She blinked and slowly turned her head to him. "Excuse me?"

"A deal with a Crossroads demon."

"What are you talking about? A Crossroads demon?"

Christian glanced at her, his expression blank by the faint glow from the truck's dashboard lights. "You don't have to lie to me. I'm a Chiasson."

"And I'm a Pierce. What has that to do with anything?"

The night was turning more and more confusing by the minute. Ivy just wanted in her favorite PJs and to sit on the couch catching up on episodes of *Game of Thrones*.

"I want to go home. Pull over, please."

Christian shook his head as he sped up. "I can't do that. As soon as I pull over, those Hell Hounds will be back. I doubt you'll get away a second time."

Hell Hounds? Crossroads demons? Was this some kind of sick joke?

Ivy quietly unzipped her purse on her shoulder and wrapped her hand around the butt of her gun. "Pull over."

"There's only one place that's safe for you. As soon as we get there, I'll explain everything."

"You'll stop now." To make him see she was serious, Ivy drew her weapon.

Christian glanced at her. Then did a double take when he saw the gun. His lips flattened into a line as he began to slow the truck.

Ivy knew the times she went to the gun range would pay off. In the cruel, vicious world it was inevitable that someone, somewhere would try to take advantage of her. But she was prepared.

Tires squealed as Christian jerked the wheel, turning them to the right and tossing her against the center console. She screamed in outrage—and surprise.

Then she heard the dogs barking again.

Christian drove like a bat out of hell down the dirt road. The night was too dark to see anything other than what the headlights showed, which was nothing but grass on either side of them.

"Hold on. This isn't going to be pretty or smooth," Christian said tightly.

The first bump jarred Ivy so much that she nearly lost the hold on her gun. She quickly shoved it back in her purse and grabbed hold of anything she could to keep from hitting the top of the truck as they bounced along.

"You left the road!" she hollered.

Christian was entirely focused on the path in front of them. "Had to," was all he said.

Ivy opened her mouth to warn him of the huge hole right before the passenger side went in. Her teeth slammed shut with the force of the hit. The truck lurched, causing her head to slam up against the window.

"Oww," she mumbled.

There was no more barking, but Christian didn't slow. He drove like he was on a racetrack and their lives depended upon winning.

All Ivy knew was that she felt a measure of relief now that the barking had stopped once more. She spotted a row of crepe myrtles lining a driveway as Christian swerved onto the drive.

When a large white plantation house came into view, Ivy assumed he would slow. He sped up instead. Words lodged in Ivy's throat when she saw the front door open and a man and woman step out.

Christian slammed on the brakes, jerking the wheel once more so that the passenger side of the truck slid toward the porch.

"Get out!" Christian ordered.

The door was thrown open by a man who grabbed her arm and yanked her out. She was unceremoniously tossed onto the porch where a woman with beautiful long blonde hair helped steady her.

"Are you all right?" the woman asked.

Before Ivy could answer, the barking started again.

"Shit," Christian said as he jumped from the truck onto the porch.

The man looked from Christian to her. "What the hell is going on?"

"She claims to know nothing," Christian told him.

Ivy had had enough. She stepped away from the three of them and reached her hand into her purse again. "I don't know what is wrong with all of y'all, but I'm done being scared. I'm through with being tossed about like a bag of potatoes. I'm leaving."

"If you do, you die," Christian said calmly. He faced her and held up his hands. "We can help, Ivy."

The man glowered at Christian. "The hell we can. She knew what she was getting into."

"I don't think she did."

The porch light came on and Ivy got a look at the man. He looked so similar to Christian that it was obvious they were brothers. They had the same coal-black hair, the same build, and the same angry looks that they were throwing each other.

"Hold up, Beau," the blonde woman said. "Listen to Christian first." She turned to Ivy. "My name is Davena."

The front door opened again, followed by the screen door. A woman with long black hair poked her head out. She looked at each of them and walked out onto the porch.

Christian turned so that he was in profile to her so he could talk to his brother. "If she knew, wouldn't she have run?"

"That's what they all do," Beau said.

"She didn't," Christian said and threw a thumb over his shoulder toward her. "She had no idea what they were."

Ivy felt as if her life was unraveling. "Look, I'm not asking for anyone's help."

"But I think you need it," Davena said.

Christian glanced at her. "I believe her, Beau."

"There's only one way the Hell Hounds would come for her," Beau said. "She made a deal, and it's time to pay up with her soul."

Ivy choked. Soul. Did he just say soul? First Crossroads demons, Hell Hounds, and now payment with her soul. Had she stepped into the Twilight Zone?

Christian walked to her and gently grabbed her shoulders. He looked down at her with eyes so bright, so vivid blue she became lost in them. "Ivy, did you make a deal for your soul with a Crossroads demon for wealth, health, or...anything? You got what you asked for, for a certain amount of time, with the knowledge that you would pay with your soul when the time came?"

"A Cross..." She couldn't even finish the sentence. "No, never."

Christian's smile was soft, his gaze intense. "Your choice then. You can leave, or you can stay here and let me help you."

As if Ivy had a choice.

CHAPTER

THREE

CHRISTIAN GLANCED at the darkness before he turned Ivy toward the house. "Let's get you inside so you can get an explanation."

He had never been so happy to have Davena and Olivia there. If the women hadn't shown up, Christian was sure Ivy would've refused his offer.

Beau stopped Christian before he could follow the women inside. "Are you sure about this? Tangling with Hell Hounds isn't something I'm crazy about on a good day, but we've got our women here now."

"And Ivy isn't important?" Christian wasn't sure why anger filled him so rapidly, but once there, he couldn't shove it aside. "I thought it was our jobs to protect the innocent."

"It is. If they are innocent."

"Ivy is."

"You just met her," Beau argued.

Christian crossed his arms over his chest. "Need I remind you of how you met Davena? Or how about how Lincoln and Ava met? Better yet, what about Vincent and Olivia?"

"I get your point," Beau said tightly.

"No, you don't. I get that you have someone to protect now, but we've always had someone to protect. We had each other and we had the innocents of this parish."

Beau ran a hand through his black hair. "It's different with a woman, Christian. I love Davena. I'd die for her."

"We could argue this point all night, but I'm not going to. I'm going to get to the bottom of this with Ivy."

"And if she's lying? What if she did make a deal? Will you really shove her off this porch and let the Hounds have her?"

That wasn't something Christian was ready to think about yet. "We protect the innocent. If she made the deal without knowing it, she's still an innocent."

"There's no getting away from a Hell Hound," Beau stated. "This house may be warded, but they'll find their way in eventually."

"I brought Ivy here. I'll be the one to protect her."

Beau turned and walked into the house without another word.

Christian blew out a deep breath. He looked into the darkness again. The Hell Hounds were out there, waiting. They weren't regular dogs. They were invisible to humans, and very intelligent. They had one mission—take the soul of whoever signed the deal with the demon.

He turned on his heel and strode into the house. As he figured, the girls had taken Ivy into Vincent's office. He stopped at the doorway next to Beau. Olivia sat in a chair while Davena took one side of the sofa. Ivy sat on the edge of the couch against the left side. She kept one hand in her purse.

Christian bit back a smile as he knew her hand was wrapped around her gun. The woman had gumption. He applauded her for that. It was too bad the weapon couldn't help her against the Hell Hounds.

But it could do major damage to them.

He cleared his throat to get her attention. As soon as he did, the idle chitchat between Olivia and Davena ended. All eyes turned to him.

Christian walked further into the office to rest one hip on Vincent's desk. "I'm sure you've got questions, and we'll be happy to answer them."

"But you've got questions for me first, right?" Ivy said in a remarkably calm voice.

That took Christian aback since he knew she was anything but composed by her rapid breathing and the way she kept fisting her left hand.

Her gaze met his straight on, and he was intrigued by their shade—a beautiful mix of green and gold. Christian had never taken much notice of a woman's eye color before.

Until that moment.

Ivy shrugged, but didn't remove her right hand from her purse. "Fine. Ask your questions. I'm pretty sure I answered them outside, but I'll be happy to repeat my answer—no."

Christian couldn't hide his smile. "You've got courage and a tough spirit. That just might get you through this."

Davena snorted. "Might? Christian, really. It will get her through this."

"Davena's right," Olivia told Ivy.

Ivy glanced at both women before turning her gaze back to Christian. "Where am I?"

He frowned. Christian had been so caught up in getting her to the house, and then inside, that he hadn't stopped to fill her in. "As I told you, I'm Christian Chiasson. This is my brother, Beau. The spirited one on the couch is his woman, Davena." He winked at Davena before he shot Olivia a grin. "The sassy one is Olivia, who is engaged to my eldest brother, Vincent. You're at our family home."

"That's apparently someplace the things after me can't get into?" Ivy asked saucily.

Davena laughed. "Oh, I like you. You're going to fit right in perfectly. These Chiasson boys have a habit of thinking they can make all the decisions."

"Now, Davena," Beau started.

Davena held up a hand and shook her head. "Stay over there, because if you get close, you'll kiss me and then we won't be able to stop."

"What's wrong with that?" Beau asked with a cocky grin.

Christian watched Ivy as she observed their exchange as if she was confused by it. Finally. He wasn't the only one who didn't understand this thing his brothers had found with their women.

"I think I should start off by telling you that the things that go bump in the night are real," Christian said, to get the topic back on track.

Ivy swallowed hard. "Meaning?"

"There are ghosts, vampires, werewolves, monsters, demons, and Hell Hounds, among other creatures."

Her gaze held his for a long moment. "You're not joking."

Christian shook his head. "You heard the Hounds tonight. You knew they were there, even if you couldn't see them. There's your proof."

"How do all of you," Ivy said, motioning to everyone with her hand, "know all of this?"

It was Beau who said, "Because we hunt them."

"Hunt?" Ivy repeated slowly. Her gaze moved from Beau to Christian. "You can kill ghosts and such?"

Christian nodded. "Just about every creature has a way to be killed." He wasn't ready to tell her the Hell Hounds were one exception.

Ivy pulled her hand out of her purse and dropped her face into her hands. "This has to be a nightmare."

"I wish it was," Olivia said in a soft voice. "The sooner

you face the reality of it, the sooner we can all figure out what is going on."

Davena tucked her legs to her side. "Would it help to tell you I'm a witch?"

Ivy's head snapped up to look at Davena. "I'm...not sure if that helps or not."

"Try to remember that we're here to help."

Christian was going to have to remember to pull both Davena and Olivia aside to thank them later.

Beau leaned against the doorway and folded his arms across his chest. "Our family came to Lyons Point generations ago to battle the supernatural that are drawn to this area. We carry on that tradition."

"All right," Ivy said with a nod. "I can't deny the sound I heard, or the fact I couldn't see what was attacking the truck. If you do battle the supernatural, then tell me what a Crossroads demon is."

Christian shifted so that he leaned back against the desk with his hands on either side of him. "There are demons who can be summoned at a crossroads to exchange something a person wants for their soul."

"I didn't do that," Ivy said confidently.

"Occasionally, a Crossroads demon will pick a place and set up at a bar for a week or two looking for those who are willing to trade their souls for advancements in their careers, money, or to save someone else."

Ivy lifted her chin. "Not me either."

"It wouldn't have been recently," Beau pointed out.

Christian studied Ivy. "Normally, the amount of time given by the demon before they claim your soul is ten years. There have been instances where the demon does five or less years, but the norm is ten."

"Not me," Ivy said with a grin. "Ten years ago I was fourteen and more focused on other things than thinking of trading my soul."

Beau pushed away from the doorway, dropping his hands as he walked into the room to stand before the fireplace. "Ivy, the only way a Hell Hound knows where to go is because a person is marked when they sell their soul. The Hell Hounds don't make mistakes."

"Well, they did this time," she stated. "My soul is mine."

Christian exchanged a look with Beau. "If she's telling the truth, then there has to be another reason the Hounds are after her."

"I've never read anything in Dad's journal about such an instance," Beau said.

Christian looked at the clock as he realized Vincent, Lincoln, and Ava weren't there. "Where are the others?"

"Lincoln and Ava took the west," Davena said.

Olivia pushed her hair back from her face. "Vincent went north. He said he'd be back around two or three."

That meant Beau had taken the south, which was easy to search quickly and return to the house. It could be hours before Lincoln and Ava returned. Christian wanted to talk to everyone before he said more to Ivy.

"It's been a long night," Christian said. "Why don't we all get some rest? We can talk more in the morning."

To his surprise, Ivy didn't argue. She rose with Davena and Olivia. As she followed the women out, her gaze met his.

Christian had the uncontrollable urge to touch her, to let her know that everything was going to be all right. He hated when innocents were caught in the middle of the monsters they hunted.

That's all it was. He was angry that Ivy had been targeted. It had nothing to do with the raw, primal desire that burned through him, demanding he learn every inch of her skin and her taste.

Once the women were gone, Christian walked around the desk. He sat in the chair and opened a lower drawer to pull out the journal their family had kept from the very beginning. It was a large book that had been rebound many times with new entries and pictures.

"If there's an explanation, it'll be in there," Beau said as he came to stand next to Christian.

"I know. My worry is if there's nothing."

"Then that means Ivy is lying."

Christian slammed his hand on the desk. "What if she's not? Have you bothered to consider that option?"

"Why are you defending her so strongly?" Beau asked, his gaze narrowed.

Christian shook his head and went back to looking at the journal. "I already explained this."

"Right. She's an innocent. You believe her."

"And you don't," Christian answered.

The back door opened as footsteps sounded through the house. Christian looked up as Lincoln and Ava slid to a stop in the foyer when they saw them. A few steps behind the couple was Vincent.

Vincent glanced at the open journal to Christian and Beau. "Why did I hear a Hell Hound close to the house?"

"Because Christian brought a woman here that the beasts want to claim," Beau answered.

Christian leaned back in the chair when four sets of eyes trained on him. He was used to having everyone looking at him for various reasons. Normally, he shrugged it off, but he knew in his gut that Ivy was innocent.

It was time he took a stand. Who better to do that for than an innocent?

A beautiful innocent with stunning hazel eyes.

CHAPTER
FOUR

"THERE'S NOTHING," Linc said as he slammed another book closed and shoved it across the floor. He leaned his head back onto the cushions of the sofa from his spot on the floor.

Christian rubbed his tired eyes. "In all the books we have in this house, there has to be something."

"Nothing," Ava said from her spot on the couch. She ran her hands through Lincoln's long hair while she looked on her laptop. "Not a single thing. Isn't that odd?"

Vincent sighed heavily from the chair near the fireplace. "Very. Either it really doesn't happen, or it's so rare that no one has bothered to mention it."

"That I don't believe," Beau said. "If it happened, then someone, somewhere would have made a record of it."

Davena made a face before she stretched her arms over her head. "I agree with Beau."

"I believe Ivy," Olivia said, smothering a yawn.

Vincent winked at Olivia. "She might be a very good liar."

Christian squeezed his eyes closed for a moment. "There's an explanation for this. We just need to find it."

"Then we start with Ivy," Ava said.

Olivia's face was grim as she gave a nod. "A background check."

Christian didn't argue, because he knew it was the only way. It didn't mean he liked it, however. While Ava and Olivia began to search the internet for anything about Ivy Pierce, Christian kept looking through the journal.

At least the family was willing to help. Beau was the only one who had voiced his concern with the Hounds being so near his woman, but Christian had seen the worry on Vin's and Linc's faces as well.

The only ones who seemed unperturbed by it were Olivia, Ava, and Davena. They each came to the Chiasson house while being pursued by the supernatural. Maybe that's why they understood.

Thirty-five minutes later Christian glanced at the clock on the wall to see that it was almost five in the morning. No one had gotten any sleep, and Ivy would be awake soon.

"Well," Ava said. "I think I might have found something."

Christian set aside the journal. "What is it?"

"Ivy's father died when she was three, along with her seven-year-old brother. There was an accident in the bayou while father and son were gator hunting."

"Ah, damn," Lincoln murmured.

Ava looked up from the screen. "Both were killed."

"That left Ivy and her mother," Olivia said.

Ava lowered her gaze to the computer again. "Yep. Ivy's life was relatively quiet until five years later. Ivy was sick. Very sick."

Christian's gut clenched at the news.

"She was in and out of the hospital for the next six years. The doctors couldn't figure out what was wrong with her. Several times she nearly died."

Vincent ran a hand across his jaw. "Is she still sick?"

"No," Davena said. "She's healthy as a horse."

"Then what cured her?" Beau asked.

Ava shrugged. "It doesn't say anything. The medical records just stop."

Olivia nodded. "Ava's right. The next thing that shows is Ivy on the debate team in high school."

Now Christian knew where she got her argumentative talents. He looked over to see Davena mumbling with her eyes closed. She was doing a spell, but he didn't know what for. Before he had a chance to ask, Beau was talking.

"We need to know what was wrong with Ivy all those years, as well as how she was cured," Beau said.

Christian sat back in the chair and glared at his brother. "You think she made a deal with a demon."

"She was a kid!" Beau shouted. "She was dying. Yes, I

think a demon might have found her and offered her a way out."

"Don't you think she would've remembered that?" Vincent asked.

Beau shrugged. "You'd think."

"Perhaps she hasn't put the two things together," Lincoln offered.

Christian shoved the chair away from the desk so hard it rolled back against the wall behind him. He stood and walked out of the room.

He didn't understand why everyone was assuming that Ivy was lying. Why couldn't they see that she might very well be telling the truth?

His name was called, but he was done with the family for the moment. He needed some time alone, some time to collect his thoughts and go over all that had happened.

Christian walked into his room, closing the door behind him. He fell face first on the bed before he turned his head to the side and closed his eyes.

All he saw was light brown curls and hazel eyes. He heard Ivy's laughter, felt her fear. He had looked into her clear eyes on the porch and accepted her answer as truth.

Was he wrong? He hadn't been before. Then again, he hadn't felt such desire for a woman either. Though that wasn't what was driving him.

It was the unshakable knowledge that he had to help Ivy. He hadn't told his brothers that, nor would he. It wasn't that he was afraid to tell them. It was because they would think he was interested in Ivy.

Boy, was he interested, but only for a night of rousing sex. Other than that, there was nothing.

A flash of her face lined with fear as she pointed her gun at him filled his mind.

She was a handful. She didn't hide her panic, but she worked through it. What else could she do after losing her father and brother at such a young age? She probably didn't remember them, but she certainly remembered all the hospital visits. That alone explained so much about her.

Christian cleared his mind and let sleep claim him.

Ivy SHOWERED and put back on her clothes before she stepped out of the bedroom she had been given. Oddly enough, she had slept like the dead once she fell asleep.

The house was quiet except for the delicious smell wafting up from the kitchen. She made her way down the stairs and followed her nose to the kitchen.

She saw Beau with his chin-length black hair cooking. He had his back to her, so she took a step back to leave when she ran into someone.

Startled, Ivy whirled around to find another man with the same intense blue eyes and black hair as Christian and Beau.

The man smiled, his long black hair hanging loose to his shoulders. "No need to leave. Beau makes the best waffles around."

Ivy opened her mouth, trying to come up with an excuse when the man gently took her arm and led her to a chair at the rectangular table in the kitchen.

"I'm Lincoln, by the way. Second eldest. Ava is still asleep. She needs at least eight hours, or she is in full on grouch mode," he said with a smile.

"Ivy Pierce," she said with a nod.

Lincoln sat across from her and folded his hands on the table. "Christian filled us in when we got home last night."

"Do you think I'm lying as Beau does?" she said. No sense in tiptoeing around it.

Beau didn't so much as twitch at her comment.

Lincoln glanced at Beau, his smile widening. "If you'd come a few months ago, I suspect things would be different. It wasn't until recently that we expanded our family. It was a house of bachelors. Then Olivia returned to Lyons Point when something was killing any woman a Chiasson so much as showed interest in. Vincent had been in love with Olivia since school."

Ivy sat back, interested in the tale.

Lincoln shrugged and reclined in the chair. "We found the culprits and killed them. By that time, Vin knew he couldn't let Olivia go. Then my Ava came to town. She knew Olivia, but she also had a history here."

"Anything after her?"

Lincoln's smile slipped. "A Voodoo priestess who had—has—a grudge against Ava's father sent our cousin here to kill her."

Ivy was mortified. "What?"

"Spells were used on Kane. He couldn't stop what Delphine had done to him." Lincoln suddenly grinned. "But we saved the day, and I got my Ava."

Ivy glanced at Beau. She jerked her head to him while looking at Lincoln.

"Davena is from New Orleans. Her mother was a witch, as was her sister, though neither had a portion of the magic within Davena. Delphine, the Voodoo priestess who tried to kill Ava, came here for Davena. Beau wouldn't let that happen. Together, he and Davena won."

"So Delphine is dead?" Ivy asked.

Beau snorted loudly. "If only."

Lincoln caught her gaze. "The point is, Ivy, we're not a house of bachelors anymore."

"You have someone you love." She nodded in understanding. "As long as I'm here, the Hell Hounds will be as well. You're worried."

Lincoln lifted one shoulder. "There is always something after us, but Hell Hounds can't be seen. They're invisible."

So that's why she hadn't been able to see them!

"I didn't sell my soul," Ivy repeated.

Lincoln leaned forward and covered her hand with one of

his. "I never said you did. I just wanted to explain why some might be acting a certain way."

Ivy couldn't exactly fault Beau for wanting to protect Davena. "I understand."

"Now," Lincoln said as he once more reclined. "Let's catch you up on us. Vin is the eldest, but I'm next in line. After that is Christian, then Beau. Bringing up the rear of the Chiasson children is Riley, our only sister. Fortunately, she's not here to be in the middle of all of this."

Ivy was raised as an only child. To have siblings was as foreign to her as the supernatural.

She listened as Lincoln went on to talk of the house and all the wards that would keep her protected. Davena was going to extend the wards to cover the back yard to give them all some room to walk.

Ivy was about to thank him when her neck heated. She touched her neck before she turned her head to find Christian in the doorway staring at her.

Their gazes met, held. He was freshly showered with his hair still damp. And too damn gorgeous for his own good.

If she thought his eyes were vivid the night before, in the light of day they were so bright she couldn't look away.

"Did you sleep well?" Christian asked as he walked into the kitchen to the coffee pot on the counter.

"Yes." Why was her voice so breathless? "You?"

He shrugged before turning and setting a mug of coffee in front of her. "I slept."

She frowned since he said it as if that answered everything. Ivy wrapped her hands around the mug. She looked down into the dark liquid. "I'll understand if y'all want me to leave. You have something precious here, and it shouldn't be shattered."

There was a moment of silence. Then a chair scraped on the floor as Christian pulled a chair out and sat.

Ivy finally gave in and looked up. Christian was once more staring at her.

"You're not going anywhere, darlin'."

FIVE

Christian stared at Ivy from the kitchen window as she stood on the porch. Her gaze was directed toward the bayou. There was a slight chill to the morning that was quickly disappearing with the rising sun.

Beau came to stand beside him. "We need to know more information about her illness."

"In other words, you want me to talk to her," Christian said.

"You brought her here."

Christian sighed, because he knew Beau was right. It wasn't that he didn't want to talk to Ivy. No, it was because he *did* want to talk to her. That alone is what had kept him from going to her all morning.

"You look at her as if you don't know what to do with

her," Beau said with a snort. "We all know you've never had a problem with women."

Christian watched as Ivy let out a deep breath, her shoulders sagging. Beau was talking again, but he wasn't paying attention.

He pushed away from the window, walked around Beau, and exited the house. Christian didn't like the way Ivy tensed when she heard the door.

"Would you rather be alone?"

She shook her head. "I've been expecting someone to want to talk. I don't like being under a microscope with everyone watching me."

He knew that had to do with her times in the hospital. Christian walked to the other side of the porch to give her some room and not crowd her. Plus, the more distance between them, the better.

"I'm going to help you with this problem," he said.

Ivy turned her head, a slight smile pulling at her lips. "I believe you're going to try. You see, I did my own research this morning on Hell Hounds. There is no helping me."

The sunlight bathed her in a red-orange light that turned her hair auburn. For an instant, she looked otherworldly, as if she didn't belong on Earth.

Then she ducked her head before returning her gaze to the bayou. The sun continued its ascent, and the moment was lost.

But Christian would forever hold the memory.

He swallowed and remembered why he was out there with her. "Demons aren't just vicious and cruel. They're also cunning and crafty. They're calculating, and if they see an opportunity, they'll do whatever they need to in order to get what they want."

"You think I was tricked?"

"It's a possibility. I need details, Ivy."

"Of my life."

He couldn't take his eyes from her. Christian leaned a shoulder against a column and crossed his arms over his chest. "Yes."

"There's not much to tell." She faced him then. "My father and brother died when I was three in an accident out in the bayou. It was just my mother and myself until last year. She had a heart attack."

"I'm sorry." Life certainly hadn't been kind to her, but then again, fate had a way of knowing who could handle such things. Ivy was a strong person. It was evident in everything about her.

Ivy shrugged. "It happens."

"Yes, it does. Our parents were killed when I was just a boy. They died on the same night."

Their eyes locked. Her gaze wasn't filled with pity. It was filled with understanding as only someone who had experienced such things could.

"It's been just us five for a long time," Christian continued.

"At least y'all had each other."

"Yeah. My brothers are a pain in the ass, but I wouldn't have survived that night without them. We were strong for Riley. She was so young. She didn't really comprehend it all at first."

"She's very lucky to have you."

Christian wasn't so sure his sister felt that way, not after the latest fiasco. How could they have been so wrapped up in things that they didn't realize she had graduated from the University of Texas?

"She came home recently. We had just defeated Delphine a second time, and we never wanted her involved with the family business." Christian ran a hand down his face. What was it about Ivy that made him want to spill his guts? "We didn't exactly give her a warm welcome. In fact, I'm pretty sure Vin told her to return to Austin."

Ivy's forehead furrowed. "Is that where she's at?"

"We don't know where she is. She called and told us she was fine, but she's still angry."

"As she should be. What were y'all thinking?" Ivy admonished. "You're her family."

If Christian didn't think he could feel any lower, all he had to do was have Ivy use that disappointed voice. "She won't answer my calls."

"Give her time. She'll come around."

"Delphine is dangerous, Ivy. We have each other here,

but we don't know where Riley is. If she's alone, she could be targeted."

Ivy raised her brows. "Then you better start leaving some heartfelt messages to get her to call you back."

"Probably." His mind was already past Riley and centered squarely on Ivy. "You've been alone for a year?"

She nodded, her gaze lowering to the porch for a moment. "I have. There are times it's bad, but the days are getting better. I work from home, so I can make my own schedule."

"Interesting."

She laughed, her eyes twinkling. "Now you're making fun of me."

"Never," he vowed, his smile growing.

Silence stretched as they stared at each other again. Christian was thankful he was so far from her, because if he had been closer, he would've kissed her.

"So, no one new in your life?" he asked after he cleared his throat.

She looked pointedly at him. "Just you and your family. Before that, no one."

"You're not seeing someone?" It was a valid question, though he wanted to know the answer for himself.

"No."

One simple word, but Christian wanted to rejoice. Then he reminded himself he didn't care. He didn't want a relationship.

Of any kind.

"Do you want to know my favorite color as well?" she asked with a grin.

Christian laughed as he dropped his arms and pushed away from the column. "I'm sorry I'm prying into your life."

"It's all right. I'll tell you anything you want to know. I don't want to die."

That wiped his smile away instantly. He didn't want her to die. "Did anything significant happen ten years ago?"

"That's right. The ten-year thing." Her face scrunched as she considered his words. "I left the hospital for the last time and got better."

Christian knew of her illness, but hearing her say it was like a punch in the gut. "You were sick?"

"Yes, but no one could diagnose what was wrong with me. I was sick for years. In and out of the hospital all the time. I missed so much school that my mother decided to home school me."

"You look healthy."

She glanced down at herself. "Now. Back then I could barely lift my hand from the bed. My mother had to feed me. My mind worked great, but my body...well, didn't. No one could get near me, because a simple cold could kill me."

"My God." Christian didn't know what else to say.

Ivy tucked a curl behind her ear and put her hands in the back pockets of her jeans as she glanced at the bayou. "All the poking and prodding of the doctors and the numerous medications I was on eventually worked. Though I fear that whatever it was will return one day."

To be miraculously healed like that wasn't something that happened often. Usually it meant that magic or a demon was involved.

"Did anyone visit you in the hospital and ask what you would do if you weren't sick anymore?"

Ivy's head cocked to the side. "I thought of that last night, but besides my doctors and the nurses, my mother was the only one who visited."

"The demon could've been a nurse or doctor."

She was shaking her head before he finished. "None of them ever asked me such a thing."

"Then I'm out of ideas," Christian said in frustration. "You're the only one who wanted you to get better."

As soon as the words were out of his mouth, he thought of her mother. The same thought must have crossed Ivy's mind, because her face crumpled.

"Ivy," he said and took a step toward her.

She raised a hand to stop him and stepped back. "My mother was devout in her beliefs. She wouldn't have traded my soul in such a way."

"She couldn't." Christian rubbed the back of his neck, feeling like the biggest ass for having to say his next words. "Ivy, the only soul a person can bargain with is their own."

"You think she sold her soul?"

"It's the only thing that makes sense."

"Then why are the Hell Hounds after me?"

It was a good question. "Your mother died last year, right?"

"In her sleep. The autopsy showed it was a heart attack."

"If that's the case, then the Hell Hounds should be satisfied. They got their soul, even if they didn't have to come to get it."

Ivy gave a little shake of her head. "That still doesn't explain why the Hounds are after me."

"It's time we found out."

Christian strode back into the house with Ivy on his heels. They walked into the office. He went to the desk and sat, once more pulling out the journal.

He glanced up and pointed to one of the laptops sitting on the coffee table. "Do you mind looking up your scenario?"

"Not at all." Ivy sat, pulling the laptop to her and opening it.

Christian thumbed through the journal until he came to the part of the Hell Hounds while he heard Ivy punching the keyboard.

"What's going on?" Vincent asked as he walked in.

Christian didn't look up from his perusal of the passages. "We think Ivy's mom might have made the deal, but she died last year of a heart attack."

"That shouldn't matter then," Vin said. "The Hounds got their soul."

"Exactly." Christian glanced up at his eldest brother. "Then why are they after Ivy?"

Vincent let out a whistle that sounded throughout the house. In a matter of moments, everyone would be in the room.

Vin walked to the bookshelf and drew out two books. "Looks like we need to alter our research."

Christian slid his gaze to Ivy to find her watching him. He gave her a nod, and her answering grin did funny things inside him.

He decided to chalk it up to the four waffles he ate.

CHAPTER
SIX

Ivy was about ready to call it a day after eight hours of research when Beau let out an expletive.

"What?" Christian asked.

She still couldn't believe how hard he was working to help her. Yet, she couldn't figure out why. He didn't know her. Sure, his family helped the innocent, but for him to go to such extremes just seemed...odd.

At least, she had never encountered anyone who would do such a thing. Granted, her experience with people was limited, but she watched enough TV to know it was unusual.

Beau's gaze landed on her. Ivy straightened, wondering what she had done.

"I found something," Beau said as he rose from his chair and walked to her. He handed her the book, his finger next to the third paragraph on the page. "Read that out loud, please."

Ivy took the book as she set the laptop next to her. She took a deep breath and started reading. "Hell Hounds, by all accounts, are simply animals doing the bidding of the Demon of Souls. They're not just beasts, however. Special care should be taken when trying to dodge them."

She paused, not liking what she was reading so far. "Once a person sells their soul, it's owned by the Demon of Souls, gathered by the many crossroads demons."

"We know all of this," Lincoln said.

Beau motioned for Ivy to keep going. "Finish the passage."

Ivy shrugged and returned her gaze to the book. "A soul can't be bought back. Once sold, it is lost forever. A person normally has ten years before the Hell Hounds are sent to retrieve their soul and take the person to Hell. For the few who trade their souls to help another, the same rules apply."

She stopped reading, because the implication that her mother had sold her soul to help her made her chest felt as if it were caving in from the weight of it all.

Suddenly, Christian was sitting beside her. He met her gaze briefly before he leaned over and finished for her. "There is one known instance where a person who sold their soul to help another died before their ten years came due. The Hell Hounds were then sent to the one who was saved and retrieved their soul. After a lengthy investigation, it was discovered the person killed themselves to avoid having to face the Hell Hounds."

Ivy shoved the book off her and stood. She paced before the fireplace. "No. My mother didn't kill herself. There was an autopsy. They would've found it."

"No one said your mother committed suicide," Christian said.

But everyone was thinking it. Including Ivy. She stopped and tried to draw in a calming breath. "What this tells me is that despite not having made the deal, the Hell Hounds are still coming for my soul."

"Actually, no," Christian said as he finished reading something in the book. "They can't."

Beau nodded. "He's right. It's not your soul that was sold."

"Then why come after me?" Ivy was getting more confused by the minute.

Christian set the open book on the coffee table before him. "They'll kill you, taking you to Hell to show the person who did sell their soul."

"Oh. Well, that makes everything better then," she said sarcastically. Ivy put her hand on her forehead. "I'm sorry. That was uncalled for."

Ava rose and came to stand beside her. "It's very much called for."

Ivy was dipping back into feeling sorry for herself like she had done as a kid in the hospital. Things were out of her control then, and it was happening all over again. Except this time it wasn't her body that was failing.

"I think that's enough research for the night," Lincoln said as he closed the book he was reading. He replaced it on the bookshelf and clicked on the CD player.

Music came over the speakers. Ivy recognized a song by Hozier as one she really liked. As if it was a cue, everyone put away their books and computers.

Ivy could only stare in confusion as the three couples came together. Lincoln and Ava began to slow dance next to her while Olivia sat on Vincent's lap behind the desk and began kissing him. Beau and Davena were smiling as she danced to him. His arms snaked out and caught her, pulling her against him as they began to kiss.

Ivy tried not to look at Christian, but she couldn't stop herself. He had his head down, as if by not looking nothing was happening.

She quietly made her way around Lincoln and Ava and walked out of the house. That morning she had watched the sun rise above the trees, now she was watching it sink behind them.

Davena told her the back property was warded, including the boathouse. Ivy stepped off the porch, waiting for a Hell Hound to take her. When nothing happened, she took another couple of steps. Then a couple more.

Finally, she walked to the door and opened it. She saw

the cages inside that drew her up short. Then she realized the guys had to have somewhere to put the monsters.

Ivy spotted the huge sliding metal door and cracked it a bit. She smiled as she finished pulling it all the way open and took in the water lapping at her feet.

She sat down and leaned against the side of the door listening to the cicadas fill the night with their music that rose and fell.

A sound drew her attention to the door she walked through. She saw a silhouette and recognized Christian.

"Couldn't take it either, I see," he said.

She laughed. "That was...awkward."

"You're the only one who understands my need to have my own place. I'm surrounded by couples on a daily basis."

"I find it hard to believe you don't have someone."

He made a face as he drew closer. "Not me."

"Relationships are complicated. I'd rather keep things simple."

"Exactly." He leaned against the opposite side of the door.

"I like to answer only to myself." His grin made her laugh. "You're looking at me as if you're not sure whether to believe me or not."

He shrugged a shoulder. "Normally women want to talk about how soon they can get married and how many kids they want while explaining how they're going to change their men."

Ivy nodded since she had a couple of friends just like that. "Why do women always want to change their men?"

"Good question. I'd like the answer as well."

She looked away when she couldn't handle his intense gaze any longer. He seemed to be able to see right into her mind, and she didn't want him to know how many times she thought about running her hands over his body or ripping his clothes off.

"No hunting tonight?" she asked into the silence.

The music from the house rose, drifting outside as if they had opened windows.

"Not with the Hell Hounds after you. We're better all together."

His voice was a seduction all his own. Ivy closed her eyes. Did he know how his voice affected her? Is that why he lowered it, making his words come out as soft as silk?

"Lincoln had the right idea. We need to take our minds off Hell Hounds," Christian said as he pushed away from the doorway.

Ivy's eyes snapped open to look at him as he sat near her. His black hair tempted her fingers to touch the strands and see if they were as soft as they looked.

"I used to come out here all the time to get away from the craziness of the house," Christian said and looked straight ahead. "I'd sit right here and listen to the sounds of the bayou, watch gators and turtles swim past, and try to pretend that my life didn't involve the supernatural."

Ivy pulled her gaze from Christian to gaze at the purple and pink streaked sky. "It's beautiful here. A place of solace."

"It's that and much more."

She felt his eyes on her. Unable to stop herself, Ivy turned her head to him. She wanted Christian, and the seductive music wasn't helping matters at all.

He turned toward her and tugged on a lock of her hair. "Curls. That's what I called you when I first saw you in the bar."

She raised a brow. So he had noticed her. Ivy would've had to have been blind not to appreciate such a fine specimen herself. She had taken plenty of peaks as he had leaned over to shoot pool.

"Having been sick for so long, I have a habit of not waiting around for things." She swallowed, hoping she wasn't about to make a fool of herself. "I'd like to take my mind off the current mess. Interested?"

"As if you have to ask," he said before his hand slid into her hair around to the back of her neck and his lips covered hers.

Ivy leaned forward, her hands going to his chest. She slowly moved them up to his shoulders and then around his neck. The kiss was fiery, passionate.

She was on her knees with him as their bodies came together. His arms wrapped around her tight, pulling her close and roaming everywhere.

His kisses took her breath away while enflaming her

already burning desire. She tugged up his shirt to feel his skin.

The kiss broke long enough for him to rip off his shirt. Their gazes met as he cupped her face. She was drowning in his blue eyes, sinking into the passion that enfolded them.

Then they were kissing again. Ivy wasn't sure when her shirt was removed, and she didn't care. She was living in the moment. Life was so fragile and could be taken at any moment. She wasn't going to wait around. She was going to enjoy whatever time she had left.

What better way than in the arms of a man who made her crave his touch?

Christian lowered them until they were lying on the concrete floor. She belatedly realized that she was on his shirt.

He rose over her and leaned back on his haunches. "You have to be the most interesting person I've ever met."

"Then you must not have met very many people," she said.

He removed her boots, and then slowly unbuttoned her jeans. Ivy tugged them over her hips. Then she was in nothing but her bra and panties.

"My turn," she said as she sat up and reached for the waist of his jeans. She unbuttoned them, opening them wide.

The trail of chest hair narrowed at his belly button and disappeared into his jeans. She ran her hands over his impressive chest and wide shoulders. His skin was warm, his muscles hard beneath her palms.

She had known he would have an amazing body, but she hadn't been prepared for such sheer gorgeousness. His skin was bronzed from time in the sun. There were marks from wounds that looked like slashes from talons, and there were even bite marks.

"I live a hard life," he said.

She lifted her gaze to his face as she traced one of his scars. "These show how powerful and resilient you are."

In answer, he claimed her mouth in a kiss that was savage and tender at the same time.

Their arms went around each other as they gave into the passion.

CHAPTER

SEVEN

CHRISTIAN BURNED. With each kiss, he yearned for Ivy even more. Her skin was soft as down, her kisses as intoxicating as the finest bourbon.

He ran his hand down her side, feeling her warmth beneath his palm. She yanked down his jeans and he quickly stepped out of them. Then he hooked his thumbs in her panties and lowered them.

With a little flick, he tossed the lace away. Her leg lifted to wrap around his hips. Christian groaned and rocked his aching cock against her.

A shiver raced along his skin as her nails lightly scoured down his back. He rolled them until he was on his back and she straddled him.

She ended the kiss and looked at him. Christian's breath locked in his lungs as her brown curls framed her face in disarray. Her lips were swollen while her eyes burned with desire.

She was the most beautiful thing he had ever laid eyes on. Ivy didn't hide her passion, didn't shield her sexuality as some women, ashamed of their bodies, did. No, his Ivy held his gaze as she sat up, her fingers caressing his chest.

Then she reached behind her and unhooked her bra. The garment sagged. She gave a little shift of her shoulders to have the straps fall away. With a flick of her wrist, she tossed the bra away.

Christian's mouth went dry as he stared at her full breasts. He cupped them, feeling their weight.

A smile pulled at his lips when her nipples hardened before his gaze. He lifted his eyes to find Ivy had closed hers, her lips parted and a look of bliss on her face.

Christian lightly tweaked a nipple, causing Ivy to suck in a breath and her nails to dig into his chest. He let his gaze devour her, putting every inch of her to memory.

He sat up and took a turgid peak in his mouth as he braced a hand on her back to hold her. Her breaths became haggard, her hips moving slowly back and forth.

"Christian," she murmured as her head dropped back.

Moving from one breast to the other, Christian lavished attention on her amazing assets. But he wanted—needed—more.

He needed her. To be inside her, to fill her and have their bodies joined in a dance as old as time.

Christian was surprised when she rose up on her knees and wrapped her hand around his aching rod. He groaned at the feel of her fingers around him and stroking up and down his length.

The pleasure was intense, deep. Ivy brought a part of him to the surface he hadn't known was even inside him. She didn't let him hold anything back, but forced him to see what was before them—and grasp it with both hands.

Her head lifted and she caught his gaze. It was the most erotic, decadent experience of his life to be looking into her passion-filled hazel eyes as she caressed his cock.

Thoughts deserted him when she brought his rod to her entrance and slowly lowered herself. He held her close, watching the desire fill her face as he stretched her.

Ivy thought she knew passion. She thought she knew what it meant to desire a man.

That was, until Christian.

He opened a whole new world to her, one where she wasn't afraid to be herself and hide her wantonness. With Christian, his every look urged her to let it all loose.

The world was spinning out of control in his arms, but it was glorious. And right. She didn't search for a way to stop it. Instead, she embraced the feeling—and Christian.

Her body tightened around him deep inside her. It took a

moment to adjust to his fullness, but oh the feeling was wondrous.

Ivy looked down into his bright blue eyes and wished she knew what he was thinking. Then she rocked her hips and it no longer mattered.

Need had been building inside her. It flamed bright with their kisses, but now it engulfed her. Her veins burned with it.

Back and forth she moved, slowly at first. His large hands held her firmly as their breaths mingled. Sweat beaded on their skin and the world fell away.

She wrapped her arms around his neck, holding on tight when he gripped her hips and began to move her up and down his length.

The desire coiled tighter, bringing her closer and closer to the precipice of pleasure.

Christian's lips were on her neck, kissing and nipping at her flesh. In the next instant, she was on her back as he leaned over her, the muscles in his arms bulging as he held himself up.

She was powerless to look away from him. He held still a moment before slowly pulling out of her and thrusting deep.

Ivy moaned loudly. Her breathing quickened and she locked her legs around his waist. His hips began to pump as he moved in and out of her, alternating from long slow thrusts to quick hard ones.

She was hurtling quickly toward release. He worked her

body expertly, leaving her no choice but to give in to all that he demanded of her.

CHRISTIAN LOVED the sound of Ivy's moans and cries of pleasure. They spurred him to push her—them—further, deeper into the desire enveloping them. It alarmed him that he so eagerly sought what he had been actively avoiding of late.

But how could he shun what Ivy so freely gave?

How could he deny both of them what providence, chance, or destiny had put in their path?

He felt Ivy's body began to tighten. Her nails dug deep into his arms. He bent and licked a nipple before lightly nipping it.

She jerked, pure ecstasy crossing her face as her body convulsed around him. Christian attempted to hold back his own orgasm, but the feel of her clutching him was too much.

He gritted his teeth until he could stand it no more. With one last thrust, he gave in to his body. The climax was powerful, taking him to a place he had never been before.

The waves of pleasure swamped them again and again, prolonging their orgasms. When Christian could finally lift his head, he looked down to find a smile on Ivy's face and her eyes closed.

"Let's stay like this for a little longer," she asked, cracking open one eye.

Christian was in no hurry to shatter what they had found. He pulled out of her and rolled to the side, pulling her against him as the first drops of rain began to land on the roof.

Ivy was the first to wake hours later. The rain was still coming down with the clouds hiding the moon and stars. She remained in Christian's arms for a little longer, enjoying the quiet and tranquility of the moment.

There had been no sound of the Hell Hounds, but she knew it was only a matter of time before they came for her. She had no wish to die, but nor did she like putting everyone helping her in danger.

She didn't know how much time passed since she woke before she gradually removed Christian's arms and got to her feet. It took her a few minutes to find her clothes and put them on.

Ivy straightened from putting on her boots to find Christian awake and propped on an elbow watching her. For once she didn't worry about what to say. They had decided on things from the start.

"Awake already?" he asked.

Ivy smiled and patted her stomach. "In need of food

actually."

"Listen, Ivy," Christian began.

She stopped him before he could go on. "There's no need. We agreed on this. We both needed each other. No strings, no ties. No need to make up excuses. It was a one-time thing."

"That's...a first for me." He flashed a grin. "I'm never very good at the excuses anyway."

"There's no need to worry. I promise not to fall in love with you."

There was a ghost of a frown quickly covered by his smile. "That's good then."

"Want any food?"

"No thanks. I'm going to remain out here and listen to the rain without having to be suffocated by the couples in the house."

Ivy laughed, watching as his muscles rippled when he laid on his back, his hands behind his head. "See you in the morning."

"See ya."

Ivy walked out of the shed with a smile. It wasn't the rain soaking her that made her frown. It was the strange, unnamable feeling within her that she had made a mistake brushing Christian off so suddenly.

Though she didn't know why she felt that way. Neither of them wanted any kind of relationship. She stopped him before he could make up some lie and excuse.

Right?

She reached the porch and shook off as much of the rain as she could. Ivy removed her boots before she walked into the house. The blast of cold air from the AC gave her a chill.

A glance found a dishtowel by the sink that she used to wipe the rain from her face and arms. It was while she was putting the towel back that she realized she wasn't alone.

Ivy turned her head and met the blue eyes of Beau. He was at the table with a tall glass of milk and cookies.

"There's food in the fridge," he said.

She nodded, feeling as if she were a teenager getting caught sneaking back in the house. "Thanks."

"I should warn you that Christian likes women. He enjoys their company and their bodies, but he isn't the kind who will give you a future."

Ivy's hackles immediately went up, even though she told herself it was just a brother looking out for his family. "No need to worry. I don't have designs on Christian. He's a good guy, but that's where things stop."

Beau frowned, his head cocking to the side. "Really?"

"Really." She laughed then and turned to open the fridge. She peered inside and found the foil-covered plates. She took one out and set it on the counter. "Even if the Hell Hounds weren't after me, my life is hectic enough without adding a relationship to the mix."

She took off the foil and looked at the large portion of

etouffee spooned over rice. Ivy popped the plate in the microwave and heated it, feeling Beau's eyes still on her.

"Why?" Beau asked.

The microwave beeped. Ivy opened the door and stirred the food with a fork before testing the temperature. She removed the plate and set it on the table. Then she poured a glass of sweet tea and sat across from Beau.

"My illness. If my mother did sell her soul to make me better, who is to say that it won't return?" She shrugged and took a small bite. "My mother's life came to a halt to take care of me. I won't put someone else through that."

"And if you never get sick again?"

Ivy gave him a rueful smile. "Let's be honest here. We both know I'm not going to get away from the Hell Hounds. I have one more day. Maybe."

His frown increased as he sat forward, putting his forearms on the table. "You're going to give up so easily?"

"I don't want to die," she stated. "I'm trying to be realistic. In all the research each of you have so graciously done, no one has found a way for me to get away from the Hounds."

Ivy took a bit of food and stared at her plate as she chewed. She wasn't giving up. How could he even think that? She figured Beau would be rejoicing since she would be gone.

Beau picked up his milk and cookies and stood. "We'll find a way, Ivy. Christian risked his life to help you. The least you could do was give him some time."

CHAPTER

EIGHT

CHRISTIAN DIDN'T SLEEP once Ivy left. He watched the rain the rest of the night until it finally tapered off and the sun rose.

Only then did he gather his clothes and dress. His thoughts had been on Ivy the entire time. He had been happy, and then confused, at her quick dismissal of their lovemaking.

Though he was puzzled at why that made him angry. He should be ecstatic. He didn't have to lie to get away from a woman for once.

He should be clicking his heels in joy. Instead, he felt...sad.

He knew he had been made to taste Ivy's kiss, to know her body. They were meant to come together and know each other so carnally.

Christian's arms missed holding her against him. Her

arms hadn't just held him in return. She had shattered him then put him back together with a simple touch.

He stood at the doorway looking out at the bayou. For once it wasn't him pushing a woman away. It was Ivy doing the pushing while he wanted closer.

How the hell had that happened? *When* had it happened?

Christian ran a hand down his face and sighed wearily. He knew how to woo women to his bed. He was a master at rejecting them. What he didn't know how to do was win one over.

He fished out his phone from his pocket and scrolled through his favorites. He dialed the number and put the phone to his ear.

It rang four times before there came a sleepy voice that said, "Hello?"

"Riley?"

There was a beat of silence, then his sister said, "It's early, Christian."

"I know. I'm sorry to wake you. Are you doing okay?"

"Yeah."

He closed his eyes briefly. "That's good."

"What is it?" she asked, her voice coming through clearer as she woke. "You sound troubled."

"It's the normal. Thanks for finally answering my call. I left you several messages."

"I got them."

He nodded, then remembered she couldn't see him.

"Good, good. I am sorry, Riley. We didn't do right, but please understand that we were just trying to protect you."

She sighed loudly. "I'm a Chiasson, you big idiot. There's no running from what is part of my DNA."

"You deserved a normal life."

"Did it ever occur to you morons that I would rather be with my family facing the supernatural every day than having a normal life?" she asked, her voice deepening in anger.

Christian felt like a heel. None of them had bothered to ask Riley what she wanted. "No, sis. We didn't."

"I know what y'all did was out of love," she said in exasperation. "I went away because it's what each of you were pushing for. I foolishly thought I'd be able to return home afterward."

"I don't want to make you angry. I didn't call to hash out what we did wrong."

"Then why did you call?" she demanded.

Christian leaned back against the doorway. "I just wanted to hear your voice."

"Bullshit. I know you, Christian. I know that tone. Something's happened. What is it?" she urged.

"I...well, I've been given the brushoff from a woman." He frowned when he heard a bubble of laughter over the phone before Riley smothered it.

"Wow. I never thought I'd hear you say that."

Christian rubbed his forehead. "Look, I don't know what I'm feeling right now. It's all confusing."

"Answer me this. Do you want to see her again?"

"Yes."

Riley whistled. "You have got it bad. You never sleep with the same woman twice."

Christian prayed for patience as Riley spoke. He hadn't intended to talk to her about Ivy, but it just all came out before he could stop it.

"If you want to see her again, then make it happen," Riley said.

"I don't know how."

She laughed. "Oh, but you do, Christian. You're charming. Win her over. She'll never be able to withstand you."

"What if she does?"

"Then she's not worth your time. Though, I'd like to meet the woman who made my brother reconsider everything just to spend more time with her."

Christian couldn't help but smile as he thought of Ivy. "Her name is Ivy. She's confident, brave, beautiful, and completely in control."

"She sounds perfect for you," Riley said with a smile in her voice.

He released a breath. "Come home, Riley. Please."

"Soon," she said and ended the call.

Christian pocketed the phone and leaned his head back

against the doorway. He did want to see Ivy again, and not just to make love to her.

After so many years of knowing he would never settle down, it felt odd to crave someone so much. If he let Ivy in his life, she could die.

"Who am I kidding?" he asked himself. "She's already in danger with the Hell Hounds after her."

He hadn't wanted to care about a woman and be put in such a position where he worried about keeping her safe, and yet somehow he ended up doing exactly that.

"Stupid fate," he grumbled.

He was perfectly fine before Ivy.

Liar. You were empty, hollow. There was a void inside you that you refused to acknowledge.

Christian squeezed his eyes closed. He had been all of those things and more. It was worth it not to feel for someone so deeply. Then along came Curls. With her confidence and pluck. He hadn't stood a chance.

He had somehow known when he saw her in the bar. It's why he had waited until he was sure she left before he went out to his truck.

So much for taking matters into his own hands and putting her safely out of reach. Nope. Fate had stepped in and made sure they met.

A regular kismet.

Christian heard the rumble of thunder. More rain was in store with the hurricane brewing in the gulf. Last he checked it was headed toward Florida, but it could turn at the last minute as they were known to do.

He opened his eyes and pushed away from the doorway. After another look at the floor where he had made love to Ivy, Christian walked out of the shed to the house.

As he opened the back door, he spied her boots. He took off his own and went inside. The house was still quiet as everyone slept, but it wouldn't be long now before they woke.

Christian moved silently out of the kitchen and up the stairs to his room. He shut his door and immediately started undressing as he made his way to his bathroom.

IVY HEARD the water turn on next door. She knew it was Christian. She sat cross-legged on the bed as she combed out her wet hair and thought of him taking his shower.

She closed her eyes, imagining her soap-covered hands running over his hard muscles. If only she was with him. She could imagine him pushing her against the shower wall and kissing her. Her lips tingled just thinking about it.

"Stupid, stupid," Ivy said as she opened her eyes and tried to push Christian out of her mind.

It was impossible. She shouldn't still be thinking about him. Yet, how could she not? They were in the same house together. It wasn't like she could leave him behind as she did other men.

What would it be like to have someone like Christian around all the time?

Ivy stopped her thoughts instantly. She knew better than to go down that road. It was better that she was alone. Now more than ever with the Hounds after her. Even if by some miracle she managed to survive them, there was still her past illness returning hanging over her head.

The worry and fear had taken a toll on her mother, aging her seemingly overnight. Then there were the nights her mother spent at the hospital so Ivy wouldn't be alone.

Even when Ivy had been released from the hospital, returning home hadn't been great. Ivy couldn't be left alone since she was too weak to do anything herself. Her mother worked odd jobs just to keep a roof over their heads and hire a nurse to help care for her.

Ivy could never put someone else through that. She might have been ill, but she watched everything unfold from her bed, helpless to do anything for her mother. How many nights had Ivy heard her mother cry herself to sleep?

She dashed away tears of her own. It did no good to cry. She might hate being alone, but she knew it was for the best.

Ivy rose from the bed and grabbed her phone. Stacy had been texting each day. Ivy had to lie to her friend to keep her from the truth, and Ivy hated that. Stacy was one of the few who knew of her past illness.

She told Stacy she was staying with friends, which was about the only thing she hadn't lied about. It's also the only thing that kept Stacy from trying to see her.

Ivy sent off a quick text to Stacy to let her know she was feeling a bit better. Then she decided to give her mind a break and play some games on her phone.

It didn't take long to be absorbed in a game of backgammon. Ivy had no idea how long she played before there was a knock on her door.

"Come in," she said.

The door opened and Davena poked her head inside. Her blond hair was pulled back in a ponytail, and she wore her usual smile. "Morning."

"Morning," Ivy replied as she set aside her phone.

"When you get a chance, come downstairs. Beau thinks he has an idea."

"Sure."

"Oh, by the way, here are some clothes," Davena said as she walked into the room and set them on the bed. "You've been in those for a couple of days already."

Ivy laughed and looked down at herself. "Thank you."

"See you in a bit," Davena said and left.

Ivy rose and looked through the assortment of sweats and lounge wear. She finally decided on a pair of black sweats and an ash-gray tee.

She glanced at herself in the mirror and shrugged before walking out. There was no sound made as she walked barefoot down the stairs to the office where she heard voices.

Ivy stopped when her gaze clashed with Christian who once more sat behind the desk. His gaze lingered with hers before he nodded in greeting.

Hoping no one else saw the awkwardness, Ivy decided to remain at the entrance. "So, what's this idea?"

Beau shut the book he was reading. "I'll be the first to admit it's not a good one. It's called transference. There is a way that we can transfer your scent to someone else."

"And send the Hell Hounds after them?" she asked confused. "Absolutely not."

"It may be the only way to save you," Christian said.

Ivy shrugged. "Then I guess I'm going to die, because I refuse to give this to another innocent."

Vincent asked, "Even if we find someone deserving of it?"

"Even then," she said. She swung her eyes to Christian expecting him to put up a fight. That's when she realized they were all smiling. "Did I miss something?"

"Just that you're worthy of saving," Beau said and opened the book again.

Ivy came to the conclusion that the Chiassons were a bit off their rockers.

CHAPTER

NINE

"You're awfully quiet," Olivia said as she stood by Christian at the desk.

He glanced up from the book to find that Vincent was also with her. Christian shrugged off their words. "We're busy."

"Since when are you too busy to give us your opinion on anything?" Vincent asked.

Christian released a breath and covertly looked at Ivy, standing with Davena at the doorway. "I'm not. I just have nothing to say."

"A first for you." Vin rested a hip on the corner of the desk. "You and Ivy were gone a long time last night."

Christian leaned back in the chair and met Vin's gaze. "What did you expect? For us to start dancing right along with all of you?"

"Y'all do make a cute couple," Olivia said with a smile.

Christian shoved the chair away from the desk and stood. He gathered his books and shouldered his way between Olivia and Vincent to walk from the room.

He needed to be alone, to stop thinking about and looking at Ivy. She clouded his mind so he couldn't sort through things as easily. And his family wasn't helping in the least.

Christian took the stairs three at a time and shut himself in his room. He locked it to prevent anyone from barging in. Then he sat against his headboard and grabbed the book he had been looking through.

"WHAT THE HELL WAS THAT?" Vin asked Olivia in a low voice.

She shook her head helplessly. "If I didn't know better, I'd say he likes her."

Beau leaned over the desk and whispered, "Because he does."

Vin frowned. Christian? That couldn't be possible. He was so against forming an attachment that he went out of his way to ensure no woman would ever want anything lasting with him.

Vincent turned his head to look at Ivy. Then again, Ivy hadn't started out as someone he took to his bed. She had been in trouble and Christian brought her to the house. Obviously things had progressed from there.

"What are you thinking?" Olivia asked.

Vin looked down at her. "I think Beau may be right."

Olivia's dark eyes widened. "It would explain why he's so...sensitive about her."

"I honestly never thought Christian would find someone he cared enough about."

Olivia smiled and rested her hand on his chest. "Things happen for a reason."

Vin frowned then. "If Christian is falling for her, it'll crush him if the Hounds get her."

"We won't let that happen."

No, they wouldn't. It wasn't just to save Ivy, but to save Christian as well. Vincent knew his brother would fight against his feelings for Ivy. Vin prayed Ivy was strong enough, smart enough—and cared for Christian enough—to get him over his trepidation.

Ivy's eyes burned from staring too long at the computer screen. Hours later she was still reeling from the "test" she had been put through.

It did make her feel better when Davena told her that Christian wasn't happy about the test. Davena assured Ivy that it was a precaution, but Ivy had the feeling everyone wanted to make sure she wasn't just worthy of helping, but of being with Christian.

The Chiasson family was a tightknit group. Ivy spent half of her time watching their dynamic because it was so foreign. As an only child with one parent, Ivy didn't know what it meant to have so many people looking after her.

Their love for Christian was visible. Their worry was as well.

Ivy looked at the ceiling. Christian hadn't left his room since that morning. Lincoln had gone up and tried to talk to him. So had Olivia, but neither could get him to come out.

"This isn't normal for Christian," Ivy overheard Ava whisper to Lincoln.

Ivy frowned as she lowered her gaze back to the computer.

Lincoln kissed Ava, then said in a low voice, "It'll be fine in the end. Christian just needs some time."

Time? Time for what? Ivy's mind raced. Surely she wasn't the culprit. She and Christian had agreed on how things would be. He didn't want any entanglements any more than she.

Ivy squeezed her eyes closed, because she knew it for the lie that it was. Why had she found Christian now? Why did he have to be so damn charming and handsome? Why did he have to be so caring and brave?

She opened her eyes and blinked several times. Ivy couldn't look at another website. She closed the laptop and set it aside as she rose and walked out of the office to the front porch.

When she spotted the swing, she smiled and sat. With one leg tucked, she used her other foot to move the swing.

The gray clouds hadn't departed the area. No doubt there was more rain on the way. Ivy braved the mosquitos to have a moment to herself.

The humidity was thick, making her skin sticky and her curls tighten even more. She shoved her hair back and savored the beauty around her of live oaks with their thick limbs that branched out like gnarled fingers and the crepe myrtles with bright pink blooms still on them.

Christian's truck had been parked with the others off to the side, giving her a clear view of the expansive green lawn and the driveway.

How many more days would she get? Was this her last one? If so, why did she even bother talking herself out of whatever feelings had begun for Christian? Who cared if she felt something for him if she was about to die?

Based on everything she had read about the Hell Hounds, if someone did manage to elude them, it wasn't for long. The Hounds always found their scent and took the souls that belonged to Hell.

"Oh, Mom," Ivy murmured.

It was hard for her to even imagine her mother selling her soul. Then again, Ivy had seen how her mother fought to keep her alive. How many times had her mom told her that a parent would do anything for their child?

Ivy didn't completely understand because she didn't have a child of her own, but she knew the depth of her mother's love. Her mother sacrificed so much for her. It wasn't a stretch to think she had sold her soul for Ivy to become healthy.

She wished her mother had told her so she could've been prepared. But that wasn't her mother. Her mom preferred to keep her worry to herself.

Movement out of the corner of her eye drew her attention. She stared at Christian as he walked across the soggy ground to his truck. He opened the bed and pulled a large box to him. After he unlocked it, he threw open the lid and rummaged through it.

Ivy watched as he pulled out a crossbow and set of bolts. Suddenly he stilled, his head swinging to her. Their gazes clashed.

Then he went back to looking in the box. "You shouldn't be out here alone."

"I'm on the porch. It's safe."

"I'd rather you were inside the house."

She raised a brow, giving him her most annoyed expression that he didn't even bother glancing at her to see. "I'd rather be out here."

"Did someone say something to send you outside?" he asked as he shut the lid and relocked the box. Then he closed his tailgate and rested an arm on it as he looked at her.

Damn but his blue eyes could impale her. His black hair was tousled, as if he had been running his fingers through the length.

Ivy realized belatedly that he had asked a question. "No," she answered. "I'm not used to so many people around all the time."

"I guess not as an only child." He pushed away from the truck and walked to the porch.

He set the crossbow and bolts down and sat on the top step to lean against a column, looking at her. Ivy grew self-conscious under his perusal.

"I can't imagine being an only child," Christian said. "Just as I'm sure you can't imagine growing up with four siblings."

Ivy smiled. "I can't. Though, I admit that I like the atmosphere here. The way each of you protect the other. You know they'll always be there for you."

"Yeah." He looked down at his hands. "Despite all the tragedies the family has suffered, we lean on each other. I never thought of that until now." He lifted his eyes to her. "You didn't have anyone to lean on when your mother died."

Ivy shrugged, trying to not feel the same overwhelming sadness that stayed with her for many months. "I was numb at first. The shock of it all, I guess. I barely remember planning the funeral. I don't think it hit me until a few days after the funeral when I woke up and walked into the kitchen calling to her." Ivy swallowed, her throat clogged with emotion. "That's when I realized I was alone. The tears I hadn't been able to shed up until that moment was like a damn bursting. I didn't leave the house for days."

"No one should have to suffer something like that alone."

Ivy hastily wiped away a tear that escaped. "I got through it."

Christian nodded and looked out over the Chiasson land. "You'll get through this as well."

"Let's be honest, Christian. Despite all you and your family has done, there's no getting away from the Hell Hounds. This could be my last day."

His head jerked to her, his gaze narrowed and angry. "So you'll give up?"

"I'm not saying that. I get through each day by being realistic. Do I hope something comes of all the research and I get the Hounds scent off me? Yes. But the odds aren't in my favor."

"Sometimes you need to forget reality."

"Reality for me was months in the hospital hooked up to numerous machines that beeped all the time. Reality was taking handfuls of pills three or four times a day to beat whatever was wrong into submission. Reality was not being able to stand on my own or even put on my own clothes. I couldn't feed myself, much less bathe myself. That was reality."

"A reality your mother changed."

Ivy looked away. When she had herself back under control, she met Christian's gaze and stood. "Now my reality is that the Hell Hounds have come to kill me to show my mother before my soul—presumably—is allowed to go free. Reality is reality, no matter how you look at it."

"Is that right?" he asked and climbed to his feet. "Hope, Ivy. You need hope. Yes, face your reality, but don't give up. You survived your illness every day because you hoped to beat it."

"Don't talk as if you were there and experienced it," she stated angrily and walked to the door.

She was yanked against Christian's hard chest a moment later. His bright blue eyes were alight with some emotion she wasn't sure of.

"I've experienced you, Ivy Pierce," he murmured before he kissed her.

CHAPTER
TEN

CHRISTIAN HAD KNOWN it was a mistake to pull her against him, but he hadn't been able to stop himself. He'd needed Ivy, like she was a basic ingredient to his survival.

The tightness in his chest loosened when her arms snaked around his neck. He deepened the kiss, his body responding instantly to the heady feel of her.

By the time he ended the kiss, they were both breathing heavily. Christian leaned his forehead against hers.

"Don't give up," he urged.

Ivy smiled and traced his lip with her finger. "I'm not. But you need to be realistic that I might die."

"There's a chance I might die every night I go out hunting," he argued.

She kissed his jaw before she rested her head on his

chest. "If the worst happens, it won't be because you didn't do all that you could."

Christian tightened his arms around her. There was a way to save Ivy. There was always a way. He just had to find it.

"I should get back inside and do more research."

Christian didn't let her move. "Not yet. You need to have a bit of downtime."

"You're probably right. I really don't want my last day to be filled with research."

He hated that she was able to joke about it. It was Ivy's way of coping with reality, but Christian didn't have to like it.

Neither of them spoke about the kiss or the fact they were embracing. Whether she wanted to admit it or not, Ivy didn't want to be alone. Since Christian only wanted to be with her, it worked out perfectly.

Every time he thought about her dying, there was an ache in his chest. It started small, but it was growing rapidly.

"Do you really never want to fall in love?" she asked into the silence.

Christian wrapped one of her curls around his finger. "My parents were deeply in love. They did everything together. There were many nights I'd wake to hear music downstairs. I'd go to the railing and look down to find them dancing."

"What a beautiful memory."

"It was. I remember barely being able to wait until I could find such love. Then my mother was killed. I can still hear the bellow that echoed through the bayous from my father when he found her body. That sound…" he paused and swallowed. "It haunts me to this day. It was like his heart had been ripped from him. The desolation, the anguish of that sound was horrible."

Her arms tightened. "I can't even imagine."

"Later that night he died. He wanted revenge. My father had such a cool head when he went hunting. He taught us patience and control, but he had neither after my mother's death."

"You fear you'll be the same."

"I know I will." He kissed the top of Ivy's head. "I know if I ever fall in love it'll be deep. It'll be the kind of love my parents had. I've always known that."

"So you've protected yourself."

He rested his chin atop her head. "I have. Even as I watched my brothers fall in love. It's in my face on a daily basis, but I know what'll happen to them if their women are killed."

"Most people don't understand why we push others away," she said. "They crave being with another, to have that connection. We do as well, but we know it comes with a price. It's a price some can't pay."

"It's a price some don't want to pay."

Ivy lifted her head from his chest and looked up at him.

"You're a good guy, Christian. You have a strong family. You shouldn't push love away if it comes your way. You deserve to be happy."

"And you don't?"

She smiled. "I'm healthy. I fear being that sick again, of being that helpless. It's terrifying. I always figured that I could have one or the other—health or love."

"Your mother sold her soul for you to be well."

"Will it last?" she asked with her brows raised. "What if a miracle happens and we get the Hounds off my scent. Will the Demon of Souls be content with things? Will he take away my health?"

"You live in fear."

"And you don't? You fear loving someone so deeply that if they die, you die."

Christian shook his head in denial. "We're talking apples to oranges."

"Says the man who has never been in the hospital for months at a time," she retorted.

Christian stroked a finger down her face. "What if the Hounds leave you alone and you stay healthy?"

"What if love finds you?"

He feared love had already found him. It stood in his arms looking up at him with hazel eyes. "I asked first."

"Those are big ifs, but if it happens, I might have to reevaluate things."

"Me too," he answered. There was no way he could tell

her that he felt something for her. Not now. Not after the talk they had the night before about not wanting relationships. She would think he said it all to get her in bed.

She returned her head to his chest. "This is nice."

"Very." Christian closed his eyes and began to pray for a miracle.

"I TOLD YOU," Beau said to the others as they stared out the window watching Christian and Ivy.

Davena elbowed him in the side. "You weren't the only one who saw it."

"I was the only one who said anything."

Lincoln turned away from the window as worry set in. "We better work faster."

"Why?" Vincent asked.

Linc faced the others. "Seeing Christian just now brought back a memory when we were just boys. Riley was only a baby at the time. Christian told me he couldn't wait to find a love like Mom and Dad had."

"That's not good," Beau said with a frown.

Ava shook her head in confusion. "Why? Wouldn't that be good news?"

Linc looked at everyone in the room. "Christian changed his mind about falling in love after our parents' deaths. If he's falling for Ivy and she dies—"

"It'll crush him like it did Dad," Vincent finished. He slammed his hand into his thigh. "Fuck!"

Olivia took her place on the sofa. "Then we better get to reading."

"Especially since we don't know how long Davena's spell to mask Ivy from the Hounds will work," Beau said.

Linc returned to the window. Christian and Ivy hadn't moved. He ached to see the chance before his brother that could very well be snatched from his grasp.

It wasn't right. Christian was the type of man who loved once and loved deep. Whether he had already fallen for Ivy or was in the process, Lincoln wasn't going to rest until they found a way to save Ivy.

THE REST of the afternoon was spent on the porch with Christian. The smell of dinner drifted to them. She snuggled back against Christian as they lounged on the swing.

Most of the time had been spent in silence. It was a comfortable silence, the kind where each was content to just be with the other.

The few times they had talked had been stories about his family and their exploits. Ivy was amazed she had lived her entire life in Lyons Point and never heard of the Chiassons.

If she had been well enough to go to school there was no

doubt Christian would've snagged her attention quick enough. He was too gorgeous not to.

His question from earlier still rolled around in her mind. If the Hell Hounds released her, and if she remained healthy, would she love?

She would only admit it to herself, but she would if it was with Christian. Ivy was able to be herself with him. He made her feel safe and sexy. He inspired wicked thoughts of tearing off his clothes and having her way with him.

It didn't help that she had come to realize he was the type of man who would stay by her side whether she was healthy or not.

"I feel bad that we've been out here," she said.

Christian chuckled. "I don't."

"Okay. I don't either," she said with a smile as she tilted her head back to look at him.

He touched her face with the pads of his fingers. "I've enjoyed this."

"I didn't know I needed this. Thank you."

Christian flashed a charming smile. "Anytime."

Ivy lowered her head. "We'll have to go in soon."

"No we don't. We can eat out here."

"Won't that be rude?"

He tugged on her earlobe. "Nope. We can do whatever you want."

"Eating out here sounds fun. If you're sure the others won't be upset."

"They won't," he assured her. "What else do you want to do?"

It began to mist, with the droplets growing in size a few moments later.

"Well, there goes me lying on the ground to look at the stars."

"I'd have taken you to the roof to get you that much closer."

It was such an innocent sentence, but Ivy smiled in joy because no one had ever done anything like that for her.

"After that?" Christian asked.

Ivy sat up and turned to him. "Will you sleep with me tonight?"

"Absolutely."

She smiled and leaned in to kiss him when a distant howl turned her blood to ice. Ivy froze. Christian jumped up from the swing and pulled her protectively behind him.

"They're a ways off," he said as he scanned the front yard.

"Not that far." They found her. Davena's spell had given her a few days, but it looked like her time was up.

Christian took her hand and walked to the door. He yanked the screen open so hard it busted one of the hinges. The front door flew open before he could reach for it.

Lincoln stood in the entrance. He pulled Ivy inside while Christian grabbed his weapon and rushed in the house.

All around her was chaos as they gathered weapons and

Davena began to chant. Ivy however, had eyes for only one person. Christian.

If only she had been able to stop time and have a few more hours with him. She wouldn't have left him that morning after they made love. She would've stayed in his arms watching the rain. Now her choices were about to be taken from her once and for all.

CHRISTIAN HELD HIS CROSSBOW, knowing that the weapon would do him no good against the Hell Hounds. The Hounds went after only their target—unless someone tried to stop them.

He was going to try and stop them. There was no other choice for him. He hadn't just promised Ivy he would keep her safe, and it wasn't just his duty as a Chiasson. He would do it because...he loved her.

"Get Ivy to the shed!" Vincent bellowed.

Christian's head swung around to Ivy. He looked into her eyes and saw the stark fear in her hazel depths. She was waiting on his agreement before she did anything.

He rushed to her, grabbing her hand as he walked past her, tugging her after him into the kitchen. Beau ran around them and out the back door. He held the screen open, his shotgun pointed up as he looked around.

"Go," he told them.

Ivy stayed next to him as they ran from the porch, across the wet grass, to the shed. Christian whirled around once she was inside to cover Beau as he followed them.

"You should be with Davena," Christian said.

Beau grunted. "She told me you would need me out here."

Christian glanced at Ivy who stood against one of the large cages. Then he looked at his brother and said in a low voice, "Don't put yourself in the way of the Hounds. You'll die and Davena will be pissed off enough to bring me back from the dead only to kill me for letting you die."

"You think you'll be killed tonight?"

"I'm prepared for it."

Beau nodded slowly. "Does Ivy know?"

"Know what?" Christian asked.

"That you love her."

He looked away. "No."

"Interesting."

Christian returned his gaze to his brother when he heard him dialing someone from his cell phone. He gave Beau a questioning look, but Beau just smiled as he turned the speaker on. After two rings a male voice answered.

"Kane, we're in a bit of a rush. We need y'alls help."

Their cousin in New Orleans said, "Hang on. Let me get

the others." With the phone held away from him, Kane yelled, "Hey! Everyone in Myles's office now. It's an emergency!"

Christian looked at Ivy to find her still in the same spot, her arms wrapped around herself. She was doing a good job of holding it together, but it was obvious by the way she shook that she was unraveling.

"We're all here," Kane's voice came through the phone. "What's going on?"

Christian turned his attention to the cell phone. "Hell Hounds."

"You're fucked then," the eldest LaRue brother, Solomon said.

"The woman we're protecting didn't sell her soul," Beau explained.

Christian sighed as the weight of what they were trying settled over him. "It was Ivy's mother. She sold her soul to get Ivy well ten years ago."

"Then what's the problem?" Kane asked.

"Ivy's mother died a year ago. We suspect it was by her own hand," Beau explained.

There was a string of curses. Then Court said, "We haven't done that much research on them, but we'll see what we can find."

"We don't have the time," Christian said through clenched teeth.

Beau put his hand on Christian's arm and told the others,

"Davena spelled Ivy so that she was hidden from the Hounds. It gave us a few days to do our own investigation, but the spell is wearing off. The Hounds are near."

"You should've called earlier," Solomon said.

Christian hung his head. Their cousins had been a last resort, and it was turning out to be a bust.

"Call Minka."

Christian jerked his head up at the voice. His gaze pinned Beau, but his brother wasn't at all surprised to hear Riley's voice. "You knew."

He wasn't sure whether to be furious with Beau for keeping their sister's location a secret, or for Riley for staying away.

"Yes, he knew," Riley said. "I asked for some time, Christian, and Beau gave it to me."

Beau shrugged. "It was the least I could do after what we did."

"We'll talk about that later," Riley said, her voice growing stronger as if she walked closer to Kane's phone. "Minka might be able to help."

Christian frowned, wishing they were with him instead of over the phone. "Who the hell is Minka?"

"A witch. A powerful one at that. She might be able to help."

"Then get her on the phone."

"Give me a sec," Riley said.

A moment later and Kane's voice came over the phone.

"Riley is calling Minka now. The witch has surprised us in the past. She very well might have the answers you seek."

"Don't get my hopes up," Ivy said.

Christian frowned and walked to her. "I asked you to give me time. Now I'm asking you not to lose hope."

"I won't have you sacrifice your life to protect me. The Hounds will get me one way or another. You and your family have given me a few days I wouldn't have had otherwise."

Christian shook his head. "There's a way out of this. We just need to find it."

"Don't lie to her," Solomon's voice said. "It's the worst thing you can do."

Christian ground his teeth together and looked back at Beau and his phone. "I'm not lying. There *is* a way, and we'll find it."

"Hoodoo," Riley said through the phone. "Minka said to use goofer dust around Ivy."

Beau's forehead furrowed deeply. "That'll only last for so long."

"It'll give Minka time. Do it!" Riley shouted.

Beau tossed his phone at Christian and rushed from the shed. More howls sliced through the night. The Hounds were growing closer. They usually ran in packs of two, but there were instances where three Hounds went after a soul.

Two was bad enough. Three would mean that two would keep them occupied while the third went after Ivy.

Christian hated the fear that filled his belly. Is this what his father felt like the night their mother died when he couldn't find her?

"Christian?"

Riley's voice pulled him out of his dark thoughts. "Yeah."

"Ivy couldn't be in better hands."

Ivy smiled up at Christian as she replied, "I agree."

Beau stormed back in the shed with Lincoln and Vincent. Christian gave Ivy a quick kiss before he stepped back so Beau could pour the dust around her.

"It's done," Beau said. "How long do we need to wait, Riley?"

Christian watched his brothers frown while Riley told them it would take as long as it took for Minka to find what she needed.

"She'll work fast," Kane said.

Vincent took a step toward the phone, but Beau put a hand on his chest and shook his head. Vin and Linc exchanged looks, but neither said a word about discovering Riley was in New Orleans.

"So," Riley said, a smile in her voice. "I can't wait to meet you, Ivy."

Ivy tried to laugh, but her fear was too great. "Same here. I've heard a lot about you."

"Don't believe everything Christian says. He tends to forget things."

Beau snorted. "Always."

Christian glared at Beau. "Hey."

"The truth hurts," Riley said with a laugh.

"Y'all can both kiss my sweet ass." Christian appreciated what Riley was trying to do, but he understood that it was a life-or-death situation for Ivy.

Ivy's eyes crinkled at the corners as she gazed at him. "If I don't get a chance later, I wanted to thank all of you here and in New Orleans for your help."

"Anytime," the LaRues said in unison.

Vin nodded his head to Ivy. "It's what we do."

"Amen," Linc said as he shot her a wink.

Beau rested his shotgun on his shoulder. "As if we could turn away the one woman who captured Christian's attention."

There was a loud boom as something slammed against the side of the shed. Ivy squatted, her hands over her ears as the Hell Hounds barked incessantly.

"Riley!" Christian bellowed.

"Hang on! Do you hear me? I'm going to be so pissed off if the four of you get yourselves killed!"

Christian set down the phone inside the circle with Ivy and turned around to take his position. He and his brothers fanned out around Ivy with their weapons at the ready.

As suddenly as the Hounds came, the noise ended. The only sound that broke the quiet were Ivy's harsh breaths. No one said a word, not even the others on the other end of the phone.

The seconds turned to minutes. Finally, Christian said, "Riley?"

"Hang on," their sister said.

Christian could hear her talking to someone else as her voice grew dimmer and dimmer.

"She's on the phone with Minka," Court explained.

Christian prayed that the witch had found something. He couldn't lose Ivy. It would break him as nothing else could.

He realized at that moment that he hadn't been the strong one of the family. He had been the weakest, erecting a barrier around his heart because he had known this day would come.

Just as he knew he wouldn't survive losing Ivy.

"Tell us you have good news, Court," Lincoln said.

Court was silent for a moment. "I can't tell. Riley has her back to us, but she's writing something down."

"You should've called us sooner," Solomon said. "We could've been there with you."

Christian wished they had called them, but it was too late now. All the research in the world hadn't given them the answers they needed.

Davena, as good as she was, didn't know magic as a witch who had been raised using spells did. Without her, however, Ivy wouldn't have had time to prepare. Then again, that might be worse than not knowing what was after you.

"Where the fuck are the Hounds?" Christian ground out.

Beau adjusted his rifle. "I like the quiet to their barking."

"I'm with Christian. I'd rather get the show on the road," Linc said.

Vin lowered his machete and turned toward the phone. "Solomon, I'd ask you and the others continue to look after Riley as well as coming to get Olivia, Ava, and Davena if the worst happens."

"You have my word," Solomon said.

Christian should have known his brothers would stand with him whether he wanted them to or not. They were Chiassons, the defenders of the innocent, slayers of the supernatural.

They were blood, family.

Those ties went too deep for them to let him face the Hounds alone.

CHAPTER

TWELVE

IVY LISTENED to Christian and his brothers to take her mind off of what was happening. It was only when Vincent asked Solomon to come for their women that she understood.

They planned to put themselves in front of the Hounds to keep her alive.

It boggled her mind. They didn't know her. Sure, they protected the parish, but that didn't mean they should sacrifice their lives and leave behind the women they loved just for her.

She was no one. She was worth nothing and left no one behind. The Chiassons, on the other hand, were the one thing that kept the parish safe. They *were* needed.

Ivy looked at Christian. Her heart ached for what could've been—what *should've* been. She saw him for what he was—the man who would cherish her, love her, protect her. No longer could she deny what had been building since the moment she met him.

Love. The one thing she had kept at arm's length for years.

But it found her despite her precautions. How sad that she only had a few hours of it. Yet, those few hours had been truly wonderful. To be in the arms of a man who was willing to risk his life for her, a man who always put others before himself.

A man who made love to her with exquisite tenderness and thrilling command. A man who knew the meaning of friendship, family, and love.

Ivy picked up the cell phone. Christian and his brothers began to talk strategy. She took the opportunity offered to her and switched the speaker off.

"Riley?" she whispered into the phone.

Christian's sister answered immediately. "I'm here."

"I know what Christian plans to do. I know that the others will stand with him, but I can't let that happen."

There was a brief pause before Riley asked, "What do you intend?"

"When Christian first brought me here, I didn't understand what your family does. During my time here, I discovered the full extent of things. Christian won't stand down, and neither will your brothers. I can't have them die for me."

"Christian won't let you face them alone," Kane said.

Ivy watched Christian. His black hair was disheveled, his face set in hard lines. "I don't have magic to stop him. But Davena does."

"Oh God," Riley said in a strangled voice.

Court said, "You'll die, Ivy."

"I'm going to die either way. Why should Christian, Beau, Lincoln, and Vincent also join me?"

She knew when no one spoke up that they agreed with her. Now all she needed to do was convince Davena to use magic to stop them.

"I'll call Davena again."

Ivy heard the sadness in Riley's voice. "Thank you. Take care of your brothers, Riley. They regret their actions, but please understand everything they did was to protect you because they love you so dearly."

Riley sniffed. "I know. The big louts are my world."

"Tell them that, will you?"

Ivy didn't wait for a response. She turned the speaker back on and set the phone down before she stood. When the time came, she would have to act quickly.

The door to the shed flew open. The sliding door behind her began to rattle before it slid open as if a giant had flung it.

Ivy closed her eyes because she knew the Hell Hounds were there, waiting to take her. She sent up a silent prayer that Davena would hurry and set the spell in place to keep Christian from stepping between her and the Hounds.

"They're here," Lincoln said.

Ivy took a deep breath and opened her eyes. Death. That's what stood just a few feet from her. She might not be able to see it, but it was there.

She was thankful the beasts were invisible, or Christian would've already attacked. Not to mention Ivy wouldn't see the Hounds coming for her. It would happen quickly, of that she was certain.

Vincent's machete fell from his hand. He blinked a few times as if disoriented. A moment later and Lincoln's Bowie knives clattered to the floor a heartbeat behind Beau's shotgun.

Christian turned and looked at her, confusion marring his gorgeous face and clouding his eyes.

"It's for the best," Ivy said. "You're needed."

"Ivy," he began, as he fought to keep hold of the crossbow.

A tear fell down her face when he lost the battle and the crossbow fell from his lax fingers. He looked from his weapon at his feet to his hands.

"You wanted to save me," Ivy said. "Well, you did. More than you can imagine. Now it's my turn to save you."

She stepped over the line of black dust encircling her and walked to Christian. Ivy cupped his cheek while his blue eyes burned into hers.

"Ivy, please."

"The only way I can do this is knowing that you'll still be

around." She forced a smile as her vision swam with tears. "Can't you see, Christian Chiasson? I fell in love with you."

"Ivy, I—"

She hurried to talk over him, because she knew it wouldn't take much for him to change her mind. It was time for her to be strong and do the sacrificing. "This is for you and your family."

Ivy kissed him quickly and walked around him to the door. She looked up and saw Davena, Olivia, and Ava standing on the porch.

"I'm sorry, Ivy. I did the first spell before the one you asked," Davena said with her hands on the screen surrounding the porch to keep out the mosquitos.

Ivy was confused. "What are you talking about?"

"Minka found a spell that would allow us to see the Hounds," Ava said. "To better fight them."

The night just kept getting better and better. Ivy shrugged. There was no use getting upset over it now. The spell was done, and it had been done to help Christian and his brothers fight.

"I think you're very brave," Olivia said as she wiped at her eyes.

Brave? Not hardly. Ivy just couldn't imagine seeing Christian hurt. That's the only thing that propelled her. Her mother sold her soul to get her healthy. Christian was willing to die to try and prevent the Hounds from getting her.

"We're going to miss you," Davena said. "You were good for Christian."

Ivy tried to smile, but failed. She stepped out of the shed and onto the grass. After a quick glance back at Christian who was watching her, Ivy turned and started walking to the front yard.

Her goal was to get off Chiasson land, but since she had no idea how much land they had, she opted to get as far from the house as she could.

"I'm yours," she told the Hell Hounds. "I'm not going to run anymore. I only ask that you allow me to get far from the house. Please."

She kept walking, her heart pounding in her chest and her body going cold from her blood turning to ice. Every step was a victory, though it took everything she had to remain upright and not give in and collapse where she was.

The tall live oaks stood like silent giants with their thick limbs outstretched as if reaching for her as she passed. The moon was hidden behind the clouds and the rain was falling lightly now.

It wasn't exactly a beautiful night to die. But when was it ever a beautiful time to die? Ivy thought back over her life and regretted so much. Was that how most people felt when they knew their time was near?

How much more she could've done and been had she opened herself up to people more. Yes, there would've been heartbreak, but that was part of life. There would also have been joy, happiness, and so many more memories.

Ivy smiled as she thought of Christian. She might regret a lot, but she didn't regret him or their time together. He hadn't let her turn away as she had so many other times.

Christian forced her to see herself. It might have been fear that pushed her to give in to the desire she had for him, but it was love that bound her to him.

Love. The one thing she had thought never to know.

How fate must be laughing at her now.

Ivy squared her shoulders as she crossed over the driveway to another field. She had no idea where she was going, only that it was far away from Christian. He would come looking for her, but he didn't need to find her at the house.

She began to hum to help calm her nerves. The longer it went without the Hell Hounds attacking her, the more frightened she became.

"Mom, I know why you sold your soul now. I wish you hadn't, but I could see myself doing the same for Christian. Your sacrifice gave me a second chance, and I let the past confine me, preventing me from living as you'd hoped I would. I'm sorry for so many things. I hope you're not suffering too much."

The sound of a growl in front of her stopped Ivy in her tracks. Her eyes might be used to the darkness, but she still couldn't see the Hound. And she was immensely grateful.

"You've let me come as far as you will, huh?" she asked the air in front of her. "I guess I owe you my thanks for that concession."

It was the red eyes she saw first. Ivy's mouth fell open when the air shimmered and the Hell Hound became visible. He was huge. His head came to her shoulders, and his body was solid black. He looked like a cross between a Doberman Pincher and a Rottweiler.

His ears were pointed, his teeth were huge as his lips pulled back in a snarl. His paws were easily the size of Christian's hand. The Hound snarled, saliva dripping from his mouth as he continued to growl.

Ivy took a step back and whirled around with a shriek when another Hound snapped his teeth behind her. With her heart in her throat, she counted six Hell Hounds that surrounded her.

She lifted her gaze to Christian's house. The porch light was only a faint glow through the trees. She nodded and held out her hands as she closed her eyes.

"I didn't sell my soul. It's not yours to take. It's mine. You might be able to kill me, but you'll never have my soul."

A scream was stopped in Ivy's throat when a Hell Hound pounced on her.

CHAPTER
THIRTEEN

Christian didn't take his eyes off the doorway that Ivy disappeared through. Rage and fear tangled within him until his stomach was in knots.

"Ivy!" he bellowed.

But it did no good. She didn't return.

He could see his brothers fighting the effects of the spell. Suddenly, three figures filled the doorway. And Christian's heart plummeted to his feet.

"Davena, release me. Now," he said through clenched teeth.

Davena walked to Beau and put her hand on his face as Olivia went to Vincent and Ava stood before Lincoln. "Please don't be angry."

"Drop the spell, honey," Beau said.

The next instant, Christian was able to move. He bent to

grab his crossbow as he ran out of the shed shouting Ivy's name. He raced as fast as he could, his lungs burning as he desperately sought to find her.

Christian didn't slow until he reached the empty field a half a mile from their house. He stopped and turned in a circle, not letting the darkness deter him. He spent too many nights in the dark hunting evil.

"Ivy!"

His only answer were the sounds of the bayou. Christian bent over to catch his breath. Behind him he could hear his brothers running toward him.

Christian braced his hands on his knees and squeezed his eyes closed. When he opened them, the clouds broke long enough for the sliver of moon to light the air for a fraction of a second.

Just long enough for Christian to see a glint of something in the grass.

He knelt on one knee and held out his hand behind him. "I need a phone," he said to his brothers as they reached him.

One was quickly placed in his hand. Christian turned on the flashlight and searched the area.

"What are you looking for?" Vincent asked.

Christian's throat closed with emotion when he lifted a single gold hoop earring. The same ones Ivy had been wearing. He stood and turned to his brothers, showing them the earring.

"Son of a bitch," Beau mumbled as he turned away.

Vincent ran a hand down his face and looked at the ground.

"Let's keep looking," Lincoln said.

Christian enfolded the earring in his hand. "She's gone. I don't hear the Hounds anymore. I lost her, Linc."

He shouldered through his brothers and walked back to the house. Though he could spend an eternity searching the world over for Ivy, he would never find her. She had popped into his life, and departed just as suddenly.

But she left her mark upon his heart.

Christian saw the girls standing on the porch, waiting. They said his name, but he was in no mood to talk or listen to Davena's reasoning for doing the spell that kept him from helping Ivy.

He didn't stop until he was at the doorway of his room. Yet, he couldn't go in. He had to be alone. Christian turned on his heel and walked back downstairs as his brothers were coming in the front door.

"Christian, we need to talk," Vincent said.

He ignored them and strode out the back.

Beau, Lincoln, and Vincent stood on the back porch watching Christian.

"He shouldn't be alone," Beau said.

Linc sighed loudly. "We could go after him, but he would keep eluding us. He needs to be by himself to deal with his grief."

"Ivy's death will kill him from the inside out," Vin said.

Lincoln nodded as Christian vanished in the bayou. "Without a doubt. I just can't believe there wasn't a way to save her."

"Who says we have to stop looking?" Beau smiled at his brothers. "We all know there are loopholes in all contracts, even the ones by the Crossroads demons."

Vincent spun and hurried back inside the house. "Get the books, Beau. Linc, call our cousins. It's going to take all of us."

IVY GROANED as she rolled onto her side. She ached all over as if she had been a punching bag for someone. With great effort she raised herself up on one elbow and opened her eyes.

"What the hell," she mumbled as she found herself on a cold black stone floor.

A glance showed all four walls also in black. There were no windows and no door that she could see. Panic began to set in. She sat up and thought of the last thing she had memory of.

"Christian."

That's when she recalled the Hell Hounds. Everything came back in a rush, including the look of the hideous Hounds.

Ivy tried to keep her breathing normal, but the longer she

sat there, the more she began to hyperventilate. Was she dead? Was this Hell? Because it certainly couldn't be Heaven.

She scooted back to the wall and set herself in the corner. Wherever she was, it wasn't good. If only Christian was with her. He would know what to do.

Despite her wishing for him, she was glad he was still with his family. He was alive to defend the parish as only his family could. She felt good for having ensured his and his brothers' survival.

Ivy dropped her head back against the wall and closed her eyes. They said the Hounds were only supposed to kill her, show her soul to her mother, and then her soul would go wherever it was supposed to. Ivy would like to think that was Heaven. She might not have gone to church every Sunday, but she hadn't committed murder, stolen, or anything vile.

Why then hadn't she seen her mother? More troubling was how had she gotten to this place? She didn't remember anything after the Hell Hound pounced on her. It was fathomable that she had already been brought before her mother and killed.

Ivy pinched her arm. She still felt very much alive. Surely she would know if she was dead? Although if she was, she missed the pain of it. Which was a good thing.

"Glad to see you awake."

Ivy's head jerked up as the voice startled her. She found the woman standing in the middle of the room. Her long blond hair was a beautiful gold color. Not a hair was out of place as the length was pulled over one shoulder in large, loose curls.

Despite the black floor and walls, Ivy was able to see the woman clearly, as if a light shown on her, illuminating the black leather jacket that conformed to her body and the white lace tank beneath.

The woman's long legs were encased in black leather pants with black stiletto boots. She was smiling when Ivy's gaze returned to her face.

Stunning didn't even begin to describe the woman. She was Charlize Theron beautiful with clear blue eyes, high cheekbones, and perfectly plump lips.

"Like what you see, huh?" she asked.

Ivy stared at her a moment longer. "Who are you?"

"You couldn't begin to pronounce my name. Just call me Liv."

"All right. Liv. Where am I?"

Liv's lips twisted as she shrugged. "You know exactly where you are, Ivy."

"Hell."

Liv nodded.

"Why am I still here?"

Liv raised a blonde brow. "That's a bit more complicated."

Ivy used the wall to climb to her feet. "Am I dead?"

"Not yet."

Liv said it with a smile that sent a chill down Ivy's spine. "You're obviously ready to meet out that deed. Why am I still alive?"

"The Chiassons. You have information on them that we'd like."

"Not going to happen."

"Then you'll be down here for awhile."

The fear within Ivy was overtaken by anger. "You can't do that."

"We can do anything we please," Liv said, with a confident smile.

"There are many who know the Chiassons. Why are you asking me?"

"Because you fell in love with Christian. You made it so easy. That family has been killing us for centuries, and it's time it stopped."

Ivy squared her shoulders. "You might stop one of them, but not all of them. There are enough that know what the Chiassons do to pick up where they left off if you do manage to kill them."

"Kill them?" Liv asked in a strangled voice. She laughed loud and long. "Oh, sweetie. We're not going to kill them. We're going to turn them to our side."

"Never going to happen."

Liv shrugged as she crossed her arms over her chest and looked Ivy up and down. "Strange things happen when you keep two lovers away from each other. Christian fell hard for you. The longer he goes thinking you're dead, the easier he'll be to turn our way. After all, we have the one thing he wants above anything else."

Ivy covered her mouth with her hand as her stomach revolted. Christian was too strong. He wouldn't fall for what was planned. Not her Christian.

"No."

"You can deny it all you want," Liv said saucily. "We have Christian right where we want him."

Ivy let Liv's words repeat in her head as she frowned. "You talk as if you've been planning this."

"Well, of course."

"What?"

Liv chuckled and walked to the side to lean against a wall. "You and Christian have been destined for each other since before you were born."

"That's not how it works."

"Denial won't change anything. You humans think you know so much, but in reality, you know nothing. The world runs very differently than you've been led to believe. There are some couples that are destined for each other like you and Christian. Then there are some that don't happen until they meet like Lincoln and Ava."

Ivy was thankful the wall was behind her, because her legs were too wobbly to hold her.

"We tried to keep Davena from Beau, but they were another couple fated for each other."

Ivy put her hands over her ears. "Stop talking."

"Is the truth too painful to bear?"

The snarky tone was too much for Ivy. She closed her eyes and thought back to one of the few perfect moments in her life—sitting on the swing with Christian, listening to the rain fall.

"Hold on to your memories while you can," Liv said next to Ivy's ear. "They'll be gone soon enough."

Ivy opened her eyes, but Liv was gone. Ivy slumped to the floor and buried her face in her hands.

CHAPTER

FOURTEEN

IT WAS two days after Ivy vanished that Christian returned to the house. He had no intention of staying. He wanted to fill up his backpack with supplies, and then he was leaving.

For good.

"Christian," Davena said as she descended the stairs and saw him in the foyer.

He gave her a nod in greeting, then started up the stairs to his room. She stepped in front of him to halt his passage. Christian released a long breath, and then met her gaze.

"I know you're angry with me," Davena began.

He smiled, but there was no humor in it. "You killed her."

"Nothing was going to stop the Hell Hounds from getting her. She wanted to make sure you weren't killed in the process."

"Tell yourself whatever helps you sleep better at night. You did the spell because you didn't want to lose Beau."

Davena's green eyes stared at him coolly. "That's true. Just as Olivia and Ava didn't want to see Vincent and Lincoln die."

"I was willing to die!"

Christian briefly closed his eyes after his outburst and got a handle on his emotions. He pushed past Davena and jogged up the stairs.

"She did it because she loved you," Davena called after him.

He didn't stop, though her words sent a slice of pain through him. Christian yanked open drawers and tossed clothes on the bed. Then he found his backpack and stuffed the clothes inside, as well as several knives.

Slinging the pack over one shoulder, Christian exited his room and descended the stairs. He paused at the bottom when he spotted his brothers, their women, Kane, and Riley.

He dropped the pack when Riley walked to him. They embraced. Christian held her tight as she sniffed.

"I'm so sorry," she whispered.

Christian closed his eyes. He couldn't talk even if he wanted to. The pain was too raw.

Riley leaned back and held his face between her hands. "We were about to go out looking for you."

"I know the bayous like the back of my hand."

Linc stepped forward. "That's not what she meant. We're not worried about you out there. We have an idea."

"Riley's idea, actually," Vincent said.

Riley beamed. It was only because of his sister that he didn't walk out right then. He hadn't realized just how much her absence affected them all until she was back in the house.

"Tell me," he urged her.

Riley took his hand and led him into the study. She gave him a little shove to sit on the sofa while the others filed in.

"We've all been looking for a way to get Ivy back," she began.

Christian leaned his forearms on his thighs and dropped his head. "She's gone."

"We're not ready to give up," Beau said. "I can't believe you are."

Christian slowly turned his head to spear his brother with a furious look. "There's no getting anyone back after the Hounds have taken them."

"That's what we thought as well," Kane said.

Christian refused to allow hope in. He had yet to come to terms with Ivy being gone. The idea that there was a chance he might get her back was too much to bear.

"I lost her once. I can't do it a second time."

Riley sat beside him and draped an arm across his shoulders. "All I'm asking is that you listen to what we've put together. After that, the decision will be yours."

He looked into Riley's blue eyes and couldn't say no. "I'll listen."

"Good." She got to her feet. "When Vin, Linc, and Beau didn't find anything here, we started doing our own search in New Orleans."

Kane grinned. "Except ours wasn't in books."

"Right," Riley smiled as the two looked at each other like conspirators. "We each went to a faction and gathered all the information they had on Hell Hounds."

"As well as what happens if the person who sold their soul committed suicide," Kane added.

Ava jumped in then. "While they did that, I called in a favor to a Medical Examiner friend and had them look over Ivy's mother's autopsy. There was a high content of NSAIDs, which, when not used properly, can cause what first appears to be a heart failure. So, our guess was right. She committed suicide."

"Meanwhile, our cousins were putting all their findings together," Lincoln said.

Riley nodded vigorously. "That's when we began to realize that they had one common theme."

"The Hell Hounds have never been stopped by a cloaking spell," Davena said.

Christian frowned as he considered what he had been told. "Then where did the Hounds go for those few days?"

"That was my question," Olivia said.

Christian shook his head. "This doesn't make any sense. They wouldn't just stop coming for her."

"True," Vincent said. "We looked at the date Ivy was last released from the hospital and never returned. The ten-year anniversary was over two months ago."

"If they had come for her soul because of her mother's suicide, they would've come for her two months earlier," Christian said.

Kane folded his arms over his chest as he widened his stance. "Exactly. We found it very odd that the Hounds waited until recently to come for Ivy, and then left her alone for a few days."

"It's almost as if they wanted the two of you together," Riley said.

Christian rubbed his eyes with his thumb and forefinger. "This still solves nothing."

"Only that the Hounds waited until you and Ivy were in the same location to come after her," Beau pointed out.

Christian lifted his head then. He looked at each of them before he came to Riley. "What is your plan?"

"I came to the conclusion that someone wanted you and Ivy to meet." Riley paused and swallowed, her excitement waning a bit. "The only one who can send the Hell Hounds is the Demon of Souls."

Christian snorted as he leaned back on the sofa. "You think the Demon of Souls wants me?"

"I think he wants our family," Riley corrected him.

"Somehow he knew what would happen if you fell in love and lost that woman."

"So he put Ivy in my path? It could've been any woman."

Lincoln shook his head from the chair next to Christian. "It had to be Ivy. You were so adamant about not falling in love that it would only work if the woman was in need and you came to the rescue."

The longer they talked, the harder it was for Christian to take.

"What we do means we have a lot of enemies," Beau said. "I'm not surprised the Demon of Souls went to such lengths."

Christian sliced his hand through the air to halt any talk. "It doesn't matter. The Hounds killed Ivy."

"Perhaps not," Kane said.

Riley picked up when Kane nodded to her. "Right. We did learn from the Voodoo practitioners that in the few instances the Hounds have come for someone like Ivy, they didn't kill them."

Christian got to his feet in a rush. "And you're just now telling me this?" he bellowed.

"You had to know all of it," Vincent said.

Christian ran a hand down his face before he looked back at Riley. "Anything else?"

"We think they're holding Ivy. The others that were taken eventually showed up. Well, some of them. It appears that, once with the demons, they are tricked to sell their soul to save the one who originally sold theirs."

Christian knew Ivy felt guilty for what her mother had done to save her. Would she in turn sell her soul to save her mother?

"We need to find Ivy," he stated.

Vin said, "You realize that means calling for a demon and traveling into Hell to find her?"

"Yes. I also know that few come out after going into Hell. Which is why I'm going alone."

"The hell you are," Lincoln said.

Kane stepped forward. "I'll go with him. You three have ties here. I don't."

"And your brothers?" Beau asked.

Kane glanced at Riley. "They understand."

"Ivy went to great lengths to ensure that you three," she pointed to Lincoln, Beau, and Vin, "remained to be with your women. Don't screw that up now."

Christian nodded to Kane. "We call the demon tonight. I'm not going to keep Ivy down there longer than I have to."

"I'll be ready," Kane said.

Christian fell back onto the couch as it all sunk in. He looked to everyone. "Thank you all. It never occurred to me that Ivy could still be alive."

"You were distraught," Olivia said. "It's understandable."

Riley pulled a piece of paper from her back pocket and unfolded it. "Minka also prepared a spell that would help you locate Ivy quickly." She paused and licked her lips. "I want to come with you."

"No," Christian said.

It was Kane who raised a brow. "What none of you realize is that she was hunting in Austin the entire time she was in college. She has been hunting with us, as well. She's good. A true Chiasson."

Riley smiled at him, mouthing 'thank you.' Christian realized that the two of them had a friendship both needed. He was glad his sister had found that in Kane when she hadn't in her brothers.

"Having said all of that," Kane continued. "I'm against her joining us."

"Thank God," Vincent mumbled.

Everyone but Riley laughed.

Christian rose and walked to her. He took her hand and waited until she met his gaze. "You have no idea how important you are to this family. You're not just our baby sister. You're the only female. I'd love for you to face this undertaking with me, but you're too precious. Please, Riley, stay here and keep those three in line," Christian said, motioning to their brothers over his shoulder with his thumb.

Riley inhaled and slowly released it as she blinked rapidly. "I'm not giving in because of all those pretty words. I'm agreeing not to go because you asked so nicely."

Christian had a feeling that one day they would all need

Riley, just as he knew that his sister would never let them down.

"The demons will figure out quick enough what we're doing," Beau said.

"And attack us," Vincent added.

Christian rubbed their hands together. "Then let's make sure we have a grand welcome waiting for them."

CHAPTER

FIFTEEN

Ivy stared at the black walls, her anxiety growing by the moment. How long would she be kept in Hell? She had no intentions of telling them anything about the Chiassons that others didn't already know.

It would be the worst kind of betrayal for her to do that to Christian and the others after they worked so tirelessly to keep the Hell Hounds away from her.

She owed them so much, especially Christian. No matter what the demons did, she wasn't going to break. She was strong. She could withstand whatever they threw at her.

Ivy must have dozed off, because when she opened her eyes there was someone standing in the far corner. She couldn't make out who it was with the lack of light. She didn't like how the demons could come and go so easily and she never knew when they would arrive.

With a door, at least she would have a second or two at the opening to prepare.

"Who are you, and what do you want?"

The person moved away from the corner, and Ivy's heart stopped when she recognized her mother. She could only stare, taking in her mother's short brown hair and hazel eyes.

"Mom?"

"It's me, sweetie pie."

Ivy jumped up and ran to her mother, throwing her arms around her neck and holding tight. The black dress Ivy had buried her in felt smooth beneath her palms. She blinked back tears. "It's so good to see you."

"I know," her mother said and squeezed her tight. "I've missed you so much."

Ivy leaned back and smiled as she took in her mother's face. "How did they let you in here?"

"They told me they had you, and then I was here. Ivy, what is going on? What are you doing in this place?"

She stepped back and shrugged. "Mom, why didn't you tell me you sold your soul?"

"As if," her mother scolded. "Why would I tell you?"

"Why did you do it?"

Her mother rolled her eyes. "Why do you think? I had already lost your father and brother. Doctor after doctor couldn't treat you. They had you on so many medications that I knew weren't good for you. You were dying. Slowly. I saw it month after month, year after year. I couldn't lose you, too."

"You shouldn't be in Hell," Ivy said and felt a tear fall on her cheek.

Her mother smiled sadly. "You don't understand the lengths a parent will go to in order to help their children. My soul was an easy price to pay knowing that you would be healthy."

Ivy nodded, because she couldn't get any words out. It took her a few moments to push the tears aside. "How did the demon find you?"

"I was coming out of the hospital chapel after another set of prayers." Her mother looked away, sadness contorting her face. "He approached me then, but I walked right past him."

Ivy wrapped her arms around her middle. There was so much to know and say, but now was the time for her to listen and ask questions later.

"I saw him for three consecutive days after," her mother continued. "Two days later we finally got results back on another round of testing performed, and just like before, the doctors had no clue what was wrong with you. If they couldn't diagnose it, they couldn't treat it."

Ivy had heard that all too many times from baffled doctors who shuffled her off to someone else.

"You already spent so many years watching life from your bed in the hospital and at home. You deserved a life instead of watching others on TV. I decided then that I would talk to the demon. It took me another two days before I found him again. This time I approached him."

Ivy waited for her mother to continue. When she didn't, Ivy urged, "And?"

"I was desperate to heal you. I accepted his offer of my soul for your instant recovering. I would have ten years with you before my soul would be claimed."

All this Ivy knew, but to hear it from her mother. It was so...wrong. "You died a year too soon."

"I did."

"That doesn't normally happen."

She shrugged her shoulders. "It does sometimes."

"You killed yourself, didn't you?"

For a long silent minute her mother simply stared at her. "Yes. I didn't want to chance you being around when the Hell Hounds came for me."

"Did you know when a person who has sold their soul commits suicide that the Hell Hounds come for the one that was saved?"

Her mother blinked, a shocked expression crossing her face. "No."

"Yes." Ivy tucked a curl that kept falling in her eyes behind her ear.

"How did you figure all this out?"

Ivy thought of Christian. "I had some help from people who fight demons and the like."

"Really? Who are these people?"

She quickly changed the subject to get it off Christian. "The Hounds found me and brought me here."

"What happens now?"

"After I see you, they kill me."

Her mother put her hands over her mouth and shook her head. "I won't let that happen."

"It's too late." Ivy wasn't sure why she didn't want to tell her mother about Christian or the demons' interest in the Chiasson. It was just a gut feeling, and Ivy didn't fight it.

"What about the people who told you of the Hell Hounds? Will they come to help you?"

Ivy shrugged. "I don't think so."

"What are their names? Perhaps we can find a way out?"

That's when Ivy knew that she wasn't talking to her mother. The woman who had sat beside her hospital bed for months at a time would never care more for learning a name than finding a way to get Ivy out.

"There's no leaving Hell," Ivy said.

Her mother looked around the room. "There's always a way. We need to learn what we have that can be used to bribe the demons."

"You sold your soul," Ivy said in a flat tone. "There isn't a demon here who would release you."

"Ivy," her mother admonished. "I can't believe you would say something so cruel. I sold my soul for you."

Ivy smiled, the tears gathering quickly. "My mother

would never say such a thing to me. She would never make me feel guilty for my illness or for her selling her soul."

Her mother smiled maliciously. Then the form changed and it was once more Liv. "Well, aren't you the smart one? I'll have to be more careful in the future."

"As if I would ever believe I was talking to my mother after this," Ivy snapped.

Liv raised a blonde brow. "Oh, you poor thing. You had no idea that it was your mother at first, did you?"

For the first time in her life, Ivy wanted to hit someone. "Go away."

"We're not nearly done," she said in a sickly sweet voice. "We're just getting started."

Ivy felt her stomach churn when she heard a scream filled with pain and then recognized her mother's voice begging for it to stop.

"That's what happens when you sell your soul," Liv said. "That soul is ours to do with what we want. And we do love our torture."

"Threaten me all you want."

"You?" Liv asked with a laugh. "Why would we do that when we have your mother?"

~

THE SUN HAD BARELY SUNK into the horizon before Christian stood at a crossroads and recited the words his family had gathered generations ago to call certain demons.

Christian didn't have long to wait before a young man of Italian descent appeared before him in a suit. Christian looked into his soulless eyes and fought back a glare of disdain.

The demon looked at Christian, then spoke with a heavy Italian accent. "Christian Chiasson. I never expected you to call to me. You come to sell your soul?"

"I would never."

"Not even to save your precious Ivy?"

Christian ground his teeth together to hold back his temper. He forced a smile then. "I'll save her. Just not by selling my soul."

The demon laughed and put one hand in his pants pocket. "So conceited. How many of your family has to die before you all realize we'll win?"

"If it was so set in stone, you wouldn't still be trying to kill us."

"Good and evil. We will battle until the end of time."

Christian looked past the demon to see Kane rise up from the ditch. "With good gaining ground at every turn."

"Ne—" The demon spun at the last minute as he heard Kane. "What are y—"

His words were cut off as Kane plunged a dagger blessed

by the church in the demon's heart. The demon jerked, his face going blank with surprise.

Christian rushed to the demon and grabbed hold of his arm as the earth opened up. It took everything they had to keep a grip on the demon as his human form fell away and his demon form began to burn from the inside out.

"We better reach the bottom soon!" Kane yelled over the demon's screams as they fell.

Christian's hands began to burn. If they held on any longer, they would be killed. "Let go!"

They released the demon and tumbled through the darkness. Christian was the first to hit the bottom. He landed on his stomach. A second later, there was a boom as Kane landed.

Christian opened his eyes to the darkened corridor. He turned his head to see Kane on his back and moaning in pain. He knew exactly how his cousin felt. His entire body ached as if it had just fallen twenty stories, which they probably had.

They didn't have time to stay there. They had to get moving before the demons found them. With great effort, Christian got to his hands and knees and crawled to Kane.

"Come on," he said hoarsely.

Kane rolled toward Christian. They used each other to climb to their feet before rocking unsteadily.

"Let's hope we don't meet a demon soon," Kane whispered. "I think I broke my arm in the fall."

Christian was sure he had a concussion, but there was no time to think about that now. He had to find Ivy. Davena had done the tracking spell to find Ivy before they called the demon. It just needed to kick in.

"We've no idea how big Hell is," Christian said.

Kane chuckled and looked at him. "Copious demons. Abundant souls trapped. This place will be huge."

"Why can't anything be easy?" he griped.

Kane's lips twisted in annoyance. "And why does everything have to be dark?"

Christian was opening his mouth when he felt a pull to the right. He looked in the direction as it grew stronger.

"I feel it too," Kane said. "Let's go find Ivy."

For the first time in days, Christian smiled. Ivy was close.

SIXTEEN

CHRISTIAN PLASTERED himself against a wall after glancing around the corner and seeing two demons coming his way. He nodded to Kane who stood beside him, the knife at the ready.

Christian had his own blade, and as soon as the demons turned the corner, he and Kane killed them. That was eight in total they had killed since coming to Hell. He would gladly gut thousands more if it meant he could find Ivy.

The screams were the worst to hear. The pain and suffering echoed through the halls. It was music to the demons, but all Christian wanted to do was make it stop.

They had been walking the halls for thirty minutes. With every step, the pull became stronger as he got closer to Ivy. Yet, the farther they went, the more demons they encountered.

Neither he nor Kane mentioned it, but both knew the chances of either of them leaving Hell was slim.

They hurried to the next turn. Kane reached it first and peaked around the corner. He leaned back and inhaled deeply.

Their gazes locked. Then Kane said, "Don't worry. The others will be fine."

Christian glanced at the blade in his hand. "Their distraction isn't working as I had hoped it would. Then again, I'm not all fired up about them surrounded by demons."

"It's what we do," Kane said with a grin.

"That it is."

Kane glanced around the corner again. "There are four of them. Ready?"

Christian was nodding when there was shouting and a commotion. The uproar grew, and through all the voices suddenly coming from around the corner, he heard one name—Chiasson.

Kane took another look and let out a string of curses. "There must be over two dozen now."

They couldn't turn away. Ivy was near. But neither could they go forward and face so many with just the two of them.

"Ideas?" Kane asked.

Christian gripped the handle of the knife tight. "The distraction from the others is working. Let's hope that means the demons will leave soon."

The voices grew. Kane motioned them back to a doorway where they quickly hid just as the demons rushed passed. It wasn't the only hallway where the demons had gathered.

Kane whistled low after the demons passed. "We need to watch Riley if she survives this. Her idea to trap a second demon after us and torture him was smart, but it's moves like that that'll get her killed."

"Don't I know it," Christian mumbled.

It seemed to take forever for the halls to grow quiet once more. Christian and Kane waited another few minutes before they snuck out of their hiding place and once more followed the pull they had to Ivy.

IVY HEARD THE LOUD, angry voices seeming to come at her from everywhere. Liv's gloating was erased as she listened to the demon speak, something Ivy couldn't understand.

She desperately wanted to ask Liv what was going on, but her curiosity wasn't great enough to get the demon's attention back on her. Instead, Ivy watched Liv's face twist with fury.

Liv slid her gaze to Ivy and closed the distance between them. She poked Ivy hard in the shoulder. "The Chiassons will die tonight. They think they're strong enough to trap a demon and torture him. We'll show them who has the stronger numbers."

And then Liv was gone.

Ivy slumped forward. She was delighted the demon was gone, but she began to worry about Christian. What were he and the others thinking trapping a demon? From what she learned while staying with them, the Chiassons didn't torture. They killed.

So what the hell was going on?

Ivy walked around the square room and began to run her hands along the walls in an effort to find a way out. There had to be a doorway. She just needed to find it.

She went around the room twice before she slammed her balled fist into the wall and screamed her frustration. Christian was fighting demons, not having any idea that those demons were trying to learn anything they could to take the Chiassons down.

"Christian," she whispered.

This trap the demons set was too good. None of them had thought she was being tracked by the Hell Hounds for anything other than her mother dying before the ten years was up.

If only Ivy could let Christian know somehow. This was a nightmare that felt as if it would never end. The despair was overwhelming, but it was nothing compared to the stark fear that Christian might die.

While her mother may have been devout in her religion, Ivy wasn't. No matter how many times she prayed to find out what was wrong so she could be healed, nothing ever came of it.

As a child, her first thought was that she hadn't prayed properly. That's when she asked her mother if the priest could come to their house on occasion. Not even that seemed to help.

No matter how many times Ivy prayed, God didn't seem to be listening. As the years wore on, she prayed less and less. After she was healed, Ivy only went to church with her mother because she didn't want to tell her mom that she didn't believe in God anymore.

But now...now that she knew there were demons, there also had to be a God.

Ivy pressed her cheek against the wall and closed her eyes. "If you're listening, I need your help. Please. I know I turned away from you for many years, and I probably have no right to ask anything of you now. But I am. I'm in Hell, trapped by demons who want the Chiassons. Christian and his family are good people. They protect others. They don't deserve what the demons have planned. If there is a way to let Christian know they're about to be swarmed by demons, please tell them."

Ivy sniffed and pushed away from the wall. She tried to remain calm for all of a minute, and then she snapped.

She slammed her hands against the wall and began to shout until her throat was hoarse. "Let me out! Let me out!"

"Ivy!"

She paused in her screaming. That was Christian's voice she heard in her mind. Was she breaking that quickly? She had to be stronger.

"Ivy?"

She squeezed her eyes closed. He wasn't there. That sexy voice wasn't close. It was all a trick from the demons or her mind—or both.

"Ivy Pierce, turn around and look at me!" Christian demanded.

She laughed then. How quickly she had gone insane, to believe that Christian was really there. She slowly turned and looked at the wall where his voice had come from.

"Go away, demon! I won't be tricked by you again," she declared.

"Dammit, Ivy. It's really me. I came to find you."

Ivy threw back her head and laughed, the sound hollow to her own ears. "Right. Just as you were my mother not that long ago while trying to find out all you could about Christian and his family. Not going to happen, bitch."

The silence that followed felt like a punch in her gut.

"Ivy, sweetheart," Christian's voice said in a low tone. "I'm standing right here. See me. See that I'm real."

She threw her hands out. "I'm in a room. You're not here!"

"Listen to my voice," he said calmly. "Track it to where I am. Look past the walls the demons erected in your mind and understand that there is nothing holding you."

Nothing holding her? What did that mean? Did he actually mean there weren't walls around her? Ivy fisted her hands and shook her head.

The demons and their tricks. If they could make her think she was talking to her mother one minute and it be the demon the next, why couldn't they also make her think she was locked in a room?

"That's it," Christian said in encouragement. "You can do this, Ivy."

She closed her eyes and concentrated on Christian's voice. Even if he was a figment of her imagination, he was calm in a storm of chaos. She would listen to him only because he gave her the confidence to face what was before her.

When she opened her eyes, the walls weren't as thick as before. She looked at the one she had been banging on and tried to hit it again, only to have her hand go through the stones.

As if that was all her mind needed, the walls vanished.

She turned in a circle to find herself in a large room with corridors leading in different directions. It wasn't until she saw Christian and another man beside him that she felt her knees weaken.

Ivy wanted to run to Christian, but she kept still for fear it was a demon again.

Christian smiled widely. "This is Kane," he said and motioned to his cousin. "He came to help me find you."

"You can't be in Hell," Ivy said.

Christian shrugged. "It seems I would walk through Hell itself for you, Ivy Pierce."

She shook her head. "I've been tricked before. This isn't you."

Kane held up a large knife that dripped with something dark and kicked at a burning body at his feet. "Trust me, Ivy. It's us. We went through a lot of pain to get here and have killed many demons. If we don't get out of here soon, then the demons will figure out what's going on."

Ivy noticed Christian had his own blade. She looked into his face and gave him a sad smile. "Make me believe it's you."

In two strides he was before her, yanking her against him and kissing her.

No one else could kiss like Christian Chiasson. Ivy wrapped her arms around his neck and returned his kiss, overjoyed that it was really him.

She ended the kiss and hugged him. "It's really you."

"I tried to tell you, sweetheart. Now, are you ready to get out of here?"

"Please," she said as she released him.

Christian entwined his fingers with hers. "Let's go."

Together, the three of them ran down first one hallway and then another and another. They began to blur together with Ivy soon getting turned around.

"Where are we going?" she asked.

It was Kane who said, "Back where we landed."

Ivy wanted to ask how they were going to get home, but she trusted Christian to have already thought of that. He wasn't the sort to go into a place without having a way home.

They rounded another corner when Christian said, "It's just up ahead."

Before they could reach it, six demons appeared before them, led by Liv.

Ivy took the knife from Christian and rushed Liv. The demon never saw the blade until it plunged into her heart. Christian grabbed Ivy and the blade and spun them around. He bent over her while Kane battled two demons.

And then suddenly there was no more sounds of battle. Ivy lifted her head and blinked at the bright light to find Davena sitting in the middle of the living room with candles all around her.

Davena smiled at them. "It's good to have you home, Ivy."

Kane and Christian jumped up and ran out the front door. Ivy moved slower, but when she stood on the porch and saw the demons and the Chiassons fighting them, Ivy couldn't breathe.

With Christian and Kane joining in the fray, it was enough for Olivia and Ava to get back to the house. Ivy couldn't take her eyes off Christian.

He was right in the middle of it all, fighting demon after demon as they fought to get at him.

"Davena!" Beau shouted.

With a few simple words, the demons burst into flames. Their screams filled the air for a few seconds before they disappeared.

Ivy ran down the steps and straight into Christian's arms. "You came for me."

"I didn't lie when I said I would walk through Hell for you. I love you, Ivy Pierce. Don't ever leave me again."

"I wouldn't dream of it," she said as she pulled his head down for a kiss. "How can I when I love you so?"

EPILOGUE

A week later...

Ivy sat in Christian's arms in the swing. The Chiasson house was getting very crowded. Kane returned to New Orleans after the demon battle. Riley remained, but she was packing her bags to return.

"This isn't going to be good," Christian said when voices from inside drifted out.

Ivy patted his leg. "Vin needs to let her go."

"He's right though. Riley belongs here. We need her."

"And she needs New Orleans right now. Give her time. She'll return."

Christian's arms tightened around her. "I hope you're right."

"I'm always right."

"Oh, really?" he asked with a laugh as he nuzzled her neck.

Ivy nodded. "Get used to it."

"I've already gotten used to quite a lot of things. Like going to bed with you and making love all night." He turned her so that she could look at him. "And watching the morning sun come through the window to touch your face before you wake up and give me a smile."

She touched his face. "I never wanted to love, but now that I do, I'm surprised at how fast it grows. I didn't think it was possible to love you more than I did yesterday, but I do."

"I know," he said, and kissed her.

She turned so that she straddled his lap and began to tug his shirt up. They were interrupted by the sound of a car approaching.

"Marshall," Christian said.

Ivy got off his lap and straightened her clothes. Christian stood at the top of the porch steps and waited for the patrol car to park.

A tall man with longish dark hair got out of the car and put on his cowboy hat. He wore jeans, shirt, and boots, with a holster around his hips.

"You look like hell," Christian said with a smile. He held out his hand for Ivy who took it and stood beside him.

Marshall walked to the front of his car and leaned back

against it. He crossed one ankle over the other and hooked his thumbs in his pants pockets. "I feel it. I never thought I would get the US Marshals out of my office."

"Did they find anything?"

"No, but that huge burst of flames the other week didn't help matters. I had calls coming everywhere." Marshall pinned Christian with his eyes of gold. "A little heads up would've been nice."

Christian laughed and walked down the steps, pulling Ivy with him. "Yeah, we'll work on that. Sheriff Marshall Ducet, let me introduce Ivy Pierce."

Marshall touched the brim of his hat. "Ma'am." He blinked and looked closer at Ivy before his smile widened as his gaze moved to Christian. "I knew you had a thing for her. You couldn't stop looking at her at the bar."

"I know," Ivy said as she leaned into Christian. "I couldn't stop looking either. The demons said we were fated to be together."

Marshall's brows raised. "Really? I guess that makes things easier."

"Fated or not, Ivy is meant to be mine," Christian said as he gazed down at her.

"I'm going to have to stop coming here," Marshall said when they kissed. "Couples everywhere. Looks like my pool partner is gone. There goes my Friday nights."

At that moment the screen door flew open as Riley

walked out of the house with her bag over her shoulder. She walked to her truck and yanked open the door even as Vincent and Lincoln were calling her name.

Ivy and Christian turned to see Beau watching it all with a smile and an arm around Davena. Olivia and Ava were trying in vain to call their men back.

RILEY HAD KNOWN it wasn't going to be easy to leave again, but she had to do it. Not because she wanted to, but to prove to everyone—including herself—that she was capable of doing it.

"It's not for good," Riley said, quieting her two eldest brothers instantly. She took a deep breath. "I'll be back."

"When?" Vincent demanded.

She cocked her head and gave him a stern look. "I'm an adult. I have been for awhile, but none of you were able to see it. I've made a life in New Orleans."

"Delphine is there," Lincoln said.

As if she didn't know that. Riley started to say something, but the words evaporated when she saw the sheriff's car and the hunk leaning back against the hood. His gold eyes watched her fervently. His black hat covered most of his hair, but there was enough hanging out the sides and back with a bit of wave to it that had Riley itching to take the hat off him.

"It's just Marshall," Vincent said. "What were you going to say?"

Was she going to say something? For the life of her Riley couldn't remember. Then all thought fled when Marshall tilted his hat back enough that she got a good look at his face.

Lean and rugged. He had a shadow of a beard that accentuated his amazing jawline and entirely too full lips.

He pushed off the car and stood straight. Lord, was he ever tall. His jeans fit his long legs perfectly, as did his white button-down shirt with the sleeves rolled above his elbows.

"Riley!"

She jerked at Lincoln's voice. Riley glared at them again. "I'm just a few hours away. You know where I am now. There's no cause for any worry."

"Are you kidding me?" Vincent asked in shock.

"Vin, careful now," Olivia cautioned him.

Riley nodded to Olivia. "You need to listen to her. You're walking dangerous ground here telling me I can't leave."

"We're better with you here," Lincoln said.

Vin turned and looked at Beau and Christian. "And why the hell aren't you two trying to keep her here?"

"Because she's happy in New Orleans," Beau said. "I saw that firsthand. Besides, she's good for Kane."

When Vincent turned his attention to Christian, he merely shrugged. "I'm sorry, Vin. Did you say something? I was kissing my woman."

Ivy giggled and kissed him again.

Riley shook her head with a smile. "I never thought I would see the day that my brothers found love, but each of you have. Vin, you and Olivia are about to be married. Lincoln and Ava aren't far behind. It won't be long after that before Beau and Davena, and Christian and Ivy are also married. We can't all live in the house."

"There's someone in New Orleans, isn't there?" Lincoln asked.

Riley glanced at Marshall to see a small frown. She waved away Lincoln's words. "Maybe. Maybe not. It doesn't matter. I'll call y'all when I get there."

She got in her truck and closed the door before there could be any more arguments. Riley started the truck and put it in reverse when she saw Marshall had taken a few steps toward her.

He was handsome. Too handsome. A man like that would break her heart, and she had had enough of that.

Riley backed up before she put the truck in drive and started down the long driveway. She looked in the rearview to find everyone was going back inside except for Marshall.

He stood staring after her.

Thank you for reading **WILD FLAME!** I hope you loved

Christian and Ivy's story as much as I loved writing it. Next in the Chiasson series is WILD RAPTURE.

LOST BUT NOT FORGOTTEN...THE ULTIMATE SACRIFICE.

One click to BUY WILD RAPTURE now!

If you love the Chiasson series, you'll love the next book in reading order from the intertwined LaRue series, MOON STRUCK...

***HIS FIGHT TO BE WHOLE,
HER REASON FOR BEING.***

Click to BUY MOON STRUCK today!

To find out when new books release
SIGN UP FOR MY NEWSLETTER today at
http://www.tinyurl.com/DonnaGrantNews.

Join my Facebook group, Donna Grant Groupies, for exclusive giveaways and sneak peeks of future books.

Keep reading for an excerpt from MOON STRUCK and a
glimpse at WILD RAPTURE…

WILD RAPTURE

DONNA GRANT

NEW YORK TIMES BESTSELLING AUTHOR

PROLOGUE

March

SOMETHING WAS WRONG. Terribly wrong.

Riley squeezed her eyes closed to shield them from the blinding light as she came awake on her side. She attempted to sit up, but was wracked with pain all through her body.

What the hell had happened?

She finally managed to open her eyes to find herself on the floor of a room. There were boards placed over the windows, many of them smashed or rotting. The curtains that were barely hanging on had fabric ripped and were so filthy the color was indiscernible. Dirt, debris, and broken furniture littered the floor.

Riley gritted her teeth and pushed up onto one hand. Images of the battle she'd fought in New Orleans with Minka and her cousins—the LaRues—flooded her. Fear threatened to swallow her whole, but she refused to allow it. Because she knew who had her.

Delphine.

If the priestess thought she could make her cower, Delphine was in for a rude awakening. Riley was a Chiasson, a hunter of the supernatural, one who was ready and willing to fight anything. Delphine was just another evil monster that had to be taken down.

"Bring your worst!" Riley shouted to whoever might be listening—or watching.

She climbed to her feet and dusted off her hands, her gaze scanning the room for a way out. Then she whispered, "I'll be ready for you."

CHAPTER
ONE

May

Lyons Point, Louisiana

EVIL HAD COME TO TOWN. There might not be a physical body, but Marshall Ducet knew it was there all the same. He'd left New Orleans because of it.

He snorted as he drove down Highway 13 on patrol. Somewhere out in the universe, someone was laughing, all because Marshall had unknowingly chosen to relocate to another paranormal hotspot.

If he thought New Orleans was bad with all the various factions of the supernatural—werewolves, witches, djinn, vampires, and Voodoo—it had nothing on Lyons Point and the surrounding area.

The sleepy little town looked idyllic. Right up until he

discovered that some unknown force drew the paranormal here. And there was a family—the Chiassons—who hunted the evil and kept everyone safe.

Marshall got involved with the Chiassons after arriving at a murder caused by a Voodoo priestess, and once he knew of the hunters, he gladly helped out when he could.

He slowed and turned down a road. The sun was bright in the cloudless sky, allowing the temperatures to come close to ninety degrees. The previous sheriff had been killed after succumbing to the paranormal, so as acting sheriff, Marshall spent most of his time driving around and helping those in need. Though there was still the occasional robbery and B&E.

And then there were the murders.

Few and far between, the killings nine times out of ten were supernatural. Marshall had quickly learned how to tell them apart. Mostly because, if any of the Chiassons were there, it was supernatural.

Marshall turned down the crepe myrtle-lined drive. He was paying his daily visit to the four Chiasson brothers and their women to see if there was any word on their only sister.

When Riley had gone missing in New Orleans while fighting Delphine, a Voodoo priestess, the Chiasson brothers were at first in shock. Then came the anger. Not that he could blame them. Marshall suspected he would act very much the same in a similar situation, but it was all a guess since he was an only child.

He had an inkling that the chaos of the Chiasson home was what drew him back time and again. He'd always dreamed of having siblings, and while his wish never came true, he could briefly live it when he was around the hunters.

Marshall parked the patrol car and turned off the ignition. He met his gaze in the rearview mirror and sighed. Riley hadn't been alone during the battle. In fact, she'd been standing alongside her cousins, the LaRues—who happened to be werewolves and the ones who kept the factions within New Orleans playing nice with each other and the humans.

The LaRues had scoured the city. And then the Chiassons had joined in the search before doing one of their own. And still, there wasn't a single sign of Riley. It was like she'd disappeared.

Grabbing his Stetson, Marshall exited the car and stood. He set the hat on his head and pushed the car door closed as he headed toward the front porch. On his way, he saw movement in the building off to the side of the main house. He altered his direction and came to the doorway of the large boat shed that had various metal cages within to hold supernatural creatures.

The cages had been used fairly recently with Kane LaRue after he was cursed by Delphine to kill Ava Ladet in retaliation for her dad, Jack, pissing off the priestess. Luckily, one of the Chiasson brothers, Lincoln, had taken a fancy to her, and the Chiassons were able to intercept their cousin before he could carry out the curse.

As Marshall looked at the cages, he recalled how close Ava had come to dying, and how both the Chiassons and the LaRues would've been impacted by her death.

For one, had Kane killed her—or any human—he would've remained in werewolf form for eternity.

Then there was Lincoln. He would've lost the love of his life.

It was the quick thinking of the Chiassons and how well they worked together that stopped the Voodoo priestess out for revenge. And it brought the two families back together again after drifting apart.

Now, however, it seemed as if Delphine had taken the ultimate revenge by kidnapping Riley. Because while no one had any evidence that it was Delphine, there was no one else who'd made it clear they would get their vengeance on the two families.

Marshall's gaze went to the eldest Chiasson, Vincent. He stood with his back to everyone, gazing out the open door of the shed to the bayou beyond. Vin's dark hair fell in waves to his shoulders.

"Hey," Christian said.

Marshall gave a nod to the middle brother and met his bright blue eyes—a family trait for the Chiassons and LaRues. It made Marshall recall the only time he'd seen Riley. She'd been on her way back to New Orleans. She'd walked from the large, white plantation house as he'd driven up.

Her steps had been assertive, her smile confident, while

her gaze dared anyone to get in her way. He'd seen the dimple in her left cheek as he leaned against his hood and watched her drive away.

It was a good thing they hadn't spoken because Marshall was certain he wouldn't have been able to form words. Riley Chiasson wasn't just stunningly beautiful, she was also a force to be reckoned with. Though, it was her beauty that most people saw—not that Marshall could blame them.

She was tall and lithe with just the right amount of curves. Her long hair was so dark it was nearly black as it fell in waves down her back. She sported the same piercing blue eyes as the rest of her kin, but it was the dimple in her left cheek that he loved most of all.

"Any news?" Marshall asked.

Lincoln shook his head of dark hair and continued sharpening his knives.

Beau put away his shotgun and said, "Linc wants to return to New Orleans to do another search."

"We can't," Christian said. "Not with the nest of vampires that arrived last week. We can't leave those who count on us."

Linc spun around to face his younger brother. "And what about Riley? It's been weeks, Christian! Weeks! We don't have any idea what horrors Delphine has inflicted on her."

"Solomon, Myles, Kane, and Court continue to look for her," Christian argued. "And if you think it's easy for me to stay here and do nothing, then you're a bigger dick than I thought."

In a split second, Beau was between his brothers, a hand on each of their chests. "This isn't doing Riley any good."

"Beau's right," Marshall said. "I'm not taking sides because I don't think I could stay here if it was my sister, but at the same time, Lyons Point needs this family. And from what all of you have told me, no one knows New Orleans like the LaRues."

"Then why haven't they found her?" Vin asked without turning around.

All three brothers swiveled their heads to Vin. Beau dropped his arms and turned to face his eldest brother. Marshall waited with the rest of them to hear what Vin might say next.

Seconds ticked by before Vincent turned around. He looked at each of them. "I was so adamant that Riley have a normal life. I sent her to Austin for her degree, and I got so caught up with everything that I didn't even realize she'd graduated. She didn't tell us. Or maybe she tried during one of the calls that I cut short because it was too painful to talk to her. But I pushed her away, believing it was the right thing to do. What did that get us? Our sister living in New Orleans, away from us."

"She was with our cousins," Christian said.

Lincoln crossed his arms over his chest. "Who let her hunt."

Beau glared at Linc. "As if you would've been able to stop her. At least our cousins made her hunt with them so they could keep an eye on her."

"She wouldn't have been taken had she been home," Linc stated.

"I'm not so sure of that," Vin said before the argument could continue.

Marshall waited for the brothers to ask what Vin meant, and when they didn't, he finally did. "What do you mean?"

"That Delphine wanted to hurt us," Christian said.

Linc nodded. "If the Voodoo bitch wanted Riley, it wouldn't have mattered where she was."

"And by taking her while our cousins were watching over her, it ensured that there would be a rift between our families," Beau finished.

Marshall returned his gaze to Vin. "Then don't let that happen. Everyone respects and fears the LaRues because they don't hesitate to put people in their place. The LaRues run New Orleans. The Chiassons run Lyons Point. Imagine if the two of you joined forces."

"Like Christian said, we can't leave the area," Linc said.

Marshall set his hand on the butt of his gun at his hip. "There has been an increase in activity since Riley was taken, hasn't there?"

Vin's brows drew together. "We rarely get a night off, but now that you mention it, yes. Instead of us hunting one creature a night, we're tracking down multiple, forcing us to split up."

"It's Delphine," Beau said with a shake of his head, a vein ticking in his temple.

"No doubt, but that doesn't help us." Linc looked at Vin and shrugged. "What do we do?"

Vin ran a hand down his face. "What can we do? Save our sister, or keep the parish safe."

"What if I went to New Orleans?" Four pairs of vivid blue eyes turned Marshall's way. He looked at each brother before he locked eyes with Vincent. "I still have a lot of friends in New Orleans. I grew up in the area, and I worked there for seven years, so I know it well. The LaRues have been searching the paranormal world, but perhaps someone needs to take a look at the human one."

Vin walked toward him, stopping a few feet away. "You would do that for us?"

"Like you said, you can't leave. I can. I can put my deputy in charge here. And Delphine won't be looking for me."

Linc shrugged when Vin looked his way. "Marshall has a point."

"I say yes," Christian chimed in.

Beau smiled and clapped Marshall on the shoulder. "There are some things you're going to need."

CHAPTER
TWO

New Orleans

THERE WAS SOMETHING DIFFERENT. Riley could feel it deep within her, but she couldn't put a name to it. She walked the streets, holding a bag in each hand from her run to the grocery store.

The sun felt glorious on her face. If only she didn't have to get back and start cooking, she would climb on top of the roof of the house in her bathing suit and catch some rays. After so many days of rain, she didn't want to pass up the opportunity.

She blinked through her sunglasses at the people passing her. The sight of two brothers good-naturedly teasing their younger sister made her stop and stare. There was something about the siblings that stirred an emotion within her, a feeling she couldn't quite name.

"Something wrong?"

She jerked her head around to find Delphine beside her. Riley smiled in welcome. "I was just watching the kids."

"You should've brought George with you," Delphine said. "He could've helped with the bags."

Riley rolled her eyes as she shook her head. "I'm more than capable of carrying them. George doesn't need to follow me everywhere. Besides, I've been doing really good this week."

"So you have."

Riley stood still so Delphine could inspect her with her black eyes that seemed to see through everything. She noted that Delphine had once more covered her long, black hair with a white cloth piled high atop her head.

Riley was quite envious of Delphine's umber skin and seemingly ageless face. But how could she remain jealous of a woman who had taken her in and given her shelter while healing her?

"Come, child," the Voodoo priestess urged.

Riley didn't give the siblings another thought as she walked beside Delphine back to the streets that she ruled. The area was the only place Riley felt safe, so she didn't venture outside of the ten-block radius.

Because, outside of Delphine's domain, lurked the monsters who had attacked her.

"Any headaches today?" Delphine asked.

Riley shrugged. "Minor. I can handle it."

"And the nightmares?"

"None." Riley wasn't sure why she lied. The word was out of her mouth before she realized it, and she couldn't take it back.

Delphine smiled, showing even, white teeth. "That's wonderful news."

"I told you. I'm getting better."

"Yes, you are, my dear."

Riley preened when Delphine put an arm around her. Everyone they passed stared in awe because every one of them wanted to be in Riley's place. She was well aware how lucky she was to have Delphine take her in. Why the priestess had chosen her when there were thousands of others she could've picked, Riley would never know. But she would never turn on Delphine.

Once they reached the house, Riley made her way to the kitchen, looking for her friend, Elin, as she did. She couldn't remember ever having trained to cook—or even where she learned—but she was decent at it. And she liked the activity. It was her way of repaying Delphine for everything.

She set the bags of groceries on the table and took each item out before putting them away. Then she got out a knife and sharpened it before peeling and chopping the garlic and onions.

Riley turned on the radio and smiled when an Eagles

song came on. She continued the prep for the spicy shrimp fettuccine while she sang. She didn't know how long she stood there before she felt as if someone were watching.

A glance over her shoulder confirmed that someone was. She flashed a quick smile at the young man who had deemed himself her protector while trying not to shiver in dread. George was nice, but there was just something about him that set her on edge.

"Delphine said you went out alone," George said as he ran a hand over his short black hair.

Riley rinsed the knife and nodded, not looking into George's black eyes. "I needed to do it. Besides, it was a quick trip. And I was fine."

"No one bothered you?"

She laughed and set the knife down as she faced him. "The only person who spoke to me was the cashier. It was actually good. I feel good, too."

He moved closer, his eyes searching her face. She wasn't able to back up, and while he had a nice body and an attractive face, he made her uncomfortable.

"I can see that," he said.

"I'm getting better."

"It's only been a couple of months. You should take it slow."

She glanced away. He'd made it known that he was interested in taking their relationship further, but she didn't have those types of feelings for him. The fact that she'd leaned on him for so long allowed him to think they were getting closer like that. It was one of the reasons she'd gone to the store by herself.

"I am taking it slow," Riley said before turning back to the food.

But he didn't take the hint. George drew closer as he came up behind her. "I worry about you. The way I found you that night—"

"I know," she said before he could continue the sentence.

He tenderly spun her around. "That's just it. You don't. You didn't see what I saw."

"You explained it to me." She sidestepped to put some distance between them. "I don't want to talk about that night again. I want to put it in the past."

His face fell as his hands dropped to his sides. "Put it in the past then, but don't ever forget it."

She didn't move until he turned and walked out of the kitchen. Only then did she resume the prep. Riley turned up the music and immersed herself in the meal creation to drown out the thoughts that were growing louder in her mind.

If she were lucky, she'd get some time alone with Elin to share her feelings. It seemed Riley wasn't the only one Delphine saved from an attack. Elin had also been brought to the house to recover. Riley was thankful for her friend, because Elin had been a comfort during all the horrible recovery days.

RILEY LOVED THE MOON. She could stare at it all night, just as she did now. Every evening, she sat beside her window on the second floor and gazed up at the orb. It didn't seem to bother Delphine that Riley wasn't part of the Voodoo religion. If Delphine asked, Riley would have gladly joined in, but the priestess had never pushed.

Muted music reached her. Apparently, there was another gathering of Delphine and her followers. The drums beat a rhythm that was both steady and sensual.

Movement below her caught Riley's attention. She saw George walking in a pair of white linen pants that billowed around his legs. His muscular chest was bare, and his skin gleamed in the moonlight. He paused and looked up at her before continuing on.

Curious, Riley rose and hurried down the stairs to the back entrance of the large manor. The family next door had given their home to Delphine to use for her gatherings. For long minutes, Riley stood in the entryway, looking across the lawn. Finally, she took a step out and closed the door behind her. She walked barefoot toward the house, the beating of the drums seeming to match her pounding heart.

The music held her in thrall. The concrete was still warm from the sun, but the grass was cool under her feet. She walked toward the open door where she saw a red-orange glow from the many candles within the dwelling.

She reached the entrance, but hesitated. There was something about the house that seemed familiar, which couldn't be right. She'd never been inside it before.

The music subtly shifted. Her eyes wouldn't stay focused, and her limbs grew heavy. And through it all, something drew her forward, into the building.

Someone touched her. It took a great amount of effort for her to turn her head and see that one of Delphine's followers had taken her arm. The older woman was chanting something as she guided Riley.

Soon, someone was on her other side. She couldn't tell them no, couldn't refuse them. Nor could she yank herself away. She was powerless, but she wasn't scared. In fact, she was calm.

And that worried her.

Something in her mind shouted for her to run, to get far away.

Suddenly, Riley was on her knees in the middle of the room. Delphine came to stand before her with her arms raised upward. Riley tried to keep her eyes open as people gathered around them in a circle, their chants strident—but not as loud as the music.

Riley realized it held her captive. There was something in the notes, some rhythm or melody that made her a prisoner.

Delphine put her hand atop Riley's head as she shouted something. Riley's arms were taken once more and held out at her sides. Someone came up behind her, pressing against her. Then they were gone.

Riley could feel sleep calling to her, but she fought it. She wanted to know what was going on. And she needed to know who was touching her. It had been nothing sexual… yet. But she could sense the carnal, wanton atmosphere within the room.

It took several tries before she was able to open her eyes. The women holding her were rocking, causing her to sway upon her knees. Delphine released Riley's head and took three steps back, her eyes closed the entire time.

Riley couldn't understand the words of Delphine's chant, but she felt their power. Hell, she could feel the magic within the room. It pulsed, growing with each beat of the drums.

No longer could she keep her eyes open. She let them fall shut, listening to the music and the murmur of the people around her. She didn't know how long she remained that way before the women released her arms and slowly laid her on the floor. Though Riley fought the blackness that threatened to claim her, it was too strong. She was lulled to sleep by the sensual tune.

Somehow, she clawed her way back to consciousness. The music still filled the room, but it was…different. Riley slit open a lid and saw that the group around her was gone.

Yet she wasn't alone. She could hear heavy breathing and soft moans. Without having to see, Riley knew someone was having sex. She wanted to leave, but her body wouldn't obey. It was as if it belonged to someone else.

She opened her eyes further and caught sight of a foot. She followed it up until she saw George lying naked on his back with Delphine atop him, writhing in lust—all while George's eyes were on *her*.

Delphine looked over at her and grinned. Then she leaned over George and stroked his face. "Soon," she whispered.

Riley could only watch as Delphine rose and walked toward her, her breasts jiggling with each step. Riley noticed the priestess was clean-shaven between her legs.

Delphine kneeled beside Riley and stroked her hair before moving her hand along Riley's cheek and then down to her breast. Riley tried to tense, but once more, her body denied her control.

"Shhh," the priestess said in a low tone. "Stop fighting this. We won't hurt you. We're protecting you. Remember? We saved you. We're making you stronger."

Safe. Yes, Riley knew she was safe and protected with Delphine.

"Yes. That's it," the priestess said. "Let my magic work to finish healing you. It called to you tonight, and you answered. That means there is something special in store for you." Delphine leaned closer after glancing at George. "And you have a man who longs to have you as his own."

Riley tried to shake her head.

"Shhhhhhhhh," Delphine insisted. "Not tonight. Tonight, he's mine. But soon, my dear, you'll want him as much as he wants you. Think of the beautiful babies the two of you will make."

Delphine let her hand continue down Riley's side as the music grew louder. The last thing Riley saw before sleep claimed her again was Delphine taking George within her body once more.

CHAPTER
THREE

THERE WAS something about the city of New Orleans that set it apart from anywhere else in the world. There were those who believed it was the people that made it stand out. And that was true.

In a sense.

Marshall drove down Charles Street in the heart of the French Quarter, looking at the people—and the supernatural beings. Because it was the mystical aspects that made New Orleans a mecca, boasting the largest concentration of such individuals on the continent.

He meandered through the streets until he came to Gator Bait. The bar owned by the LaRues was a favorite of both locals and tourists, but Marshall didn't stop. For now, he was going to search for Riley on his own. He knew without a doubt that he'd eventually have to come to the LaRues, but not until he had no other choice.

For the next hour, he drove all over New Orleans until the sun went down. He made a stop at a local store to pick up some food. Then Marshall pulled into the driveway of his old partner's house and turned off the ignition. He sat in his truck for a moment before he grabbed his duffle bag and headed to the front porch.

Marshall was glad that Donnie was out of town for the next week on a cruise with his girlfriend. It would allow Marshall to go about his business without having to hide anything from his friend.

Inside the house, he made his way to the spare bedroom and dropped his bag on the bed. He unzipped it and pulled out the files of everything he had on Riley. Then, he walked to the kitchen and laid it all out on the table.

Marshall got out a steak and seasoned it while reading over everywhere the LaRues and Chiassons had looked for Riley. Like the rest of them, Marshall was sure she was still somewhere in the city.

The problem was the city itself. There were so many places for her to be hidden away, especially the area that Delphine had claimed as hers. The Chiassons hadn't ventured into that district, not that he blamed them. They'd gotten as close as they could, but their clashes with the priestess made them targets. The four LaRue brothers, as guardians of the city, were able to freely walk the streets, but they'd gleaned nothing that could help either. Marshall hoped he would have better luck.

He went out back and lit the gas grill before returning to the kitchen to open a can of baked beans. In no time, he was sitting at the table eating his steak and beans and studying the map of New Orleans.

Without a doubt, the first place he needed to look was in Delphine's district. He'd agreed to contact the Chiassons twice a day, every day, with his location. If he didn't, they would assume that something happened to him and would know where to begin searching.

He'd been a damn good detective with the NOPD. He loved the city, but he didn't love how the supernatural had important and influential people of the community in their pockets. Those high-ranking individuals—including his superior—had made Marshall repeatedly let guilty parties go because they happened to be supernaturals.

The only sect who hadn't given the NOPD any shit were the werewolves. Mostly because the LaRues were the only ones around back then, but that was changing with the reemergence of the Moonstone pack.

After his meal was finished, Marshall sent a quick text to the Chiassons, letting them know he was at the house and settling in for the night. Then he began to go over the different factions within the city to mark off who wasn't involved with Riley's disappearance.

Obviously, the weres weren't involved. The LaRues

would've sniffed out if someone from another pack had taken their cousin, so that faction was quickly scratched off.

The vampires could have done it, but it wasn't likely. They liked to make a statement, so if they had been the ones to abduct Riley, they would've either turned her or killed her—and either way, they would've shown her off to the LaRues afterward.

The djinn were a possibility. They certainly had the power to do it, and their victims weren't usually recovered. Though they generally kept to themselves, they had been consorting with vampires recently. Still, if a djinn had Riley, a vamp would've found out and quickly told everyone, thinking it would give them an advantage over the LaRues.

As for the witches, they had no reason to want to harm Riley, the LaRues, or the Chiassons since it was one of their own, Minka, who'd stood up to Delphine recently. And the LaRues had helped to band the witches together as they all stood and fought the priestess.

So that only left Delphine.

It was the same conclusion the LaRues and Chiassons had come to. And it meant that Marshall would have to tread carefully.

He'd seen Delphine when she came to Lyons Point to try and get Davena to join her followers. The sheer amount of power the priestess possessed terrified Marshall because he had nothing to combat it. Neither his gun or his knife could damage Delphine.

But she could do a number of things to him with just a thought.

That wasn't going to stop him from searching for Riley, though. It had been over eight weeks since she was last seen. That was eight weeks of suffering at Delphine's hand. Just as Marshall was sure Riley was in the Voodoo district, he was sure she was alive. If Delphine had wanted her dead, she could've killed Riley on the street.

No, the priestess had something else in mind for Riley, a plan that would strike at both the LaRues' and Chiassons' jugulars. The question was: what? What could she possibly do that would stop two such strong families from coming for her?

Because it would happen. It was simply a matter of when. Right now, they were waiting to locate Riley. Once that was done, the two families would unite and descend upon Delphine and her followers.

All that was holding them back was Riley.

Marshall shook his head as a thought took root. It was a dangerous one, and something that left him a bit sick to his stomach. He rose and went to the fridge for another lager. He twisted the cap and lifted the longneck bottle to his lips to drink deeply.

He set the beer down on the counter and braced his hands on either side of it, hanging his head.

"Fuck me," he murmured.

Riley's brothers and cousins were so wrapped up in

locating her while praying she was alive, that none of them had stepped back to try and determine what Delphine wanted with Riley.

And Marshall wasn't so sure he wanted to tell anyone his theory just yet. Because if he was right, and the Chiassons and LaRues learned that Delphine was using Riley as a shield of sorts, that would keep both families from ever attacking. Marshall wasn't sure what they would do.

He ran a hand down his face and straightened. Damn. His job had just gotten harder, not that it had been easy to begin with. If his prediction were correct, then Delphine would be watching anyone in her district closely—especially outsiders.

She'd need a place to keep Riley so that she couldn't escape, but also someplace that Delphine could show the Chiassons and LaRues to get them to back off.

Marshall didn't know the Voodoo area as well as he knew some of the other parishes. He hadn't been stationed there while still in uniform, and once he'd made detective, the police were rarely called into that area.

He grabbed a cupcake that he'd bought and walked back to the table. Once back in his seat, he studied the map again, memorizing the streets of Delphine's area as he ate the sweet. Between the map and looking at various pictures of Riley that all the Chiassons had sent to his phone, he was at the table for hours.

At midnight, he stretched his back and rose to walk

around. His feet took him to the front door. He opened it and looked out the screen to the world beyond. A full moon was coming, and that meant the LaRues would be on full patrol because things really went crazy in the city during that time.

The night air was cool, the crickets and frogs noisy between the sounds of the passing cars. But it was the creatures beyond that he was concerned with.

He'd been given all sorts of weapons to fight with. They were in his truck, but now he wished he would've brought them in. Though, honestly, this was probably the only night he could sleep without them.

Once his search began, he would have to place them all over the house, on his person, and even in various places in his truck so a weapon was always near. Imagine, at one time, he'd believed the worst thing he would ever track down was a serial killer who had murdered six blonde college girls.

That was eight years ago, when the monsters he protected innocents from were both human and supernatural alike.

His phone rang behind him. Marshall shut and locked the door before going to answer it. "Hello?"

"Hey," Christian said. "Everything good?"

"Yep. Didn't you get my text?"

There was a bit of a hesitation. "I did. I was hoping for more information."

Marshall smiled because he'd been expecting this from

one of the brothers—if not all of them. "I don't know anything yet. I just got here, remember?"

"Yeah, I know. I just...well, shit. The thing is, I wish I was with you."

"There's a part of me that wishes you were here, as well. But it'll be better if I search on my own."

Christian released a long sigh. "Give me something, man. I'm going crazy over here."

"I drove around all over, even in Delphine's area, but I didn't see anything."

"Yeah," Christian replied in a desolate voice.

Marshall stared at the map. "I'm going to do everything I can to find her."

"I know you will, but she's not your sister."

"No, but that's not going to stop me. She's your sister, and you and your brothers are my friends."

Christian said, "You're a good man and a good friend, but I'm worried—"

"That I'm out of my element?" he finished.

That made Christian chuckle. "Well, yeah."

"No one is more aware of that fact than I am. I might have helped y'all out a few times, but that's much different than being on my own. And it's Delphine."

"She scares the shit out of everyone, including me."

Marshall grinned. "That's saying something."

"If you knew something, or figured something out, you'd tell me, right?"

"Of course," he lied. There was no need to get Christian and his brothers riled up before Marshall had more information.

Christian cleared his throat. "I know. I'm sorry. I just had to ask."

"None of you have told the LaRues I'm here, have you?"

"Give us some credit, man. You've only been gone twelve hours."

Marshall rolled his eyes. "Who wanted to call them?"

"It might have been me."

"Dude."

"I know, I know. I'm just worried you're going to step into something you can't handle."

Marshall made a sound in the back of his throat. "For fuck's sake. You do know I was a cop in New Orleans for seven years, right? And I was a Marine."

"Yeah."

"I survived that just fine."

Christian let a lengthy pause grow before he said, "But you didn't have Delphine to worry about."

CHAPTER

FOUR

FOR SOME REASON, Riley couldn't stop staring at the house next to Delphine's. It was smaller and uninhabited and didn't look the least bit inviting. But that had nothing to do with the look of the house.

It was clean, and the yard was maintained, but for the life of her, Riley didn't like the building. And the longer she stood out in the sun and stared at it, the more she disliked it.

"Riley?"

She jumped at the sound of George's voice behind her. Riley grabbed her throat and forced a laugh when she turned to him. "Oh, hey, you scared me."

"I'm sorry," he said with a soft smile. "What are you looking at?"

Her gaze shot to the house before she quickly looked

away. "What do you know about the people who used to live there?"

"Nothing much. They had to move away, and they signed the house over to Delphine."

There was the briefest moment where Riley thought she knew that, but it vanished as quickly as it had appeared. "Does Delphine use it?"

"Occasionally. Why are you asking?"

"I don't know."

His brow furrowed as he stepped closer to her. "You had another migraine last night, didn't you?"

She couldn't remember much of the evening before, and that usually signaled that it had been a migraine. Thank God she had someone like Delphine to look out for her. "I think so."

"You shouldn't overdo it today," he advised.

"I appreciate your concern, but I'm fine."

She moved past him and walked back into the house through the back door that brought her immediately into the kitchen. When the door didn't shut directly behind her, she knew George had followed her.

"Riley," he began.

Grabbing her shopping list, she turned to face him. "Please, don't. I'm fine."

"I'm concerned about you."

"Because Delphine told you to be?" She had no idea

where that thought had come from or why it even left her lips.

Hurt cut across his handsome features. "No. Because I care about you."

"Because you found me that horrible night eight weeks ago. You feel responsible."

He gave a shake of his head. "That's not it at all."

"I went to the store yesterday by myself, and it was amazing. I need to be able to do things on my own again. So, I'm going to walk out the door and do as I did before. I'm even going to take a little more time today."

His brows snapped together. "I don't think that's a good idea."

She rolled her eyes and shoved her hair away from her face. "I'm not a prisoner. Delphine said I could come and go as I please."

George took a step back. His hands clenched, and his frown deepened while his gaze dropped to the floor as if he were searching for something to say to change her mind.

But there wasn't anything that would alter the course she had set for herself. She might not remember much of her past, but she knew she had been independent, and she was going to get back to that.

"I'll return soon," she said and looped her purse strap over her shoulder before she headed out the door.

Her steps were quick and light as she bounded down the

porch stairs and then over the path to the sidewalk. This time, she left the sunglasses off, even though she had to squint against the sun.

The rays felt too good on her face.

Unable to help herself, she looked at everyone she passed, trying to discern if they had been the ones responsible for her attack. Yet, she knew those responsible wouldn't be in this part of the city—because they feared Delphine.

Just as she had told George, Riley took her time, leisurely strolling along the concrete and taking in the glorious city. The plants had begun blooming weeks ago when the weather warmed. She'd missed that, and it was usually one of her favorite things.

That thought made her halt. Every once in a while, a thought like that popped into her mind. She didn't know why it felt as if it had been buried, but now, at the surface, she knew it for a fact.

Moreover, she knew she loved plants. She loved planting and cultivating them. Her favorites were hibiscus, snapdragons, and daisies.

Recalling more of her past that had been taken from her the night of the attack was another sign that she was growing stronger. If only the migraines would stop, because each time they came, she lost time. Sometimes, small bits. Sometimes, hours.

Riley began walking again until she spotted a bench near a street performer. The sound of the violin was a call she couldn't ignore. Somewhere, sometime, she had gone to a symphony and enjoyed it.

She sat on the bench and closed her eyes while the rays of the sun bathed her face, and the music filled her ears. The soft melody drowned out the sounds of conversations around her as well as the cars.

Several songs were played before she finally opened her eyes. Just as she was about to get up, her gaze landed on a dark-headed man off to her left. His wavy hair was just a bit on the longish side, enough that he shoved it out of his face with his hand.

He was lean and rugged, his skin bronzed by the sun. His gaze was locked on the woman playing the violin, his toe tapping along with the music. He wore a simple navy V-neck tee that stretched across his wide shoulders and around his defined arms. Faded denim hugged his trim hips.

While his body was certainly nice, it was his face that she found herself staring at. His cheekbones, jaw, and chin were cut with chiseled perfection. And the slight shadow of a beard only made him sexier. Yet his wide lips were slightly turned up at the corners, softening his look.

Suddenly, his head turned slightly, their gazes clashing. She was mesmerized by his beautiful silver eyes. Maybe that's why she saw the slight widening of his gaze as if he recognized her.

But he didn't approach her right away. Instead, he turned back to the performer. When she finished her set, he walked to her and dug out some money from his wallet before tossing it into her opened violin case.

Riley sat up straighter when the man then turned her way. She wanted him to come talk to her. For someone who was so terrified of her own shadow a few weeks earlier, she was making great headway now.

He smiled and gave her a nod as he approached. "Hello."

"Hi," she replied. "The violinist was quite good."

He glanced over his shoulder. "That she was."

"Are you from New Orleans?"

"I grew up close to the city, and I've worked here for some time. You?"

She was shocked when the answer came out of nowhere—again. "I've only been here a short while. I'm Riley, by the way. Riley Chiasson."

"Marshall Ducet," he said and held out his hand.

Riley couldn't stop smiling when she shook his hand. Reluctantly, she released him, suddenly at a loss for words.

"What brought you to the city?" he asked.

She looked away as her mind shut down. "I don't remember."

"Did something happen to you?"

It was the concern in his voice that drew her gaze back to him. He looked at her as if all he cared about was her. It warmed her heart in ways she couldn't explain. And there, just for a millisecond, she thought she knew him. "Yes, something happened."

"Are you okay now?"

She didn't know why she felt so at ease with him, but she did. "I am. I'm sorry, but have we met before?"

"No."

There was some emotion in his gray eyes, almost as if he were holding something back. "There was an attack. I hit my head, and I lost some of my memory."

"An attack?"

Two words. That's all it took for the grin to vanish and his gaze to turn hard in anger *for* her.

"What happened?" he demanded in a soft voice.

Normally, she didn't like to talk about it, but she found herself wanting to share with him. But she hesitated.

His dark brows drew together. "What's wrong?"

"I can't explain it or my reaction to you."

He blinked and sat beside her. "I think I'm confused."

She gave a shake of her head. "That's my fault, I apologize. I don't usually like to talk about the attack, but there's something about you that I innately trust, something that makes me want to tell you."

"And that frightens you?"

"A little," she confessed. "It could have been that same trust that caused the attack in the first place."

His lips thinned for a moment. "I doubt that."

"You sound sure of yourself."

"I work in law enforcement. I've seen and heard about all sorts of attacks, and trusting your gut isn't ever the cause of one."

She blew out a breath. "Maybe."

"You don't have to tell me if you don't want to. I just couldn't imagine anyone wanting to harm you."

She smiled, liking him more and more. "If I tell you the truth, you might think I'm crazy."

"Never," he said and leaned back. He turned his head to her. "If you want to talk, I'll gladly listen."

"Are you married?" She had no idea why that was important, but she had to know the answer.

He chuckled softly. "No. I've never been married. You?"

"No." Of that, she was sure. Just like she'd known she liked flowers.

"Good."

Yes, it was good. Riley held Marshall's gaze and said, "There are supernatural creatures in New Orleans."

"I know."

His casual response was all she needed to continue. "I was out walking one night when I was viciously attacked by a werewolf. It was trying to kill me, and in the struggle, I slammed my head on the pavement. My friend, Delphine, heard my screams and came to rescue me. She brought me to her house and has given me shelter as I healed."

"Delphine?" he asked in a voice devoid of any inflection.

But his eyes said it all. He didn't like the priestess.

"You know her?" Riley asked.

He lifted one shoulder in a shrug as he looked away. "Everyone who knows about the paranormal knows of Delphine."

"And you don't like her."

Silver eyes returned to her. "I didn't say that."

"You didn't have to. It's in your gaze."

He glanced down before shifting to face her. "I'm glad she helped you."

"I've known nothing but kindness from her. Nothing bad can get to me in her district."

He smiled, but it didn't quite reach his eyes. "So you don't need to worry about werewolves."

"Exactly."

Marshall ran a hand over his mouth, a frown forming. "I'm sorry for what happened to you, Riley. I imagine your family has been worried about you."

"I don't have family."

"No one?" he pressed.

She shook her head. "It's why I'm so blessed to have Delphine in my life."

"Indeed."

Riley looked at her watch. "Shit. I need to go, but I've enjoyed talking to you. I'm sorry I can't stay."

"Meet me here tomorrow."

Her heart nearly erupted in joy. "I'd like that. Until then, Marshall Ducet."

"Stay safe, Riley Chiasson."

She rose and walked away. After a few steps, she looked back over her shoulder to find him watching her. He waved, causing her stomach to flutter in excitement.

CHAPTER

FIVE

MARSHALL SAT at the kitchen table with his elbows on his knees as he stared at his cell phone. Though he'd promised to call the Chiassons and update them, he knew he couldn't tell them anything.

He kept going over his accidental meeting with Riley in his head. While only seeing her once before—briefly—and staring at her photos on his phone, her image was branded in his mind.

It's why he'd recognized her instantly.

To think, he had almost turned down the previous street, but the performer had sounded so good that he needed a closer look.

As soon as his gaze clashed with her bright blue eyes, Marshall had known it was Riley. The fact that she had sat there as if she didn't have a care in the world is what tightened the ball of worry in his stomach.

It was why he hadn't gone to her right away. He'd needed time to gather his thoughts on how to approach her. But it was nearly impossible not to look at the Cajun beauty.

Luxurious dark hair tumbled down her back in soft waves. She'd had one side tucked behind her ear, showing off her long, slender throat. Her wide, slightly angled eyes looked at everything as if seeing it all for the first time.

With her high cheekbones, simple beauty, and lips so full and sinful that he ached to touch them, Riley had people of all ages looking her way. And she seemed completely unaware of her allure, which made her even more attractive.

He'd approached her cautiously, not entirely sure what to say. Yet, she'd smiled in welcome, though there hadn't been any recognition in her eyes. Why would there be? They had never actually met. The one time she'd seen him, she was leaving to return to New Orleans and her cousins. Her thoughts had been on anything but him.

The fact that she thought she was with Delphine because of a werewolf attack made Marshall sick to his stomach. Just as he'd guessed, Delphine planned to use Riley against her family. He just hadn't expected the Voodoo priestess's actions to be quite so sinister.

To take away the one thing the Chiassons cared about above all else, all while making Riley believe she had no family. And ensure that the LaRues could never convince Riley to return to them.

Marshall hung his head and blew out a long breath. Obviously, Delphine believed in her magic enough to allow Riley off on her own. Then again, Riley believed every word she said. The conviction had been in her voice and her actions.

Where exactly did that leave Marshall? It wasn't like he could tell Riley the truth. She wouldn't believe him, and then he might lose the only chance he had of getting her away from Delphine.

But how did he convince Riley of what was really going on?

His phone rang. Marshall lifted his head and pursed his lips when he saw the Caller ID. He lifted the phone to his ear and said, "Hey, Vin."

"Hey. I wanted to see how things were progressing."

Marshall closed his eyes as he sat back in the chair. He heard the anxiety and worry in Vincent's voice, and he could only imagine how the eldest Chiasson was handling things.

"Slow."

"I'm going insane here, Marshall. My siblings are my responsibility. If anything happens to Riley—"

"It's not going to," Marshall interjected. "Don't go down that road. You need to stay positive for your brothers."

Vin sighed loudly. "Where did you look today?"

"Look, I know you're worried, and I know you want to be

here searching yourself, but perhaps it's better if you don't second-guess everything I'm doing."

Besides, Marshall didn't like lying to his friends, and with every call where he didn't tell them about Riley, it would eat at him.

"Shit. That's not what I'm doing," Vin said. "I'm sorry. I just want something to hold on to, something that says my sister is going to come back to us."

Marshall tilted his head back to look at the ceiling. "We all know how strong Delphine is. Her magic is powerful."

"Davena was telling us all the different ways Delphine could hurt Riley. I had to ask the question, which made Davena answer it. That Voodoo bitch wants to destroy our family, Marshall. And she's going to use Riley to do it."

"I know."

Vincent snorted. "Christian said you'd probably figured that out."

"It makes the most sense."

"Well, at least my sister is alive."

Marshall closed his eyes. "Yeah."

"You shouldn't be there, and you especially shouldn't be going up against Delphine alone. This family has lost a lot of friends over the years. We don't want to lose you, as well."

"Since I'm not ready to kick the bucket just yet, I'm treading carefully."

Vincent was silent for a moment. "Be safe, Marshall. And don't trust anyone."

Vincent's words rang in Marshall's head the next day as he waited on the bench for Riley. Though Vin hadn't said it, he was telling Marshall to be wary of Riley if he encountered her.

And after his brief conversation with the youngest Chiasson the previous day, Marshall planned to take everything she said with a grain of salt.

He glanced at his watch. It was thirty-seven minutes past the time Riley was supposed to meet him. Since everything hinged on their speaking again, he didn't intend to leave. He'd stay there all damn day if he had to.

At least the violinist was back. Marshall spread his arms along the back of the bench and stretched out his legs, one ankle crossed over the other.

The detective in him took in everything around him, cataloging it in his mind—because details were important. He noted the people walking past him, the ones listening to the performer, and those who milled about for other reasons. It was easy for him to spot and separate the tourists from those who lived in the city.

In many ways, he missed the vibrant hum of New Orleans, the mix of the old and new, and how it seemed to seamlessly mesh together. Fun and danger mingled together like dance partners, each trying to take the lead.

And thrown into the jumble was the supernatural.

Someone approaching on his right caused Marshall to turn his head in that direction. The concern that had been courting him each minute Riley was late vanished when he saw her.

"I can't believe you're still here," she said with a relieved smile as she stopped beside the bench.

Marshall motioned for her to sit beside him. He looked over Riley's gray jeans and white shirt, appreciating how both garments showed off her body. "I had nowhere else I wanted to be."

She pushed her hair back over her shoulder and turned so that she faced him. "I'm sorry for being late. I couldn't get away."

"Everything all right now?" he asked as he covertly looked around for anyone who might be following her.

It didn't take long for Marshall to find the tall man who stared at Riley as if she were his favorite toy, one that had been stolen by someone else.

Riley laughed softly and leaned back. "Yes. I'm glad you waited."

They stared at each other for a few minutes before she looked away. Finally, she asked, "How do you know about the supernatural?"

"You can't be a cop in this city and not see something. I also know people who hunt the evil creatures."

Her head cocked to the side as a small frown puckered

her brow. "You make it sound as if there are monsters who are good."

"Would it shock you to know that I know for a fact that some are? Just as humans are both, the same is true for the supernatural."

She looked forward, lines of thought bracketing her mouth. "I always assumed they were all evil."

"Always as in forever, or since the attack?"

Blue eyes slid back to him. "I can't recall what I thought about them before the attack."

"Does that mean that you knew of the supernatural before?"

"Yes," she answered immediately. Then she frowned.

He shifted his body some to face her. "What's wrong?"

"Sometimes, I can answer things like that without knowing how the information is there."

"It's locked in your mind."

A grin curved her luscious lips. "You make it sound as if my memories have been secured away."

"In a way, they have." The longer the tall man stared at Riley, the angrier Marshall became. "How long do I have with you?"

"As long as you want."

"Is that so?" he asked with a grin. Then he got to his feet and held out his hand. "Do you trust me?"

She took his hand and stood. "Yes, though I don't know why."

Marshall wrapped his fingers around hers. "Let's walk."

They talked of easy things like the weather and tourists. Riley laughed and joked right up until they reached the edge of Delphine's domain where she came to a halt. Marshall said nothing as he watched Riley, whose gaze was glued to the invisible line before her. On the surface, she looked calm, but he noticed that her breathing had quickened, and her fingers now gripped his hand tightly.

"If I leave this section of the city, the supernatural can get to me."

He turned her to face him. "I don't want to scare you, but the fact is, the monsters can get you anywhere—even in this part of the city."

"No. Delphine wouldn't allow that."

"I'm sure she wouldn't," he answered. There was no need to try and persuade her differently.

Riley licked her lips and glanced at the ground where the invisible marker was that sectioned off Delphine's part of the city. "I don't like living in fear. The longer I hide from it, the longer it's going to take me to get my life back."

"We can turn around," he offered.

She looked at him and lifted her chin. "No. We're going forward."

"Lead the way, Miss Chiasson."

Riley was smiling—and still holding his hand—when she stepped over the boundary into the vampire sector of the city.

They walked quietly for some time before she glanced at him. "You look at me as if you know me."

"What would you say if I said I did?"

She shrugged and shifted to allow another couple to pass on the sidewalk. "I'd want to know from where and how."

As they passed a restaurant, Marshall looked in the windows and saw the tall man's reflection from across the street. No matter where they went, he was going to follow them. And Marshall wanted Riley alone.

He looked down at her lips, his balls tightening.

Oh how he wanted that kiss.

"How do you feel about boat rides?"

Her eyes grew large as she grinned. "I love the water."

"Good," he replied.

In a matter of moments, they were at the water's edge, where they jumped on one of the tour boats. Marshall inwardly smiled when the vessel pushed away from the pier with no other passengers getting on behind them.

He and Riley walked to the opposite side of the boat to the railing. Someone bumped into her from behind, sending her straight into his arms.

Marshall held her protectively as he gazed down into her eyes. God, how he wanted to taste her lips.

CHAPTER

SIX

God, how she wanted to kiss him. Riley's palms were flattened against Marshall's chest, and she could feel the heat and hardness of his sinew through the black shirt. Desire scorched her, leaving a trail of need in its wake.

The way his gunmetal eyes looked at her, truly seeing her as a person and not an object, made her skin tingle. She enjoyed being in his arms and feeling his strength. He walked and looked like a man who could take on anything, and she felt safe with him.

Before she could think about it, she rose up and pressed her lips briefly to his. As she was drawing back, he captured her mouth and slid his tongue along her lip. Riley opened for him immediately.

The taste of him was heady, intoxicating, and caused her body to warm, and longing to quicken her blood.

He kissed her slowly, thoroughly. Gradually deepening the kiss until she was clinging to him, need thrumming through her as her sex ached. His arms were the only reason she was still on her feet.

When he ended the kiss and looked down at her, she struggled to get herself under control, fought not to pull his head down for another taste of his amazing lips. Because, damn, the man could kiss.

"I've been wanting to do that for a long time," he said in a low, soft voice.

"Then why in the hell did you stop?"

He smoothed hair away from her face. "I didn't want to. In fact, I don't ever want to stop."

Something was happening between them. Desire, yes, but something more primal, more untamed swirled between them. Though it frightened her a little, she didn't want it to end. Ever. It felt so good, like basking in the glow of the sun.

Whoever Marshall Ducet was, she knew she could trust him, and that he would keep her safe. She didn't question that—or the craving she had for him.

His hand splayed on her back, pulling her against him so she felt his arousal. Her stomach fluttered, and desire pooled low in her belly. She lifted her face, silently begging for him to kiss her again.

"I can hardly think with you near," he murmured.

"Stop thinking."

His eyes darkened as he stared at her, his craving blatant. And palpable.

Breathing became impossible as she struggled not to tear his clothes off. The crush of people was a constant reminder that they weren't alone.

His other hand came up along her side, his thumb stopping at the base of her breast. He held it there, teasing her while he leaned forward and brushed his lips along her throat. Her moan was drowned out by the person speaking through the speakers while pointing out sights. Marshall's hot mouth made a trail from her neck to her ear.

"I want you," he whispered.

She took his head in her hands and moved it so that he was looking at her. "Yes," she said just before pulling him down for another kiss.

The rest of the world fell away, leaving only the two of them and the raging, rampant desire that burned uncontrollably between them. He felt so good, so right. Like they had been destined to meet. Now, all she had to worry about were her brothers.

She jerked back, breaking the kiss as she searched her mind to continue the thought. The thread she clung to evaporated, taking the certainty of family with it. She didn't have any brothers. She was alone in the world.

Then what happened to your family?

"Riley?" Marshall asked as he studied her, worry in his slate-gray gaze.

She swallowed and shook her head, facing the railing to look over the water. "I'm sorry. I just...I..."

"Shhh," he said and put an arm around her. "It's all right."

She stood there, waiting for him to press for more. When he didn't, she looked over at him. "This is normally the part where people ask what's going through my mind."

He pulled his gaze from the water and shot her a half smile before raking a hand through his dark locks. "Something traumatic happened to you. Your mind is trying to work it all out. The less you worry about giving answers, the quicker they'll come to you."

"Is that your professional opinion?" she teased.

A soft chuckle fell from his lips. "Actually, yes. I've seen a lot of horrible things working in law enforcement. There are times to push someone for answers, and there are times when we can tell that a person just needs some space. Right now, you need someone to stand with you while you sort through everything."

"Have you had much experience with head trauma?"

There was a slight pause before he turned to her, leaning his other arm on the railing while still touching her. "How do you know you had head trauma? Did you go to a hospital? Did a doctor see you?"

With every question, she found herself frowning. "I... No. Delphine found me and took care of me."

"Do you remember the attack?"

"Bits and pieces," she said with a shrug.

He nodded slowly. "Then how do you know what happened?"

"George told me how he found me."

"George, huh?"

The wind coming off the water was cooling her heated skin. "George is one of Delphine's followers."

"I thought Delphine found you."

"She did."

"But you just said George found you."

Riley rubbed her temple. "He did."

"Were they together?"

"I don't know," she snapped. Then she took a deep breath. "I'm sorry."

Marshall rubbed his hand along her back. "No, I'm sorry. I shouldn't have pushed you. Old habits, and all that."

She gave him a quick smile. "The thing is, your questions have merit. They made me revisit what I've been told, and I can't answer your last question. Mainly because I'm not sure if they were together or not. Neither has said they were with anyone."

"Will you tell me about the attack when you're ready?"

Riley scooted closer to Marshall and looked back out over the water, shaking her head to loosen the strands of hair that clung to her face. "I remember being scared. It was nighttime. I want to say that there were others with me, but I can't see them. Like there's a fog. It's like my brain is telling me I wasn't alone, but if that's the case, why can't I remember them?"

"You will in time," he assured her.

She sure hoped so. While she'd been content these last few weeks without knowing her past and getting over the migraines, she suddenly yearned to recapture the memories —good or bad—of her past so she knew who *she* was.

"I wanted to run," she continued. "I think I might have even tried. My memory is just so murky about the details. But I remember the terror. And the pain as I was slammed to the ground." She lifted her hands, turning them over to look at her palms. "I recall how the pavement cut into my hands. There was a broken bottle near. I reached for it to use as a weapon, but I couldn't grab it."

She fisted her hands and slid her gaze to Marshall. "I can't remember anything clearly after that. George tells me that I fended off the werewolf while it was trying to bite me."

"What color wolf?"

She blinked. "Color?"

"Yes. Every were is different. If you can recall the color, we might be able to find him or her."

"I don't know," she said, shaking her head.

He straightened and wrapped his arm around her again. "It doesn't matter. How long ago was this?"

"About eight weeks or so. George said I was out of it for a while."

"And they didn't get you to a doctor?"

She shrugged while wrinkling her nose. "Voodoo and all that. Delphine is apparently pretty powerful."

"And you trust her?"

"She saved me. Why wouldn't I trust her?"

He bowed his head. "Point taken."

"Do you not like her?"

"I've never met her."

"That's not what I asked," she pressed. "You don't necessarily have to meet someone to like them."

Marshall's smile was tight. "I've not heard very good things about her."

"And?" Riley pressed. "I hear an 'and' in there."

He stared at her a long moment. "She tried to hurt a few of my friends."

"I'm sorry. I didn't know. Delphine has only ever been good to me."

"Let's hope it remains that way."

Why then did Riley have a feeling that there was another meaning to his words? She wanted to press him for more, but there was a part of her that was a little scared of discovering anything else.

After all, she had thought Delphine bordered on sainthood. Now, she learned that the priestess had tried to hurt others. Riley wanted to say that perhaps Delphine was defending herself, but the words wouldn't come.

"You're thinking too hard," Marshall said.

The sound of the motor slowing made her sad. "The ride's over."

"That doesn't mean our day has to end."

She smiled and turned to face the city. But the sight of George and Delphine standing on the pier wiped the expression from her face.

"What is it?" Marshall asked. Then he followed her gaze. "Ah. I see."

Delphine had said she could do whatever she wanted for the day, so why were she and George there? It infuriated Riley. Especially since Delphine told her she wasn't a prisoner.

"Is he your boyfriend?" Marshall asked, referring to George.

Riley pulled Marshall behind a group of people. "He wants to be. He won't take no for an answer," she replied, letting the frustration ring in her words.

"You don't have to go with them."

She stopped and faced him. "I do. I can't explain it, but I have to go. I need you to hide, though."

"Hide?" he asked with a quirk of his brow.

"Please."

He looked over her head to the shore before he gave a single nod. "I want to see you again."

"Tomorrow," she said. "There's a little store two streets over from the bench. Meet me there at two."

He pulled her against him for a quick kiss as the boat

docked. Riley pulled away and shoved him back so he could hide.

In all the time she spent with Delphine, there had never been an occasion for her to lie to the priestess, so she wasn't sure why she did it now. Only that her gut told her to, and she trusted that instinct.

Riley looked back over her shoulder to have one more look at Marshall as she fell in line with the others to disembark, but he was now out of sight.

When she walked from the boat onto shore, she smiled when she saw Delphine and George. "What are you two doing here?"

"You left my area," Delphine said, disappointment tinting her words.

Riley widened her eyes. "I know. I wanted to push myself. I figured during the day would be better. I'm not that far from your section, so I knew I could get back if I needed to."

"And the man you were with?" George demanded as he looked at the face of every dark-haired man who exited the boat.

"I don't know who you're talking about."

Delphine raised a brow and folded her arms over her chest. "George followed you today. He said you spoke with a man and took his hand."

Riley's first instinct was fury over being followed, but her gut told her not to show it. Not yet, at least. Instead, she gave a hollow laugh. "Oh, that man was a tourist. He was lost and looking for his way back to the French Quarter."

"That's not what it looked like," George said.

Delphine put an arm out, blocking him from advancing on Riley. The priestess's black eyes bored into her. "So, you weren't meeting anyone?"

"Who would I meet?" Riley said with a frown. "I'm alone except for you, my friends."

And her brothers.

The thought drew her up short. That was the second time in less than an hour that, for just an instant, she thought she had siblings, but she couldn't get any more from her memories than that. Not how many, not their names. Nothing.

"You had me worried," Delphine said with a sigh. "It's time to go home, child."

As Riley walked away with them, she had to fight not to look back for Marshall. Already she missed the safety of his arms—and the heat of his kiss.

CHAPTER

SEVEN

IF MARSHALL THOUGHT NOT TELLING the Chiassons he had
found their sister was hard, it was nearly impossible to keep
from letting them know he had spent a few hours with her.
Yet, somehow, he managed to keep his mouth shut.

Mainly because the things Riley had told him worried
him greatly. She said she was able to do what she wanted,
but there had been a healthy dose of fear in her eyes when
she spotted Delphine and George.

Whatever the priestess was doing to Riley, it wasn't
working fully. The truth seemed to be making itself known
to her slowly and at odd moments, but it was coming back to
Riley.

If he tried to tell her everything now, she might very well
bolt and inform Delphine of it all, which would send the

priestess after him. Frankly, Marshall would rather not go up against Delphine on his own.

He needed more time with Riley to slowly get the truth to reveal itself to her. Only then would she believe anything he had to say.

Thankfully, none of the Chiassons called him. It was a reprieve, but one he appreciated. Though he didn't get much sleep. He kept thinking about Riley's kisses and how he hadn't wanted to let her go. Ever.

He was literally counting down the minutes until he could see her again, to hold her. To taste her.

Night finally gave way to dawn, but his anxiety only grew. He couldn't shake off the sense that something had happened. A scan of the internet showed that while there had been crimes committed in New Orleans, none had involved anyone that fit Riley's description.

Why then did a feeling of dread fill him?

The morning crept by, during which he worked out and did more research on Delphine and the Voodoo culture. When noon finally came, he ate a quick meal before jumping into the shower. He was ready over an hour early, but he couldn't stay within the confines of the house anymore.

Marshall got into his truck and drove toward Delphine's area. He parked on the outskirts of the sector and decided to walk as he had the past two days. The violinist wasn't performing, so he continued on until he found a pantomime.

With time to kill and an affinity for watching others, Marshall found a bench and sat. There was so much he could tell about someone just from a few minutes of observation. It was a skill he liked to hone. And it helped pass the time.

When it got closer to two, Marshall rose and found the store Riley had spoken of. He walked inside and picked up a handcart while leisurely strolling through the aisles. Since he needed a few things, he began to fill the basket. When he checked his watch, it was ten minutes after two. He glanced toward the door and discreetly walked down the center row to look down the aisles. But there was no sign of Riley.

He remained calm since she had been late the day before, as well. It was no great feat to position himself so that he could see the door and everyone who entered. He moved often so as not to draw attention to himself. Especially since any of those around him could be Delphine's followers.

The time stretched to three, and it became impossible to remain. He made his way to the cashier and got in line, thankful that there were people in front of him. Then, another cashier opened and motioned him to her. Marshall tapped the woman's shoulder in front of him and pointed out the waiting cashier. But not even that could stop him from eventually reaching his turn.

All too soon, he paid, and his groceries were bagged. Marshall was thankful that he hadn't bought anything that needed refrigeration because he didn't intend to leave yet.

He walked around, keeping an eye out for Riley's tall form and dark locks.

Every time he caught a glimpse of someone who might be her, his heart raced. But disappointment soon reigned. The more time that passed with no sign of Riley, the more worried he became.

It was nearing five o'clock when he finally gave up and headed back to his truck. Anger and frustration and regret rolled through him in waves. Not to mention the heavy doses of fear that something had happened to Riley.

Two hours later, he'd nearly paced a hole in the floor of Donnie's house. Knowing he was probably going to regret it later, Marshall drove to Gator Bait. He only knew Kane and Solomon—barely—but if anyone knew the underbelly of the city, it was the four werewolves.

He parked on the side of the street and shoved a hand through his hair after he got out of the truck. The bar was situated in a prime corner location with the large wooden sign that looked as if a huge gator had taken a bite out of it.

Music from within wafted out onto the street. Loud, noisy places weren't his particular cup of tea—unless it was for pool—but this was a necessity.

With a sigh, he walked across the street to the door and stepped over the threshold. A quick glance showed that every table was full with only a couple of barstools open. There were several pool matches going on, and all four dart boards were occupied. If he weren't there on business, he would have made his way over to a pool table and gotten involved in a match. But that was for another day.

"Find yourself a place," said a woman with long, black hair and dark, smoky eyes.

Based on Beau's description, that was Skye Parrish, Court LaRue's woman. It didn't take long for Marshall to locate Kane acting as bartender.

He walked to the bar and lowered himself onto the stool. When Kane's blue gaze landed on him, the werewolf froze. Marshall clasped his hands together on the glossy bar and gave a nod.

"What can I get you to drink?" Kane asked, studying him.

"Bourbon."

Kane raised a blond brow as he set a glass on the bar. "That kind of night, is it?"

"You've no idea."

After pouring the alcohol, Kane shoved the glass to him. "How about you share?"

"I'd love to."

Kane jerked his head to the side as he walked away. Marshall grabbed his glass and downed the whiskey before following. He wasn't surprised when Kane took him to the back of the bar and into the kitchen area before turning right to an office.

"Myles, you're going to want to get off the phone," Kane said as he motioned Marshall to a chair.

Marshall nodded to Myles and put his hands on the arms

of the chair before lowering himself down. When Myles hung up, Marshall said, "Hello."

"And you are?"

"Marshall Ducet."

"Ahh," Myles said, nodding. "The sheriff in Lyons Point. What the hell are you doing here?"

Kane said, "We all want to know that."

Solomon, the eldest LaRue, walked in, followed by the youngest, Court.

"Marshall," Solomon said. "I'm surprised to see you here. Can I hope this trip is one of pleasure?"

"Unfortunately not," Marshall said. He blew out a breath and pressed his lips together. "I wouldn't be here if it wasn't important, and I need all of you to understand that what I'm about to tell you, no one else can know."

Court crossed his arms over his chest. "We're waiting."

"It's about Riley, isn't it?" Kane asked, his blue eyes filled with worry.

Marshall cracked his knuckles and wished he had another shot of bourbon. "Yeah."

"Don't keep us in suspense," Myles said.

Unable to stay seated, Marshall rose to his feet. There wasn't much room to pace with the four brothers standing around the desk staring at him, but he couldn't keep still. He rubbed the back of his neck, giving himself one last second to make sure he was doing the right thing. Not that the LaRues would let him leave now that they knew what had brought him to New Orleans.

"Do my cousins know you're here?" Solomon asked.

Marshall glanced at him and walked a few steps before turning around. "They do. It was my suggestion not to alert any of you to my arrival."

"Why?" Court demanded.

Myles leaned back in his chair. "Because if we'd known, we would've pushed ourselves on his search, making it impossible for him to look on his own and thus drawing attention to him by being associated with us."

"You found her, didn't you?" Kane asked.

Marshall halted and looked at Kane. From what he'd heard, Riley and Kane became close friends after she arrived. They shared an apartment, which allowed Kane to keep an eye on her, and for her to keep an eye on him. The bond that developed between the two had stabilized Kane and given Riley purpose.

Marshall blew out a deep breath. "I did."

With two simple words, Solomon, Court, and Myles began bombarding him with questions.

"Is she all right?"

"Did you talk to her?"

"Why isn't she with you?"

"Do you have her hidden somewhere?"

"Can we see her?"

"When can we kick Delphine's ass?"

"Enough!" Kane bellowed, putting a stop to the questions.

Marshall looked at each of the brothers. "Riley is hale and hearty. But she's...not herself."

"How do you mean?" Myles asked as he braced his arms on his desk, a frown furrowing his brow.

Marshall struggled to find the words. "For one, she believes she doesn't have any family."

A look of fury erupted over Court's face. "What the fuck?"

Marshall held up his hand. "I came to the same conclusion that you four and the Chiassons did. Delphine had to have her. Since I don't register on the priestess's radar, I decided to stroll through the section of the city she's claimed as hers. Imagine my surprise when I saw Riley that first day."

"I think I'm going to be sick," Court mumbled.

Solomon's blond brows drew together in concern and disbelief. "The first day? You mean, you had only just begun looking for her, and she was there?"

"Yes," Marshall answered. "I walked over to the bench where she was sitting, and we had a nice chat. She told me that Delphine found her after an attack. That it's the priestess who's been sheltering her and keeping her safe."

"Actually, I know I'm going to be sick," Court stated.

Kane issued a growl to Court before turning his gaze back to Marshall. "What kind of attack?"

This was the part Marshall didn't want to tell them, but there was no way around it. "A werewolf attack."

The four brothers displayed varying degrees of shock. It was Solomon who clenched his fists at his sides and said, "It's so damn obvious. Of course, the bitch would make our cousin believe she was attacked by the very creatures we are so she won't trust us."

"We underestimated Delphine," Myles said with a shake of his head. "And how the hell did we do that after everything she's done to this family?"

Kane glanced at the ceiling. "So, the very thing we're trying to kill took Riley, somehow erased her memories of us and her brothers, made her believe she was attacked by a were, and now, Riley thinks Delphine is her friend."

"Yeah," Marshall said.

"It's probably a good thing you didn't tell Vin and the others. They would've been here immediately, wanting to attack Delphine," Solomon said.

Court issued a loud snort. "Hell, I want to attack her."

"You can't," Marshall said. "Not yet anyway."

"Then why did you come to us?" Myles inquired.

Marshall suddenly found that his legs couldn't hold him. He sank into the chair he'd abandoned moments ago. "Riley wanted me to meet her yesterday. She was followed by a man named George. She didn't see him, but I was able to get us away. We even left Delphine's area and got on a tour boat. Her memory is there, but it's being blocked. I think she recalls things at times, but she questions them. Anyway, when we docked, Delphine and George were waiting for her."

"Did they see you?" Solomon asked.

He shook his head. "Riley asked me to hide, which I did. But we made plans to meet today. And that's what brought me here. She never showed up."

CHAPTER

EIGHT

HER BODY WAS ON FIRE. It burned from the inside out with desire that felt as if it would never be quenched. Yet Riley knew that there was one who could ease the ache within her —Marshall.

She tried to move, but her arms and legs were held down. Thrashing her head, she attempted to call out. But no sound fell from her lips.

Her hair tangled in her face. She felt it stick to her skin, just as she felt the wind whisper over her bare legs and the sweaty hands that pinned her down. The hard floor vibrated from the stomping and clapping of those around her, which was only matched by the loud singing.

Was this a nightmare? Because she couldn't remember any of her dreams being so...vivid. It had to be a nightmare. Otherwise, someone was doing this to her.

"Shh," a voice said near her ear. "Stop fighting."

Delphine. Riley recognized her voice and soft hands smoothing the hair away from her face. She stopped struggling, thinking that she might wake from this horrible dream.

Instead, she felt the hem of her gown being pushed up her thighs to her hips, exposing her panties. Riley's heart began to pound as fear consumed her when she couldn't open her eyes.

"She's coming," Delphine whispered. "Open yourself up for the spirit to possess you, child."

No. Riley didn't want to be possessed. She, more than anyone, knew that doing such a thing opened a person up to all sorts of events afterward.

But wait. How was she so sure of that?

Lincoln had told her.

No sooner did she think of her brother than she felt someone over her. There was only a fraction of a second before the body rested atop hers.

Marshall. She could picture his face, recall the taste of his kiss, feel the heat of his body. He wouldn't let anyone hurt her. She was as sure of that as she was that—

"I want you."

George's rough, lust-filled voice made her panic, but now, she couldn't even move her head. She screamed as loud as she could in her brain as he ground his arousal against her, humping her.

"Now, Delphine?" he asked.

"Soon, my sweet. Soon, Riley will be yours. Until then, Elin awaits you."

RILEY STOPPED CHOPPING the bell pepper and lifted her gaze out the window.

"What's wrong?" Elin asked as she walked into the kitchen carrying a basket of homemade jams someone had delivered.

Riley looked over and met Elin's green gaze. "I just feel like I was supposed to do something today."

"You had a terrible migraine last night. I heard you call out."

How come she didn't remember that? "It must have been a bad one."

"You don't remember, do you?" Elin asked, her lips turning down in a frown.

Riley shook her head.

Elin walked to her and put a hand on her arm. "I was like that for months after Delphine found me. They'll go away, just like they did for me."

Months of pain and lost time? Riley wasn't sure she could stand another day of it, much less longer.

Something pulled at her mind again. She was sure she

was supposed to be somewhere else. The more she fought to remember, the farther away the memory seemed to go.

"What's on your arm?" Elin asked.

Riley looked down and saw the bruise on her left wrist. A glance at her other arm showed the same thing. "I have no idea."

And that's what frightened her. Lost time, bruises she couldn't explain, and the feeling that she was forgetting something vitally important that plagued her.

"I did hear you yell," Elin said. "Maybe they had to restrain you."

Suddenly, a flash of images filled Riley's mind. They came at her so quickly that she dropped the knife and grabbed hold of the counter to remain standing.

Delphine leaning over her.

People holding her down.

George pulling up her gown.

George on top of her.

Then George having sex with Elin.

Riley jerked her head to her friend. Though she wouldn't be able to explain it, she knew those images weren't fragments of dreams. It had actually happened, but she couldn't say when or where.

Elin scrunched up her face as she took a step back. "Why are you looking at me like you know something that I don't?"

"Are you having sex with George?"

Elin's face went slack before her eyes widened. "What?

No. He showed interest in me for a while, but then you came. Everyone knows he wants you."

"So you aren't sleeping with him?"

"No," Elin stated more firmly, her eyes hard. "I already said I wasn't. What's wrong with you today?"

Riley licked her lips. "I'm sorry. I don't know why I asked that."

The lie was an easy one since she used it often enough. But it was the first time it hadn't been the truth. Riley wanted to clutch her head and shake it. She began to wonder if her mind wasn't more affected by her attack than she originally thought. Perhaps she should talk to Delphine.

NO!

Her inner voice issued the bellow so loudly that Riley thought it had come from Elin for a second.

Riley backed away from the counter. She wished she could see the one person she did trust, M.... His name was on the tip of her tongue, but more troubling, was that she couldn't dredge up his image in her mind.

"I'm not feeling well," she told Elin. "I'm going to go lie down."

Elin nodded worriedly. "I'll be up shortly to look in on you."

Riley left the kitchen and started up the stairs. Halfway to her room, she looked down to find George at the bottom, staring at her with such a covetous expression that it sickened her.

Once in her room, Riley shut the door, only then noticing that there was no lock on it. She glanced around, but there was nothing that she could easily move to bar the entrance. Which meant that she would never sleep easy again.

What was going on that she was suddenly wary and nervous in a house where she had always felt safe?

Always?

Well, maybe not that long, but as long as she had been recovering.

She turned and walked to the bed. There, she lay down and threw an arm over her eyes. It took her several minutes before she was able to calm herself enough that her breathing evened out.

That's when she began going through every male name that she knew that started with the letter M. She got to the name Mark, and it gave her pause, but she knew it wasn't quite right. But it had to be similar.

So she started over, using all the "Mar" combinations she knew until she finally landed on it.

"Marshall," she whispered.

As soon as she said the name, she recalled their two meetings, the boat ride, the kiss, and her promise to meet him today at the market.

Riley jerked upright and looked at the clock on her nightstand to see that it was after five. She could try to get away, but George would only follow her. Hopefully, Marshall would return to the store tomorrow.

She had no way of contacting him, nor did she know where he lived. Everything rested on hoping that she could get away the next day and that he'd return.

Approaching footsteps had her quickly lying down again, though this time, she put her back to the door as she curled on her side. She waited when the footsteps paused outside her room for a few seconds before moving on.

Riley didn't so much as move a toe. She stared at the wall, waiting to make sure no one was there, wondering all the while why she would forget Marshall. He was the one thing she wouldn't forget. He'd been charming, gorgeous, and nice. Not once had he hurt her or made her do anything she didn't want to do.

No matter how many migraines she had, none of them would make her forget a person. And then there were the flashes. They happened. She would bet her life on it. But she couldn't recall any more than those brief seconds she saw in her mind.

She looked down at her wrists and the bruises. Then she covered her left wrist with her right hand and found that the bruises lined up with her fingers. Which meant that someone had held her down.

Riley knew at that moment that she had to get away from Delphine, George, and the house. She didn't know who was involved and who to trust, and that meant she couldn't even tell Elin her thoughts.

Whatever was going on, she wanted to be far from it.

Maybe then the migraines would stop, and she could remember things. Like... She fisted her hands. Something had happened yesterday on the boat with Marshall. She recalled a memory that had distressed her, but it was now gone from her recollection.

She sighed loudly.

Why wasn't she scared like Elin, who refused to go farther than Delphine's yard? No matter how much anyone coaxed her, Elin wouldn't go another step. She said it was her fear of another werewolf attack that kept her at Delphine's. Only, now that Riley thought about it, Elin, like her, didn't have a bite from a were.

How was it that both were attacked yet neither of them sustained any type of injury?

Riley sat up and glanced at her door before looking out the window. It was too far of a drop for her to try and get out that way, and there was no way she could go out any of the doors without George knowing it.

He was always near, always watching. And, somehow, she knew that if she remained at the house, George would have her body—even if she didn't want him.

Once more, she had no proof of that, only a feeling, a sixth sense that she felt all the way to her soul. So she couldn't go to Delphine or Elin or anyone with her thoughts. No one would believe her.

But at least her memories of Marshall had returned. If she could get to him, then she had a chance. It was just finding him. And in a city the size of New Orleans, that might very well be impossible.

Riley didn't remain in her room long. To do so meant that Delphine would pay her a visit to check on her, so Riley rose and returned to the kitchen to finish preparing the evening meal. She ate with the others, keeping involved with the conversation while making sure never to look at George, who sat across from her. After she and Elin cleaned up, Riley went upstairs and took a long bath.

Thankfully, there was a lock on that door. She hated having to leave the bathroom, but others had need of it. Inside her room, she sat with her back against the wall, staring at the door. Waiting to see what would come for her.

THE WITCHING HOUR WAS REAL. Marshall stood on the roof of Gator Bait with Kane as the other three LaRue brothers shifted and took up their posts throughout the city.

After spilling everything to the brothers, they had simply asked Marshall what he needed. The problem was, Marshall didn't have a clue. All he knew for sure was that he had to get to Riley.

And soon.

"Do you hear it?" Kane asked.

Marshall looked over at him. Kane stood as still as stone, his lips rarely lifting into a smile of any sort. All because of Delphine's curse, a curse that had made Kane her weapon against his will and changed him.

"Hear what?" Marshall asked as he strained to pick up whatever it was Kane heard.

Kane's blue gaze was directed toward Delphine's section. "Beneath the noise of the city beats the heart of magic. It's why New Orleans is a mecca for the supernatural. Anything magical lives and breathes here. Thrives. Magic drives everything. If you listen closely, you can hear it."

"I know it's there, but I don't feel it like you do."

"You may be lucky in that regard."

Marshall wondered what Riley was doing. Years on the job and encountering all sorts of vile people allowed him to imagine dozens of ways Delphine could be hurting her. "I don't consider myself lucky to not be able to fight the supernatural."

"You're fighting." Kane swiveled his head to him, pinning him with his ice blue eyes that flashed yellow, showing the wolf within. "You fought while you were a detective here, and you fight alongside my cousins."

"It's not like I do much good. I've learned a few things from the Chiassons, but I'm not nearly as skilled."

Kane let out a long breath as he resumed his watch. "In many ways, I envy my cousins. If anything supernatural arrives in Lyons Point, they immediately hunt it. We don't have that option here since this is a Safe City."

Safe City meaning that any supernatural creature could find solace there—as long as they obeyed the rules. If they didn't, then the LaRues would hunt them down and kill them.

"Your job is very much like mine," Marshall said. "I can

usually pick out the ones who are going to be trouble, but I have to wait for them to do something before I can arrest them."

Kane shook his head slowly. "Then you have the ultimate monsters like Delphine. The one time she was weak enough that we could've taken her out was when we were just boys, and she killed our parents. If she hadn't run off the Moonstone pack, we could've ended this."

"She's smart. I'll give her that," Marshall admitted.

"In all my life, she's the one thing I've feared." Kane drew in a deep breath. "The only other person who knows that is Riley."

Marshal glanced at Kane. "I don't think less of you for being afraid of Delphine. She cursed you."

"And has wreaked havoc on everyone in my family. It has to stop."

"It will."

Kane rotated his shoulders as if it was killing him to stand still. But the brothers alternated, and it was his turn to stay behind. "Will it? Or will Delphine finally triumph? She has the one thing neither our cousins nor we will harm. And because of that, she has the ultimate control."

"Not if I can talk to Riley again."

The were's gaze returned to him. "You sound confident. Why?"

"Riley and I had a connection."

"Apparently a serious one by the way you gave a slight pause before saying it."

Damn. Kane would've been a great detective. Marshall decided there was no need to go into detail. "Yes."

Kane raised a brow, his gaze knowing. "I see."

"Riley is special."

"Very much so. A lot of people are putting their faith in you. Don't get in Delphine's crosshairs, and don't get killed."

"It isn't my plan."

Kane's face went cold. "It wasn't mine to be cursed either."

"One way or another, Riley and I will meet again."

"It's time we don't have. The longer Delphine has her hooks in Riley, the harder it will be to bring my cousin back."

Marshall put his hand on his hip where the holster of his gun usually hung. He had a pistol in his truck, and he wished he were wearing it.

"There might be something you can do to help," Kane said.

He turned to the werewolf. "Name it."

"When we hunted together, I taught Riley the symbol my brothers and I learned from my parents. We mark it on things to let each other know where we've been. The sigil is altered slightly for each of us, and I made Riley her own."

Marshall nodded, liking what he was hearing. "That sounds good, but how is it going to help?"

"Put it someplace Riley goes often. Then leave a trail that

will bring her to you. If she recognizes the symbols, she'll find her way."

"That could work."

Kane squatted and looked down at the street below where a man was following three girls. "You'll be on your own. We'll head into Delphine's district to keep their attention on us, but we won't be able to mark anything."

"Understood."

"Good," Kane said right before he jumped from the third-story roof to the ground behind a man.

Even from the distance, Marshall heard Kane's growl as he landed. The man whirled around and attacked. That's when Marshall saw the guy's red eyes, signaling him as a vampire. In seconds, Kane ended his life as the three women walked on without ever knowing they were in danger.

RILEY FOUGHT to keep her eyes open. It felt so good to close them, but her life depended on remaining awake. She glanced over at the bedside table to the clock that read 1:57.

This night was the longest of her life. She yawned and stood to get the blood flowing. That's when she saw something outside through her window. She immediately recognized Delphine's form in her usual all white, and George, walking shirtless beside her toward the vacant house. They were talking when George looked up at Elin's window.

Delphine was the first inside the darkened dwelling. Within minutes, candles along the windowsills were lit, casting everything in a soft glow.

Riley's head jerked to the side. Elin was in the room next to hers, and she was now moving around. Riley silently tiptoed to the wall that separated them and put her ear against it, listening.

The sound of Elin's door opening had Riley yanking her ear away as she looked at her own door. The floorboards creaked as Elin made her way past Riley's room to the stairs.

Riley's heart pounded as she debated whether or not to follow. Elin could be going to get something to drink. Or it could be something much, much worse.

The image of Elin and George having sex flashed in Riley's mind again.

She squeezed her eyes shut and shook her head to dislodge the scene, but it held fast. Then she moved to the side of her window and looked out, praying that Elin remained in the house.

But it wasn't long before she spotted the woman making her way toward Delphine and George.

Riley didn't hesitate this time. She quietly left her room and hurried down the stairs. When she reached the back door, she opened it just wide enough to slip through before softly closing it behind her.

She flattened herself against the house, looking across the yard to the abandoned structure. For some reason, Riley's hatred of the dwelling grew. She didn't want to go near it, but she had to. For Elin.

Looking all around her to make sure no one was about, Riley darted across the lawn to the other residence and once again flattened herself against the support.

She didn't know how she knew to do these things, only that they came naturally to her. As if she had learned them years ago. Whatever the reason, they were aiding her now, so she was thankful.

Listening carefully, she could hear Delphine talking to Elin, but couldn't quite make out what was said. With the house on piers, she couldn't easily look through the windows since she couldn't reach them. But that didn't stop her.

Riley began searching for something to climb up on to allow her to see inside. After a bit of searching, she found a cinderblock and carried it back to the window. Then she stood on it and peeked inside.

She was so shocked to find Elin standing naked in the middle of the room surrounded by dozens of candles on the floor that Riley jerked back, falling off her makeshift step. It would be so easy to return to the safety of her room, but Elin was her friend. How could she leave now?

With her mind set, Riley climbed back on the block and resumed her watch.

Delphine stood at the front of the room with her eyes closed as she sang. George then walked to stand beside Elin. He grabbed a fistful of Elin's long, dark hair and yanked hard. Elin kept her gaze on him, never flinching or crying out.

"Get on your knees," George ordered.

Elin dropped down, waiting. Riley couldn't look away as George demanded she remove his pants and then take him into her mouth. By the vacant look in Elin's eyes, she had no idea what she was doing.

Riley closed her eyes and gagged, even as she wondered if they had done the same thing to her. She forced herself to look back at Elin.

George now had her on her back, her legs spread. The glee on his face at his total domination of Elin sickened Riley. She knew then that her *dream* of George grinding against her had been real.

And it put into question everything Riley believed. More than anything, she no longer trusted Delphine. How could she when the priestess was part of such horrors?

Riley covered her mouth as George claimed Elin, taking her body roughly. Tears spilled down her cheeks. It was all Riley could do not to bust inside the house and kill George and Delphine—but something held her back.

A deep-rooted fear that loudly cautioned her to be careful.

Riley stepped off the cinderblock and returned it to where she'd found it, and then she stealthily made her way back to her room. There, she stood watch next to her window, hidden from view as she waited for them to finish with Elin.

It was after 4:30 before George and Delphine escorted Elin up to her room. As soon as Riley saw them exit the other residence, she slid beneath her covers and curled on her side, anxiously waiting as she focused all her energy on her hearing. Every sound in the house was as loud as a rocket, but none more so than the footsteps leading up the stairs and past her door.

Minutes after they'd *tucked* Elin into bed, Riley heard her door open. She kept her breathing even, and her eyes closed even though she was screaming inside.

Her blood ran cold when two sets of footsteps approached her. Soft fingers ran along her cheek. She wanted to jerk away, to plunge a knife into their hearts, anything but lie there and let them do as they wished.

"I ache for her," George said.

Delphine slid her long fingers into Riley's hair. "It's not quite time. She's fighting this harder than Elin. We can't push her too soon, or we could break her. And I've need of her yet."

"I have need of her."

"Your lust is never-ending."

George's voice lowered in anger. "Don't fuck with me, priestess. You gave me this body to possess, but you don't rule me. I'm tired of waiting for Riley. I want her. Make it happen tomorrow night. Or you won't like the consequences."

"But the La—"

"I don't care about the werewolves. You'll find another way to wipe them out. I've chosen Riley as mine."

With that, George strode from the room. It was several more tense minutes before Delphine followed.

Even after her door was shut, Riley didn't move. While she had been fighting sleep earlier, she couldn't sleep now if her life depended on it. She counted down five minutes and didn't hear anything. Finally, she opened her eyes a slit and looked around before she sat up and leaned against the iron headboard.

Without a doubt, she and Elin had to get away.

Tomorrow.

CHAPTER

TEN

THE LARUES COMMANDED ATTENTION. Marshall was never more aware of the brothers' reach than observing everyone in Delphine's district watching them as they paired off and walked the streets.

Those staring after the LaRues were Delphine's followers—and there were many.

Marshall tossed money into the case of the violinist who had returned and made his way to the market where he was supposed to meet Riley the day before. He'd already left the symbol Kane taught him on the bench with an arrow pointed toward the store. Outside the building, he hastily drew a circle within a circle, making sure the lines met on the left side. Then he added another arrow.

It took Marshall forty-five minutes before he was finished in Delphine's district, marking the symbols discreetly. A text to Kane let him know the LaRues could leave, but they were using the opportunity to search for their cousin.

Two hours later, Marshall carved the last of the symbols on the lamppost on the sidewalk outside of Donnie's house. Marshall looked back, hoping that Kane's suggestion worked. Otherwise, Marshall might go knocking on every door searching for Riley. Because he wasn't sure how long he could wait before he saw her again.

HER THEATRE TEACHER would've been proud, especially since Riley had all but failed the class in high school. Yet, she'd become a master that morning when she left her room and proceeded as she had every other day that she could remember.

She looked for minute details in everyone to catch anything that would tell her they didn't buy her act. But so far, so good.

Unfortunately, she didn't get time alone with Elin until after lunch. They sat out in the back yard beneath the cloudy sky sipping ice tea.

"Why do you keep looking at me like that?" Elin asked.

Riley rubbed her finger along the condensation of her glass before taking a long drink of the sweet tea. "How did you sleep last night?"

"Like a baby."

"Did you get up?"

Elin rolled her eyes. "No. What's going on?"

"I have to tell you something, and I'm afraid you won't believe me."

Elin turned her head to look at Riley. "We'll never know the answer to that unless you tell me."

Riley knew she was right, yet once the words were out, there was no putting them back. And there was a chance that Elin would tell Delphine.

But Riley would be long gone by then.

"Yesterday, when I asked if you were having sex with George, it was because I saw you."

Elin's brows grew together, half in shock, half in denial. "I think I'd know if I was giving my body to someone."

"I also remembered being held down as he ground into me." Riley held up her hands to show the bruise again. "Then there was the fact that I was supposed to meet someone yesterday, but I forgot all about them."

Elin turned her whole body to face Riley. "Who were you meeting?"

"Did you hear the part where I said I couldn't remember them?"

"Yes," Elin nodded slowly, anxiety growing in her eyes.

Riley licked her lips and pushed onward. "Something within me told me there was something wrong. I stayed awake all night because I had a feeling something would happen. And it did. But not to me."

It took a moment, but Elin's eyes widened as realization dawned. "Me? It happened to me?"

"Yes."

Elin looked forward again and swallowed. "Do you recall things that don't make sense? Like having a family even though I know there's no one looking for me?"

"Brothers," Riley admitted. "I think I have brothers, but I don't know their names or faces or even how many."

Elin looked at her with widening eyes, nodding. "I have brothers. Two of them."

"You remember?"

"Just now, after you said something."

Riley smiled and reached across to grab Elin's hand. "That's good."

"Tell me about last night."

With those words, Riley's grin faded, and she released Elin. "I saw George and Delphine head there," she said, nodding toward the adjacent house. "Candles were lit, and then you walked out of your room."

"No," Elin said as she scooted to the end of the chair.

Riley continued. "You walked from the house to where Delphine and George were. And I followed. I could hear Delphine singing, but I had to see. So I looked through the window."

"And?" Elin demanded when Riley paused.

Riley glanced away. "You were naked. George came to stand before you and ordered you first on your knees to remove his pants and then to take him into your mouth."

Elin slowly fell back on the chair. "And then he took me."

"You were aware?"

"No. Those images come to me through a thick fog, like a dream. They've been going on for months, but I didn't think they were real."

Riley leaned close and said, "I don't know what they're doing to us or why, but I think we need to leave. Now. Today."

"Yes. I want to find my brothers. And to stop the dreams."

Riley was about to tell Elin her plan when Delphine exited the house. She wore a bright smile as her long, black braids fell past her hips.

"Are you two enjoying the day?" Delphine asked.

Riley forced a smile. "As much as we can before the rain comes."

Delphine kept her gaze on Elin. "And how about you, Elin? How are you feeling?"

"Fine," Elin replied, but she couldn't quite meet Delphine's gaze.

Riley watched as Delphine's brow furrowed. She then leaned over Elin and put her hand on her stomach. Riley's heart fell to her feet.

"What is it?" Elin asked as she moved the priestess's hand away.

Delphine straightened, a huge smile on her face. "Life is growing inside you, child."

"That's not possible," Elin said, her face going white.

"With Voodoo, anything is possible," Delphine said and turned on her heel. "I'll spread the news."

Elin turned to Riley once Delphine was out of earshot and said, "I can't stay here another second."

Riley tried to reach for her, but Elin was already up and running into the house. She hurriedly followed in time to see Elin collide with George in the kitchen. Riley prayed Elin would keep going, but the anger and betrayal were too much to contain. Elin confronted George. She barely got two words out before he had her by her throat up against the wall.

Elin looked at Riley. Riley glanced at the set of knives, contemplating using one as a weapon when she noticed one was missing.

"Run!" Elin shouted to Riley as she plunged the blade into George's chest.

Riley took a step toward her friend, but the crack of Elin's neck halted her. Riley watched as Elin fell to the ground in slow motion. Then Riley looked back at George, who pulled the knife from his chest without so much as flinching.

Shouts and approaching footsteps filled Riley's ears as loudly as a rushing wave. She gave Elin one last look before she turned and ran out the door. Knowing how everyone was a follower of Delphine kept Riley off the streets, moving between houses and ducking behind anything that could keep her hidden.

So many times she was sure someone had seen her, but miraculously, she was able to keep moving without being stopped—or chased. For once, she was happy when the rain began. She stole an umbrella from a porch and opened it, mingling with the others on the sidewalk. She kept her head down and walked as quickly as she could without bringing notice to herself.

Riley had no idea where she was headed. Though she wasn't surprised to find herself near the bench where she had first met Marshall. She paused to look at it. The rain sent everyone for cover, including the violinist. With a sigh, Riley continued on, not stopping again until she was in front of the market.

She glanced inside, hoping she might spot Marshall within, but he wasn't to be found. Just as she was turning away, something caught her eye. The symbol was no bigger than the palm of her hand, and though she couldn't say how she recognized it, she did. And she was sure it hadn't been there before.

The arrow pointed in the direction she was headed, so she decided to follow it. All the while, she kept her eye out for more of the symbols. And as luck would have it, she found them, each pointing her a certain direction.

The heavier the rain came, the more people hurried indoors. It allowed her to find the symbols easily enough.

She shivered as her jeans from the thighs down were damp, and her bright pink Converse were soaked through.

As soon as she walked out of Delphine's section, she breathed a sigh of relief. That's when she began moving more quickly from symbol to symbol. Yet, she wasn't stupid. She stopped often, taking cover and looking behind her to see if she were being followed. Because she knew Delphine would come for her.

She ached for Elin's needless death, and she was terrified of what awaited her if Delphine—or George—found her. It's what kept her moving instead of hunkering down in a corner somewhere and letting the tears fall.

Because Riley wanted to make sure she wasn't followed, it took her hours before she found herself standing in front of a house. This was where the symbols had led her.

Suddenly, the door opened, and a man stepped onto the porch. Her gaze collided with gray orbs. When she saw it was Marshall, her composure crumbled. Without a word, he walked into the rain and down the path to her before pulling her into his arms.

"I've got you," he said.

She clung to him, soaking in his warmth and his strength. He took the umbrella and turned them. With his arm around her, he walked her to the porch and then inside the house.

He led her to the bathroom and turned on the shower.

"I'll leave some dry clothes on the bed for you. Take your time."

Riley only stayed beneath the hot water until she was warm. She dried off and found the sweatpants and tee shirt waiting for her. Then she went looking for Marshall. She found him in the living room, staring out the window.

He smiled when he saw her. "I wasn't sure you'd find your way here."

"I don't know what to believe anymore. I've seen...some horrible things, and I know Delphine has been lying to me."

The smile faded as a frown took its place. "What do you mean?"

She lifted her arms to show him the bruises.

"Who did that?" He was careful to keep his face even, but his words were laced with fury.

"I'm not sure. I only recall bits and pieces, but I know I was held down."

"Did they...hurt you?"

"I don't think so. But they did harm Elin."

He ran a hand down his face. "There is another woman with you?"

"She's dead because I told her I saw them taking her last night. Then Delphine told Elin she was pregnant."

Marshall closed the distance between them and put his hands on her arms. "Is that why you didn't meet me yesterday?"

"I didn't meet you because they made me forget you."

"But you remembered," he said, his face softening.

Riley grinned. "I couldn't forget you for long. But I want to know who I am."

"I can tell you that."

She released a thankful breath. "I was hoping you'd say that."

CHAPTER
ELEVEN

MARSHALL WOULD NEVER KNOW what made him walk to the front of the house and look out the window. But when he'd seen Riley, he felt a rush of relief so great that it made his knees buckle.

He'd managed to catch hold of the back of a chair before he hit the ground, but that was only because he had wanted to get to Riley quickly. It took all of his control to calmly open the door instead of rushing out to her. The look of fear on her face made him want to hurt the ones responsible—and he intended to do just that.

Marshall hadn't cared about the rain when he walked out to her. He was immensely grateful when she didn't push his arms away, and instead, let him hold her before leading her into the house.

He walked around the house trying to find something to

do while Riley warmed up beneath the hot water, but all his mind could focus on was wondering how she had gotten away from Delphine.

And when the priestess would come for her.

Marshall needed to call Kane and the others, but he wanted to talk to Riley more before he bombarded her with family that she didn't remember.

Then—*finally*—Riley was standing before him once more. She was no longer shivering, but as soon as she showed him her bruises, he found it nearly impossible not to go out into the storm and start bellowing for Delphine.

Riley wanted to know who she was. And it was up to him to tell her.

They sat in the living room facing each other in opposite chairs. He was sure someone else would be better at filling her in on her past, but he was selfish and didn't want anyone else with them.

"Is something wrong?" she asked.

He gave a shake of his head. "No."

"You're just sitting there. Normally, that means there's something you don't want me to know. At least that's been my experience with others."

Marshall ran a hand through his damp hair. "That's because I'm probably not the one who should be telling you about yourself."

"Why?" she asked with a frown, cocking her head to the side. "I thought you knew me."

Shit. He'd really stepped in it this time. "I know your brothers."

"So I do have brothers," she said with a grin. "I knew it! How many?"

"Four."

"Four!" she repeated with wide eyes. She looked at the ceiling and laughed. "Four."

He watched her curiously. "You're the youngest, which makes them very protective of you."

Her blue eyes returned to him. "Beau. That's one of my brothers' names."

"Yes," he replied, unable to stop the smile that pulled at his lips.

"Tell me more," she urged eagerly. "Why aren't they here?"

Each time Marshall tried to answer her question, he realized she needed to know more before she could fully comprehend what he was saying.

Finally, he said, "They looked for you extensively, but Delphine wants to hurt them. That's why I came instead. She doesn't know me."

"And she knows my brothers," she replied with a nod.

"Yes."

"How long have I been gone?"

He swallowed. "Over eight weeks."

"I see," she murmured and sighed.

"There was an attack, but not like you were led to believe. You were fighting with others against Delphine."

Riley's face shuttered as if she were searching her memories. "I don't recall that. Tell me more. How was I fighting her? Who were the others?"

Marshall rose and began to pace. He'd delivered all kinds of news to people before, but this time, he couldn't find the words. Because it was Riley.

Because he cared about her.

"Marshall," she said, standing before him so he had to halt. "I can handle whatever it is you don't want to tell me."

"It's not that I don't want to tell you, it's that there are years of information that bitch took from you. Things you lived through and did. My words won't be the same."

She put a hand on his arm and smiled. "But they may lead me to those memories."

He knew she was right, but he also knew that it should be one of her brothers talking to her right now and not him. Yet, he was prepared to fight anyone—even Delphine—to remain by Riley's side.

"Your family fights the supernatural. Any evil that comes into the parish, your family hunts down and kills."

She blinked, nodded. "Wow. Tell me more."

"You were raised by your brothers when your parents were killed. Vin sent you off to Austin to attend college, and after you got your degree, you came to New Orleans."

Her gaze narrowed. "Why New Orleans? What's here? I wouldn't just randomly pick a place."

"Your cousins are here."

She looked away, her brow furrowed. "I...think my cousins are men, but I feel like there are women I'm close to, as well."

"You're very close to the women who have fallen in love with your cousins."

Her smile was back in place when she looked at him. "More memories are being unveiled, but it's going slow and only fragments at a time."

"Delphine had a lot of time to work her magic on you and wipe away all that you knew."

"She might have won had I not met you."

He tucked her wet hair behind her ear. "You're much too strong for Delphine to have kept a hold on you much longer."

"You know me, which means we did meet before."

"I wish we had, but I only saw you once. I'm the sheriff in Lyons Point, and I help your brothers when I can. I came to the house when you were leaving to return to New Orleans. We briefly looked at each other, but we never spoke."

She raised her brows. "How stupid of me."

"I know you, Riley, because I've listened to stories from your brothers. They sent me so many pictures of you from throughout your life that I almost feel as if I were with you all those years."

She glanced at his mouth, making his balls tighten. "How

lucky my family is to have you as a friend, but I think I'm the really lucky one."

His blood rushed in his ears. He put a hand on her hip and lowered his head. "From the moment I saw you, I wanted to pull you close. Nothing would stop me from finding you. Not this city, not Delphine, and not magic."

"Here I am. In your arms," she murmured as she lifted her face to his.

Their lips brushed. He kissed her softly even as his body demanded he bury himself inside her. But as she moaned and sank against him, an image of her bruises popped into his mind. Marshall put his hands on her shoulders and ended the kiss.

She blinked up at him, confusion filling her gorgeous eyes. "What?"

"It wouldn't be right for me to do this without knowing if someone...if...."

"Raped me?" she finished.

He gave a nod.

She cupped his face. "I want you. The past doesn't matter. The future doesn't matter. This moment does. And I ache for you."

He was powerless when she pulled his head down to continue their kiss. And as soon as their tongues touched, he was lost in a sea of desire, swept beneath the tidal wave to surrender to the siren that had captured him, body and soul.

Fire burned through him, heating his skin until he was

consumed. And it was all because of Riley. Her kisses were as sweet as honey and as scorching as a desert. Yet he couldn't get enough.

His hands moved around to her back, holding her close as he plundered her mouth, his kiss fiery. She pressed against him, trying to mesh their bodies closer.

Marshall knew exactly how she felt. So when she tugged at his shirt, he reached to yank it off.

And then someone pounded on the door.

They jerked apart, breathing heavily as they stared at the front of the house. He glanced to where the rifle was behind Riley. Pointing to it, he put his finger to his lips and motioned for her to grab it. Once it was in her hands, he palmed the pistol he had hidden near the door and put it behind his back. Then he opened the portal a crack. His gaze met bright blue ones.

Kane lifted a dark blond brow. "You going to let me in?"

"What are you doing here?" Marshall asked, looking over Kane's shoulder.

"I thought you might want some company. Actually, that's a lie. I'm here because you were the last one to see Riley, so that means you're the best hope of finding her."

Marshall glanced over his shoulder to Riley behind him, who held the rifle pointed at the door like someone who knew how to use it. He then stepped back and widened the gap.

Kane took a step inside and came to an immediate stop.

As soon as his gaze landed on Riley, he stared for a moment before glaring at Marshall.

"What the fuck?" Kane growled.

Riley lifted the rifle to her shoulder. "Marshall?"

"Easy," he told her. "Lower the gun. And look at him."

It took her a moment, but Riley did as he asked. She propped the weapon against the wall and stared hard at Kane for a long time.

"Riley," Kane said as he took another step toward her. "You know me. Search your mind."

She gave a shake of her head. "There's nothing there, no memory of you."

Marshall closed the door. "Don't try so hard." Then to Kane, he said, "Try sharing a memory with her."

"Right," Kane said as he glanced Marshall's way.

Riley watched him skeptically, as if she wasn't sure she wanted Kane in the house with them. But she remained, waiting.

"Around Christmastime, when the weather dropped into the thirties, you wanted ice cream at midnight. We went out in—"

"The rain," Riley interrupted him. "You found a place that was open, and we ate ice cream together."

Kane nodded, his face tight.

A tear rolled down Riley's face. "Kane," she said and rushed to him.

Marshall watched the stoic LaRue envelop his cousin in

his arms and squeeze his eyes closed as he held her. The two remained that way for several minutes.

Then Riley pulled back and turned her gaze to Marshall. "I remember."

"All of it?" Kane asked worriedly.

She gave a nod. "All of it. Including what Delphine did to me."

"What did she do?" Kane's voice had lowered, his eyes flashing yellow.

Marshall kept his gaze on Riley. "And?"

"No," she whispered, smiling.

He let out a sigh, glad that Riley understood what he was asking.

Kane looked between them. "What the hell are you two talking about?"

"He wanted to know if I had been raped."

Marshall winced at Riley's words. She didn't realize how protective her cousins were of her. By the growl rumbling in Kane's chest, though, she got a reminder.

"I'm fine," Riley told him.

Marshall fisted his hands to stop from reaching for her each time her gaze landed on him. Would it be rude if he kicked Kane out of the house so he could have Riley to himself, and they could resume their kissing?

TWELVE

DELPHINE STARED down at Elin's lifeless body. Everything she had worked years to achieve had been wiped away in seconds. Because of George.

His obsession with Riley had clouded his mind, making him forget the goals they had set together.

"Elin was carrying your child," she said.

"Riley is who I wanted to have my seed."

Delphine glared at him. "And now she's gone after witnessing this."

"I'll get her back," he stated.

"Perhaps it's better if you remain behind. She'll be frightened of you. It is why she ran."

George's lips turned into a sneer. "You have twenty-four hours, priestess, or I go looking for her myself."

Delphine turned and walked from the house. The streets

were lined with her followers, each awaiting orders. They ignored the rain, standing without umbrellas or coats. This was New Orleans, and the rain came as often as the heat.

She removed her headscarf and let her hair down. Then she made her way from the porch down the steps and out into her people, walking among them.

"You all know Riley Chiasson. I took her from the LaRues when they attempted to best me. She is mine now. I've taken her memories so that she believes she's without family. We're her family. But she's scared.

"We must find her and bring her home. She has yet to fulfill her role, and until she's back among us, she never will. Spread out, search for her all through the city. Go to the LaRues—their homes and their bar—and watch them. I want to know of any increased activity that means they might know where Riley is."

She stopped and turned in a circle to look at the faces that came to her for advice and help. These were the ones who would aid her in wiping the LaRues and Chiassons from this world for good.

"We need to find her before the LaRues do. Go!" she commanded.

As one, they all turned and spread out, doing her bidding.

Delphine watched them until they disappeared, then she turned back to her house. George stood on the porch, watching her. He had been her greatest achievement. One of her most faithful followers, he had opened himself up to the spirit of a famed Voodoo priest who had been cut down by the LaRues before he could carry out his grand plan.

With him by her side, Delphine knew she was unstoppable. He added to her already impressive depth of magic, and they had worked together perfectly. Until Riley.

As soon as he had seen her, desire had ruled George. He wouldn't listen to Delphine as she tried to explain that Riley was stronger than Elin, and it had taken Elin months to fully succumb to Delphine's magic.

Riley would take even longer, and to push her too soon would break her. Or return her memories. And neither option was one Delphine wanted.

George turned on his heel and walked back into the house. Delphine sighed and blinked the rain from her eyelashes. If only he had been patient, he could've had a child from both Elin and Riley.

Delphine looked over her shoulder toward the French Quarter. The LaRues continued to find ways to best her. They had come so close this last time. Minka was incredibly strong, much stronger than Delphine had ever dreamed she could be.

That had nearly cost her everything. But Delphine wouldn't underestimate Minka or the LaRues again. Because they too were growing stronger.

At least she had stopped the Moonstone clan in their tracks. Taking Elin had brought her Griffin. The Alpha had done everything she wanted in exchange for keeping Elin alive. Griffin had been stronger than both his parents put together, but he'd let family and love rule him. Now, he was gone, having slunk away with his tail between his legs, no doubt.

One werewolf down. And with Griffin gone, the Moonstone pack was floundering. Now, all Delphine needed to do was take care of the LaRues and Chiassons.

She rubbed her hands together, calling up ancient magic from her African ancestors. She began humming, allowing herself to grow louder and louder.

"Find me Riley," she whispered.

She turned in a circle, waiting for the magic to direct her. But nothing happened. She attempted the ritual twice more, with no better results. Yet she wouldn't give up. There were many more tricks up Delphine's sleeve. She would find Riley, and if she had to slaughter each and every person in New Orleans, she would bring the girl back into the fold.

MARSHALL CAREFULLY LIFTED Riley in his arms and stood. She had fallen asleep between him and Kane thirty minutes earlier. Once Kane left to do a sweep of the area, Marshall knew it was time to get her in bed.

Her eyes opened when he laid her down. "Stay with me."

As if he could resist such a request—or the temptation.

He climbed in beside her and smiled when she snuggled against him. It felt so good to hold her.

"I wish I would've talked to you that day I first saw you," she said.

"Why didn't you?"

"I knew you were the type of man I'd fall hard for. And the kind who could break my heart."

He looked down at the top of her head. "Why do you think I'd hurt you?"

"You're very much like my brothers and cousins. You're used to taking charge and risking your life. You think of others before yourself. It's a great quality, but it can be hell on relationships."

"Your brothers seem to make it work."

She nodded. "Yes, they do."

"So do your cousins. Well, except for Kane."

Her head lifted, and she shot him a grin. "I have hope for Kane. He has a big heart, but it's filled with so much hurt and regret right now. The right woman could change him."

"The right woman could do a lot of things," Marshall said as he held her gaze.

She glanced down as she came up on her elbow. "The way I feel when you kiss me is like I'm flying through the clouds."

"It's like coming home."

"Your kiss sears me to my very soul."

He ran his hand up her back to tangle his fingers in her hair. "You slay me. I want nothing but you. Only you."

"Always you," she murmured.

He cupped the back of her head as their lips met. As their tongues dueled, he rolled her onto her back and settled between her legs. She moaned in contentment.

Marshall rose up on his knees and removed his shirt. When she rose from the bed and began to strip, he quickly did the same.

As soon as their clothes were gone, they were back in each other's arms, kissing. He smiled when she pushed him backward onto the bed. Her blue eyes were dark with desire. With her dark hair falling haphazardly about her, he took in her slender form, and the pert breasts with their dusky nipples that he yearned to taste.

His gaze traveled down to her smooth belly and slim hips to the trimmed patch of black curls between her long legs.

"Keep looking," she said huskily while rubbing her hands over his chest. "I get to look at your amazing body."

Marshall felt as if he had waited his entire life to have her. He wrapped an arm around her and yanked her close. Searching her eyes, he looked for...hell, he didn't know what it was he wanted to find.

"It was your kiss," she told me. "You began to unravel all that Delphine had done. And you took me down a road I'd never been on before. Take me again."

"Yes," he whispered before he kissed her slowly, thoroughly.

He ran his hands up her back, learning the feel of her warm skin. Her hips rocked against him. God, she felt so good. Like she had been made just for him. Or maybe it was the other way around. Maybe he'd been made for her. Marshall didn't care.

As long as he got to have her.

"If I don't have you inside me right this instant, I might die," she said between kisses.

All thoughts he had of going slow and kissing every inch of her went right out the window. The need in her words, and the way her voice turned raspy from desire sent him careening into a haze of hunger only she could quench.

SHE HAD NEVER *ACHED* SO in her life. It went bone deep. Riley didn't fight it, she accepted it, reached for it. Grabbed it.

Whatever *it* was, it was amazing. Surprising.

Mind-blowing.

With every kiss, every touch and sigh, she could actually feel herself growing closer to Marshall. It defied logic, but she came from a world with the supernatural. Who was she to question such things? Which was why she marveled at her fortune and ate up every millisecond.

Because it could all end in the next minute.

But she wasn't going to think about Delphine or the epic battle she knew was coming. Instead, she would glory in the magnificent man beneath her.

She ran her hands over the thick sinew of his chest and the dark hair that covered him. The quick glance she'd gotten of his chiseled abs and corded arms and legs was forgotten when she saw his thick arousal.

There would come a time—really soon—when she paid that particular member a lot of attention.

Her breathing quickened, and her mind went blank when his hands moved over her ass and held her as he ground himself against her.

She gasped, her sex clenching as desire spun wildly through her. Her inhale turned into a moan when his fingers found her. He slipped two inside, pumping slowly.

"There are so many things I want to do to you," he said in her ear before he nipped at her lobe.

She shivered from his words, his bite, and the way his fingers played her. Riley wanted to reply, to tell him that she wanted him to do all of them and more, but the words were lost as he pushed his fingers deeper.

"Is this what you want?"

She nodded, her throat refusing to form the words.

"Or is it this?"

His fingers left her. In the next instant, she felt the head of his cock rubbing against her swollen clit before he slipped inside her. As their bodies merged, it was like a key fitting into a lock.

She braced her hands on his chest and sat up. Their gazes clashed, held. With his hands on her hips, she began to slowly rock back and forth.

There was nothing that could stop their passion now. It hadn't just taken them. It consumed them. And through it all, though every tingle of pleasure, each quiver of need—she rushed toward it eagerly.

As her tempo increased, Marshall sat up. His silvery gaze raked her face as if he couldn't believe she was there. She understood how he felt because she feared this was all a dream. That she would wake up back in Delphine's house with her chest hollow from where her heart used to be.

His hand slid around her neck and held her head as their bodies moved together, the friction building their desires and bringing them closer and closer to the peak.

"Come with me," he urged.

She nodded, already more than halfway there. But at his words, it propelled her past the point of no return. All that was, all that mattered, was Marshall and how she felt in his arms.

And that's all she needed.

His grip tightened, and his face pinched as they both held back their pleasure as long as they could. Riley's breaths were loud, her body moving on its own as it careened toward the climax.

"Now," Marshall rasped.

Her head fell back as she gave in to the ecstasy. The pleasure slammed into her, cocooning her in light and decadence. The tremors ran through her body as she felt him shudder in her arms.

CHAPTER

THIRTEEN

UTTER CONTENTMENT. That's what Marshall felt after making love to Riley. Their bodies were still joined, their breathing loud, when he realized for the first time in his life, he'd forgotten all about a condom.

As if Riley needed something else to worry about.

He watched as she lifted her face. He'd never seen anything so stunningly beautiful in his life. In every way, she was gorgeous, but now, with her face flushed and her lips swollen, she was exquisite.

They stared at each other, no words needed. Their bodies had said it all, and it was glorious.

She leaned forward and pressed her lips against his. Marshall hungrily kissed her, desire surging through him again. And he knew with the same certainty that the sun would rise in the east in the morning that he was falling for Riley.

Or perhaps he already had.

Hell, he didn't know. And honestly, he didn't care. At one time, he would've been afraid of loving someone, but it was different with Riley. *She* was different, unique. A woman all her own, and he loved everything about her.

From the living room through the closed door, Kane cleared his throat loudly, breaking their kiss. Riley's eyes widened as she smiled. Marshall couldn't believe he hadn't heard Kane walk back inside the house.

"Um...just thought I should let you two know that you might want to get dressed. Now," Kane said.

Riley rolled her eyes. "My cousins are on their way."

Marshall nodded. "Appears so."

"I'm not ready for this moment to end," she said softly.

He ran his hands down her face. "There will be others."

"Promise?"

"Promise."

It was the look in his eyes, the look that said he would move Heaven and Earth to be with her again that made her smile. She reluctantly rose and dressed.

"Riley."

She finished putting her hair atop her head and turned to Marshall. He looked so out of sorts that she frowned as she took a step toward him. "What is it?"

"I...we didn't use a condom."

There weren't too many men that would own up to such a thing, and it made her—

Her mind stopped because she'd nearly said love. How could she love him? She barely knew him. Yet, in the few days that she had, it seemed as if they had walked through Hell and clawed their way back again.

"It's all right," she assured him. "I get a shot every three months for that. Thankfully, I had one right before Delphine took me. Though I'm going to need to get that updated soon."

"Good. You have enough to deal with right now. You shouldn't have to worry about having children."

No sooner had the words reached her ears than she imagined a little boy running around the Chiasson house in Lyons Point with dark waves and gray eyes.

"Right," she said, feeling a yearning she'd never experienced before.

"Riley!"

She winced at the sound of Solomon's booming voice. With one last look at Marshall, she walked out of the bedroom and was surrounded by Solomon, Minka, Myles, Addison, Court, and Skye.

It seemed impossible that she could forget her cousins and their women, and yet Delphine had wiped them from her memory. Just as the priestess had done with Riley's brothers and their loves.

To be held by her family was a wonderful thing. It made

Riley realize how easily she could've lost it all. Thanks to Marshall, she was back where she belonged.

Well...sort of.

She pulled out of her cousins' arms and turned to the bedroom where Marshall was leaning against the doorframe, watching her. Though she couldn't explain how or why, she knew she should be with him. That that's where she belonged.

One side of his lips curved into a smile as if he too recognized what was going through her mind. She made her way to his side and looked up at him in wonder.

"Thank you," she said.

He quirked a brow. "For?"

"Coming to look for me."

Marshall straightened and put his hands on her arms, drawing her close. "Like your family, I knew you were here. And I didn't intend to leave without you."

"It worked."

"You can thank Kane for the idea of the symbols."

She turned so that she stood beside Marshall and looked at Kane and winked at him. "Thank you. All of you."

Myles glanced worriedly outside. "While I like this reunion, and I want to know everything that crazy bitch did to you, Riley, we need to prepare."

"He's right," Addison said as she put an arm around Myles. "Delphine will come for you again."

Minka snorted as she walked to stand before Riley. "My

wards on you weren't strong enough last time, but I won't make that mistake again. Even if Delphine manages to take you again, she won't be able to hold you after I finish my spells."

Riley slid her gaze to Marshall as Minka began her magic. "It's nice to have a powerful witch as a friend."

"You have two," Solomon reminded her.

Riley nodded slowly. "I need to call my brothers."

"Already done," Court replied as he stood behind Skye, his hands on her shoulders.

Her eyes widened. "All of them?"

"Beau and Davena have already left with the others on their way," Solomon said once Minka was back by his side. "Since both Davena and Minka have gone up against Delphine before, we all figured it would be best to have both witches in the city."

Because of her, Riley realized. She was bringing the Chiassons and LaRues together—which was most likely exactly what Delphine wanted. What better way to wipe them all out?

"What is it?" Marshall whispered as the others talked amongst themselves.

Riley leaned against him, loving his strength. He wasn't offended or intimidated by her independence or the fact that she was a hunter. Instead, he was like a wall around a fort, giving her courage and strength.

"This could be exactly what Delphine wants." She looked

at her cousins. They had found happiness—well, all except for Kane, but she wasn't giving up on him—and she didn't want to be the cause of destroying that.

Marshall leaned his head down so that he whispered in her ear. "That won't stop them from wanting to go against Delphine again."

"They survived three times already. The odds aren't in their favor. Then there are my brothers." She swallowed, emotion choking her as she imagined Delphine killing them.

"It won't happen," Marshall stated firmly.

But she knew it could. Easily. Delphine was that powerful. And while Delphine hadn't killed Riley's parents, the priestess had been responsible for murdering her aunt and uncle.

"We need the Moonstone pack," Court said.

Kane crossed his arms over his chest. "No."

"Though I don't want to call for them, we need them," Solomon said.

Myles shrugged. "The last we heard, Jaxon was still searching for Griffin."

To her horror, Riley then remembered Elin. "There was another woman with me. Delphine had her for much longer. She was—"

"Elin," Addison interrupted.

Riley blinked, her mind working to sort out how her cousins knew the name. She took a step back as more memories flooded back. "Oh, God. Griffin's sister."

Kane's arms dropped to his sides. "We need to get her from Delphine."

"You can't," Riley said and found herself reaching for Marshall's hand—and his strength.

"What happened?" Minka asked in a soft voice.

Riley squeezed Marshall's fingers. He remained composed beside her, a rock upon which a steady foundation could be built. "George snapped her neck. We were going to leave together, but then Delphine told Elin that she was pregnant. It didn't help that I told Elin I saw her in some kind of a trance the night before where George had had sex with her."

"This isn't good," Minka said as she turned her head to look at Solomon. "At all."

Myles cut his eyes to her. "Meaning?"

"That is dark magic," Minka explained. Then she turned her gaze back to Riley. "I need to know everything about George."

For the next twenty minutes, Riley told them all that she knew about the man who'd followed her everywhere. She relayed every detail of her time with Delphine and everything that she saw and heard—including her last night with the priestess.

"I'm going to fucking rip her head from her body," Kane said with a low growl.

A muscle ticked in Marshall's jaw. "I know exactly how you feel."

"We need to be careful," Minka said as she glanced at the door.

Solomon looked at her and asked, "What do you mean?"

Minka's gaze swung from him to Riley. "George isn't just anyone. From the things you told us he said and did, that body is housing a spirit."

"And Delphine wouldn't just call up any spirit," Skye said.

Minka shook her head. "No, she wouldn't. That means, whoever is inside George is powerful. His fixation on Riley means that he's chosen who he wants as his."

"Over my dead body," Marshall declared.

Riley looked up at him, and in that moment, she knew that she was falling in love with him. And, somehow, that made facing what was to come easier.

Because she had someone as solid and strong-willed as Marshall by her side.

"We need to get Riley out of the city," Court said.

Minka stopped him before he could continue. "It won't do any good. George won't stop until he finds her."

"Then we take the bastard out," Marshall suggested.

Myles and Solomon exchanged a look before Solomon gave a nod of his head.

"Should we be doing this in the middle of the city?" Skye asked, her face filled with concern.

Addison nodded in agreement. "Exactly. Innocents could be killed."

"There's my place in the bayou," Minka offered.

But as her family talked, all Riley could think about was Marshall. She and her cousins had been born into this life. Minka, Skye, and Addison, as well as Olivia, Ava, Davena, and Ivy had all chosen it because of their love for the LaRues and Chiassons.

Riley faced Marshall and turned him to face her. "If you remain, she'll turn her focus on you."

"I'm not leaving you."

"You have a life," she said. "A career. You can get out now without her ever knowing of your involvement. She won't touch you."

He gave a small shake of his head, his lips twisted. "That's where you're wrong, sweetheart, because she's already touched my life by coming after you and your family."

"Then think of your future."

"I am."

Emotion welled within her so fast that she was choked by it. There was no denying that he meant *she* was his future when he said the words.

"Marshall," she began.

He put a finger to her lips. "I'm not leaving you. I can't. Don't you understand that? Can't you *feel* it?"

"Yes," she said breathlessly.

"Then you should know it'll take more than a Voodoo priestess to tear me away from your side."

Riley nodded.

And fell completely in love with Marshall Ducet.

CHAPTER

FOURTEEN

Marshall stood before the living room window with all the lights off inside the house. Myles and Court had taken Addison and Skye to safety since neither of them had magic. Once the girls were set, the brothers planned to find Jaxon, who was leading the Moonstone pack until Griffin was found.

Riley sat behind him while Minka meditated in a bedroom. Marshall was aware of Riley's gaze on him, which made it difficult to keep an eye out for anyone because he kept thinking of how it felt to slide inside her.

"I'm scared."

Her confession hit him square in the chest. They were words he'd never thought to hear from her. Mostly because she was such a strong individual that he assumed she would keep it buried. And he loved that she was sharing it with him.

He turned to the side to look at her. "Any sane person would be. You've fought Delphine. You know what we're up against."

"My cousins and brothers worry about me," she said as she drew her legs up to her chest and rested her chin on her knees. "I've made it my mission for them to believe that nothing frightens me."

Marshall nodded slowly. "I won't tell them."

She lowered her gaze to the floor. "So much could go terribly wrong."

"And it could go right. This isn't the first fight for your brothers or cousins. Or me."

Her eyes lifted to him. "It's the first time I've realized that I could lose absolutely everything in a heartbeat. Everyone I care about wants to fight her."

"Would you not do the same for anyone in your family?"

"Yes. Just as I would for you."

He glanced out the window to make sure no one was near. "I suspect this is why Vin fought so hard to keep you away."

"Now I understand how he and the others feel every night when they go hunting."

"This is different," Marshall said. "This isn't about hunting some monster or keeping the peace in New Orleans.

This is about a priestess who has specifically targeted you and your family."

Riley rose from the sofa and walked to stand before him. "I can't lose them. Or you."

"You won't."

She shot him a dry look. "You can't promise such a thing."

"You're looking at your family through your eyes. Step back a moment and look through mine. Your brothers are a cohesive unit. They've been hunting together since they were kids. They know the bayous and every house in and around Lyons Point."

"But we're not there anymore."

He slid his fingers around hers. "No, we're in New Orleans where your cousins know every alley, street, and building around all districts and are just as unified as your brothers. Then you take those two organized groups and combine them with the Moonstone pack and the witches. All of which stood against Delphine before."

She released a long breath. "The way you say it gives me hope."

"Then cling to it."

"I can't just sit here while my family fights."

He grinned down at her. "I'd never suggest such a thing. I plan on being right beside you."

"And if I told you I wanted to run away from all of this?"

"I'd be with you."

He didn't say more because he knew what kind of woman Riley was, and the type of family she had. No matter how much she wanted to run, she would never do it. Her sense of duty to her family and the innocents she helped to protect drove her too hard. He understood that because it was part of what had made him want to become a cop.

Movement out of the corner of his eye had him whirling around and pulling his gun even as he shoved Riley behind him. He glared at the shape before him that stepped out of the shadows into the light that came through the window.

Vincent's gaze was steady, unflinching. Though no words passed the eldest Chiasson's lips, Marshall knew Vin had seen him and Riley together and most likely heard them talking.

Marshall lowered his arm. As soon as Riley saw her brother, she ran to him.

Vincent caught her in his arms and held her tight. "I've never been more worried in my life."

"I'm sorry."

"You're back now. That's all that matters," he said as he released her. Then he raised his gaze to Marshall. "You did what we couldn't. We owe you."

Marshall shook his head. "You owe me nothing."

"Where are the others?" Riley asked. "I want to see Christian, Beau, and Linc."

"They're with Solomon," Vin said.

As an only child, Marshall had always been fascinated

with anyone who had siblings. He had seen the Chiasson brothers interact with one another on multiple occasions, but to watch them handle their sister as if she were a prized possession was fascinating.

Hell, even the way the LaRues treated Riley was interesting. While both families were in instant protective mode with her, the LaRues allowed Riley to be herself while her brothers tried in vain to keep her a little girl.

Despite the differences, there could never be any doubt that Riley was loved fiercely by all eight men—and the women who had come into the families.

Marshall turned to face the window and allow Vin and Riley some privacy. He tucked the gun back into the holster that he'd put on earlier and let his eyes move slowly over the area.

It wasn't long before Riley stood beside him. "Vin is staying close to the house and waiting on Beau to bring Davena. Apparently, she wanted Beau to drive her through the city a few times."

"She's getting reacquainted with the streets," Marshall said. "It's been a long time since Davena ran away from New Orleans and Delphine."

Riley drew in a deep breath. "There's something bothering you."

He glanced at her. "I find it intriguing to watch families, particularly how your brothers and cousins interact with you."

"Why?" she asked with a frown.

"I'm an only child. My parents tried for years to conceive without any luck. They decided to adopt and found me." He turned his head to her. "My birth mother was a twenty-year-old who got pregnant by her boyfriend before he was deployed—before either of them knew it. He was killed in action, and she decided she didn't want to raise a baby on her own."

"Oh, God. I'm so sorry," Riley said as her face lined with pity.

He shrugged. "My parents were amazing people. They loved me like their blood. I regret nothing."

"Except having siblings."

Marshall shrugged, even though it was true. "I would rather have had my parents."

"Have you tried to find your birth mother?"

"My parents gave me her name as well as my father's. I know where she is, but I've never wanted to see her. I don't hold any animosity towards her for what she did, but I also don't see a reason to have a connection with her."

Riley said nothing more. She merely wrapped an arm around his waist. He draped his arm over her shoulder and smiled. Who would've thought he would return to New Orleans for the very reason that he'd left?

Who would've thought that he would not only go looking for the supernatural but be prepared to fight it?

And who would've thought that he would find

contentment during it all with a woman that made desire burn within him?

"If none of this had happened, how long do you think it would've been before we met?" she asked.

He thought about it a moment. "You'd be able to answer that better than I. How long before you returned home?"

"I didn't intend to for a very long time."

"Then I guess you have your answer."

She leaned her head against him. "When I think about not having you in my life, it makes what I went through with Delphine okay."

"I would've found you one way or another."

"I don't think anyone in my family can find love without some major event or someone's life being in danger."

Marshall's heart missed a beat. Had she just said love? Could she mean...was there even a chance that she felt as he did?

From the first time he'd seen Riley's photo at the Chiassons' he'd thought her beautiful, and had felt an inescapable, relentless need to know more about her. So he set about posing questions to the brothers until he began to formulate an idea of who Riley was.

It wasn't until he saw her at the Chiasson house that he knew his life would be tied to hers. He didn't know how or why or even when, but he'd known it as fact.

A truth he didn't try to ignore or discount.

Everything made sense when the weeks went by, and she

couldn't be found. He'd known he needed to come look for her. Even if her brothers had not agreed, Marshall would've made the trip. Because he'd known he would find her. That somehow, something would lead him to her.

"Why does it feel as if I've known you my entire life?" she asked.

He rubbed his hand up and down her arm. "You mean, like we've already spent a lifetime or two together before?"

"And have found each other again," she said as she lifted her head to look at him.

"Yes."

She moved to stand in front of him, wrapping her arms around him as she did. "I'm going to tell you something I've never told anyone else before, but when I was a little girl of about five or six, I dreamed of a man and a woman deeply in love. I saw them fall in love, have a beautifully long, happy life, and die." She glanced down at his chest. "Even as a child, I knew the woman was me. All I needed to do was wait for the man who I belonged with."

"For me," he whispered before he kissed her.

Everything Riley had said resonated with him, striking a chord within his soul that he recognized. It explained so much. And how could he even think of discounting it now that he knew magic and supernatural creatures existed? Why not soul mates finding each other across lifetimes?

The kiss grew heated quickly, and he regrettably ended it because he knew they didn't have time to let pleasure overtake them again. He cupped her face, amazed at what he was feeling—and how deeply he felt it.

"Tell me we'll have more than one night together," Riley said.

"We will," he assured her. "One night isn't enough."

She grinned. "I'm not sure a million would be sufficient."

"Forever wouldn't be long enough."

"I don't think we should wait for Delphine to find me. I think we should go to her."

Marshall considered that for a moment. "It would allow us to set the time and location and use it to our advantage. And we could make her think she stumbled onto you."

Riley's eyes went wide. "I like the idea of tricking her. She'd be focused on me."

"And not see the rest of us coming."

"No doubt her followers are looking for me even now."

Marshall glanced toward the utility room. "Your clothes should be dry now."

"No time like the present to get things rolling, right?" she said with a forced smile.

He didn't want to let her out of his arms, but if they were going to have a shot at defeating Delphine, they had to take this chance. "Right."

She blew out a breath. "You better get Vin while I change."

Marshall turned and headed to the back door. If they were lucky, no one had seen Beau and Davena yet. The other

Chiassons were coming in separately in secret so Delphine wouldn't know of their arrival.

And maybe, just maybe, if everything fell into place, then Marshall's plan would work—and Riley would be free of the priestess once and for all.

CHAPTER

FIFTEEN

HER FAITH WAS BEING PUT to the test. Though it was her belief in herself and not her family—or Marshall.

Riley's heart raced, and her blood rushed in her ears as she looked out of the abandoned building into the darkness of the night. Her hands fisted as she wished she could reach over for Marshall. It would be so much easier to carry out her role in the trap if Marshall could stay beside her.

But she had to do this alone.

Which brought her back to her faith. She had fought vampires, ghosts, demons, and a number of other supernatural creatures, but none of them terrified her like Delphine did.

The fact that Riley had lived in the priestess's house for weeks as a *friend* sickened her. Actually, the very thought of Delphine made bile rise in Riley's throat.

So how was she going to stand there and not say the things she wanted to shout at Delphine? How was Riley supposed to act as if she still didn't have her memories?

And how did her brothers and cousins expect her not to try and kill the priestess herself?

The plan had come together quickly, and all of them had decided to act on it that night instead of waiting and allowing Delphine to discover that the Chiassons had come to the city. Now, her family was in their designated places with Davena and Minka each waiting to use their magic on Delphine and any of the other followers who got involved.

Riley tried not to glance over at Marshall, who stood beside her, because she might not be able to leave him if she did. She was glad that he would remain behind and take his position on the second floor as a sniper. Marshall's plan was solid, as was his confidence in her. That would get her through this.

"I won't be far," Marshall whispered.

God, how she wanted to touch him. "I know."

"I'll remain with you until you tell me you're ready. Everything is on your time. And you don't have to do any of it."

The more he spoke, the harder it was for her to keep her gaze straight ahead. But if she looked at him, if she touched him, she would never walk out there. "I do. Besides, this plan is the best one. She won't be expecting any of it."

He faced her and raked a hand through his dark, wavy hair. "I don't think you shou—"

She broke her rule and looked into his gray eyes while forcing a smile. He was struggling with the plan. And she knew he would stay with her if she asked it of him. That's how she knew it was time to get things moving. Because to remain with him, to continue living in fear of Delphine, allowed the priestess to win. And Riley couldn't accept that.

She started to walk away when Marshall grabbed her hand, halting her. Riley briefly closed her eyes before looking at him over her shoulder. He was the kind of man who would never falter, who would stand beside her in the very worst of times—like now—and during the best of times.

He was the kind of man who would love her deeply and never let her down. The kind of guy who would always put her first. The kind of male who would love her from one life to the next.

She wouldn't let anyone break what she had found with Marshall, and that included Delphine. Riley was going to fight with everything she had because she wanted a life with Marshall more than she had ever wanted anything before.

"I love you," she said.

His eyes widened, but she pulled her hand out of his grasp and walked from the building before he could say anything. With her heart thumping wildly, Riley wrapped her arms around herself and kept her head down.

It wasn't an act. She was chilled, bone-deep, from

walking away from Marshall. The anger and fear were so intertwined now that she could no longer tell one emotion from the other. And she didn't think it would get any better, at least until either Delphine was dead—or she was.

Riley stayed close to the building, making it look as if she were attempting to hide. Every once in a while, she would look over her shoulder or duck into an alleyway and peek around the corner.

She counted eleven of Delphine's followers, but no doubt there were others she didn't see. It wouldn't be long now before the priestess showed. And since this was the place her cousins had said was the best for battle, Riley walked slowly.

The streets were never deserted in New Orleans, but this district wasn't Delphine's. That made it significantly more dangerous because they were in the djinn's territory.

Riley had only encountered the djinn a few times, and quite frankly, they were scarier than the vampires. Still, the djinn were smart. They didn't kill everyone who walked their streets. Only a few individuals went missing from here. Most were taken from other parts of New Orleans.

As if sensing something in the air, people hurried away from her. Riley wanted to yell at anyone who remained. The idea of innocents getting brought into this war angered her, but she knew her family would make sure that those who were caught in the crossfire were protected.

Her thoughts drifted to the Moonstone pack. Tensions had

run high since Griffin—the Alpha—and Solomon clashed over Minka. Yet, in the end, the pack had stood beside the LaRues to fight Delphine, even though Griffin had disappeared.

That battle was when Riley was taken. Not that she blamed her cousins. They'd all been fighting for their lives. It was no one's fault but hers that Delphine managed to get her hands on her. But she wondered if Delphine had gotten to Griffin, as well.

Riley shivered at the thought of how close Delphine had come to getting everything she wanted. While Riley wasn't entirely sure what the priestess and George had in mind for her, Riley knew it was probably very close to what they had done to Elin.

She cringed at the thought of her friend's death. If only Riley hadn't told her everything, perhaps she and Elin could've gotten away together. Maybe even now, Elin would be reunited with her brothers and her pack.

But thanks to Delphine and George, that was never to be. Just one more crime the priestess needed to pay for.

Riley was so deep in thought with her head down that she lurched to a stop when she saw the hem of a white skirt. Her head jerked up to find herself staring into Delphine's black eyes.

Riley took an unconscious step back while her gaze raked over Delphine's long, black braids hanging loose. The hatred that rose up in Riley was so powerful that she instantly fought against it so she wouldn't attack the priestess and ruin Marshall's plan.

Delphine could use that loathing against Riley, so she had to be careful.

"Hello, Riley," the priestess said in a pleasant tone.

Riley didn't answer. Simply took another step back.

Delphine's head cocked to the side. "Riley?"

"He killed Elin," she finally said.

Delphine's lips pressed together briefly. "I know."

"What are you going to do about it?" Riley demanded.

"I'm taking care of it, my way."

Riley hunched her shoulders. "I saw him snap her neck. He could do the same to me."

"He won't. George cares about you too much. Riley," Delphine said, taking a step closer. "You had me so worried. Where have you been?"

"Wandering the streets, trying to get away from George. I don't want him anywhere near me again."

"He's part of our family. It's going to take some time, but it'll all work out. Come to me, child."

Riley stood her ground. "I won't go back as long as George is there."

"He's family."

"And I'm not." Riley held Delphine's gaze. "I think it's best if I go, then."

"No!" Delphine bellowed when Riley turned to walk away.

Slowly, she turned back to the priestess. "You told me I was free to do as I wanted. I'm not a prisoner."

"You're returning with me," Delphine stated firmly.

Riley wrinkled her nose as she shook her head. "Actually, I'm not. While your magic worked for a while, your hold over me was broken days ago."

Delphine's gaze narrowed. "You stayed because you wanted to and because you had nowhere else to go."

"That's not entirely true, is it?" Riley asked. "Since my cousins live in the city. You know, the LaRues."

As soon as the words were out of her mouth, Solomon, Myles, Kane, and Court stepped from their hiding places to surround Delphine. Even though the bar was being watched, they had snuck out of Gator Bait and made their way to Riley as soon as she walked out of the building.

"You're also well acquainted with my brothers," Riley continued.

Vin was the first to make an appearance behind Delphine. Then Christian, Beau, and finally Linc as they surrounded her.

Riley smiled as she watched Delphine's expression tighten. "Oh, and did I forget Minka and Davena?"

The two witches came to stand with the men.

"Is that all you have?" Delphine asked her. "I'm not without my own backup."

With a snap of her fingers, Delphine's disciples made a circle around Riley's family.

Riley smiled and raised her hand. Witches and members of the Moonstone pack—in werewolf form—filled the area.

"You've fought my brothers and Davena," Riley said. "You've even battled my cousins on several occasions, as well as Minka and our allies. But you've not faced all of us."

Delphine's chin lifted defiantly. "If you're trying to scare me, you're not doing a good job."

"I'm laying out the facts."

"Then let me lay one out for you," the priestess said. "I was able to kill two powerful LaRues to get them out of the way. I'm more than ready to wipe out not only your cousins but also your brothers and everyone who stands against me."

Riley yawned, covering her mouth as she did. Then she widened her eyes as she looked at Delphine. "I'm sorry. Did you say something? Because you keep reiterating the same shit."

"It looks like it's past the time for words," Delphine said.

In the back, one of the weres yelped loudly in pain. A second later, the sound was cut short. Riley didn't need to ask to know that the werewolf was dead. She kept her gaze on Delphine, using every ounce of control she possessed not to show any weakness.

She wanted to call for Marshall, to run to him and stand in his arms. But he was hiding, waiting for the final part of the plan. Except Riley wasn't sure she could make it to that finish line.

Someone who'd been helping her was now dead. She

might not have known the werewolf personally, but it didn't matter. Delphine wasn't striking out at Riley's family—yet. But it was coming.

If Riley was already ready to break, she wouldn't survive once Delphine turned her brand of evil on the Chiassons or LaRues. Or Marshall.

Riley somehow stood her ground. Her knees knocked together, and her blood ran like ice through her veins. It was a horrible feeling, and she wanted it to end. Really, she was just ready for Delphine to die.

"Well?" Delphine asked. "Is this really what you want to do? Do you really want to go up against me and know that it'll mean the death of your family? Or will you walk away with me now? If you do, I'll allow them to live. I'll even take away your memories again. You were happy, Riley. Remember? You had no fear and no worries."

"But I wasn't me," Riley insisted. "Everyone here has chosen to rise up against you. We all know that this could be our last night on this earth, and we're all prepared to give our lives. If it means your death."

Delphine's eyes hardened. "Wrong choice."

Riley took a step back, and a second later, all hell broke loose.

CHAPTER

SIXTEEN

From his position on the second story of the building across the street, Marshall never took his eyes off Riley and Delphine. His gun was on his hip, but he held a rifle in hand, ready to lift and fire at the priestess.

All he could think about was Riley telling him that she loved him before walking away. He hadn't had time to respond, or even formulate a reply before she was gone. He'd wanted to pull her back, to tell her that he felt the same. Now, he had to wait until the battle was over.

Though he couldn't hear what Riley and Delphine were saying, he could tell by their expressions that things were heating up quickly.

Marshall lifted the rifle and peered through the scope. It was killing him not to be down there with the others, but he was Riley's backup. Because they all knew that Delphine was either going to either try and take Riley again—or kill her.

As long as he had breath in his body, that wouldn't happen.

He turned the gun and glanced through the scope at Lincoln, who was the closest to Riley. Linc was as still as a statue, a bowie knife in each hand. While Lincoln never turned to look at Delphine's disciples behind him, he was very aware of them by the way he shifted just slightly in order to see them better.

Marshall gave a quick look at the rest of the Chiassons and LaRues before glancing back at Riley. Delphine's face was filled with fury, while Riley was smiling in triumph.

He lifted his head and glanced around at Delphine's followers. None had moved, but they were waiting for the priestess's decision. However, it was the werewolves who were crouched low and ready to spring that drew his attention.

Right about then, a were let out a shrill cry before everything went eerily quiet. Marshall knew the werewolf was dead.

So, this was how Delphine wanted to play it.

He once more gazed through the scope at Riley and Delphine. The grin Riley had worn slipped as they exchanged more words. Then she took a step back.

In that instant, Marshall moved his finger over the trigger. He was prepared to take the headshot on Delphine when the quiet was broken by a low growl before a melee the likes of which he'd never seen broke out.

He lost Riley in the chaos, and then he lost sight of Delphine. Lifting his head, he scanned the crowd of witches, werewolves, and humans for some sign of the priestess. Though he wanted to keep an eye on Riley, he knew her family would remain close.

It was Delphine that Marshall truly needed to find. As long as he could keep her in his sights, then Riley and the others had a fighting chance.

But everywhere he looked, there was no sign of her. It should be easy to pick out the white clothes in the darkness, but the crush of people clawing, slashing, hitting, and stabbing one another prevented him from seeing anything clearly.

He debated running up to the roof for a better view, but it was time he couldn't take. Instead, he caught sight of one of Delphine's disciples coming up behind Kane. Without hesitation, he fired off a shot.

Kane whirled around and saw the dead man behind him. Then he gave a nod to Marshall before he returned to the fighting.

Marshall continued looking for Riley and Delphine while picking off more and more of the enemy. Delphine and her people were seriously outnumbered, yet that didn't seem to factor in their decision to fight.

All Marshall could be thankful for was that this battle

playing out in the middle of the streets of New Orleans hadn't drawn any policeman, nor had any innocents been affected. Yet.

But it was only a matter of time.

RILEY WINCED as she fell back and slammed against the side of a building. She saw a fist come at her, and she quickly ducked. When she straightened to deliver her own blow, Beau had already taken down her opponent.

"Where's Delphine?" Beau asked.

She shrugged. "I haven't seen her since the fight began. One minute she was in front of me, and the next, she was gone."

"That's not good," he murmured as he pivoted to continue fighting.

Riley looked around for someone to battle, but everyone was already matched up. Thankfully, more of Delphine's followers lay dead than anyone in her group.

The sound of a rifle firing had her lifting her gaze to the window where Marshall was stationed. She hoped that he'd found Delphine and could end all of this with literally one bullet. But he fired two more rounds in quick succession in various places.

She saw one of the disciples fall and knew that Marshall was helping in the battle while looking for Delphine. He was their secret weapon, though with every bullet he fired, he drew attention to himself.

Riley felt the hairs on the back of her neck lift. She looked around, seeking the source, and found George standing off to the side, watching her. Then his gaze slid to Marshall's position before George turned on his heel.

She lost him as the crowd shifted, blocking her view. She pushed against a witch while trying to hurry after George, but it felt as if, suddenly, everyone was closing in around her.

"Marshall!" she yelled.

Her cry was swallowed by the sounds of battle.

The harder she tried to move through the throng of people, the less distance she was able to achieve. She kept glancing up at the window. Every time Marshall fired the gun, relief filled her.

She was finally able to push through the last of the group and stumbled out onto the deserted street. Her gaze jerked to the window where Marshall's rifle barrel no longer poked out.

Riley ran toward the building, praying with each step that he wouldn't be hurt in any way. She reached the door and threw it open to run inside when Kane suddenly appeared beside her.

His hand on her arm halted her. "What?"

"Marshall."

That's all that was needed. Her cousin gave her a nod and

rushed inside. He reached the stairs first, taking them three at a time while she followed as fast as she could.

The battle raged on outside, the sounds dimmed by the walls of the structure. But it was the silence from above that scared her.

They reached the top of the landing, and Kane motioned to her that he was going to come in another way. Riley didn't care. She just wanted to find Marshall.

Her heart was in her throat when she ran to the doorway and looked inside to find George and Marshall glaring at each other. Riley glanced at Marshall, but she kept her full attention on George.

"You don't belong up here," she told George.

He turned his cold, dark eyes to her. "And you do?"

"Leave."

"I'm here for you."

Riley could feel the tension and anger rolling off Marshall. If George were just a man, she would let Marshall take him down, but George was something much more. And that's what made her leery of him.

"I'm not going anywhere with you or Delphine," Riley stated.

George cut his eyes to Marshall. "Because of him."

"Because I don't want to be with you. Because I'm not a possession. I'm a woman who has the right to choose, and I choose my family."

George turned his head back to her. "I can give you

everything. Power, wealth, status, and the ability to rule all of New Orleans."

Out of the corner of her eye, she saw Marshall frown. Riley shrugged. "First, I don't care about any of that. Second, Delphine wants to run New Orleans."

"I can give it to you."

The way he said it sent a chill of foreboding down Riley's spine. She spotted Kane coming up behind George, but she wasn't ready for his attack yet. Moving the fingers of her right hand, she waved Kane off for the moment.

"What do you mean you can give it to me?" Riley asked.

George smiled, his gaze locked on her. "I can give you anything you want. All you have to do is come with me."

"Tell me how you can do what you claim."

He waved his hand around him and glanced out the window. "Once, a very long time ago, I ran New Orleans. Nothing went on in this city that I didn't approve of. My magic was unbeatable. I was the strongest around. And everyone knew it."

"But you died," she said, before Marshall could.

George lifted one shoulder in a shrug. "I was betrayed by those who wanted someone else in power."

"Who?" she asked.

"A family. The LaRues came to the city and began driving out the worst of the supernatural. They were chosen to regulate the city. And their first order of business was to get rid of me."

She took a step closer to George even as Marshall whispered her name, and Kane glowered. "Why do you want me?"

"Because only my spirit is here. I control this body since Delphine summoned me, but I want more. I want to take my place at the head of this city once again. And you can give that to me."

"How?"

"A blood sacrifice. And a child."

She grimaced. "You mean you'll be reborn?"

"No. The sacrifice will make sure that I can never be removed from this body."

Even though she knew she didn't want to know the answer, she asked, "And the child?"

"We'll create a dynasty so strong that no one will ever be able to destroy it."

She shook her head. "LaRue blood runs in me through my family. I'm your enemy."

"You can see it that way, or you can be my ally. I'll spare your family—all of them—but they must leave New Orleans forever."

Riley swallowed. "Who is to be the sacrifice?"

"Delphine, of course."

Riley could barely believe his response. But she didn't have time to answer as there was a loud shriek that made Riley bend at the waist and cover her ears with her hands.

She looked over to find Delphine striding into the room

with her gaze full of vengeance and death. Another blood-curdling scream filled the air as the priestess sent George flying backwards.

He slammed into the wall and dropped to the floor without an ounce of pain showing. He got to his feet and blinked as if he'd suspected such a show.

Marshall was suddenly at Riley's side. He took her hand and was leading her out when she gasped as an arm wrapped around her waist and jerked her back out of Marshall's grip. He spun around at the same time Kane made himself known.

The five of them stared at each other in silence. And then Riley felt as if something were tightening around her throat. She clawed at her neck and struggled to breathe, gasping for air.

"Delphine," George warned.

Riley was unceremoniously dropped. She fell to the floor with her mouth open wide and her lungs burning for breath. Marshall was immediately at her side, but there was nothing he could do.

The corners of her vision began to swim as black dots appeared. Riley knew she was dying. Marshall looked on helplessly as Kane made to attack Delphine. Except George beat him to it.

George was fast and strong, and he moved as if he knew what Delphine was thinking. It allowed him to get close and slam her head against the wall.

Riley choked as the pressure on her neck vanished, and she dragged in mouthfuls of precious air. As her lungs filled, the rushing in her ears ceased so she could hear again.

"I love you. I love you. I love you," Marshall repeated over and over again.

She looked up at him and smiled.

CHAPTER

SEVENTEEN

IF THEY REMAINED, they were going to die. Marshall pulled Riley to her feet as George turned to them. Delphine pushed herself up onto her hands and knees and slowly turned her head to George.

The rage in the priestess's eyes warned of retribution and violence. And Marshall didn't want Riley anywhere near such happenings. She'd already been through too much already.

And he'd come so very close to losing her.

Delphine used the wall to climb to her feet. George turned back to her while Kane kept his gaze locked on the priestess. Both stood against Delphine, but even then, Marshall wasn't sure who would come out the victor.

For the moment, Kane and George were on the same side, but how long would that last once they took down Delphine?

Probably no more than a few seconds before George realized that he wasn't going to get Riley, and then he would attack all of them.

"Fuck," Marshall murmured.

Riley was still wobbly on her feet, but with each second, she gained strength. He glanced behind him out the window to see that the battle was still raging, but there were few of Delphine's followers left standing.

"How dare you," Delphine said to George through clenched teeth.

He smiled, but it was cold, unfriendly. "You shouldn't be surprised."

"We were supposed to work together," she stated.

"I would have said anything to come back. Now that I'm here, I'm going after what I want."

Marshall's gut clenched when George turned his head and looked right at Riley.

"Over my fucking dead body," Kane declared.

George's black eyes met the werewolf's. "That can be arranged."

"Not if I kill you," Delphine said.

Riley leaned close to Marshall and whispered, "Get ready."

Marshall debated turning and getting his rifle. Though he would be better served with his pistol—if he could get a shot off.

The tension ratcheted up so high, the air fairly vibrated

with it. George and Delphine stared at each other, while Kane's eyes moved from one to the other. And all three were ready for anything.

Riley took Marshall's hand. He palmed his gun with the other and pulled it from the holster. While he wanted to kill Delphine, his attention was on George. With him and Kane, surely they could eliminate at least one of their enemies this night.

Marshall's gaze darted to the two doorways. To get to either meant getting near George and Delphine. The two windows behind him were out of the question since it was a straight drop to the pavement below.

If only the building had a balcony, then that would give them several options. But there was no use wanting something that wasn't there.

"Get to your brothers," he whispered.

Riley shot him a flat look that said she wasn't going anywhere.

The sound of Delphine's laughter sent a chill down Marshall's spine. Even Kane was affected by the maniacal cackle. The only one who didn't seem bothered was George.

He tilted his head to the side and calmly said, "Let's get on with this, shall we?"

In the next instant, Delphine launched her attack.

Marshall grabbed Riley and dove to the side as George slammed into the wall where they had been standing.

Marshall briefly met Riley's gaze before they jumped to their feet.

Kane went after Delphine, but he only got a few steps before she had him hanging in midair. Then her head snapped to George as he got to his feet and dusted himself off.

It was all casual right up until he lifted his gaze to Delphine. Marshall saw the evil within the man then, the malevolent spirit that was prepared to do anything to get what he wanted.

And right now, he wanted Delphine dead.

George moved so quickly that Marshall couldn't keep up with him. One moment Delphine was standing, and the next, she was gone. Kane dropped to his knees as he fell to the floor. And then George turned his attention to Riley.

Marshall shook his head and tried to move her behind him. "She doesn't want to go with you."

"I can give her everything you can't," George said.

Then, without missing a beat, George looked over his shoulder at Kane and used magic to lift Kane and toss him out of the room.

"As I was saying," George replied once his attention was back on Marshall. "I'm going to give you one chance to step away from what's mine. If you don't, I'll kill you."

Riley gave a loud snort. "Yours? I'm not yours. I never was, and I *never* will be."

"What a pity," George said in a soft voice. "I'd hoped you

would come willingly. I didn't want to force you, but I'm prepared to do whatever is necessary."

All the fear that had been pressing against Marshall from the moment they put this plan into motion evaporated. He'd been in this position countless times before—only this was his first time where everything directly connected to him.

He wasn't going to watch George take Riley away. Nor would he stand aside and give in to George's demands. While Marshall might not be a werewolf or have the skills of a lifelong supernatural hunter, he did know bad guys.

And he was in love with Riley.

All of that meant one thing—he had to give Riley time to get to her brothers and cousins. With them, she had a chance of fighting against George.

He didn't think about all the dreams that had flooded his mind over the past few hours of having a life with Riley. Or of a love so deep and profound, one that he'd never expected to find.

If all he was meant to have were these few precious hours with Riley, then he would take them with a smile, knowing that he was about to ensure that she continued to live. That the world would be a brighter, happier place with her in it.

Marshall pulled her behind him as he took a step back and to the side. He was trying to inch closer to the door, but by George's raised brow, the bastard knew exactly what Marshall was attempting.

"You've chosen poorly," George said and lifted his hands.

Marshall turned and pressed Riley against the wall, shielding her with his body as he waited for whatever magic George was about to unleash on them.

Instead, a scream of rage rent the air. Marshall's gaze cut to the doorway to see Delphine stride into the room with her lips peeled back in a snarl as she advanced on George.

The building began to shake from the force of the magic between Delphine and George. The two were utterly focused on each other. Or so Marshall thought. Just as he was about to lead Riley to the door, Marshall felt himself being lifted and tossed against the far wall.

He hit the ground with a thud, his head slamming against the floor. Pain exploded through him even as he fought to stay conscious.

"Marshall."

He heard the worry in Riley's voice as she kneeled beside him, her hands on him as she helped him sit up. "You need to leave," he said, holding a hand to his throbbing head.

"Not without you."

Of course, she'd be stubborn. Not that he could find fault in her words. He'd do the same in her position.

"Come on," she said as she slung his left arm around her shoulders.

He tightened his grip on his gun even as he struggled to his feet. His gaze was riveted on George and Delphine, but now he realized that while it appeared George was focused on the priestess, the bastard was always aware of where Riley was.

"What are you thinking?" Riley whispered.

There was no way they were getting to the door. It would be easier to get out that way, plus they could check on Kane. But Marshall knew they couldn't get close to either of the two doorways. George had positioned himself in such a way that they would have to get near him in order to get out.

The only other option was the windows.

"Are you afraid of heights?" he asked.

Riley shook her head. "Windows, then?"

"I'm afraid so."

"And Kane?"

"We'll come back."

She glanced out the door. "Yes, we will."

Marshall jerked his chin to the nearest window. "Get it open. I'll watch the two psychopaths."

As she worked to open the old windows that had been painted shut, the ceiling began to crumble and fall from the magic being thrown between George and Delphine. Marshall raised his gun and sighted down the barrel. The moment he got a shot, he fired at George.

Except the asshole moved at the last minute, causing the bullet to lodge in the wall. And then George turned his fury on Marshall.

His pistol heated in his hand, causing his skin to smoke. Marshall fired off two more shots, both going wide before he had no choice but to drop the weapon. The only thing that kept George from coming straight for Marshall was Delphine, who hadn't let up her assault.

There was a loud bellow followed by Kane leaping into the room. His eyes were bright yellow as he rushed George. When Kane tackled him to the ground, Delphine came in for the kill.

"Get out!" Kane bellowed to Marshall.

He didn't hesitate. He grabbed Riley's hand and ran to the door. Large chunks of the ceiling fell all around them. The stairs were separating from the floor that swayed beneath their feet.

Marshall never slowed. His hold on Riley was tight as they ran down the stairs toward the doors. No sooner had they sped from the stairs than they crumbled behind them, filling the air with a dust cloud that enveloped them.

"Kane!" Riley screamed.

Marshall paused long enough to wrap his arms around her waist and haul her against him when she tried to go back for her cousin. He glanced up and saw the massive cracks in the ceiling. The entire building was about to come down.

He barreled through the doors when he heard the loud crack that split the air. The sight of friendly faces had relief pouring through him.

Riley was pulled from his arms and engulfed in her brothers', but her gaze never left the building.

"Where's Kane?" Court asked.

Myles came to stand beside his brother. "Listen."

The street quieted as everyone raised their gazes to the second floor where the sounds of growls could be heard over George's bellows and Delphine's screeches.

Solomon pushed past his brothers and started toward the building even as Kane released a howl. Solomon paused, glancing upward, before continuing on. Right before he reached the doors, the building gave a great yawning noise before collapsing in on itself.

Marshall reached for Riley. She slammed into his arms before he turned and shielded her from the flying debris of the building. It felt like an eternity before the dust began to settle. Marshall heard the approaching sirens and straightened.

He glanced at everyone before his gaze landed on Riley. "All of you need to leave. Now."

"No," she said.

Solomon nodded. "He's right. We should all go."

"What about Kane?" Christian asked.

Court raked a hand through his hair, dislodging dirt. "There's a very good chance he got away. His howl told us that."

"We won't do him any good in jail," Myles said.

Beau held out his hand for Davena as she and Minka walked up. "Then let's head out."

The others began to walk away, but Riley stayed with Marshall. "You should go with him," he said.

She raised her blue eyes to his. "My place is by your side."

"They'll want to question you," he warned.

She shrugged. "It won't be the first time."

Marshall wrapped an arm around her shoulders and waited for the first responders to arrive. The sky was turning a soft gray with the first hint of dawn.

"So many dead," she murmured.

He glanced at her. "But we're not."

"Do you think we could be lucky enough to have both Delphine and George dead?"

"It's a possibility."

She blew out a breath. "Kane can't be gone."

Their talking ceased as the first police cruiser arrived, followed by fire trucks and an ambulance. Soon, the entire area was bathed in red and blue flashing lights.

Just as Marshall had known, detectives repeatedly questioned them while others searched through the rubble of the building for bodies. The story he and Riley told of walking through the streets on a date and coming across a massive gang fight seemed to be accepted. Though no one had an explanation for why the building came down.

The soft light of dawn was soon replaced by the bright light of day. Riley was wrapped in a blanket in the back of an ambulance as paramedics checked her over while she drank a cup of coffee.

Someone said Marshall's name. He turned his head to find John Gallagher, who he had known well before leaving the city. Marshall's eyes immediately went to the badge hanging around his neck.

"Captain now, huh? I'm not surprised. Congrats," Marshall said.

John gave a nod. "Thanks. Now, how about you tell me what really happened."

"I don't know what you mean."

"Bullshit. You always pretended you didn't know about the supernatural in the city, but I knew you did. You were too careful."

Marshall studied John a long minute. "You plan on putting this in your report?"

"Hell no," he said with his face scrunched up. "I'd like to continue on my career path. This will be for my information only."

Marshall glanced at Riley to find her watching him. He returned his attention to John and took a deep breath before condensing the story for his old friend.

"Fuck me," the captain said and ran a hand down his face.

Marshall shrugged one shoulder. "Aptly put."

"We've got a body!" someone shouted from the remains of the building.

Marshall held his breath, praying it wasn't Kane. Riley came to stand beside him and took his hand in hers. Both anxiously waited for the men to clear the debris from the body and pull him out.

"It's George," Riley said as soon as they got a glimpse of him.

Marshall winced when they saw the odd angle of George's neck, but it was the gaping wound that showed Kane's ferocity.

Even with fatigue weighing heavily upon both Marshall and Riley, they remained for hours until the authorities deemed that no other bodies could be found.

As one, he and Riley turned and walked from the scene arm-in-arm. They were quiet, letting the horror of the night fade with each step they took.

They were a few blocks from Gator Bait when Riley stopped and faced him. Marshall smoothed his hands down either side of her face. Her cheeks were smudged with dirt, and he was sure he didn't look any better.

"I was almost positive I was going to die last night," she said.

He nodded slowly. "I feared you would, as well."

"It's why I left so quickly after telling you my feelings. I knew if you said anything that I'd never walk out those doors."

Marshall pulled her against him and wrapped his arms around her as he kissed the top of her head. If he lived a hundred years, he would never forget what it felt like to helplessly hold her as Delphine choked her to death.

"I love you," he said. "I'd stand beside you every day battling evil if it meant I got to hold you in my arms."

She lifted her head and smiled at him. "Life with me isn't going to be easy. I've got four interfering brothers and four nosy cousins."

"I've always wanted a big family."

"I'm afraid you've bitten off more than you can chew," she teased.

He glanced to the side, twisting his lips. "I'll have you beside me through it all."

"Always."

Neither could stop smiling as they walked into the bar. The mood was subdued as everyone waited for word about Kane, but Marshall didn't have long before he was pulled from Riley and surrounded by the Chiassons and LaRues.

"I love her," he told them.

Vin's smile was huge. "And we wholeheartedly approve."

"To Marshall and Riley," Beau said as he held up his beer.

As everyone toasted, Marshall looked beyond the men to find Riley at the bar with the women. Their gazes met. Love and warmth spread through him.

Against all the odds, he'd found the one woman who was meant to be his.

And the one person who he was meant for.

Life couldn't get any better.

EPILOGUE

Three weeks later...

RILEY WIPED at a tear that escaped and adjusted the bouquet of flowers in her hand. She stood at the front of the church as a bridesmaid, watching Vin and Olivia say their vows. Beside her, Ava had stopped all attempts to hold back her tears.

Looking out over the pews, Riley spotted Christian and Davena, and Beau and Ivy as well as Solomon, Minka, Myles, Addison, Court, and Skye. The absence of Kane was felt by all, but each of them held onto hope that he was still alive.

Riley glanced at Vin, who was grinning like a fool at Olivia. Lincoln, who was best man, only had eyes for Ava, and Riley suspected that they were thinking of their own wedding since they had gotten engaged after they all returned from New Orleans.

But it was the man on the other side of Linc who drew Riley's attention. Marshall Ducet was her everything. She loved him with her whole heart.

They shared a secret smile. It had killed Riley not to put on the ring this morning after he proposed the previous night, but both had agreed that the day was for Olivia and Vin. There would be time enough later to celebrate their engagement.

As a matter of fact, there would be a lot of celebrating. Along with Linc and Ava, both Beau and Christian had proposed, which meant Davena and Ivy would officially become her sisters soon, as well.

Riley cut her gaze to Minka, who was staring up at Solomon with so much love that it made Riley smile. She spotted the sparkler on Minka's left hand, but she wasn't surprised. Solomon and Minka belonged together, and they weren't going to wait.

Riley didn't think it would be much longer before Court and Skye were also engaged. Yet there would be no more weddings until they learned what had become of Kane. And Riley planned to be right there with them searching.

Everyone erupted in applause and cheers when the priest told Vin that he could kiss his bride. And then they were walking back down the aisle. Riley smiled as she took Marshall's arm.

"Your thoughts give you away," he said with a wink.

She grinned at him. "Is it that obvious?"

"Only to me," he admitted.

Once they were out of the church, he took her in his arms and pressed her against the side of the building before kissing her deeply. When he lifted his head, she was clinging to him breathlessly.

"Not fair," she said.

"It's going to be us up there soon."

"And I can't wait."

Marshall moaned as he kissed her again. "Me, either."

They broke apart and hurried after the others to begin the reception where the entire town was invited. The celebration was amazing, but Kane's absence was glaring.

"We'll find him," Marshall said. "Just as I found you. But that's for tomorrow. Tonight, we party."

She laughed as he led her out onto the dance floor. Marshall was her future and everything she held dear. Nothing and no one would ever tear them apart—not even death.

Afterword

Thank you for reading the **CHIASSON SERIES!** I hope you loved these stories as much as I loved writing them. The Chiasson and LaRue series are intertwined. First in the LaRue series is book one, MOON KISSED...

BROUGHT TOGETHER BY CHANCE,
BOUND TOGETHER BY CIRCUMSTANCE.

BUY MOON KISSED today at
www.DonnaGrant.com

If you love the LaRue series, you'll love the fan favorite world of the Kindred series which starts with EVERSONG...

She is a hunter, trained from birth.

He is a man sworn to vengeance.

Nothing can stop them. Except each other.

BUY EVERSONG today at
www.DonnaGrant.com

To find out when new books release
SIGN UP FOR MY NEWSLETTER today at
http://www.tinyurl.com/DonnaGrantNews.

Join my Facebook group, Donna Grant Groupies, for
exclusive giveaways and sneak peeks of future books.

Keep reading for an excerpt from MOON KISSED and a
special sneak peek at EVERSONG…

EXCERPT OF MOON KISSED

NEXT IN INTERTWINED READING ORDER: LARUE SERIES, BOOK 1

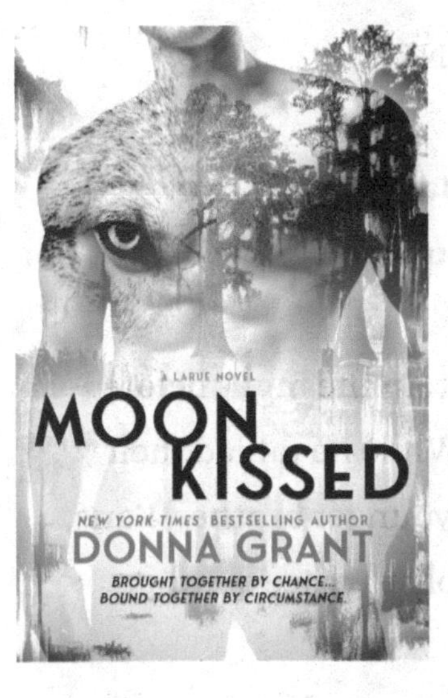

BROUGHT TOGETHER BY CHANCE

For years, Addison Moore worked herself ragged to achieve her goals. Close to earning her degree, the contents of a shocking letter rip her world to shreds. In an attempt to forget, she wanders into a bar, unknowingly changing her life forever. Suddenly she's surrounded by the supernatural she thought only myth and stalked by an evil priestess intent on her death. Her only chance is with an enigmatic man who makes her want to forget everything just to be in his arms.

BOUND TOGETHER BY CIRCUMSTANCE

Myles LaRue was content owning a bar and hunting evil in the French Quarter. He wasn't looking for love, especially after the tragedy his family already experienced. But when the exquisite Addison Moore walks into his life, he can't help but be charmed. Despite the dangers surrounding them, Myles comes to one conclusion – against the odds they found each other, and now that they have, he will do whatever it takes to keep her safe.

CHAPTER ONE

Gator Bait Bar
New Orleans, Louisiana

Myles looked through the receipts from the night before from his seat at the end of the bar. While he tallied their profits and balanced the books, his younger brother, Kane, was going through their liquor supply to place another order.

A shout from the pool tables interrupted Myles as he was inputting numbers in his laptop. He turned his head to the side and glared at his other two brothers—Solomon and Court—who were enjoying their daily pool game.

The game began when Court was barely tall enough to

play properly. Solomon was the one to teach Court the game, beating him soundly every time. It was a LaRue trait that once they set their minds to something, they didn't relent until they had whatever it was they wanted. For Court, that had been beating Solomon. When it had finally happened, Solomon had been unprepared, thinking he still had years of winning.

From that day onward, there had been few things that disrupted their daily games, and that included hurricanes.

"You'd think they would've ended the rivalry," Kane said, without looking up from his clipboard as he wrote down numbers.

Myles watched his brother closely. After the fiasco with the daughter of the Devil himself, Delphine, and their cousins in Lyons Point, Kane hadn't been the same.

Then again, who would be unchanged after being cursed by a Voodoo priestess out to annihilate your family?

"They'll be using walkers and still playing pool," Myles said. He closed his laptop. "You know you'll have to talk about what happened one day."

Kane was in the process of replacing a bottle of Ciroc vodka on the shelf when he froze. There was just the slightest tightening of his shoulders before he turned his head and glowered at Myles with his bright blue eyes—eyes that every LaRue had.

"I've done all the talking I'm going to," Kane stated in a hard voice.

Myles didn't respond as Kane turned back around. Everything about Kane was perfectly tailored, from his golden blond hair, to his shirt tucked into his jeans, down to the laces of his shoes exactly the same length when tied. This was not the Kane of old. That Kane would roll out of bed with his messy hair, throw on a tee shirt and jeans, wearing a smile that stopped women in their tracks.

This new Kane was too uptight, too...controlled.

"It's not your fault."

Kane whirled around, his eyes blazing with fury, but there was no shouting from this new Kane. His nostrils flared, his hands fisted. "It's my fault I caught Delphine's attention. Wasn't it bad enough that one of our ancestors screwed with a Voodoo priestess that caused us to be werewolves? Apparently not for me. I thought I could do whatever I wanted. Delphine wanted to teach me a lesson." Kane snorted derisively. "She wanted Ava killed, and who better to do it than the cousins of the Chiassons who were protecting her?"

"You didn't kill her," Myles pointed out.

Kane rolled his eyes. "It's a good thing too, or Lincoln would've killed me. And I would've welcomed it. We know what we are when we shift, but if I had killed Ava, all of my memories would've been wiped. I'd have been a monster we hunt."

"It's why we called our cousins, remember? We couldn't come after you because we captured Delphine." Myles always wanted to scrub himself in acid after he thought of that vile bitch. It had taken almost every trick they knew to confine Delphine, and then it nearly backfired on them.

Kane braced his hands on the bar and let out a deep breath. "I was reckless, Myles. I didn't just put our family at risk, I put our cousins' as well. If Ava hadn't been with them..." he trailed off, unable to answer.

It was a feeling each of them experienced. Kane was dealing with nearly losing himself to the wolf within, but he had no idea how the events had changed the rest of them. And Myles wasn't about to tell him.

It hadn't been just the curse from Delphine, or even capturing her, it was Court with his fangs around Delphine's throat, ready to clamp down. It was Solomon ready to kill every last one of her followers. It was Myles sprinkling the goofer dust around them so none of Delphine's people could get to her.

That night, all three of the brothers had been prepared—and willing—to do anything and everything to save Kane.

"It'd been too long since we saw our cousins. Each side of the family has been so busy fighting the supernatural that we forgot family." Myles shrugged with a grin, hoping to take both of their minds off Delphine. "You changed all that."

Kane shot him a look and tossed a towel at him. The softening of Kane's mouth was as close to a smile as they would get, but it was enough for Myles.

Since it wasn't yet ten in the morning, all four LaRue's were surprised when the door to the bar opened and in walked a woman with hair so brown it was almost black. She shoved the long hair over her shoulder as the door shut behind her and she looked around the room with bright blue eyes.

Myles slid off the stool as he realized he was looking at his only female cousin, Riley Chiasson. He stopped in front of her and smiled. "The last time I saw you, you were in pigtails and running roughshod over your brothers."

Riley's smile was slow, showing a dimple in her left cheek. "I wondered if you'd know who I was."

"With eyes like that?" Solomon asked as he set down his cue stick and walked to her. "There's no denying our family. What brings you to our neck of the woods?"

Riley swallowed and looked at each of them until she met Myles's gaze. "Since you so graciously pointed out that I was a little girl the last time we saw each other, names put to faces would be great."

Myles pointed to Solomon. "That's the jackass who thinks just because he's the eldest that he can make decisions for us."

"Solomon," Riley said with a nod at him.

"Next up in the order is me," Myles said, waiting to see if she would know.

Riley raised a dark brow. "Then you're Myles."

"Very good," he said. "The scowling one behind the bar is next."

Riley's smile slipped as she shifted her gaze. "Kane." They stared at each other for a heartbeat before Riley turned her head to the pool table. "Which leaves the youngest, Court."

Solomon crossed his arms over his chest. "Now that that's settled, why not tell us why you're visiting."

When she hesitated, Myles wrapped an arm around her and walked her to the bar where Kane filled a glass with ice and then water. She sat on one of the stools and closed her fingers around the glass.

Myles exchanged a look with Solomon. By the way Riley was acting, it was obvious she hadn't told her brothers where she was.

"Do you know I was sent away?" she asked, her gaze on the bar. "Vin said he didn't want me to be a part of the family business."

"You're his only sister. I'd have done the same," Court said as he joined them.

Riley shrugged. "I'd have liked to have some say in it. All of my brothers agreed with Vin, even Beau. The day after I graduated high school, Vincent drove me to Austin. For years I've lived in Texas, going to college. I wanted to go home."

"Did you tell Vin that?" Solomon asked.

Riley shook her head. "I thought since Vin was marrying

Olivia, and Lincoln and Ava were together, that it would be okay to go home."

"You just showed up, didn't you?" Kane asked softly.

Riley looked up at him. "Olivia and Ava knew what I planned. They told me how Beau had met Davena. There were three women at the house now. Surely that meant Vin wouldn't keep me away."

"But you didn't know about what all happened," Myles guessed.

Riley snorted and said, "The Chiasson and LaRue's have been fighting the supernatural since before I was born. My mother had five children and still fought beside her husband. I should be able to go home."

"Your brothers just want what's best." Solomon took the stool on her left. "Surely you understand that."

"I do, but I've not seen my home in over four years. They always had some crises around my breaks that prevented me from returning."

Myles saw the desolation and unhappiness in her gaze, a look he recognized all too well in Kane's eyes of late. "What happened?"

"There was no big family reunion as I'd hoped," she said with a laugh, her lips in a tight smile. "Vin was furious. He and Olivia got in a huge fight because she tried to convince him to let me stay. It didn't take long for all of them to begin arguing. That's when Vin told me to go back to Texas. I told him to kiss my ass, and I stormed out to my car. Then I started driving. Before I knew it, I was here."

Court leaned his forearms on the end of the bar. "I spoke to Christian yesterday. He filled me in on Delphine's appearance in Lyons Point. These are dangerous times, Riley."

"They're always dangerous. She's a Chiasson. She knows how to fight," Kane said to Court. He then turned his gaze to Riley. "What's your plan?"

She tucked her hair behind her ear. "I'd like to stay here a couple of days to figure out what I'll do next."

"Next?" Solomon repeated. "You're not going back to Austin?"

Her smile was sad. "I graduated in June. My brothers didn't even know it. All the times I called home, they didn't have time to talk because of something they were hunting. I had no family in attendance. I even remained for a few months thinking they might realize their mistake, but there's always something to keep them from remembering me."

Kane covered her hand with his. "They remember. Trust me. You had the chance at a normal life, Riley. They didn't, and neither did we."

"Of course," she said too quickly.

Myles wasn't fooled. Riley was hurting and she needed someplace to lick her wounds. "You're welcome here for as long as you need."

His brothers were nodding in agreement before he finished talking.

"Thank you, but I can only accept on one condition," Riley said.

Court shrugged, not understanding. "Name it."

"None of you tell any of my brothers' or their women."

Riley might be beautiful, but she had a sharp mind. Myles realized the trap she led them into at that moment. If they didn't allow her to stay, they couldn't keep an eye on her, and as hunters and her family, that was their duty. By agreeing to her terms, she ensured that she wouldn't have her brothers descending upon her to get her back to Texas.

"I never saw that coming," Kane said, one side of his lips lifted in a grin.

Myles caught Solomon's and Court's gazes. Perhaps Riley was just what Kane needed to remember to smile and laugh again. Kane could look out for her, which would help him heal.

"You do know the full moon will be here in a few days?" Solomon asked her.

Riley looked at him as if he were a simpleton. "I'm a Chiasson. Of course I know. So don't bother trying to lecture me. I know the divides in New Orleans where vampires, witches, demons, werewolves, and djinns are housed. I also know enough to stay away from Delphine and anything to do with Voodoo."

"She's a Chiasson all right," Myles said with a grin.

Riley was a breath of fresh air that seemed to be just what the LaRues needed. Vincent might lament having a sister and the worry it took to keep her safe, but Myles wondered how different their lives would've been had they had a sister among them.

"I'll get her settled," Kane said as he came around the bar.

Myles, Solomon, and Court watched the two of them walk from the building with Riley talking and Kane nodding his head.

"I don't know if this is a good idea," Solomon said.

Court ran his hand through his chin-length butterscotch-blond hair. "It's done now. She knew we couldn't let her leave."

"She got Kane to smile. That's a vast improvement over the last few weeks," Myles pointed out. "He needs something to do, and Riley just gave him the opportunity."

Solomon slid off the stool. "Let's hope you're right, because when Vin discovers Riley is here, we may well have the entire Chiasson clan here."

"Think how we could clear out New Orleans with all of us," Court said. "No more pacts with the five houses. New Orleans could be clear once more."

Myles knew Court had been joking, but it made sense. "We can't bring Delphine and her followers down by ourselves. With four more, we'd stand a really good chance."

"Especially with Beau's woman being a witch," Court pointed out.

Solomon pinned Myles with a look. "First, we make sure nothing happens to Riley, because Chiasson or not, she's not been hunting as we have. If anything happens to her—"

"You don't even need to say it," Myles said.

Maybe it wasn't such a good idea that Riley was there.

BUY MOON KISSED now at
www.DonnaGrant.com

SNEAK PEEK OF EVERSONG

KINDRED, BOOK 1

She is a hunter, trained from birth. He is a man sworn to vengeance.

Nothing can stop them. Except each other.

Leoma does not back down from a fight. She must bring down the Coven before they awaken the First Witch to unleash an unimaginable evil. And there is nothing standing in her way.

Except the sexy, infuriating man who keeps crossing her path.

Wracked with grief, Braith is not looking for love. Hell-bent on revenge, he can't rest until he finds the witch that murdered his heir.

He finds Leoma instead.

These two hunters are tracking the same prey. They could fight together.

But they have to trust each other first.

West Morland, England
September 1349

It was a good day for hunting witches. Then again, Leoma believed every day was a good day to hunt.

She kept the hood of her cloak pulled forward to conceal her face as she meandered through the crowd. The few days of fair weather they'd enjoyed, allowed the soggy ground a chance to dry so that mud no longer squished beneath her shoes. The market was filled with people, and while she detested the crush of bodies, it gave her cover.

Chickens squawked, men yelled, women haggled, and even a dog or two barked. The smell of freshly baked bread and raw fish, along with rank body odor, clung to everything. Leoma ignored all of it, including the children that ran through the market without a care or worry—picking pockets when they could.

With her pace unhurried, it was easy to blend in with the

crowd while her gaze was focused on her quarry—Brigitta. The witch was easy to pick out with her flagrant beauty that she happily showed off.

Leoma battled the rising hatred within her. Edra, her mentor, warned her about letting anger rule. But it was becoming more and more difficult to keep it at bay.

While Leoma had begun learning to battle witches the day Edra and Radnar found her starving on the streets, it hadn't been until Brigitta cruelly and viciously killed Leoma's closest friend that she truly understood vengeance.

"Ease your mind."

Leoma inhaled deeply as Edra's words came back to her. While releasing her breath, Leoma centered herself. It had been six weeks since she left the safe haven of the abbey ruins Edra and Radnar had made into a home.

All those years of training with various weapons and learning how to fight against witches were being put to the test. This wasn't the first time Leoma had gone hunting, but it *was* her first time alone.

For weeks, she had been steadily closing in on Brigitta. Two days ago, Leoma finally found her. It was obvious by the way the witch traveled with determination that she had a specific destination in mind.

It was really too bad she would never make it.

Leoma smiled, her hand on the hilt of her sword hidden beneath her black cloak. She couldn't wait to sink the blade into the witch's heart. Or better yet, slice off her head.

Meg's face popped into her mind. Leoma had to close her eyes against the assaulting image of her best friend's decapitated body.

If only Leoma hadn't insisted they split up in order to corner the witch. If only she'd realized that Meg was terrified. If only....

There were so many regrets that haunted her, and Leoma was sure they would remain until her dying day.

She touched the inside of her left forearm. Before she left her family, another tattoo had been added to her body. The Vegvisir.

The Icelandic word meant signpost, but the magical stave was much more than that. It helped the bearer find their way and never become lost. The Vegvisir would not only help Leoma track Brigitta, but it would also bring Leoma back to her family.

She dropped her arm and moved away from a cart to continue following the witch. It was only Brigitta's habit of remaining right in the mix of people that kept Leoma from attacking. Because Leoma wouldn't have the weight of any more innocent deaths on her conscience.

If she had to track the witch for a year in order to get her alone, then that's what Leoma would do.

Brigitta suddenly halted and looked over her shoulder. Leoma ducked behind a building. She peered around the corner, her gaze taking in Brigitta's stunning face with her long, black hair up in braids, and bright blue eyes that seemed to hold everyone entranced—everyone except Leoma.

A few moments later, the witch continued on. Crowds parted without Brigitta ever saying a word. It was as if others recognized the power within her without understanding what they felt.

While men stared after Brigitta in a lust-filled haze, none were brave enough to approach. It sickened Leoma that so many were so easily manipulated by a beautiful face. Couldn't they tell the witch could end them with a thought? Did they even care?

To Leoma's surprise, Brigitta stopped again and simply looked around as if searching for something.

Or someone.

Leoma remained hidden, wondering just what the witch was up to. Had it not been for Edra, Leoma would never know that there was magic in the world, or that there was a Coven who recruited the most powerful witches in order to grow.

For what exactly, no one knew. Yet.

But that knowledge was something Leoma hoped to bring back to the abbey.

The Coven once sought Edra. They had hunted her for seven years until Edra took a stand. With the love of her life, Radnar, by her side, Edra defeated the witches sent to either bring her into the fold or kill her. That's when Edra decided to create her own coven—a Hunter's Coven.

Leoma was the first of the homeless, abandoned, and starving children that Radnar and Edra found. Some trained like Leoma, and others, like Meg, found different duties at the abbey.

No one was forced to do anything they didn't want to do, but everyone pulled their weight. It allowed Radnar and Edra to supply a safe place for anyone who wanted or needed it.

Leoma couldn't imagine growing up any other way. While Radnar had been her first teacher, he hadn't been her only or her last. Other knights and warriors found their way to Radnar and helped train those wanting to be a part of the Hunter's Coven.

The sword Leoma carried had been designed by Radnar and created by Berlag, their master blacksmith. And then Edra had filled it with magic so Leoma could kill witches.

Because a witch could survive a normal blade. It took something special to make sure a sorceress remained dead. And Leoma would make damn sure Brigitta never hurt anyone again. It might very well cost Leoma her life, and she accepted that.

As soon as she saw the witch move, Leoma scanned the crowd, looking for anyone who could be meeting up with Brigitta. Leoma might get lucky and find a second witch. It wouldn't be the first time she fought multiples.

She had the scars—and the tattoos—to prove it.

Leoma counted to twenty before she slid from her hiding

spot to follow Brigitta. To her surprise, the witch walked into the Three Moons. Leoma flattened her lips as she eyed the tavern.

It wasn't that she minded going into such establishments, it was just that she spent most of her time fending off advances from drunken idiots who thought that anyone with breasts was fair game for a tumble into bed.

But she wasn't going to let that stop her from discovering all she could about Brigitta, just in case Leoma did survive the battle and made it back to the abbey. Any information—no matter how inconsequential—was needed.

She made her way around the building made up of small stones and wooden pillars to make sure the witch didn't sneak out the back. Then Leoma waited until she found a group of men walking into the pub. She snuck behind them and went unseen by most.

The tavern was packed. Loud, boisterous groups singing and laughing occupied several long tables. Those enjoying food and drink took other, smaller tables.

Leoma noted the hearth and roaring fire, as well as the shadowed parts of the interior. She quickly found a smaller table with an elderly couple who didn't bat an eye when she sat with them. Leoma gave the woman a nod and set a few coins on the table before sliding them toward her.

The woman took the money and didn't look at Leoma again. That allowed Leoma to let her gaze wander the tavern as she inhaled the delicious aroma of food, which was probably why the place was so popular.

With little effort, Leoma picked out the men she knew could be trouble. Danger filled the air around them like a dark cloud despite their laughter and noise—or perhaps *because* of it. They drank too much and made sure everyone could hear their boasting. But so far, the men were content to focus on imbibing instead of fighting.

Just before her gaze moved away, she spied someone she had somehow previously overlooked—twice. He sat motionless in a shadowed corner with a mug of ale before him and his gaze directed toward the stairs.

She eyed him, wondering how she could have missed him in her perusal of the occupants. She put his face to memory. Dark hair, thick with just a hint of wave, that fell loose to his shoulders. A lean, rugged face that had sharp cheekbones and a square jaw with a slight indent in his chin ensnared all her senses.

His lips were wide and sinfully full. Thick brows slashed over piercing eyes a deep color she couldn't quite discern from the distance.

Leoma couldn't remember ever encountering a man with such a striking face before, and the fact that she didn't want to look away disturbed her greatly.

But it wasn't just his features that captured her attention. There was an air about him that declared he and battle were well acquainted. If he were a knight, his plain brown cloak and leather jerkin beneath hid the chainmail. He reclined in the chair as if he didn't have a care in the world, and yet his expression told a different story. He was intent on something.

Perhaps he was hunting, as well.

She regretted that she wouldn't find out for sure because she was intrigued. And she almost felt sorry for whoever the man was after. He seemed the type who would not give up until he ran his target to ground.

Leoma pulled her gaze away and looked at the table. This would be the time when Meg told her to flirt. Meg had always pushed Leoma to do the things she watched others do. Her friend made her a part of the world instead of just someone observing it.

But Leoma was better at watching. The few times she tried to do as others did, it hadn't turned out well. It's why Leoma was so suited to witch hunting. It was a solitary business. And she was damn good at it.

She began to wonder how long she would have to wait for some sign of Brigitta when the witch walked down the stairs with a young woman. Their heads were close together as they whispered.

Leoma saw Brigitta pass a small bag to the woman before they reached the bottom step. The woman hugged Brigitta and hurried to the back of the tavern with a bright smile in place as silence fell over the occupants.

Brigitta's grin was coy and sly when she caught men

staring. She gave them a little wave before walking out. Leoma glanced at the back of the tavern. A part of her knew she needed to see what the witch had given the woman, but Leoma didn't want to lose Brigitta.

Yet, if Leoma found her once, she could again. Leoma waited until the conversation in the taproom resumed, and then she discreetly rose and made her way to the back.

"I got it," came a feminine voice.

Leoma leaned around the corner to find the woman showing the bag to a man.

"We can have a child now," the woman said excitedly.

The man eyed the bag. "I'm not sure about such methods."

Leoma knew the risks involved with using magic for such things. The couple would be indebted to Brigitta forever. And the witch wouldn't hesitate to take what she wanted from them—most likely their firstborn child. There was no way Leoma could allow that to happen.

She put a smile on her face and walked toward the couple. "My apologies. I don't mean to interrupt, but I think I'm lost."

The woman set the bag on a table near the hearth as she turned to Leoma. "It sometimes happens. Would you like something to eat?"

The tavern owner hurried out to the customers when someone shouted for more ale, leaving Leoma with his wife.

The first thing Leoma had learned in her training was to be swift of hand.

She walked closer while the woman spoke. "This is a wonderful place. I'm glad I stopped in."

"That pleases me greatly to hear," the woman beamed.

When the wife glanced out the doorway, Leoma swiped the bag. "Can you show me the way out, so I do not get lost again?"

The woman's smile grew tight, most likely irritated at being interrupted, but she replied, "Of course."

Just before Leoma followed the woman out, she tossed the bag into the fire.

Leoma began searching for Brigitta as soon as she was out of the tavern. She caught a glimpse of the witch heading west and made to follow when the same gorgeous man from the tavern snared her attention. She allowed herself a moment to stare while he saddled a horse. But it was the way his gaze kept returning to Brigitta that made her frown.

Leoma hoped the man wouldn't interfere. She'd hate to have to put him on his arse, but she'd do it in a heartbeat. The witch was her prize.

BUY EVERSONG now at
www.DonnaGrant.com

ABOUT THE AUTHOR

New York Times and *USA Today* bestselling author Donna Grant® has been praised for her "totally addictive" and "unique and sensual" stories.

She's written more than one hundred novels spanning multiple genres of romance including the bestselling Dragon Kings® series that features a thrilling combination of Druids, Fae, and immortal Highlanders who are dark, dangerous, and irresistible. She lives in Texas with her dog and a cat.

www.DonnaGrant.com
www.MotherofDragonsBooks.com

facebook.com/AuthorDonnaGrant

instagram.com/dgauthor

bookbub.com/authors/donna-grant

amazon.com/Donna-Grant/e/B00279DJGE

pinterest.com/donnagrant1